Bamboo Grove

Bamboo Grove

Romy
Wood

ALCEMI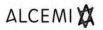

First impression: 2010
© Romy Wood, 2010

Published with the financial support of the Welsh Books Council

Editor: Gwen Davies
Cover: Marc Jennings

ISBN: 978-0-9560125-1-7

Printed on acid-free and partly-recycled paper.
Published by Alcemi and printed and bound in Wales by
Y Lolfa Cyf., Talybont, Ceredigion SY24 5HE
e-mail ylolfa@ylolfa.com
website www.alcemi.eu
tel 01970 832 304
fax 832 782

To my family; every messy, far-flung part of it.

PART ONE

1

I asked my mother once what made her choose Bangkok. Jessica was in an enigmatic mood and she laughed and said it was Bangkok that chose her.

"I was supposed to be born in the East," she said. "But there was a mix-up and I ended up in Surrey."

Surrey. The Thais would have pronounced it 'Sulley'. Jessica pronounced it with an accent like the Queen of England and a quite ridiculous expression on her face.

"And my father?" I said, just for the hell of it. "Did you meet him in Surrey?"

Jessica tried to do a handstand, screwing up her face and grunting.

"My arms are so weak," she said crossly. "It's horrible, getting old."

I must have been about twelve, which would make her all of thirty-one.

Jessica stopped trying to do a handstand and started combing her hair with her fingers instead. She had white hair that fell in soft, loose curls to her shoulders. If anyone asked, she'd say, "I bleached it into submission." My own hair was a dull, colourless blonde. I used to wonder sometimes if from the back I looked like a scruffier, less vibrant copy of my mother.

"Yingyang, sweetheart, you know your father never set foot in Surrey," said Jessica. "He was an Eastern Prince who smelt of incense and could cure people by touching them."

Yeah. Right.

Over the years, she'd told me many different stories about how I came to be. As a little girl, my favourite story was that a fortune-teller gave her a sweet like an opal and told her to wish while she sucked it. She wished never to be alone and the opal-sweet became the seed of a baby inside her. When I grew too old for this story, I realised my father must have been white. I didn't get my blue eyes or my mousey blonde hair from an Asian man. I was no Thai Princess. I felt twice the size of the local children, bulky and pink with fat ankles and big flat feet.

Jessica rummaged in a box on the elm wood apothecary cabinet that took up a whole wall. At the top were rows of tiny drawers with Chinese characters on the front and charms hanging from the handles. Lower down there were larger drawers and tall shelves with lines of jugs, bottles and a cut-glass decanter.

"Do you think this stuff matures?" she said, gulping something yellow from an eggcup. "Or goes off? Oh, bloody hell."

The air-conditioning unit had shuddered to a halt and she kicked it with her bare foot.

"Ow. It's prehistoric, this building. We should find somewhere a bit more twentieth century, I suppose. Don't you think?" She was hopping on one foot, hooking her little red shoes on and grabbing her bag.

I said nothing. I watched her swing open the door and start down the steps, going to buy Coca-Cola from the shop across the street that was really just someone's garage. Our apartment was on the third floor of a lopsided block less than half a mile from the sprawling slum at Phetbin. On the ground floor was a shop with a display of wind chimes that tinkled whenever someone went in or out. There were racks of second-hand shoes outside and glass-fronted cabinets full of dusty ornaments on the inside.

When I was thirteen, I stopped talking altogether. At first, I shook my head and clamped my mouth shut, as much to remind myself as anything else. But quite soon, silence became my natural state and it no longer occurred to me to speak. They had meetings. Jessica sat in a little office with my teacher and the headmaster while I waited in the corridor, listening to the cleaners talking softly in Burmese and laughing. I remember she came out quite flustered the first time, looking as if she might cry. But after that she was defiant. I heard her say, "I respect my daughter's choice. The world is too full of words and most of them are bullshit."

She relished the *bullshit*, speaking loudly so that the words hung conspicuously in the air. I hurried her away; the embarrassment was nothing in comparison to what she was capable of.

I wrote more than ever. I wrote and wrote, spilling words onto the page as easily as other people spoke them. I bought notebooks with butterflies on the front and wedged them between my mattress and the wall, tying complicated knots in ribbons to keep Jessica out. And at night I invented stories in my head, while the moon shone through the window onto the silk screen where a turquoise sunbird spread his feathers in a perpetual state of take-off. Each feather was rimmed with gold and the bird looked upwards through spiralling branches at a whole flock that was already far in the distance above him. I would lie on the mattress, my eyes tracing the fine swirls of the branches and the outspread wings. If I stared patiently without blinking then after a while they'd begin to shimmer. The colours rippled and shifted, turquoise became silver then palest blue, and the sunbird cocked his head ever so slightly.

I remember once lying on my mattress behind the screen, watching my mother's shadow, her arms outstretched as she spun faster and faster in the centre of the room. I dug my nails into my palms.

"Yingyang!" she cried.

I held my breath.

"Yingyang, you are a Thai Princess and you must prepare yourself for your people."

She spun herself around the screen and the sunbird stiffened as she steadied herself against it.

Striking a match, she lit a stubby candle and put it by the screen. I wanted to move it, just a little, because the sunbird looked uncomfortable. But I didn't move. Jessica flung open her special bamboo box and a rainbow came pouring out. Scraps of silk in strawberry-pudding pink, palm-tree green and burning orange, twisted knots of embroidery thread, glass beads like miniature crystal balls, sweet wrappers like jewels.

Her eyes reflected every colour. She dropped to her knees and pulled on my hands. I sat up, rigid, swallowing a yawn.

"Princess Yingyang, wise and honoured. Descendant of Emperors and Kings!" She combed my hair briskly with her fingers, tearing painfully at a tangle. I pressed my teeth together.

"Revered Princess, the ritual begins—"

She twisted my hair into hundreds of delicate little plaits, decorating each one with thread and beads. It took her so long I fell asleep sitting up. When I opened my eyes, she was sucking the end of a plait to slide a sequin on. Sleep dragged on my senses so hard it hurt.

"You know your father was a great man, Yingyang." Her voice was muffled from the plait in her mouth. "You have his wisdom and his power." Her hands shook as she scrabbled amongst the beads on the sheet.

"He loved me very much, your father."

I sneezed, trying hard to stay still.

"He did. He loved me more than life itself and he visits me from the Spirit World." She ripped a piece of silk printed with cartoon children whose eyes took up half their faces. "You have his strength." She began to cry and blew her nose on the cartoon children. "Can you keep a secret?" She put her hands around my face and pressed her forehead to mine. "I was raped. Do you know what that means?"

I didn't move.

"He was someone I trusted, back in England." Jessica took a white ribbon and tied some of the plaits so that they sat like a fountain on top of my head.

"You are ready!" she cried, scrambling up and tugging on my hand. "Let's go."

She grabbed her lipstick, which was the same red as her shoes, and rubbed it approximately onto her mouth.

I shook my head and rubbed where one of the plaits was too tight.

"Come on," Jessica insisted. "Together, we can save the world. Just think of that. Me and my Yingyang."

2

Jessica was eighteen the day her mother clicked on the television without looking at it and set an eggcup and a teaspoon on the table.

The upstairs cistern hissed. The toast popped up. Maureen placed it squarely in the rack beside the eggcup. As Geoff approached, she transferred his boiled egg to the eggcup and rinsed her hands.

On the television screen, a starving woman was trying to breastfeed her baby.

"That is out of sight," said Geoff, beheading his egg. He flicked

11

his eyes to the solidified yolk and prodded it. Maureen took out a clean tea towel and arranged it in its holder.

Jessica crammed cereal straight from the packet into her mouth, staring at the television.

"Jess love, put it in a bowl and pour milk on it. I shouldn't have put the telly in the kitchen. It's just when I'm on my own, I like to—"

Jessica grabbed a biro and copied a number onto her arm. Maureen sighed.

Geoff stood.

"If you want to do something for charity," he said, "there are causes much closer to home you could start with. Hmm? People in need in the city we live in. We walk past them every day, then come home and sign a cheque to some organisation that may or may not use it to feed Africans."

"Geoff—" said Maureen.

He peered at Jessica. There was a fleck of egg-white stuck to his lip.

"What are you planning to do with yourself today? Shops and friends again? Quite the lady of leisure."

Maureen made a little squeak.

"She's going to look for something part-time, aren't you, Jess? Just while we think through the next step. It's natural that she needs a bit more guidance than—"

"I am not extending the mortgage to pay for some fancy course she'll abandon halfway through."

"Halfway through…" repeated Maureen.

Geoff pecked her on the cheek and left. On the television, diamonds sprayed in a fountain from a huge bottle and people leapt in the air to catch them.

"Your father's tired," murmured Maureen, sweeping toast crumbs into her hand.

"Strictly speaking," said Jessica, tossing her head, "he's not my father."

Maureen held on tightly to the tea towel. A woman in a suit was talking about mortgages.

"Sorry," whispered Jessica. She shoved the heels of her hands across her eyes.

Maureen coughed. She fixed her eyes on the biro Jessica had discarded on the table.

Jessica began to cry and she didn't know if the tears were for the starving stranger on the television or for herself. Or for her mother whose pain was stretched so clearly across her face. She didn't know how to rub out what she'd said. She gritted her teeth in an effort to stop the crying.

"For God's sake, child," hissed Maureen, "turn off the waterworks."

Jessica's cheeks flamed. She stormed out of the kitchen, rammed her feet into her shoes and slammed the front door behind her.

~

Moses actually believed the flying carpet would work. It had hovered, definitely hovered – if only for a few seconds – but then the phone rang and the vibes got in the way.

It was Bristol.

"They are woven," Moses told him, "from the wool of a sheep/goat hybrid found only in the mountains of Vietnam."

"Wool?" said Bristol. "I remember more a straw/double knit hybrid."

Moses looked at the carpet.

"There's something very other-worldly about them. And it works. I'm still floating, man."

"I'll get you a hundred," said Bristol, "if you promise you'll shift them."

Moses frowned. He'd have to drop the 'man'. It was too cannabis-in-a-caravan.

Pippa shoved open the door with her bum. She was carrying a large cardboard box that was in danger of spilling its contents.

"Moses, stop staring my bottom and give me hands," she said and thrust the box at him.

"Hang on, Bristol, we've got the fliers here. Just wait a mo–"

Mo? Where did that come from?

He slid the box onto the desk and took out one of the fliers. There was a slightly distorted photo of the carpet and underneath, in comic sans, the words:

Look at the carpet and breathe.
Be still.
Be present.
Some people begin, after a short while,
to feel a sensation of hoovering.

"Pippa, you've typed 'hoovering'."

"I photocopy already two hundred," she said. "And a 'o' is not too much a problem."

Moses placed the flier carefully back in the box and swallowed at length.

Pippa folded her arms.

"We make some tippex," she said. "OK?"

"Bristol? You still there? Listen – here's the concept: *Meditation for Levitation.* Thirty-six sessions of one hour each. Money-back guarantee."

On the other side of the world, Bristol laughed.

"A refund if they don't leave the ground? Moses, you've surpassed yourself."

"Thank you."

"OK. I'll get *two* hundred but you'll have to shelve the levitation course. Nice outside-the-box thinking, but–"

"Bristol," said Moses, patiently, serenely, "the point is no one ever manages all thirty-six sessions. If they would only commit, really commit, they would reach undiscovered echelons. I have to open people's eyes to the abundance of experience. It would be rude not to."

Bristol sighed.

"Just word it carefully. The money-back shit. Thirty-six pre-specified, fully attended hours."

Moses grinned.

"The undiscovered echelons bless you and await you, Bristol. I bid you farewell."

14

"Bugger off. Fax me the flier."

Pippa grabbed her bag and grunted a goodbye, letting the door wobble shut behind her. Moses put the phone down and stretched his arms until his elbows clicked. He looked down at himself in the mirror he had propped against the wall and it struck him that it seemed appropriate to shave his head in the nude. So he pulled off the collarless shirt he'd been in for a while and stepped out of his jeans. Then, cross-legged on the floor, he brought his hands together in front of his heart and bowed his head.

He listened to the sounds from the street below. To feet climbing the endless stairs to the floor above. Then, slowly, reverently, he took his razor and put it to his hairline. With each stroke, he let out a long 'Omm.' Very dark, very unwashed hair fell in tufts onto his shoulders, his lap and down his back, but, in the advanced state of mindfulness he had reached, he wasn't in the slightest bit bothered by the itching.

~

The train carriage smelt of ketchup and sweat. Jessica stared at the dark window where she was a ghost in the glass. Her teachers had said she'd go far. If she only stopped falling flat on her face. That she wore her heart on her sleeve. That she bottled things up. She was her own worst enemy. And the clichés were so much a part of her that she no longer knew how to be.

She was as seduced by the idea of the 'Gap Year' as her father was repelled by it. She had a vague notion of herself as a missionary, though without the religion. Teaching, perhaps. Guiding people. Somewhere like Africa, probably. Or India.

She gazed down at her feet. She could just walk – not literally, not all the way – and see where her feet took her. Her head hadn't exactly proved itself worthy of taking charge. In fact it had taken her nowhere; had failed to make any decisions at all so that she was now adrift in exactly the way her father had feared. If she could clear her mind, let her feet take over, she might find herself beginning to take shape. She might find that she could breathe without thinking about it, speak without replaying the words in her head. When the train stopped, Jessica let her feet take her onto the platform and out into the street.

It was still early, but already people carried shopping bags. Crumpled supermarket carriers. Precise little paper bags. A vast shiny one bulging with the corners of some grotesque plastic toy. She wanted to burn them all. Bags of things. Endless clutter. She felt she couldn't see for the mess, was wading in it, choking on its stench. She trod on a slimy crisp packet, watching it curl round her grubby white pumps.

What would happen, she wondered, if you rubbed it all out? Would people just fill it with rubble again? The shuttling mass of people and plastic bags grew thicker. Jessica wondered what would happen if she screamed. She imagined tipping back her head and yelling. She clamped her mouth shut and slid down onto the pavement with her back against a bin.

A polystyrene cup spun over her head, spraying dregs of synthetic milk. She thought of the starving woman breastfeeding her baby on the television and wanted somehow to send them the drops. The idea revolted her and she stood up quickly as if she could escape it. A young man in a suit handed her a half-eaten packet of sandwiches without looking at her.

Seeing the crust leaking lettuce and grated cheese, Jessica knew that she had to disappear. To rub it all out and start again. She threw the sandwich in the bin, wiped her hands on her jeans and began to walk quickly. She cleared a path through the mindless shoppers, cut down a side street, walked round the four sides of an office block. She shook off clutter as she walked, imagining she could move faster and faster until she spun away from the scribbled mess in her head. If she kept moving, she might never have to go home, never have to feel the peach-pink nylon sheet pricking her skin. She would go far, far away, somewhere where different was commonplace.

Tripping on a paving slab where weeds had dislodged it, she sliced a flap of denim and skin from her knee. She felt the thud across her face as she fell onto her nose and lay staring at the thorn so thick it could shift concrete.

"Are you OK?"

"I'll call an ambulance."

"Don't be ridiculous. She's only fallen over."

Jessica staggered to her feet and her head rushed with nausea and dizziness. Someone helped her to a small set of steps and sat her on the bottom. She could see dog muck on the pavement and brushed her arms and legs in revulsion.

"OK?"

"Careful, you're spreading blood all over yourself."

"I'm thinking ambulance."

"I'm OK! Please. Thank you." Jessica held up her hands. "Sorry." She fixed her gaze on the dog muck until they left her, blood running down her leg.

The skin flap on her knee turned thick and white above the blood. She dug a piece of grit from the wound and wiped it on the step.

After a while, she rested her arms and her head on the step above and shut her eyes. She thought of the goodbyes, the leaving. The cornflower blue dress; the declarations of love. As if it were all a beginning and not an end. As if any of it had ever been real.

And then there was a gentle hand on her shaking shoulder. It felt so soothing she stayed as she was, her face pressed into her arms. After a while, the hand stroked her hair. She looked sideways, afraid suddenly. It was a young man. A very tall young man wearing orange Buddhist robes. He had a recently shaved head and the whisper of a beard.

"Guidance comes in many forms," he said, sounding like the vicar at Maureen's church.

Jessica frowned and sniffed. She rubbed her nose with her hand and realised she'd streaked her face with blood.

The Buddhist monk sprawled across the steps, oblivious.

"How can you tell I'm in need of guidance?"

It was meant to be a joke. She gestured feebly at the blood, the snot; she felt responsible somehow even for the dog muck. But the gangly young man in the orange robes pressed his palms together as if in prayer. She looked at his bare feet on the steps. He had six toes on each foot.

"You are in a place of uncertainty," he said.

She looked up at the sky and blinked.

"Yup."

"You aren't sure what to do or where to go. But your aura tells me that you already know."

He waited, while she watched the blood on her leg congeal.

"I want to go far away. I can't be – here – anymore."

"I know. I know." The monk put his fingertips to his mouth and nodded. The too-bright orange of the robes made his skin look even whiter than it was. His eyes seemed to swim as they looked through her own and into her soul.

"The clutter," she said. "I can't stand the clutter."

"I can see that," he said. "In your aura."

When he kept looking at her, she said, "There was a woman on the television, in some African country, trying to feed her baby. But she was starving–"

The monk laid his hands either side of Jessica's head and breathed in at length.

"You wanted to feed that woman."

"And I can't even remember the name of the country. I am so f–"

She'd been going to say *fucking useless*. Remembered just in time that she was addressing a monk.

"What is your name, child?"

"Jessica. Jessica Jane."

"I believe, Jessica Jane, that the redistribution of the world's wealth may be in your hands."

The young man's nostrils flared with passion.

He stood. This took a while as there was so much of him to unfurl. Jessica slowly raised her neck, her eyes following him from the long untrimmed toenails to the drape of the robes, to the beard that seemed to be longer already. Eventually, she let her eyes meet his. He stretched out his hand and she took it.

"My name," he intoned, not letting go of her hand or her gaze, "is Moses."

3

I remember when I was about seven, Jessica was walking me to the bus stop and she talked faster and faster all the way. She kept saying that Buddha would protect us. He would look after me at school; he was so huge he could do this and still be with her in Phetbin while she worked. Buddha shone in the sun because he was made of gold, and I mustn't touch him because he was burning hot. His eyes were precious jewels which changed colour with his mood. (Hers was a Buddha who could rage and storm between bouts of serenity. He was, apparently, very angry with Bristol and Sam at the time because they were so materialistic and selfish. I wanted to stop her and check on this point – I had some idea even by then that it was them who paid for me to go to school.)

She dragged me down the steps and along the street so fast I tripped over myself, telling me about her plans for a shrine on the roof of our apartment building. I waved at the old man who squatted all day in front of the little shop over the road, but Jessica tugged me away without so much as looking at him.

"We need animals," she said. "A cow, an elephant and some chickens."

"*Real* ones?" I dodged a motorbike and clung to her hand. It was early, but already the smell of food was in the air. Woks were balanced on carts all along one side of the street, sending up bursts of steam. The vendors shouted to each other above the sound of the traffic, slicing fish and crushing chillies without looking what they were doing.

"As many varieties of fruit as we can find," said Jessica. "Pomelo. Buddhas like pomelo. And strawberries, because they're a lucky colour."

A woman in a faded floral pinafore pushed a supermarket trolley with five little children inside. They pressed their faces up against the bars and squashed their noses. It made me smile and they giggled when they saw me looking.

We reached the bus stop, where schoolchildren were gathered in the shade of a tree. A boy in the class above me sucked on a lollipop as his nanny retied his shoelaces.

"Hello, Yingyang," said the nanny, reaching out to touch my shoulder.

"Leave her alone!" cried Jessica, grabbing hold of me by the pigtails.

All the children stared and then turned away, pretending to hide their laughter. I grew hot and prickly behind my eyes and decided to hold my breath until the bus came.

"They will never know the peace of Buddha," hissed Jessica. "The love and the path to enlightenment."

The sun grew stronger with every minute that passed but I couldn't move into the shade without standing right up close to the others. I shut out the sound of the children's laughter and fixed my attention on an elegant young woman with a mobile phone. She stood in the centre of the sidewalk, where people had to step round her, and flicked up the aerial. I watched her punch in a number, her long fingernails flashing bright pink, and put the phone to her ear. She chattered brightly, oblivious to the heat, the dirt and the noise.

When the school bus drew up, yellow and shiny with a foul exhaust, the children jostled for space at the door and I bit my lip and waited until last.

"Stay and help me," said Jessica suddenly, "with the shrine."

She pulled me back and we watched the door shut and the bus nudge its way into the traffic. The nanny gave a tight little half-smile without looking at us and set off on her errands. The young woman with the phone was gone.

"Now," said Jessica. "We'll start with the fruit."

She bought oranges, pomelos and melons, loading me up so I couldn't see over them. She fussed because she couldn't find a stall with strawberries but she said we'd pray for forgiveness. I trailed after her back through the streets and up the steps. All the time she talked, and her words made less and less sense. When we reached the door of our apartment, I stopped, ready to drop my load.

"Keep going!" she said, already halfway up the next flight. "We're building the shrine on the roof so it's as near to the sun as possible."

My nose ran and I had to keep sniffing because I had no free hand to wipe it with. I wondered how we would get the animals up to the roof.

"Stop sniffing. That is foul. We need to transcend our bodily filth…"

Her words disappeared with her up the steps and I tramped up after her. I'd never climbed higher than our apartment; from outside, the building seemed so tall I hadn't thought of it as *having* a roof. Where the steps ended, there was a dusty landing with a ladder up to a skylight. Jessica climbed to the top and shoved hard at the window above her head, still talking.

"Fuck it," she said, "fucking open, will you?" and thumped on the glass with her fist.

I gaped up at her, biting my lip.

Finally, she forced open the skylight. She made me pass the fruit up to her while she sat on the roof with her legs dangling down onto the ladder. I had to carry things in one hand and hold onto the ladder with the other to climb halfway up so she could reach them. Then she swung her legs up and disappeared entirely from view. My breath came fast. With both hands free now, I went further up the ladder and peeked over the edge. Jessica was chasing oranges that rolled in all directions on the uneven surface of the roof. One wedged itself between the railings and she lunged at it, but her scrabbling hands pushed it further through until it popped out the other side and fell to the street below. She thumped the railings and cursed and I wanted to shout that it wasn't safe, that the railings weren't strong enough, but my throat was so tight I couldn't form a sound.

From where I stood, my chin level with the skylight, it looked as if you could jump from our block to the next, or grab hold of a window ledge on one of the buildings even taller than ours that stretched up into the hot, dirty sky. There were men working on a scaffolding platform attached to a great white tower on the other side of the slum, and people hanging out washing on balconies almost as high, but no one was looking our way; no one knew how wobbly the railings were and how careless Jessica could be when she was busy like this.

She arranged the melons, the oranges and the pomelos, shuffling on her knees, muttering to herself. My own knees started to shake and my knuckles hurt from gripping the ladder.

"Mum," I whispered. "Please."

Jessica didn't hear me. She looked at the sky as if that would tell her something and I stepped rung by rung back down the ladder until I was on firm ground at the bottom. I crouched on the floor waiting and worrying that she might lean too hard against the railings. From time to time, I could hear noises from the apartments below; doors shutting, telephones ringing, but the sound was muffled as if it were far far away. I was scared someone would come up and find me sitting under the open skylight but I was even more scared that they wouldn't. I imagined myself sitting there for hours and hours, Jessica never coming back.

~

Jessica stood awkwardly outside the door, checking the address Moses had given her. The building looked grim from outside, grey and old. She coughed and swallowed, thinking she might go away again, walk around the block or something so that she didn't have to wait so conspicuously. He'd smiled when he handed her the scrap of paper, as if he knew she would come. And she'd watched him walk away, his arms loosely by his sides, his steps easy, confident. Now she was anxious that he might have forgotten. Or that he rescued so many lost people as he peacefully wandered the streets of London, that he'd be inundated with visitors desperate for his help. But he'd said she should come. He said he'd take her to the East, to Thailand, and she could change people's lives as he was changing hers.

"Jessica Jane."

Suddenly he was there, across the road, looking as if he'd been watching her forever. She smiled.

"Moses."

He crossed the road without turning his head, without taking his eyes off her, ignoring the honk of a car's horn.

Inside, the building was as gloomy and dusty as it had promised. Just flights of stairs and closed doors with peeling paint. Jessica peered upwards as they climbed, spiking her hand on the banister.

Moses stopped at a door with a pale sand undercoat and a rainbow that snaked and twisted all the way up from bottom to top.

"Welcome," he said, "to Eastern Vision."

He smiled at her, pushed open the door and pulled her gently in behind him.

Hundreds of precious stones lay on an ancient rug. Emerald, topaz, opals, onyx, sapphire. Orange teardrops, squares of fuchsia pink, ruby flowers, hypnotic black and deepest indigo, elegant green ovals and tiny pink jellybeans. And everywhere, gold rims and diamond studs glittering.

To Jessica, every stone was a wish. In every shining jewel she saw a dream. In an emerald, she saw her birth father, and this time he was a broad-shouldered man with square glasses and a gentle smile wrapped up in a serious face. In an opal, she saw a child of her own. A beautiful baby girl whose head smelt of warm soap. In the ruby, her birth mother became a queen, strong and loving, with only one hole in her robust heart – the daughter she'd been forced to give up for adoption because she was too young and no one must know.

From the corner of the room, a woman coughed. Jessica looked up and blushed. The woman was very young and dressed in a sarong and a rugby shirt. She had a mousey ponytail right on top of her head so that she appeared to sprout a fountain of hair.

"Who that is your friend, Moses?" said the woman, with an accent that was perhaps Polish or Russian. Moses looked at Jessica.

"Jessica, meet Pippa," said Moses benevolently. "Pippa, this is Jessica who is going to work for us in Thailand. She's going to head up the charity side of things."

Pippa squinted at Moses.

"I want to help the poor people," said Jessica quietly.

Along a shelf on the opposite wall was a row of six crystal angels with moonstone wings and tiny aquamarine eyes.

Moses beamed. He strode to the desk and took a file from a drawer.

"Eastern Vision, Charitable department. Jessica–?"

"Cotton," said Jessica, embarrassed by the banality of her surname and mesmerised by the crystal angels. Outside, a cloud shifted and sunlight ignited the prism within each one.

Sitting cross-legged on the floor, his back against the wall, Moses attempted a lotus posture.

"Practicalities," he said, holding out a hand, balancing the file on his knee. Pippa threw him a pencil, which he caught. "Do you have a passport?"

"Mark," said Pippa. Moses ignored her. "Sorry, Moses. Sam is knowing this?"

"Bristol," he mumbled, jotting some notes on a sheet of paper, "Bristol's fine with it. I'll confirm it with him when we've got the details sorted."

"Passport?" repeated Moses, and Jessica couldn't help noticing that right there in the centre of his half-lotus was a bulge underneath his robes. She shook her head.

Pippa stopped searching through a drawer and looked at Jessica. "You are not going some place already?"

"Dorset," said Jessica. "And the Isle of Wight."

Pippa stifled a noise that might have been a belch or a laugh. Moses glared at her.

"We'll get you a passport," he said. "Sam and Bristol can fast track it. It's no problem." Sliding up the wall, his hand adjusting his robes where they stuck out in the middle, he went to the desk and opened another drawer.

Pippa found a gold spray with a B & Q label and began to spread newspaper in the corner.

Moses installed himself at the desk, opening a fat envelope full of forms.

"Pippa," he said, without looking up. "We need two identical photos." He pointed at Jessica. Pippa said nothing. She peeled the rubber mould from a plaster cast Buddha, taking extra care over the facial contours. Positioning it in the centre of the newspaper, she shook the gold spray can vigorously.

"I am doing like this," she said. "Cannot *Jessica* go alone?"

Jessica shut her eyes, speaking so quietly they had to strain to hear her.

"Could someone – come with me? To find a photo booth?"

Pippa snorted. She began to spray the Buddha gold. "You want going to Thailand," she muttered, "and you cannot go alone for a photo."

24

Jessica opened her eyes and looked at the stones, swallowing. She felt inexplicably that she might never find her way back again, that the room might vanish if she left it.

"Has Sam in fact make a interview with her?" said Pippa, shaking the gold spray again. The Buddha's first coat was almost complete.

Moses stood up, unfolding his endless arms and legs and cracking his knuckles above his head. "Come on, Jess," he said, "we'll do it now."

~

I woke to the sound of angry, hurried footsteps.

"Yingyang? Thank God you're OK."

It was Bristol, with sweat in his eyebrows and under his nose. He crouched beside me and put his hand on my cheek.

"Where's your mum? Is she up there?"

I nodded and he shut his eyes and sighed.

"She cries when you're cross with her," I said, staggering to my feet with pins and needles everywhere.

Bristol looked at me. He took off his cufflinks and put them in his pocket, then he rolled up his shirtsleeves.

"Stay there, OK?"

I chewed my pigtails. He climbed the ladder and his top half disappeared through the skylight so I could just see the backs of his legs and his shiny black shoes.

"Jessica?" he said. "What the fuck are you doing?"

I glanced down the steps and sucked on my hair. *Please don't be angry.* I couldn't make out what she said but I strained to hear her mood in the tone of her voice. Was she happy building the shrine or had it gone wrong? I had no idea how long I'd been asleep.

"Pull yourself together, Jessica. Yingyang's frightened."

"No I'm not," I said quietly.

"Leave them there then. So what if the birds are eating it? Please, just come down. It's dangerous up there."

He thumped his fist on the skylight and scrambled up out of sight. Then his face appeared.

"Good girl. I won't be long, OK?"

I shrugged as if it were nothing to me either way and he sighed and vanished. I hoped she was right about Buddha protecting us. I hoped he was in control right now. Perhaps it was Buddha that had sent Bristol to get her down.

"If you keep this up, I'm going to call an ambulance," shouted Bristol. "Is that what you want?"

"Mum!" I called up the ladder. "Can we do the shrine another day? Please?"

I needed the toilet. I was hungry and thirsty and my nose was running again. I knelt at the bottom of the ladder, squinting upwards, willing them to come back.

By the time Bristol's feet appeared, searching for the top rung, I'd wet myself. He came down slowly, one hand poised to steady Jessica as she followed him. They had to step over me because I wouldn't move.

Jessica was shaking. She sat on the floor beside me and held out her arms.

"I'm sorry, Yingyang. I'm sorry, baby."

I said, "I'm not a baby."

Bristol climbed back up to the skylight and slammed it shut.

"Let's get you both downstairs," he said.

Neither of them mentioned the patch where the grime had turned muddy underneath me or the way my school skirt clung to my legs as we processed down to our apartment.

I shook with relief, to be inside with the door shut and Jessica safe. I found my jeans in the drawers beside the sunbird screen and Bristol stood staring out of the window while Jessica helped me change, crying all the time.

4

The next time Jessica went to the rainbow office, Moses said, "Come. I want to show you something."

Jessica let him take her hand, and she loved the sense that hers was so small in his, that his incredible height draped in orange robes was like a looming, solid rock. They went out through the rainbow door and across the landing.

Moses reached inside the flap of his robes and pulled out a bunch of keys on an orchid key ring.

"There's no light switch in the store," he said, letting go of her hand. He unlocked the door and reached inside to the right, producing a torch. "Look." He swept the torch slowly around a small, dark space which smelt of spray paint and spice. The shaft of light hit rows of miniature Buddhas; gold, silver, shocking pink, crystal blue. Identical in size and shape, mesmerising in their colours. Jessica's eyes grew round. The torch settled on a huge glass jar filled with precious stones jumbled in a mass of heart-stopping colour. *We're keeping your dreams safe*, they whispered, *we're holding them tight*. Sweeping the torch past some plaster cast figurines with monstrous phalluses, Moses found swathes of fabric in a pile. He slid an arm around Jessica's shoulders.

"Silk," he said, and his voice was melted chocolate. "Jessica Jane, I feel deep inside me that your spiritual home is in the East."

The silk was shot through with coloured threads and edged with gold and silver. Jessica wanted to throw off her clothes and wrap herself in it. Moses moved the torch again and lit up bunches of wooden orchids painted purple, pink and white.

"The real thing lasts a long time," said Moses, "but these last forever." He pulled her gently into the store, letting the door shut behind them.

"You import these from Thailand?" breathed Jessica. Moses' arm fell away from her shoulders and slipped further down her back.

"Some of it," he said. "There's a big market for Eastern objets here. We're looking to – expand. And the charitable arm is going to be a big part of that. I feel some higher power has brought you and I together."

Jessica trembled. "I feel it too," she said. "I must go to Thailand. It's my destiny."

"You may be right. The higher power has plans for you."

"And my future is hidden in the stones."

Moses pushed a pile of fuchsia-coloured fabric flip-flops to one side and made a space in the middle of the store. Taking both Jessica's hands, he lay down with his head on the silk and his legs tucked under his robes. She knelt beside him, their hands entwined.

"I love this room," he said. "Thailand is my spiritual home but when I'm here, this is the closest I can get."

"I think I understand," said Jessica. He shone the torch up under his chin so that his face looked like a ghost. She giggled. Despite his size, his wisdom, and his shaven head, he didn't look much older than she was.

He pulled her down next to him. His body radiated warmth.

"You are beautiful," he murmured. "And you are exactly what Eastern Vision needs. You are unique. Unique." His words became kisses, covering her head softly, moving down to her ears, licking the creases, sucking the lobes. Jessica kept still. She let him slide his hand under her top and lay his palm across her belly. Her breath caught in her throat for a second and the words, "I want–" came out of her mouth.

"Mm? What do you want?" Moses drew a circle round her tummy button with his finger. She shut her eyes and breathed.

He turned off the torch and continued his trail of kisses down her neck and between her breasts.

When he came, rather theatrically, she suddenly felt his weight. Cramp took hold of her legs and she tried to move, shuffling awkwardly.

"Sorry, I'm squashing you." Moses rolled off her and lay flat on his back in the dark, breathing deeply. Jessica curled into his side.

"I feel," she said, "that my life has just begun."

~

Jessica was a queen in Phetbin, the slum she was proud to call her second home. She was happy in the alleys of huts made from plaster board and old fence posts, bits of scaffolding and torn canvas. The children followed her round, elbowing each other aside to be closest to her, and the women pressed fried nutmeg cakes into her hands. There was a bench by the tap, made from one big log with stubby legs of smaller logs. It was shaded by an overhanging tree with beaming bright pink flowers and I liked to sit there with Poey and her friends.

Jessica would leave me while she went to talk and eat in the shacks where she was always welcome, handing out the things she'd collected from the rich families.

People donated clothing, food, money, cooking pots and scissors, towel rails and radios. When a family moved away, there was sometimes a whole houseful of stuff for us to sort. And Jessica seemed to hold an inventory in her head of what was needed in the slum. She knew where an armchair could go and who wanted a stove or a mattress. She knew, too, who needed someone to care for their children because they were sick, and who was looking for work. There were expat families near us with more domestic help than was strictly necessary because Jessica was hard to turn away when she was set on an idea.

But I remember one morning, we were at the far edge of Phetbin where the air was filled with gnats and the stench of the stagnant overflow from the khlong. The shacks here were squashed right up against each other. A little girl I hadn't seen before peered out from behind a bulky old lady.

"Sawadee ka," said Jessica, *hello,* pressing her palms together and dipping her head in a wai. She stayed like that for a while, as if she'd forgotten what she was doing.

"Sawadee ka," said the woman. Jessica shook herself and handed her a carrier bag of toilet rolls.

The little girl popped her head around her grandmother's other side and frowned at me. I put my hands together in a wai, trying to smile.

"Yingyang," snapped Jessica. "What are you doing?"

I looked at my flip-flops in the dust. I had a blister in the usual place where they rubbed the inside of my toe.

"Kop khun ka," murmured the old lady, *thank you,* and she bowed herself backwards so that the sacking doorway shut in front of her.

A fly circled my ear and I batted at it.

"Stop fussing," hissed Jessica, "I can't think."

I pinned my hands to my sides and shook my head to keep the fly away. A young man wrapped in a blanket emerged from a heap of cardboard boxes and stared at me. I sniffed. He shuffled to the edge of the khlong and splashed his face.

"I can't. Can't do this. Can't do anything." Jessica dropped the last bag and started to scratch at her head. Two boys ran towards us, laughing.

"Khun Jessica," panted the first one. "Make me fly again!" He tried to take her hands. She pulled them away.

"What the fuck is going on?" she muttered, looking all around her and then at her hands. The boy shrugged and ran off, whooping and dodging the stones his friend was throwing at him.

I picked up the bag from the ground and led Jessica home. With every step, she had less strength. She was sobbing by the time I dragged her up the steps to the door.

Jessica lay down on the mattress in her little room, still in her clothes and shoes. "Sorry," she said, tears coming out of her mouth. "I'm so fucking useless. Can't do anything."

I held her hand and stroked her head. Jessica let out a desperate, whispered scream, stretching her mouth until the corners split, forcing it like vomit until she had no breath left.

When she finally slept, I sat cross-legged on the floor with my notebook. I remember I had my period. My stomach cramped heavy and sore and my head ached. My pen would not move fast enough across the page to rid myself of the mass of words crowding my mind. The first time I bled, I panicked that I would end up like Jessica, who often started bleeding when she was at her worst. I used to wonder if it was something I'd inherited. Or caught from Noah, who died of rotten blood when I was only a few years old. But Noah got thinner and thinner and I was growing taller and fatter all the time. I felt like Alice in Wonderland who got so huge she burst a house. I saw myself expanding until I filled the apartment, sweating and straining.

That day I wrote a story about an opal sweet that would shrink me to the size of the precise little Thai women who trotted on high heels through the dust. I wrote about butterflies and sunbirds, flying weightless and careless. I wrote about the hero who pulled me in my dreams from the murky waters of the khlong. And, as the room grew darker, I let my eyes blur and dropped single words onto the paper, words that seemed to come from nowhere and to make no sense.

I was nearly asleep when Jessica crawled into the room, her hair

30

twisted and tugged and fuzzy. She looked like a drawing scribbled by a child.

I shut my book and held it tight.

Jessica lay on her side with one arm bent under her head. She opened her mouth, closed it and let her eyes sag shut. I thought she'd fallen asleep again but after a while she said, without opening her eyes, "We're having visitors. Imagine that. Geoffrey and Maureen." She laughed sourly, as if the sound exhausted her. "Your grandparents. What have we done to deserve this?"

~

Pippa stood in Oxford Street, thrusting fliers into the fists of passers-by. The fliers were round, printed with the black and white symbol of Yin and Yang. The two swirled halves opened up to reveal an image of a golden Buddha, surrounded by gemstones in garish colours. In a spiral between the Buddha and the stones, so that you had to turn the flier round to read it, were the words, 'Eastern Vision. Exclusive Exhibition Today Only. Discover how the secrets of the East can change your life.' The typeface resembled an Eastern script, as though it were brushstrokes made by the hand of a wise old monk. Moses took one for Jessica and Pippa glared at her.

"And you swap me what time?" she said.

Jessica glanced at Moses, clutching the flier. Moses laid a hand on Pippa's shoulder and she threw it off, spitting at him like a snake.

The exhibition studio was filled with pastel-coloured dry ice. Sky-blue from one corner, baby pink, soft yellow, mystical mauve. The visitors were up to their knees in multi-coloured smoke, floating on clouds. Displays of lanterns, butterflies, fish made from translucent film. A giant mobile hung from the ceiling; twirling insects catching the light. Pinned to the wall beside the mobile was a notice 'For luck to all who enter the room wherein this hangs' and another, '£22.50'. Jessica looked at a shocking pink satin-covered Buddha the size of a small dog. It had crystal blue eyes. She imagined the line of its mouth moved and spoke to her. Whispered of secrets from far away.

There was a stall that sold magic carpets. These were £120 but they promised that if you enrolled on a course they would make your dreams come true. Moses circled his arms round her waist and said, "I'm your magic carpet. I'm taking you where you want to go."

Beside the carpets was a row of outsize candles in bright pink and orange, with Thai characters down the length.

"What does it mean?" asked Jessica, reaching out to touch the inscription.

"It means, 'take the path your aura promotes.' Sounds better in Thai, really." Moses cleared his throat and pointed above their heads where bells dangled on gold chains with long pink tassels.

"Look," said Jessica, wading through the rainbow ice to the next trestle table. "These pigs are great." They were chubby, smiling pigs sticking their bottoms in the air, and they came in lavender, blue or pale clementine.

"They're surplus, actually," said Moses, "it's the Chinese year of the rabbit now. Should be bunnies waggling their arses."

A young man in a pale tan jacket tapped Moses on the shoulder. "Are you going to introduce me?"

American. Jessica blushed. The man was so adult and confident, she felt scruffy and childish.

"This," announced Moses, "is Jessica. She's going to run the charitable arm. Bristol is really into it."

"Sam," said the American, shaking her hand firmly. "Welcome aboard. I have to say I've not been too involved in the development..." He trailed off, looking at Moses. "Of the charitable side of things. But if Bristol's keen then so am I. Why don't you come by the office and you can fill me in?"

"I'll leave Jess with you," said Moses. "If I don't go and see Pippa she'll be casting gypsy spells on us."

"Look," said Sam. "These are new. What do you think?" He turned away to gesture at a screen, three-fold, tall enough to hide behind and painted with tiny birds. The painter had given each feather and each eye a change of expression, a touch of movement. Jessica saw the birds' wings flutter gently as she watched.

"Sunbirds," said Sam. "Hell, I'm jetlagged. Come back to the office. I want to hear all about this do-gooding we're getting into."

In the office, Sam took off his jacket and hung it on the back of the door. He opened a drawer and poured himself a shot of vodka. Sighing, he poured a second and knocked it back. He looked at Jessica.

"No, thank you," she said. Sam looked out of place somehow.

"Take a seat." He moved some files off a chair and she sat.

He leaned against the desk, breathing loudly.

"So, Eastern Vision is to develop a benevolent face. Excellent. And you look just the person. Have you travelled much?"

Jessica shook her head.

"But I very much want to be part of Eastern Vision. To go to Thailand. To help the poor people."

"Very admirable," said Sam. "And how much have they told you about the work of Eastern Vision?" Absent-mindedly, he twisted his wedding ring, watching Jessica's face.

The half-unpacked boxes and crates of shiny gold pigs, fat little Buddhas and grotesque figurines swirled into one. Jessica felt as if the dry ice from the exhibition had caught up with her and was smothering her. Her eyes were heavy and her body began to shake. Sam's features blurred in front of her. She told herself firmly that now was not a good time to pass out; that this was effectively an interview. And even semi-conscious, she knew how important it was that she went to Thailand.

"Moses," she began, trying not to slur her words, "showed me some of the stock. And took me to the exhibition today. I think it's great that you support the Thai artists. Ethical Trading." She hoped she had the words right, she'd read them somewhere.

Sam nodded. "Good, good," he said. He seemed faintly amused. "I'm based in Bangkok. As is Bristol. But we come over here from time to time. Moses and Pippa keep things running smoothly. Keep all the balls in the air so to speak with the whole East-West–"

Jessica's head fell forward and she snapped it up, hoping he hadn't noticed.

A voice in her head spoke witheringly: *You won't get a second chance. Fuck this up and you're lost.*

Sam watched her eyes fall shut and snap open and wondered what Moses had been feeding her.

"I'm sorry," she said. "I don't feel too well. This is not good timing. Normally I'm fine. You mustn't think-"

Sam couldn't make out what she was saying exactly; she seemed to be sinking into sleep. He caught her as she fell off the chair.

He looked down at her lying at his feet and chewed his lip. What the hell–? Where was Moses when he needed him?

He tried shaking her.

"Jessica? Wake up. Jessica?"

She mumbled and dribbled a little.

Sam thought about having another shot of vodka but what with the jetlag, he thought he might end up in the same state himself.

Pippa opened the door.

"What is–?"

"Pippa, thank God. I think she's fainted. Do you know where she lives or anything? I wouldn't put it past Moses to–. She looks very young."

"There is copy of her papers for passport in that desk," she said, and went to look.

Moses arrived as Sam was telephoning Maureen, trying to explain who he was and where they were and that in fact he'd only met Jessica an hour ago. He knelt down beside Jessica and pulled her up to sitting. Then he put his hand under her chin and put his forehead to hers.

"Mark. Moses," said Pippa crossly. "Leave her alone this goodness' sake. You are not bloody Jesus."

"Ssh," murmured Moses, rocking Jessica gently to and fro. "I'm sharing my energy with her. She'll wake up in a minute."

Jessica opened her eyes. She sat opposite Moses, straight-backed and peaceful, looking into his face.

"There. Better?"

Pippa grabbed her bag and banged the door behind her.

On the telephone, Maureen said weakly, "Give me the address. I'll come and get her."

"She's woken up," said Sam, relief and wonder in his voice. "She's OK."

So, when Maureen pressed the buzzer labelled 'Eastern Vision' and dragged herself up the stairs, she found Sam at the desk checking through paperwork, and her daughter sitting on a faded rug opposite a very tall and rather grubby Buddhist monk.

"Mum," said Jessica. "This is Moses. And Sam. They're taking me to Thailand."

5

My grandparents were grey all over. Grandfather Geoff had no hair and a permanent squint. The intense light bothered him. He was built on a different scale to the Thai men. He was as tall as the Americans, but his shoulders were hunched over where theirs were broad and squared. With the fingers of one grey hand, he worried at a cigarette, flaking ash onto his clothes. His other hand was raised as if he was about to catch Grandmother Maureen, and I was glad because she seemed alarmingly brittle.

I looked at my grandmother's fragile bones and wrinkled skin and knew that Jessica had been adopted. I couldn't imagine the old woman ever having had thighs or a bosom and I was certain her eyes had never caught fire the way Jessica's did when she said we'd save the world.

"We'll have tea at the hotel," said my grandmother, looking at the camping stove.

Jessica shrugged. "If you like. Are you coming, Yingyang?"

"Of course she's coming," said my grandmother, wincing at my name.

We walked through the side streets where shops jutted out over the road and rails of clothing thrust themselves into the path. A man squatted beside a defunct motorbike and a boy sat on a tower of newspapers.

Jessica walked faster than usual, her red heels scraping the tarmac. My grandparents clung to each other, shrinking from mopeds that appeared from nowhere and nearly ran over their feet. I watched them edging their way through a cluster of children begging from a food stall, unaware that a truck was passing inches from them. My grandmother pinned her handbag to her side.

We turned into the main road and right across the sidewalk was an elephant. Its feet were decorated with bunting and it wore a headdress of bells and feathers. It had blinkers to keep it from veering off-course as it was led slowly along the street. Knots of electricity cable swung slightly from the vibrations of the traffic. The elephant could have hit them with its trunk.

Jessica strode past. My grandparents came to a halt just behind the elephant, glancing at me.

"Does she always walk this fast?" they complained. I blinked. They looked at each other and tutted.

The elephant swished its tail and farted. Grandfather thrust his arm across Grandmother's chest and stepped backwards into a cyclist cutting across to an alley. I put my hands over my mouth and laughed.

The air-conditioning was turned right up in the hotel lounge. A large white fan whirled above our heads, freezing the air so that my skin pimpled. We sat on white cane settees with green cushions that matched the tablecloths.

"Now then – Yingyang." Maureen sat forward and held out the menu, smiling. "What would you like?"

I looked at her, thinking that later I would write a story about an old lady who turned to stone.

"Yingyang?" she said again. Her smile and her hand holding the menu quivered a little.

Jessica took the menu from her. "Banana milk," she said. "Yingyang and I will have banana milk. Please." She winked at me and I smiled.

Grandmother sighed and sat back against the green cushions. I watched the fan. It had sharp edges. I imagined it letting go of the ceiling and spinning out of control around the room. It would decapitate the guests.

"It's time she came home," Grandfather was saying. I looked at Jessica.

"Thailand is home," said Jessica, taking a banana milk before the waitress had a chance to set the tray down. "Bangkok is all Yingyang's ever known."

"Exactly," said both grandparents together. The waitress picked up the teapot and poured hot, fragrant liquid into their cups. She put her palms together and dipped her head.

"Kop khun ka," murmured Jessica.

"Thank you," said my grandparents. They looked into their tea.

I slurped the banana milk and Jessica smiled.

~

Sam was sitting at the desk. Moses was practising the lotus position, which he still could not quite manage in full. And the telephone rang.

When he put the telephone down, Sam had an odd expression on his face; almost beseeching. His eyes quivered and didn't seem to focus.

Moses unfolded his legs. The left one had developed such bad pins and needles he could hardly put his weight on it. He stood beside Sam, who looked untouchable, unreachable, and waited.

After a while, Sam took out the vodka.

"Sam?" said Moses.

Sam drank, wiped his mouth, and put his elbows on the desk.

"My wife," he said. And, after a minute, "Anna. She has—"

His eyes bulged a little and then quivered again. "She has killed herself," he said.

It was difficult to shock Moses. Although he was young, only just twenty, he had developed an enviable strength in his aura. But faced with the rawness of Sam's pain, he found he had no words. And he couldn't so much as put a hand on his shoulder. He watched him drink too much, put his head on the desk and shut his eyes.

"Sam, where are you staying? Can I call you a cab to your hotel?" Moses had never used the word 'cab' before.

"I have to go home," Sam slurred, screwing up his face as though his pain were physical. "Get me a ticket organised. And a cab to the airport. Please."

Moses nodded. He chewed his lip, which was a very un-Moses like action. He sniffed, and glanced at the door.

"I'll need you to sign for the funds," he said quietly, "and for Jessica's ticket too. Can you manage that? I'll get the forms and the pen. You just sit there."

Sam grunted.

His signature was acceptable, if perhaps a little shaky. And Moses was able to buy two one-way tickets to Bangkok. He considered three, but he felt that it was not yet his destiny to travel East. His time would come, but for now he had further business in the West.

~

"Maureen," said Geoff, turning the page of a journal he was reading in bed. "You're cross."

It was the way she was rubbing cream into her hands. As if they'd let her down in some way.

"I'm not cross. I'm concerned. Quite justifiably."

Geoff glanced up. He took off his reading glasses.

"Concerned," she repeated, her voice cracking. "And you were always so very *against* the Gap Year thing."

"Ah, but this is apparently *much more* than a Gap Year," he said. "She tells me she's emigrating." He polished his glasses on the sheet and set them carefully by the bedside. "Characteristically perverse. But she will make her bed and she will have to lie in it. I have said my piece."

Maureen nodded. She went to the toilet, grimacing when she passed gas as she peed because Geoff could hear. She blew her nose, set her jaw and turned off the landing light.

Geoff had folded his journal and his glasses beside him on the little pine shelf unit. He pulled back the duvet on Maureen's side and patted the sheet.

"My dear," he said, as she sat beside him and adjusted her pillows. "Jessica will be nineteen in the autumn. I was in the office every day at her age, earning my own way in the world. Hm? You've been a good mother to her and now it's time for her to grow up."

"I won't stop being her mother, Geoffrey, just because she's not going to be home for a while."

Geoff rubbed his eyes.

Maureen repeated tightly, "I'll always be Jessica's mother."

"I know you will. But this isn't a school trip. She's not coming back next week with her dirty washing."

"She can come back whenever she likes. This is her home." Maureen's eyes swam.

Geoff grabbed hold of her wrists. "It is also my home. And yours. And it has not been a pleasant one these last few years. Hm? She has – poisoned the place."

Maureen's arms hung limp in Geoff's grip. "No," she whispered. "Don't say that. I know it's been—"

"It's been poisonous. And I am not prepared to put up with it any longer."

"Geoffrey, please." Maureen's nose was running and she couldn't free her hands to wipe it.

"Jessica is going to Thailand. Or wherever else she decides she fancies. Hm? But she is not staying here longer than it takes for her to pack her rucksack."

When he let go, there were red marks on Maureen's wrists.

Maureen cried in the dark, while her husband's breath loosened to a snore. Eventually she said into her pillow, "She's your daughter too."

Geoff's breathing grew shallow. He didn't move. "I never had a child," he said quietly. "You wanted one so much you adopted someone else's. And I went along with it to make you happy. Instead it has—"

Neither of them moved.

"We weren't to know," he continued. "But now I want my life back. And my wife. Hm?"

Maureen wrapped her arms around herself. She felt choked, strangled. Thailand might have been on another planet it was so far away. It was on a different *continent,* for heaven's sake. Jessica would have to travel on an aeroplane.

"Enough said on the subject," said Geoff, punching his pillow into shape.

Crouched outside the bedroom door, her head resting on the faded wallpaper, Jessica grit her teeth.

6

The sunbird shook his head. The movement was so delicate that it might only have been the fabric of the screen vibrating as a truck went past. But he was listening to the conversation, and he meant to say that simply because someone is silent does not mean that she is deaf or fast asleep.

"Jessica, you gave us no indication the child had problems."

"None at all."

"Everyone has problems."

"Not of this magnitude."

Magnitude. I saw myself under a magnifying glass, my eyes as big as a cartoon, my cheeks bulging scarlet.

The door to the central steps creaked. Jessica had left it open. My grandmother coughed.

"Do they have special schools in Thailand?"

"Yingyang doesn't need a special school. She's fine."

A motorbike revved its engine and stopped with a sound like a gun being fired.

"Autistic children need special schooling," said the mother quietly.

"Yingyang's not autistic, Mum!"

Mum. She called her Mum. After all these years. I didn't care if Maureen thought I was autistic. I had learnt long ago not to care what people thought. But Jessica was furious. The sunbird told me she was sorting the donations. Folding T-shirts, counting them, unfolding, shaking them out.

"She will speak when she chooses to. What does it matter? There's nothing wrong with her."

"Do you know that?" said Grandfather. "Has she seen a doctor?" He was pacing in front of the open door. "A paediatrician. Or a – psychiatrist?"

"Oh God," whispered Grandmother.

"Talking of which. Are you keeping up with your medication?"

"Why now, Dad? Why are you asking me now when you've not asked for thirteen years?"

"You left!" shrieked my grandmother. "Don't you tell us about

40

thirteen years!" She was crying. I didn't need the sunbird to tell me that. She made little shuddering breaths and sniffs and my grandfather muttered to her. Jessica sat down on the floor.

"I knew that – when we came – you would want us to take the child," said Grandmother in a whimper. "I wasn't ready."

"And now?" said Jessica, but I couldn't read her voice. The sunbird held its breath.

"I had thought – well, as you know," Grandmother's words were muffled. "But I'm not sure I can go through – that sort of thing – again. And psychiatrists." She spoke as though the word smelt.

"Silence isn't an illness, Mum. It's a choice."

"How much choice has Yingyang had in her little life?"

The magnifying glass vanished and I shrank until I was as small as the silhouette sunbirds that were high in the sky. I flew weightlessly with the flock, and it felt like swimming. Kicking my tiny legs behind me, I soared through clouds and felt the air on my face. But the sunbird on the ground looked up through the silver branches and said *don't go, wait for me.*

"Who pays the rent on this establishment, hm?" Grandfather patted his head and looked at the room and the apothecary cabinet coated in grime.

"Eastern Vision. The Americans who run it made their fortunes from this city." Jessica was drinking through a straw stuck into a plastic bag of ice. "And they've seen the slums fill up as quickly as they've been making money, so it's quite natural they want to support what I do."

I stuffed my notebook between my mattress and the wall and shuffled round the screen without looking at anyone. My grandfather huffed down his nose.

"And what exactly do you do? Hm? That makes married men pay out for your upkeep?"

"Geoffrey, for goodness' sake." The old woman reached out an arm to Jessica but stopped just short of touching her. "That's a terrible thing to say."

"I'll say what I like."

I knew that we would be living in the stinking slum if it weren't

41

for the Americans. I'd heard them call Jessica *Robin Hood*, something about taking from the rich and giving to the poor, and I was never sure which we were ourselves. Jessica still brought Sam or Bristol home from time to time to share her bed and she'd make ugly, elegant sounds from behind the door of her little room. The visits were less frequent and more discrete now that I was older and I sensed Jessica's unspoken resentment.

I squatted by the camping stove, reheating pancakes we'd bought in the street.

"Jessica, I think what Geoffrey, what your father, is concerned about, is Yingyang's schooling. She's clearly not making, well, progress." My grandmother's voice became quieter and quieter as she contorted herself in a pitiful pantomime, turning her back as if it would stop me from hearing.

"And you've been here long enough to know that, have you? Have you read her stories? Yingyang, where's your notebook?" Jessica grabbed a pancake, burning her fingers and stuffing it into her mouth. She made to go behind the sunbird screen and I jumped up.

"No!"

The sound came out shrill and cracked. Jessica froze. The grey grandparents looked like startled rabbits. They stared at me. I shook my head and Jessica laughed, spraying pancake crumbs from her mouth.

Grandfather blew his nose and rammed his handkerchief back into his pocket.

I sank down to the floor again, my eyes fixed on my mother, and began to roll a pancake.

Grandmother bent down, a movement which caused her to purse her lips and frown. Then she faced me and asked, "Would you like to come to England? Just to see—"

"How dare you?!" screamed Jessica.

"Don't shout at your mother. I've had enough of this."

"And so have I." Jessica pushed past to the door and held it open.

I backed against the wall. I'd read "Malory Towers" at school and I knew that England was a place where groups of girls had feasts at midnight and played games with nets on sticks. They got in trouble and played tricks on each other, but they were never ever lonely. And not *all* of them were English. I looked at Maureen, knelt painfully in front of me. Would they send me to such a place?

The thought was fleeting because I could never have left Jessica alone. Who would hide the knife when she threatened to slit her wrists? Who would lead her home when she forgot who she was in the street or walked without looking into the road?

I lowered my eyes and shook my head.

"You're saying you don't want to come? You want to stay here with your mother?" Grandmother's voice was tight.

I shook my head more fiercely.

"Get up, woman," muttered my grandfather. "This is out of sight. And I am not paying one more night in that hotel if I can possibly avoid it."

The old woman's lips trembled. "She's shaking her head. I'm not sure which she's saying no to. If I can–"

"I said get up, woman." My grandfather pulled his wife to her feet. Her knees clunked as she straightened up.

She patted her hair and blinked a lot.

"Well," she said, "we'll be saying goodbye, then."

I felt a sound forcing its way to my throat again but I clamped my mouth shut and prodded my uneaten pancake.

Jessica held onto the door and stared long after they were gone. I mashed the pancake into a mess on the hot metal plate. It was soft, almost rubbery, and it became sticky in my hands.

Sucking my fingers, I went to Jessica's side. I looked at the forbidden drawers of the apothecary cabinet and wished for a magic potion to take away her fury.

Resting her head on the door, still clutching the handle, Jessica whispered, "Maureen has never got on a plane before in her whole life."

I tugged my hands through my matted hair and endless strands came out. I rolled them together like a twisted knot of straw.

Jessica slammed the door shut.

"They came to see you, Yingyang. You know that, don't you? They crossed continents to see you. How does that make you feel?

And," she grinned. "You wouldn't even speak to them. We'll save the world, just you and me. And the stench of those two ancient people will never fill this room again. Open the windows."

I looked down at the floor.

"Get a grip," said my mother. "Open the windows. It's stifling in here."

PART TWO

7

As a child, I took my pick of the stories Jessica told me. I wrote of a glittering romance between her and a father I conjured up for myself. I imagined their parting; tearful, beautiful and for some reason inevitable, though I could never quite decide why. But now when she talks about the past, she stays closer to the truth. She understands my need to hear it, and she will talk for hours if I prompt her; about how she felt when she first saw Phetbin, how I came along and rocked the boat and how she's finally beginning to grow up at the age of thirty-seven.

The story of our life together begins with Jessica stepping groggily off a long-haul flight at Bangkok airport. I don't come into it for a while. She has no idea I'm on the way. She left Pippa and Moses behind in England, and Jessica laughs and cries telling me about the rise and fall of Eastern Vision London.

Jessica clutched her passport. Her shoulder hurt where her schoolbag dragged on it. She stuck close to Sam, who moved like a zombie but at least one who was familiar with Bangkok airport.

They queued forever to have their passports stamped and then they were thrust forward into the squash of people round the luggage carousel. Sam shoved his way past two boys with new rucksacks strapped to their backs. He pushed aside a trolley where a Chinese family were loading cardboard boxes wrapped in cling film. Jessica couldn't see him then. She chewed her mouth and stayed where she was. A Dutch couple argued over a suitcase handle as if one had broken it on purpose.

Sam came back with his bag over one shoulder and Jessica's in the other hand.

"Thank you," she said and tried to take it from him.

Wordlessly, he kept it, setting off toward the exit. She followed, memorising his appearance from behind in case she lost him. The crumpled linen jacket, the sweat on the hair at the back of his head.

"Taxi, madam."

"Taxi?"

"Madam, taxi?"

A tunnel of men called out to her and a crush of people hailed each other from either side of the ropes that divided them. A woman stopped abruptly in front of her to shake hands over the rope, and Jessica had to step sideways to stop herself slamming into her.

"Here," said Sam, taking her arm roughly. She let him lead her through the people. Then she watched as he leaned forwards into the arms of a young white man and began to cry. Keeping one arm round Sam, the man held out his hand to Jessica.

"Bristol," he said. "Welcome."

Bristol's hair was blonde and messy. He was tall and his shoulders were beginning to square themselves into adulthood. His skin was tanned and dirty but his T-shirt was pristine white, somehow immune to the sweat and dust that stuck to his stonewashed jeans and converse trainers.

Bristol clasped Jessica's hand long enough to tell her he was in control now. Thank God.

She felt somehow that she recognised him. They were very close, less than a foot between them now as people shuttled and squashed for a path through the crowd.

"Jessica," he said.

She nodded, still looking up into his face.

He stood Sam in front of him and brushed his chin with his fist.

"We can get you through this," he said, stiffly, quietly. "Give." He took Jessica's rucksack and led them to the exit.

The air smacked Jessica hard in the face, in the gut, on her knees and her feet that ached where she'd sat cramped for so long on the plane.

"Fuck," she mouthed.

"Hot?" asked Bristol, jerking his head at a taxi.

Jessica murmured a reply, sliding gratefully into the air-conditioned taxi.

Sam slammed his head back against the headrest. Bristol instructed the driver in Thai. Jessica gaped out of the window. She couldn't see clearly because her eyes flickered everywhere, drawn to the shop fronts that spilled onto the streets, to people squatting and shovelling food into their mouths, to the barrows where food was cooked in vast woks. A man with no hands sold tickets from a tray round his neck. A rail of clothing stretched right across the pavement. A man and a woman on a moped edged round it, the woman side-saddle in a pencil skirt and peep-toe heels. Piles of rubble where the pavement wasn't finished. Endlessly tall new buildings growing like elegant weeds from amongst the life below them. And everywhere the beautiful, inconceivably difficult Thai script on billboards and banners, handwritten signs and shop fronts.

"We'll go to my apartment. You can sleep if you want. Are you hungry?"

Hungry? Jessica couldn't tell. Her gut was bubbling as if the flight had filled her with air. Sleep? She wasn't sure she would ever sleep again.

A group of children in immaculate white shirts and navy bow ties crossed the road in front of them; the taxi's headlights missed them by inches.

Bristol spoke to the driver in Thai again. The taxi couldn't move; the crossroads were jammed with miniature open-sided trucks crammed with passengers.

"Tuk-tuks," said Bristol, without turning round. Jessica had an unnerving sensation that he could hear her thoughts. Immediately, her head filled with all that he mustn't know. He mustn't see that she was in fact a child in an adult's body who knew almost nothing and understood even less.

The taxi turned onto a side street. A building site was bordered by sacking on bamboo poles and a large canvas banner reading 'Luxurious Condominiums. Build for you tropical lifestyle.'

After that was a high whitewashed wall. Jessica could just see what looked like dolls' house temples poking out over the top.

"Spirit houses," said Bristol. Jessica choked on a cough. "For protection."

They pulled up at a wide iron gate where two uniformed guards saluted them. They had handcuffs in their back pockets and truncheons hanging from their belts.

"For protection?" said Jessica.

"It's a job," said Bristol.

The guards slid open the gate. One of them carried the bags to the sliding glass doors of the apartment.

"This is me. Ground floor." Bristol unlocked the door and gestured for Jessica to go in. Sam leaned his head on the glass.

Jessica didn't sleep. Not that afternoon or that night, when Bristol insisted she have his bed and he'd sleep on the futon in the other room. Sam drank until Bristol wouldn't give him any more and then he fell asleep on a pile of cushions.

In the morning, the maid fried samosas filled with minced pork and cabbage. Bristol pushed the plate towards Sam.

"Eat."

Jessica ate hers silently, aware of the crumbs of mince falling onto the table and floor.

"Tutu will clear up. You're in Thailand now." Bristol smiled at her. She wanted to say something in support of Tutu, but his smile was so warm and so especially for her that she was wrapped in it.

Tutu placed a bowl of tea in front of her.

"Thank you," said Jessica, who never drank tea.

"It's green tea. You'll like it, it's good for you. Sam, eat. You have to pull yourself together for a while or Anna's parents will take the twins back to the UK. Are you listening?"

Jessica blew on the tea and sipped. It was cold.

"Your in-laws want to adopt your children?" She looked from Sam to Bristol. Sam's face was as crumpled as his shirt, his hair sticking to his forehead. He'd kicked off his shoes and his socks stank.

Bristol spread his palms flat on the table. His nails were square. He wore a gold signet ring on the little finger of his right hand with the initials BJC.

"Jessica, will you be all right here if I go to Sam's this morning?"

She swallowed the rest of her tea and tossed her head. "Sure," she said. She thought, *I've never said, sure, like that before. Did I sound ridiculous?* "I'll maybe have a walk around. I'll be fine."

Bristol looked at her as though he really were trying to read her mind. She laughed.

"Is there a problem?" She wanted to stroke the signet ring.

"Don't go too far, Jessica. You're a lone farang female so don't get foolhardy on me. I have enough crises to handle right now."

"Farang?" said Jessica, trying to adopt a nonchalant expression. Did he think she was a child? Why had he agreed to take her on? Had he ever agreed? Really it was Moses who had got her here and he was still in London, where the streets made sense.

"It's Thai for foreigner," said Bristol. "Alien. You'll get stared at."

Jessica didn't put her sun hat on. Sun hats were for holidays and she didn't want to look like someone on holiday. She wore a camouflage green skirt and a black vest. But she still stuck out. Her skin was so white, her hair was so fair and seemed to take up so much room. The Thai women had smooth flat black hair. And she was so big. The Thai women were small and neat, even those that squatted in the dirt. So compact, so sure of their place in the vast ever-shifting jigsaw of the streets.

She walked fast. She found herself giving prim little smiles to the people who sat on the edges holding cups, bowing their heads silently at her or murmuring, "Madam?" People carried small plastic bags of food from the barrows that were made of bicycle wheels and baskets.

She tripped, the front of her shoe catching in a drain cover. The hole underneath splashed dirty water across her feet and the hem of her skirt. Beside her, three boys idling beside mopeds laughed. She ignored them.

She walked until she was dizzy with heat and the balls of her feet throbbed. Sweat dripped from every pore and she wiped at her face. She couldn't remember now if she'd turned corners or gone straight because every stretch was so new, so different and so much the same as the last.

A girl stood in an open shop front, framed by gold and fuchsia. Joss sticks, piles of limes, plastic flowers and Buddhas holding offerings were all around her and strung over her head, so that she must surely have all the luck in the world.

At a table sat a dumpy, wrinkled woman in a paisley apron, stringing tiny white buds, orchids, miniature roses and jasmine. Beneath her feet sat a skinny dog foaming slightly at the mouth.

Her father had told her to beware of dogs and muggers. But the dogs looked harmless enough; they lay cooking on the ground, droopy with fatigue, too hot even to look for food in the bin bags that sat on the road. And the people she passed were either too busy to mug anyone, shuttling to and fro on the uneven paving, or too calm and relaxed, leaning, lying, resting, breathing.

She decided she would step firmly away from her upbringing and assume the best of everyone. She wouldn't 'hmm' and sniff distrustfully like her father or mumble nervously like her mother. She would stop smiling primly. From now on she would beam at the world and the world would beam back.

~

Pippa swivelled her chair away from the desk. She glared at the stacks of fertility symbols she'd unpacked that morning. Grinning faces, contorted limbs, alarming phalluses like drill bits protruding from the middle. Available in five colours.

· The crates for next week's exhibition needed sorting. And Moses had been out all day. She kicked a luminous turquoise figure right on his spike.

Mick was no use. He said, "Pippa, it's a job, it's paid in pounds. Nod your head and take the money." He said it was harder for him to find work, that he stood out more and people might ask questions. And anyway, he said, he'd got them somewhere to live, hadn't he? Meanwhile he watched his girlfriend's television.

Last night, he had sat on the armchair, rolling himself something to smoke.

"What did they say at the bar?" Pippa asked.

"There is some work. Not every day."

Pippa heard the telephone ring through the wall. There was no telephone in this flat.

"Good," she said.

"Come here, sister." He squeezed her hand, holding the cigarette between his teeth.

As they listened to the sound of Marina's key in the lock, and Sasha whining in the pushchair, Pippa dropped his hand and turned away. She kept her back to the door. She felt the cold air as it opened and Marina bumped the pushchair over the loose step. The door fell shut again. In Pippa's head, it sounded exactly as the door at home did. If she closed her eyes, the scrape and shunt of damp wood might have been her mother returning from the bread queue. Or her father finished in the factory for the day. She might still be in their little apartment, knowing that tomorrow life would be the same as every day since she could remember.

Instead she was in London, sleeping on the floor while her brother shared Marina's single bed and the little boy woke them all up three times a night.

She righted the figure she'd kicked and wiped her nose on her sleeve. She needed this job. She needed Moses and Bristol and Sam and the whole web of half-truths that was Eastern Vision. With no idea what the future held for her or for the country she had fled, she could only – as her brother said – nod her head and take the money.

~

The kitchen smelt of lemongrass and ginger. Bristol sat at the table with his head in his hands. Tutu leant against the hob, watching a simmering pan. Jessica knocked and slid open the door.

"Sawadee ka!" she sang, *hello!*

"Very good, so quick learning," said Tutu, smiling.

"I've been talking to people." Jessica's feet and shoes were black. Her clothes were soaked through with sweat. "Bangkok is – I can't find a word for it. Mad, crazy. Like a jungle but it's not, it's very much a city. And the people are incredible, they've got such incredible karma, as Moses would say. I don't know how I imagined it would be but it's–"

Bristol sat up. He spread his hands flat on the table.

"I'm glad you've been OK." He turned his signet ring full circle. "I'm sorry you've come at such a bad time. I wouldn't have left you alone."

Jessica sat opposite him. She reached out and laid her hand on his. Her fingernails were dirty and she made a face.

"I understand," she said softly. "Poor Sam."

"Yup. Poor Sam." Bristol looked at her hand on his.

"God, sorry, I'm filthy." She snatched her hands away and sat on them.

He smiled. "I haven't even had a chance to ask Sam about his plans for you. I heard you were coming the same day I found out about Anna."

"I'm going to help with the charitable side of things. The benevolent face of Eastern Vision, Sam said."

Bristol nodded slowly. "Did you hear that, Tutu? Eastern Vision is to have a benevolent face."

Tutu giggled and said, "Your face, Easter' Vision uh?"

Bristol drummed his square-tipped fingers on the table, looking at Jessica.

She held eye contact without blinking.

"And what form is our charitable side going to take?"

"It's a simple matter," said Jessica, "of collecting from the rich and distributing amongst the poor. This is a city of extremes. I've seen both today. I've walked miles."

Tutu poured the steaming lemongrass potion onto two bowls of rice. She placed them carefully on the table.

"Kop khun ka," said Jessica, *thank you*. She grabbed her spoon and stirred. The first gulp burnt her mouth with boiling water and chillies.

Bristol looked into his bowl.

"Was this really Sam's idea?"

Tutu put her hands together and bowed slightly.

"You need some else?"

"No, Tutu. You are too too kind. Thank you."

"He always say that," murmured Tutu and left the room.

"I'm not sure," said Jessica. She felt the chair sway a little beneath her.

Bristol swallowed three large spoonfuls of food. Leaning back in his chair, he said, "I'm sensing more than a hint of Moses here. I'm right. You're blushing. But clearly he's talked Sam into it and some of Moses' worst ideas can turn out to be worthwhile."

Jessica dipped her chin. "Am I a worst idea?" she said.

"That remains to be seen." Bristol raised his bowl of tea and winked at her over the top.

~

On the bridge over the canal, Jessica stopped. From here, she could see the roofs of the slum houses. Tin huts and lean-to shelters, crumbling concrete and canvas tents. Two vast pipes lay to one side on the rubble of a demolition site. In one sat two little boys, their bodies moulded to the curve. In the other was a dog that lay awkwardly and didn't move. A statue of an elephant stood in the midst of the nothingness, draped with flowers and bells, ribbons and tinsel. At its feet were plates of limes, plastic bottles of oil and cards with handwritten messages.

In her hand was a bag of outgrown clothes Bristol's neighbours had given her. And in front of her were narrow alleys and rows of shacks. She took a deep breath, stepping off the bridge onto the walkway. It swayed under her feet. The planks were on stilts but they were soft with spray from the longboats that sped along the khlong. The smell was fish sauce, sewage, landfill, petrol and sweat.

A passing motorbike hooted at her. She smiled but it had gone already, bumping over the uneven walkway.

I can do this, I can do this. I will beam on the world like sunshine.

She would find someone friendly who would know who to give the clothes to. She'd keep smiling until someone smiled back and then she'd stop and somehow talk to them.

A plump old woman squatted at the foot of a reclaimed staircase, making little tutting noises. Her home was a corrugated lean-to; the staircase led to nothing. And her possessions apparently consisted of six cats and a toaster.

Jessica bowed in the wai greeting, pressing her palms together and dipping her head. The old woman stared for a moment and then returned the greeting.

Jessica took a step closer. She bent down within reach of the nearest cat.

"Lovely," she beamed, and stretched out her hand. Now she saw that the animal had little fur. Most of its scraggy frame was covered in rotting flesh. It had three legs and no ears.

She emitted a squeak and snatched her hand back. The old woman rocked with laughter until she coughed the contents of her lungs onto the bottom step.

Jessica had just decided to laugh as well when the coughing began and she stood quickly, glancing about to see who was watching. But the alley was quiet. The residents were out. At work? Begging?

"OK?" Jessica asked the woman, who was wheezing her breath back in strained gasping sucks.

The woman didn't reply but her breathing gradually eased and she continued to look at Jessica, picking her remaining teeth with her fingernails.

Jessica flailed about her for something to say.

"You have many cats," she said, pointing at them and holding up six fingers.

The woman heaved herself upright, frowning. She held up her hand and disappeared behind a wall of sacking.

Jessica waited. She rubbed the sweat off her face for the hundredth time, leaving dirty marks on her cheeks. I will beam and the world will beam back. I will soar in the sky like the sunshine. I am all the colours of the rainbow.

A beautiful girl came to Bangkok. She had hair like spun gold and people stopped in the street to touch it.

She carried a backpack covered in diamonds, rubies, emeralds and sapphires. Each precious stone was a wish that she had made and she wanted to carry her wishes with her all the time.

The children saw her coming because she glinted in the sun and they ran to her and took her hands. She whirled them so fast their feet came off the ground and they flew around her in a breathless circle.

The women stroked her golden curls and smiled at her sparkling wishes, and—

The woman returned with a young man whose eyes swivelled. They spoke in short, furious sentences, gesturing at the cats, shrugging.

The man lurched towards Jessica, swivelling his eyes all over her.

"OK?" he said, pointing at a grey cat with all its limbs and both ears.

"Oh no, I don't want to buy one, no!" Jessica backed away.

The man screwed up his face. "Hnh?" He shrugged. "Hnh?"

"Lovely, they're lovely cats. But they're yours." She shook her head, tripping backwards over a jagged concrete rock. "Thank you, kop khun ka, sawadee ka." She bowed in a deep wai, dropped the sack and walked quickly away in what she hoped was the direction of the road.

8

Moses made the office as dark as possible for one-to-one Psychic Therapy sessions. Pippa refused to do any cleaning at all, on the basis that he already gave her all the worst jobs and if she did it once, he'd expect it of her. So he shut out the grime and conducted his sittings by the light of several candles, cradling his clients in a sanctuary of warmth.

He buzzed the door open for Alexis, who had made the appointment following a visit to an Eastern Vision exhibition. Another American in London. Moses seemed to attract them. He drew in a deep breath. In his stomach was a flicker of anticipation – nerves? – which was an unfamiliar sensation.

He opened the rainbow door and bowed, gesturing for his client to sit on the rug, then he shut out the strip light from the hallway, which would time itself out after five minutes.

Alexis sat, unsure where to put his knees and feet. Moses sat opposite in his usual half-lotus. He began by looking at the client in the candlelight.

Alexis swapped his weight from one buttock to the other, first meeting Moses' gaze and then flicking his eyes down to the little flame beside him.

Moses was careful not to let his face show surprise or recognition. Alexis George was an actor. Only a few years before, when Moses had still been living with his parents and watching television after school, Alexis had been on his screen three nights a week. He looked older now, despite the candlelight, but he still had that ridiculous wide-eyed button-nosed face that would keep him a boy forever. Moses gave himself time by passing his fingers through a flame and nodding slowly.

After a while, he said, "You are in a place of uncertainty," and he watched Alexis's face.

Alexis grimaced and nodded.

"You aren't sure what to do or where to go. Even which continent to live on."

Alexis sighed. He looked pained.

"It hurts you to hear this spoken aloud," continued Moses. "It feels wrong to admit how insecure you are."

Alexis swallowed and watched Moses' fingers hover by a tea light.

"But your aura tells me that you already know. That you have plans but that the part of you that is suffering is not listening. You have become so – unsettled, that you cannot hear what your inner voice is saying."

Alexis ran a hand through his hair. Moses waited.

"I need a new direction," said Alexis at last, in a croak. "Is that what you're seeing?"

Moses drew in a deep breath, nostrils flaring, and pressed his fingertips together.

Behind the filing cabinet, Pippa tried hard not to sneeze. She concentrated on breathing through her mouth. She'd been hoping Moses would play some sort of atmospheric music in the background. The silences were long – she tried holding her breath but she had to let it out in little puffs. If she shut her eyes it was all too easy to imagine she was back in the truck, or under the seats in the coach.

"I'm getting travel," said Moses. He swivelled his eyes up and left. "Do you know someone in Spirit who had a soft spot for you?"

Alexis thought quickly.

"A man or a woman?"

"A man," said Moses, stretching his neck so that his head followed his eyes in the effort to maintain the connection with the Spirit world. "He wasn't that old when he died. He went too early."

Alexis's eyes were wide.

"There was an ex-cast member who had cancer," he said quietly. "Trevor was in his fifties when he died. "

Moses' eyes fell shut and his face became a picture of serenity.

"Trevor says you did something for him. Something kind and he hasn't forgotten. It meant a lot to him. He wishes you well."

Alexis looked shame-faced; perhaps he hadn't taken as much notice of Trevor as he should have.

"Trevor says listen to your inner voice. The future will come to you if you let it."

Pippa's toes had gone numb. She wriggled them, wondering how long these sessions lasted, and how long after Moses left she would have to wait until she could stand up and slip out.

~

Bristol came back late. Jessica had showered and washed her hair and now she sat on the floor eating biscuits and circling areas of her map of Bangkok. Her cotton pyjama vest and shorts felt unnervingly like a piece of home. Her legs were covered in large pus-filled insect bites.

"Hey," said Bristol.

"Hey," she said.

"Have you eaten?" Jessica held up a biscuit. "I'll tell Tutu I'm home."

Tutu appeared magically at the door.

"You wan' dinner Mister Bristol? I make already, come now."

"You're a gem, Tutu one-two." Bristol unbuttoned his shirt and tugged it off, using it to wipe the sweat from his chest.

"Have you been busy today?" asked Jessica shyly and her voice sounded childish in her head.

He rubbed the shirt over his face. "Today," he said. "Yes." He dropped the shirt on the floor. "Interesting meeting on the building side, actually. Luxury condominiums."

"Building? I thought Eastern Vision was about art and enlightenment."

"Eastern Vision is about anything I want it to be." Bristol made a crazy face.

Tutu picked up the shirt.

"The art of making money." Jessica folded her arms.

"I'd put it more delicately than that."

"But the materials are ethically traded. And the labour is properly paid, right?" She dug her nail into a bite on the sole of her foot.

"We are building," he said, "two apartment blocks. Which will make us money. I'm sorry if that's a problem for you."

She shrugged.

"Summer Towers and Tranquillity Place. At least admit they're cool names."

She looked at him with her head on one side, suppressing a smile.

"That's better. Now tell me what *you* have been doing."

"I've been making friends in the slum by the khlong." Bristol was looking at her legs. "I know," she said, "I've been bitten to pieces."

"In the slum? There's dengue fever in that water. You should have worn repellent."

"My body will acclimatise." She stuck out her chin. "Then they won't bite any more. The locals don't get bitten."

Tutu placed a steaming bowl on the table.

"No," said Bristol, "but you're a juicy farang with fresh white skin just asking to be eaten." He gnashed his teeth.

Jessica blushed. She sat with him and they spooned soup full of chillies and ginger over their rice.

"How is Sam?" She stirred her food.

"Sam is improving." Bristol slurped the soup. "There's a good kick in this."

"Are the grandparents still talking about taking the children?" She wondered if he'd say this wasn't her business.

He shook his head.

She ate. After a while, he put down his spoon and stretched his arms.

"If we can keep him sober and roughly upright, we'll be OK. Although…"

Jessica traced Bristol's hairline with her eyes, watching the sandy blonde tufts that fell where they chose.

"Although?" she murmured.

"Although," he breathed in deeply, "maybe it would be better if they did go back to the UK."

"How can you say that? They'd grow up wondering why. And the grandparents will get *old*." Jessica's voice cracked. She knew her face had turned blotchy.

"Hey," said Bristol. He threw her a kitchen roll. "Issues?" he said.

She blew her nose and tossed her head.

"No issues. I was adopted. That's all."

Bristol nodded slowly.

"OK," he said. "OK." He took her hand for a second across the table and she saw that he wasn't wearing the signet ring.

~

Moses was what Sam referred to as his 'wild card'. His serendipitous bolts of inspiration could be very profitable. Diversification came naturally to him, so that each bizarre new layer of enterprise seemed to sprout almost credibly in his hands from the last.

And now he began to move on his idea for a media campaign that would bring to another level of profitability the Psychic Therapy sessions, related merchandise, courses, workshops and by extension the other lines of business that he was nurturing more discreetly.

Sam was still comatose much of the time, but Bristol had found a confidence that he hadn't known whilst his older cousin had been in control. In the days since Sam and Jessica had arrived in Bangkok, Bristol had made business decisions and investments independently. He had listened while Sam's father-in-law railed that the business had killed his daughter. And, when it came to it, he had had her body flown home. He doubled the maid's wages and told her she was an angel.

And there was Jessica. She spent her days exploring. She found the hidden parts of the city and was made welcome where no farang had ever been. She made him show her where the richest people lived.

"It's so important," she said, "that an ethical business like Eastern Vision has a purely altruistic branch. Redistribution of wealth." She laughed, and Bristol said, "You're so right," and began to wonder if he was falling in love.

He let her keep his bed and he slept on his futon. Each morning she was up early, poring over maps and scribbling plans.

And then Moses rang about Alexis.

"He was an actor. An American in a British soap. His face is still quite well known in the UK. Potentially we have a high profile Psychic success here. He's ready to be persuaded."

Bristol sighed.

"How well known?"

"It would make those composite magazine covers where celebrities tell their stories. 'Life, Death, Prizes,' those ones. *Woman's Weekly* or *Froth* maybe. But we need to move on this now if we're going to do it. Can one of you get over here?"

"Moses, Sam can't get out of bed most days. And I'm tied up with everything else. Including the last project you sent me. Who is borrowing my bed because I haven't had a chance to sort accommodation yet." As he said this, his eyes met Jessica's and he smiled.

"How is Jessica Jane?" said Moses.

"She's incredible," said Bristol, still looking at her. "I have never known anyone with so much energy." Jessica blushed and looked away, her heart beating a little faster. "And you're right, goddamn you. A charitable arm is a Good Idea."

"So I'm right again this time, Bristol. Stop shagging the new girl, get on a plane and help me set this one up."

Bristol spluttered, "I am not–" and Moses laughed. "I'll call you later. Ring the bastard and make sure this is good. I am up to my eyes here."

"And you love it."

Bristol sighed as he put the phone down, aware of Jessica's presence. He pushed back his chair and went to stand beside her. She didn't move. He'd never seen her so still. He put a hand gently on her arm.

"Jessica?"

"Mm?" She sounded different.

"I have to go to London for a week or so. Would that be – would that be OK with you?" His hand was still on her arm.

"Does it matter? That it's OK with me?"

Bristol moved his hand down her arm to stroke the inside of her wrist.

"You," he said very quietly, "are beginning to matter to me."

Jessica smiled. She let him turn her to face him and kiss her forehead.

"I will be back as soon as I can," he said, his lips still touching her skin.

She shivered. She whispered, "What sort of kiss is that? On my forehead like a child?"

"It's a promise kiss," he said. "Now is the wrong time to–. Bangkok is a place where everything happens too fast. And with Anna, and Sam like he is. What am I trying to say here?" Bristol finally put his arms round her. The new, grown-up Bristol, who could take responsibility and think ahead. "I don't want to go wrong here." He wound a golden syrup curl around his finger. "I want to see what this is between us, because–"

"Because–?" breathed Jessica, smiling, a tear forming behind her eyes.

"Because." He squeezed her, let her go, took hold of her hand and coughed. "As I said, you are beginning to matter to me. And I hope, I think perhaps, you might be feeling–?"

Jessica kissed his hand and dropped it.

"That's a promise kiss," she said.

Bristol nodded. "I'm looking forward to taking you up on that promise."

"Me too," said Jessica.

~

'*Psychic Therapy Freed Me From HIV: Alexis George's Amazing Claim.*'

Bristol's eyes widened. He swigged from the bottle of water beside him.

"It's his risk," said Moses. "It was a slow news day, they're glad to have him."

Bristol flicked the corner of the paper.

"He's asking a lot," he said.

Moses performed a plié, clicking his knees.

"He wants in on Eastern Vision."

"So take him on. You need him if Sam is as crashed as you say he is."

Bristol thought. He was in control now. His strong older cousin needed him. To make decisions and carry their weight. And maybe Alexis had come at the right time. If he really wanted in, why not give him a chance? The publicity he'd brought Eastern Vision in the UK was huge. Bookings for Hypnogem Practitioner courses and Psychic Therapy sessions were full for months. And the merchandise was selling through mail order and exhibitions faster than it could be acquired.

"Just give him some leaflets to file," said Moses, grinning, "he's not the brightest card in the Tarot deck."

~

"Sam, if you want to keep your children you have to fight for them. Do you understand what I'm saying? Anna's parents are talking themselves into coming back for them. They're changing their minds, they don't believe Gina will last. You must have seen this coming. Sam?"

Sam was kneeling on the floor, wearing only boxer shorts. His eyes were closed. He held the telephone tightly, as though it were Bristol's hand. Bristol, his little cousin, had become his rock. He had kept Eastern Vision afloat while Sam ignored it, and now he was putting a stopper on the sympathy to save him from losing everything.

He could hear Gina singing as she tucked the children into their beds.

"Tell them no," he managed to say. "I – we – can manage. I'm their father."

Bristol waited.

"I know I haven't been much of a father so far." Sam swallowed. His voice felt crusty from disuse. "But I'm going to be. And I will speak to Anna's parents. Soon. Tell them to come back. If they want." He opened his eyes, unsure what he was saying. "They can come and see how well we're doing."

"That's the man. Sam, I have to go. You will get through this. You will."

Sam got shakily to his feet. Gina came through with a stack of washing when she heard the telephone click.

63

"Gina," he said, and she stopped and looked at the floor. "I want to thank you. Thank you." He spoke slowly. "You have been like a—" he swallowed. "A mother. To Jack and Tilly."

Gina looked up, her face panicked.

"You have rescued us all." Sam held out his hands and took the washing from her. "Have a rest, yes? You can't work all the time."

"You no wan' I work here?"

"Yes, God yes, Gina, that's what I'm saying. I'm saying I can't do this without you."

Gina had been about to cry and now the tears came anyway.

"I so worried. I love those children. I like stay here."

"And the children love you," said Sam quietly, tears in his own eyes.

He dropped the washing on the floor and before he knew what he was doing he had put his arms round Gina's shoulders and pulled her to him so that they could cry together.

9

Pippa laughed in Bristol's face.

"How can I believe you are making this suggestion? Please don't think about it anymore." She made a great show of returning her attention to the book of catalogue orders. Her face was red and her fingers shook on the keyboard.

"A suggestion which brings business and employment to your country?" Bristol leaned back in his chair, watching her face.

"In Romania, business and employment are not words of joy." Pippa stopped typing. "I know, because my father works in a factory and he is looked after the same as a piece of – of machine. He is a piece of machine and his family is put in a box. Those factory workers *must* be there. They were maybe happy in their villages but they are forced to move in the town." She pronounced 'forced' with two syllables.

Bristol nodded. He breathed out noisily through his nose. "Forgive me, Pippa. You are upset."

"Yes I am upset. I cannot make contact with Romanian people.

For myself reasons. Please understand." Now Pippa watched Bristol's face for his reaction. He nodded slowly.

"We will look into other possibilities," he said, sitting straighter and reaching for his notebook. He had lists within lists of things to do.

"Not some other possibilities, Bristol," said Pippa, her arms folded. "If these stupid English people want these ridiculous toys, make them in a stupid English factory. Not in another country where people are so cheap." She looked at him, the red flush gone and a flame in her eyes.

Bristol stood and made to leave. "Those stupid English people," he said, "are paying your wages and mine. Don't forget that." He opened the door.

"There is a message," said Pippa.

He turned, arched by the rainbow on the open door.

"I write it down. There." She held out a scrap of paper, her other hand on the keyboard and her eyes on the screen so that he had to go back and take it from her.

He squinted at the note but the bulb in the corridor strip light had blown and he couldn't make it out. In the street, he read Pippa's small, cursive hand: 'Bristol phone Linda today now' and a number.

Linda. He'd been hoping to get away without seeing her. He checked his watch.

He went back to his hotel, sank a beer from the minibar and pulled off his shoes. Linda. He'd talked her out of coming to Bangkok when she wanted to use up her leave before April, inventing a trip to a hill tribe in Laos where they made interesting shawls. Coming to the UK and not calling her was supposed to be a message. But perhaps her skin was even thicker than he'd thought; he'd have to make it clearer.

He'd never promised Linda monogamy. They slept together when they got together, but they were independent, business-minded people going in different directions. Initially, when Bristol had refused to allow his own father to invest in Eastern Vision, Linda's father had financed the very first buying trip to Thailand. Sam graduated from Oxford, and Bristol hadn't known what to do, and the two cousins rented a flat in London together. The PR company Linda had been with at the time had helped set up the first "Wisdom of the East" programme. But she was older than Bristol and she was on a ladder, so she'd drifted away from Eastern Vision since. They took off on their own, with a night together occasionally for old times' sake. And the business arrangement with Linda's father continued of its own accord, enabling Bristol to leave his own father stamping and puffing that he was a "pig-headed" boy who'd be back when it all fell apart.

He didn't want to think about Linda's hard-nosed talk and ungainly love-making right now. Jessica was sleeping in his bed. It was almost more than he could bear, to wait. Those golden curls. Those turquoise eyes. How the Bangkok she saw was so different to the one he knew.

He dialled the number on Pippa's note, lying on the bed and rotating his ankles.

"Bristol? I need to speak to you. My father—" Linda was whispering and she covered the telephone to speak to someone else.

"Your father what?" He was pulling out. Bristol began to calculate how they could manage without his investment. Whether he could be made to stick around at least until the apartment blocks were up. Without Linda's father, the real estate project would collapse catastrophically. Whilst Bristol was in control. There was no way he was going to let Eastern Vision fall apart and have people say it was because Sam was out of action. Was that why Linda's father was pulling out? Because Bristol was not considered capable of handling things without his big cousin to mind him?

"Linda. Listen. Let me speak to him. Is he there with you?"

"He knows you're in London."

"Speak up. I can't hear you."

"You can't speak to him. Not yet. Meet me. Where are you staying?"

"The usual. But I'm leaving—" he thought quickly, "in the morning."

"Then I'm coming now. Don't go anywhere, we have to speak."

"What is going on here? Is this about Sam?"

"No Bristol, this is very very much about you."

He put the phone down with the old feeling of petrol fumes in his spine, the way his father had made him feel when he said, "I'm a self-made man." His voice was so loud. "This boy is entirely a product of my success. You'd have thought he'd have cut the apron strings by now but they're all knotted up with the purse strings." He shouted with laughter when he said that and people joined in. Bristol had trained himself to think *who does he think he is, asshole?* When the memory of his father grew too loud, he repeated this until he silenced it.

Reception rang to say his visitor was in the lobby. He was wearing jeans now and an old T-shirt, and in a spirit of irritation and defiance, he went downstairs with no shoes on.

He strode past reception where a pastily pregnant woman was looking at the hotel brochure. She was wide from every angle. Her hair was too short. He hated how women gave up with their looks when they got settled.

He scanned the sofas and chairs, furious to have been caught like this. Pippa must have told them he was here. If he'd thought to see Linda's father for a schmooze and a beer, he might not be in this mess. He could have got away without seeing Linda, or at least without *seeing* her. He scratched his scalp. Stress had sent his skin out of control. He peered at his shoulders to check for dandruff, brushed them with his hands and glanced towards the ladies', thinking Linda must have gone in there.

"Bristol."

Her voice, behind him, reminding him she was real. Making him feel – something indefinable to do with the past.

He turned, with his face on, ready to say her name and kiss her cheek. But he was stunned into silence. The bulky pregnant woman at reception stood before him. She had the face of Linda's mother, but she spoke with Linda's voice.

"I've surprised you," she said. Bristol stared at her. "I was somewhat surprised myself."

He opened his mouth. When nothing came out, she said, "Shall we sit down?"

The lobby was dead. She led him to a sofa in the far corner, beneath a television screen that wasn't switched on. He sat at a right angle to her, leaning his elbows on the arms of the chair.

"Well," he said.

A matronly waitress stood over them with her eyebrows raised.

"No, thanks," muttered Bristol.

"Hot chocolate with cream, please," said Linda, tucking a pleat of blouse up under her breasts and smoothing the rest over her huge belly.

"I didn't know you were – uh – in this condition," said Bristol, scratching his head.

"No, I didn't ring you."

"I thought you were anti-children."

Linda shrugged. "Not a lot of choice now is there?"

"And your father? What's his problem? Does he not trust me without Sam to–?"

"This isn't about Sam, I told you. What I wanted to tell you is that this baby is coming soon. You are going to be a father within days." She laughed softly, tiredly, "I hope it's days, anyway. I can't go on like this for long."

Bristol's mind scrambled over itself to count back – when had he last been in the UK? He wanted to tell her how ridiculous she was being, that it couldn't possibly be true. She was joking to watch his reaction. Maybe she wasn't even pregnant.

"You were taking the pill, Linda. I saw the packet."

The hot chocolate arrived. Linda ate the cream from the top with the long spoon.

"Sometimes," she said, through a mouthful, "pills fail." Bristol scratched behind his ear. "What are you thinking?"

"I'm thinking," he said, leaning back and looking directly at her, "that you have missed a pill by accident or design to trap some poor English guy into – I don't know what. But there is no way that I am responsible here. Have you spoken to the poor English guy?"

Her face flushed a deep pink and she splashed a drop of chocolate onto the shelf of her breasts.

"You are basically telling me I've been sleeping around." Linda slurped the chocolate and wiped her mouth with her hand.

Bristol made a face. "I am making no such judgment. You have always been – free – to do your own thing."

"No. You have been free to do your own thing. I have been getting fatter and puffier and completely unfree. Since I last saw you. I can't even concentrate at work. They don't take me seriously anymore. I'm off now."

Bristol laid his hands flat on the table. After a while, he said, "Is there – no doubt, no – possibility?" He coughed a little.

"You are this baby's father."

He coughed again. It made him feel quite dizzy to hear the words spoken so bluntly.

Then, she said, "Do you want to be – involved?" Quietly, looking down into what remained of her drink.

Bristol found his breath stuck halfway down his windpipe and he had to gulp the air down.

"Bristol, I have always loved you." Linda's voice was tiny. She looked up at him.

He took her hand across the table. It felt big and spongy. He remembered the feel of Jessica's hand in his.

"You've not mentioned this before." He tried a smile.

"I do. I love you. I've never loved anyone like I love you. I've always pretended our relationship was – intermittent. But all the time I'm waiting for you."

He squeezed her hand and passed her a paper napkin from a little steel holder.

Linda blew her nose on the napkin.

Bristol swallowed. He touched her arm.

"Hey," he said.

She took his hand and held it firmly, staring into the tall, scummy glass.

10

Jessica lay in Bristol's bed, reluctant to move. She wanted to hold her breath until he got back; wanted the world to pause and nothing to change until he was there again. *A promise kiss.* She smiled at the ceiling. If she wasn't so grateful to Moses for sending her here, she'd have resented him for taking Bristol away just as they were beginning. She laughed aloud at the thought of sex with Moses – she'd lost her virginity to someone who dressed as a monk. It was so outrageous and so perfect. And she was pleased that she'd done it, as if she had given him a gift, because it was he who had spirited her away from everything that was suffocating her and catapulted her into a new life. He had shown her how to live, how to breathe. She knew at last who she was and she felt pity for the memory of herself staring forlornly at her reflection in the train window the day she'd met him.

Her father had told her not to go near dogs or strangers, not to drink tap water and not to phone home. He said she would get homesick if she rang and she'd be back home with her tail between her legs. At the airport, her mother couldn't speak because she was crying so much. She clutched Jessica's hand and in the end her father had prised their fingers apart. Then he patted Jessica as if she were a horse being sent into a field and said, "Get going, girl. Don't want to miss the plane." Maureen didn't move; her hand had hovered like a claw where Geoff had separated it from Jessica's.

Jessica blinked away the memory and swallowed. She got out of bed and examined herself in Bristol's bathroom mirror. Her period was overdue and, despite the sunshine, her skin had erupted in spots since she arrived. New heads were forming like seeds at different stages of growth; flat ones and sharp ones, red and black. She squeezed a whitehead with two fingernails. Now she'd made deep ridges either side and a miniature bleeding volcano.

"I'll burn them off," she said out loud, pulling her hair back into a band and grabbing her key. She walked with her chin jutting out, willing the sun to scorch her skin. She wanted the spots gone and her period out of the way before Bristol came back. In her mind, she saw him slide open the door to his apartment and take her straight into his arms, covering her face in kisses.

Although she was thirsty and hungry, she was too impatient to stop and buy breakfast. She passed the wagons where people stirred huge woks of noodles, rice, ground meat and vegetables, but her feet were in charge and they never quite stopped. She passed Western corner stores and she went inside one but couldn't decide what to buy. In the street were rows of transparent plastic bags hung on poles holding bunches of long dried leaves, ginseng roots, grotesque fried shapes that crumbled under each other's weight, and mushrooms that looked thousands of years old. They all belonged in a witch's cauldron and she wondered who bought them and for what.

She walked the streets all afternoon, dizzy from lack of food and drink, going faster and faster, smiling at people; a trinket seller, a man in a suit and tie trying to cross the road, a gaggle of street kids, a bearded backpacker.

As darkness fell, she came to a street of bars. Outside each one were touts with menus and sales pitches.

"Pretty lady menu?" A man thrust a sheet of paper in front of her.

"Pussy blow candle, Pussy ping pong uppercunt, Pussy shoot balloon, Pussy chop banana, Pussy razorblade show."

Jessica couldn't focus on him, as if he were standing in a haze.

"You put these shows on? In your bar?"

"All time, madam. You come one minute, no like, no money OK?"

Jessica walked on fast but the next bar also had touts and their menu was the same.

"No, thank you," she said.

There was a night market, lit with precarious wiring, selling live toads in sandwich bags and fake designer watches. She approached a food cart, peering into the wok. As her eyes flicked to one side, she jumped. Beside the cook was a pig's head, smirking up at her, its snout swollen and bloody.

"You like girl-on-girl action?" said a tout, blocking her path, "Or man and girl together?"

A woman, unusually wide across the shoulders, emerged from the bar. She wore a prim waitress' uniform of black and white that would have fitted in in a hotel lounge. Jessica was curious. Maybe she would learn about what men liked. She followed the woman into a bar lit with fairy lights. Down the middle, on a raised platform, ten women shuffled from foot to foot in matching thong bikinis with numbered badges. They bounced continuously at the knee, glancing at each other, at the customers. A cartoon show was projected onto one wall showing a naked girl performing obscene little tricks with what looked like a small second world war bomb.

In the corner, a fat white man with a ginger moustache stroked the thigh of a dancer, dressed in her bikini thong and sitting right up close to him. Jessica watched his hand slide over her golden skin.

She squinted up at the dancers' faces which registered only distance and boredom. They were young, these girls, her own age perhaps. The voice in her head said, *perverse child*, and the ice in her drink shook. What was she doing here? She jumped up and left, avoiding the pleas of the tout, thinking that she could pretend she had never come.

She wanted Bristol to come back more than ever. The revulsion she felt at the bar and the cartoon was mixed with a yearning, with stirrings in her body that made her want to touch herself. Her groin, her stomach, her breasts throbbed with want. The blood she needed to release filled every part of her.

She was shaking when she got back to the apartment. Tutu was nowhere to be seen, and she was grateful; she didn't feel able to speak sense and she knew she looked a state. She showered, still shaking, and looked in the kitchen for water. There were dregs in two plastic bottles and a third one crushed in the sink, but no more. Tears came to her eyes but she was too tired to cry. She lay down on the bed and wished for sleep. The warmth she had felt over the last few days had deserted her; she felt alone and confused.

When she slept, she dreamt she was lost in the night market. Her father drove past in a car but didn't see her. Stalls selling cake were encased in glass and she couldn't see how to buy any. She woke again and again, cold from the air-conditioning, feeling sick and dizzy.

In the morning, she was woken by a man's voice. She couldn't make out what he was saying, but the rumbling tone told her Bristol was home. Jessica brushed her teeth quickly and pulled her hair into a rough ponytail. She was still shaking. She waited for him to come into his room. She thought about getting back into bed and pretending to be asleep.

"Jessica?"

"Hey," she said, grinning, coming out into the main room.

Sam stood there wearing a shirt with cufflinks, sober.

"Sam."

"How are things?"

"Good," she said, looking around for Bristol.

"What happened to your face?"

She yanked the band off so her hair fell over it.

"The do-good project going well?"

"Yes," she jutted out her chin. "Small steps."

"Jess, I spoke to Bristol."

"Is he on his way?"

"Not yet. Can we sit down?"

She laughed oddly. "If you like. It's not my apartment."

"No. That's sort of what I need to talk to you about. I'm not sure how to say this."

Jessica sat straighter. She raised her eyebrows, tried to look nonchalant and ironic all at once.

"So say it," she sniffed, looking away, yawning a little.

"Jess, Bristol has got himself engaged. To an English woman. They're having a baby. I'm sorry if you–"

The room shifted. The chair spun. Jessica gripped the edge of the table.

"Why should you be sorry?" she said. "Don't you like her?"

"Linda's OK I guess." He smiled. She was tough this kid. He'd been too deep down inside himself to notice her much, and the last moment of sanity before the bomb fell on his life was when she passed out in the rainbow office and he ended up ringing her mother. But now he could see that she wasn't the schoolgirl he'd seen that day. She was something unique, something intangible that he wanted very much to hold fast to. He wanted to absorb some of the energy that came from her. Maybe this was what Moses meant when he talked about auras. Jessica's aura was almost visible.

"They're coming to Bangkok when the baby's born."

"And they're gonna need the space, hmm?" Jessica thought, *Oh God, I sound like my father.*

"In fact Linda's dad is helping out. And she's selling up in London. They're looking for a bigger apartment."

"Great."

"Jess?" Sam reached out for her hand but she wouldn't let him take it. She couldn't bear any glimpse of comfort where there was nothing to follow.

"It's OK, Jess. We're not going to abandon you. You've got some good ideas and I'm sure you'll do good things for Eastern Vision. You could be a little Robin Hood and I'm thinking—"

"Don't patronise me!" Jessica stood, kicking her chair to the floor behind her. "Don't you dare speak to me like a child! You all think I'm useless, I know what you say when I'm not there."

She ran to the bedroom, grabbing her T-shirts from the basket where Tutu had folded them and stuffing them into her rucksack. She wouldn't cry, she wouldn't let him see that he was right, that she was in fact a useless child. And she could never let him see what she felt for Bristol; the revolting lust, the overwhelming need for his attention, his affection. He was having a baby, getting married, and he'd never said *anything*. He'd let her make a fool of herself. She crammed her wash bag into the rucksack, squeezing toothpaste onto her hands.

"Shit. Fucking shit." She wrenched at the buckles, hating Sam for standing so still, hating him for being there, scared he would leave.

"Jess, you don't have to go anywhere just yet. Calm down. If we weren't so crushed at my place, you'd be welcome there, but it's not a long-term answer. What we'll do is sort out a room over the next few days and, hold on, hold on—"

Jessica had her rucksack on her back and fire in her eyes. She made for him like a bull for a matador. He grabbed her, pushed her so that the rucksack was pinned to the wall behind her.

"I can't just let you go—"

"You can't just do anything. Let go of me or I'll say you attacked me." She lunged, biting his neck.

"What are you, a vampire? For God's sake, Jessica."

"Let go of me! Let go, let go!"

With the weight of her whole body and her full rucksack, she body slammed him and ran out of the apartment, still barefoot.

She walked fast, head down, turning corners randomly. Sweat streamed down her back, under her breasts, over her face, stinging her eyes, and she walked even faster, as if she could drown herself in her own sweat and black out the nightmare.

~

"Moses," said Pippa, "I am able to see. And to hear. I am also able to stay quiet. That is good for us both I think."

Marina said, "Thank you for the offer of work. I am looking forward to working here." Her son was crawling through a tunnel of cardboard boxes. Moses stepped back and tripped on a full potty, drenching the rug in pee.

"Shit," he hissed, checking the hem of his robes.

Marina caught Pippa's eye and they snorted, clamping their mouths shut and screwing up their faces.

"I am sorry," spluttered Pippa. "Moses, I am sorry. It is not you that is funny."

He laid a palm flat on the bristle that was growing thick now on his scalp. He widened one eye – he was still shaving his eyebrows but the skin lifted where they would have been.

"Ladies," he murmured. "Your laughter is a joy to hear. If we could bottle that sound, it would sell at a high price."

"I would believe it only of you," said Pippa. "To sell jars of laughing."

"Pippa," said Moses. "Pippa, Pippa."

Marina looked from one to the other, unsure of the tone of the exchange.

But Pippa and Moses had both stored the idea for further thought.

~

When Sam got home, he pressed the bell while he searched his pockets for his key.

Gina stopped grating ginger and wiped her hands on a cloth, going straight to the door.

"Mister Sam," she said, shutting it behind him as he slid off his shoes. "Dinner maybe fifteen minutes, OK?"

He nodded. He sat down at the kitchen table and drank the water she put in front of him. Where the hell had Jessica gone? By the time he'd found a key and locked the door, because Tutu was nowhere to be seen, Jessica had fled into the backstreets. He'd tried asking people. A motorcyclist had pointed in the direction of the khlong, but she could have walked left or right along it or even crossed on a boat not far up. The boat people couldn't understand him. They laughed when he repeated "Farang? Lady?" and tried to mime her hair.

An image of her mother standing in the rainbow office came to mind. So defeated, so old. He had failed Anna and now he had let Jessica go. He'd never known such a lack of confidence. Everything he'd thought he was seemed shaken. He had become a monster who destroyed the lives of the young women he touched.

"Mister Sam so sad," said Gina softly, placing a bowl of steamed rice in front of him.

He could report her missing but she had chosen to go. If she had any sense, she'd head for the Ko San Road, find someone else with bare feet and a backpack she could stick with. His mind was running in several different directions. He made mental lists of people to ring. At the same time, he thought of Jessica's expression and the strength with which she'd fought him.

"You no eat?" Gina hovered, close enough for him to reach out for her.

"Yeah. Yes I will. Thank you. It's Jessica, she's gone."

Gina said nothing. She poured soup over Sam's rice and made a wai gesture. Jessica. Rich farang with too much hair, a bit crazy. That was one of Gina's new words. Sam had said one night that Jessica was 'a bit crazy'.

11

The voices were loud again. Laughing at her, calling that she was ridiculous, perverse. And because they were lodged inside her head, she couldn't run away from them. That's why she banged her head so hard; trying to smash the voices. They were towards the back, on the left hand side.

She walked without stopping for six hours. A tree full of red flowers cast a wide pool of shade. For a long time, she paced a circuit over and over, skirting the shade of the tree and passing the same game of draughts, the same chestnut seller and the same line of motorbike taxis that came and went. After ten circuits, she knew she couldn't stop until all the chestnuts were sold.

She stared at tin vats of crabs, shells, pulped fish in oily water, fat grey slugs in vinegar, wanting to rub her skin with them until she stank as foul as she felt.

As darkness fell, a mirrorball hung from the tree began a dance of lights in the sky. She lost the chestnut seller. Girls in satin slips outside a bar yawned and crossed their legs, grateful for the cool of the night.

Jessica is her own worst enemy. She wears her heart on her sleeve. She bottles things up. She'll fall flat on her face. She wears her face on her sleeve. She bottles her enemies. She falls flat on her heart.

She slapped at the back of her head.

Perverse child.

"Fuck off," she muttered.

Hmm, let her go wherever she chooses.

Her body shook inside and out. Her eyelids flickered, her hands trembled. She walked until she reached the edge of an oily khlong, where mosquitoes were gathering for the night, and then she let her knees buckle. The weight of the rucksack pushed her forward. She was trapped underneath it, her face on a crack in the planks where red ants scurried in silent, frenetic business.

Mosquitoes stabbed and sucked at her calves, her arms, the soles of her feet. But she was grateful for the spiralling blackness and she let it swamp her until she couldn't see or hear or feel anymore.

~

Pippa thanked the Hypnogem therapist.

"You have now some good customer from today?" she asked, taking the wad of notes and locking it in the cash box.

"Today I have been blessed with many new clients seeking my help," said Lazuli. Her diary was full and she'd doubled her hourly rate halfway through the exhibition. She'd been on the verge of quoting her usual price when she realised she was undervaluing her skills. All these people needing her guidance, and she herself was not realising the true worth of what she was offering.

"That is Alexis, the man from the television. These customers listen to such persons."

Pippa stretched up to unhook the corner of an Eastern Vision banner, yawning.

Lazuli helped her to fold it. "It's the same story for the courses. Suki told me Cool and Karma is full and they've had to book the cottage for six more Power of the Orient weekends."

Pippa cradled the cash box. "I see you make a new price," she said.

Lazuli toyed with the long string of fabric beads around her neck. "Er, yes," she said brightly. "We must understand the full weight of what we are bringing to people's lives. It will take its toll on our own lives."

"I have so busy," said Pippa, "I have not yet a chance to change the notes of your finances." She blinked at the therapist, her face unreadable.

Lazuli's fingers were tightly woven in the string of beads now. The tip of her thumb was a little purple.

"Not to worry, Pippa," she said lightly. "You and I know what we're doing and where we're at. I'll see you next week, I'll come to the rainbow office. We could pop out for a coffee."

"I would enjoy that," said Pippa, "goodbye for today."

~

Air was blowing in her face. Someone was strumming a guitar, trying to tune it. And the smell of barbeques was strong. Memories of a summer party floated through Jessica's head. Herself as a little girl, spreading bright yellow mustard over a burger and biting into it. The shock when it hit her tongue, the splodges that stained her sundress.

A woman was talking. Jessica wanted her to slow down; she didn't understand. She felt the plastic syringe as they eased it between her lips and the trickle of water in her stale mouth. She swallowed.

The yellow stains had made her self-conscious. She was a baby who spilt her food. She needed a bib. But her mother had said they had to stay until after dessert. It was rude to leave early. So Jessica waited at the edges, hiding from the other children, looking down at her feet to avoid people's eyes.

Her stomach ached. Her head hurt. Her feet felt as if they'd been burnt off. She brushed a fly from her cheek.

The talking grew suddenly faster. The guitar stopped and footsteps hurried away. Jessica opened her eyes a little.

A young woman knelt beside her, smiling gently. She spoke in Thai and stroked Jessica's hair. Squatting behind the woman was a child, pointing an electric fan at Jessica's face. The cable hung down from a hole in the corrugated ceiling, where a light bulb might have hung.

She was in Thailand. Bristol was getting married. She'd been made a fool of. She couldn't go back to Eastern Vision. Tears pooled in her sore eyes.

"I have messed everything up again," she croaked.

"Ssh," murmured the young woman, offering the little syringe of water again. Jessica found she couldn't lift her head much.

"Kop khun ka," she murmured, *thank you*. Her eyelids dropped shut and the tears seeped out from underneath.

~

Moses preferred the fertility symbols to be collected, rather than delivered, so that a small ceremony might be performed as they changed hands.

Usually, customers needed to arrange a time after work for this and Moses was happy to meet at the rainbow office at a convenient time.

It was the women who bought them. He'd rarely sold them to a man. They arrived in business suits, hair sleek and faces made up. The calm and the incense, the soothing tones of Moses' voice as he warned them that the fertility symbols were as powerful as they wanted them to be, was welcome to these women who'd had to strut and snap their way through the day.

This one was crying. It wasn't unusual; it was the release of tension and the enormity of the hopes they were placing in the obscene little statues. As Moses showed her, she held it to her forehead, kissed the phallus, clasped it to her breast. She chanted with him, words she didn't understand but repeated with passion.

"In Thailand," murmured Moses, "to sleep with a monk brings new life. The semen of a virgin monk wakes the womb and miracles occur."

The woman looked up, frowning.

"I am not suggesting we try this." Moses smiled peacefully. "I have blessed the statue. That is enough."

"How long will it take to work?" asked the woman, her voice pained.

"A very few weeks," said Moses, placing his hands on her shoulders. "It is rare for a womb to be so stubborn that the miracle takes longer. If nothing happens for you, we will bless it again together."

"Thank you, Moses." The woman kissed his hand. She laughed briefly. "I'm sorry, I'm sure women aren't supposed to kiss monks."

"In Thailand, a woman must not touch a monk even to pass him food or water. But this is not Thailand and I am eternally adaptable. I treasure the kiss you gave me. I wish you well and I know you will soon be with child."

~

Sam came back from the Ko San Road with no information – except that a hundred curly-haired white girls with backpacks had passed that way. He'd been offered fake identity cards, bed and breakfast, visits to temples and special rate taxis by people who thought they might have seen Jessica. But he'd come up with nothing.

He eased off his trainers and slumped into a chair at the kitchen table. For a moment, he didn't notice that Gina was on the floor by the telephone, wiping her eyes.

"Gina. What's the matter? Are the twins OK?"

"Twin good."

"Are you ill? Has something happened?" His heart raced. He couldn't lose Gina; she was everything to the twins. She was more a mother to them than he'd ever been a father.

Gina shook her head. "My sister very sick," she said. "My daddy no have money hospital." She got up, washed her hands and opened the fridge. "You wan' dinner?"

"Forget dinner. What's up with your sister? Sit down."

Gina sat, her hands in her lap, looking at the table. "My daddy say sister can die. Need hospital."

Sam stroked her hair. "God. Has she seen a doctor?"

Gina hiccupped. "Doctor say medicine very expensive."

"How much money do they need?"

Gina named a figure, still staring at the table.

"Shit. The doctor said that?"

"Mister Sam," purred Gina, looking up. "I can work more for you get money."

"Gina, you couldn't work any harder than you already do. We're going to have to think about this."

"I can do some more thing you like."

Suddenly, she'd slid to the floor and was fumbling for his zip.

"Gina, what are you doing?" He pulled his chair back.

Kneeling at his feet, she put her head on one side. "You like how?"

Sam stood up. "Please, Gina, get up. Please."

She pulled herself up on the table leg and sat down, hanging her head.

"I sorry. You no like today."

"For God's sake, Gina. You're not a prostitute. I thought we had sex because we both wanted to. Shit. Don't cry. Look, it was wrong. I should never have started something with you. I don't know what I've done. No more sex. OK? No more sex."

Sam turned away, breathing heavily, his hands in fists.

"OK. No more sex." Gina's voice sounded like a child's.

Sam shuddered. "Tomorrow I will give you the money for your sister. I want her to be well. But we mustn't go to bed together any more. It was a mistake. I'm sorry."

"Mister Sam, thank you. My family pray for you." Gina bowed in a deep wai and Sam left the room, trembling.

12

When Jessica woke again, a very short Chinese man had arrived carrying a wooden chest.

"Hello, good morning," he said. "How are you?"

She blinked at him.

"You have very sick," he said. "I can help you?"

She blinked again. She could see the guitar leaning against the wall of the little shack. The child squatted still, as if he'd never moved, pointing the fan earnestly at her. His mother was pouring water from a plastic bottle into tin can cups.

"This good people, madam. Is many bad people. You lucky charm meet good people."

Jessica made a sound with her out breath. Yes, she was grateful to these people. She couldn't think what might have happened. But a part of her wished she had rolled unconscious into the canal. Drowned anonymous, sunk into the mud. Instead, she had lived. To dream of the blackness that she might have known.

"I sorry. Pressing you here," said the man, easing his fingers under Jessica's neck and rubbing tiny, precise circles. "Here, too." He laid his hand on her belly and shut his eyes. The young woman took Jessica's hand.

He opened his little chest. He spoke to the woman in Thai and she nodded. They looked at Jessica. What were they asking? Did they want her to go?

"You baby here, yes." The man put his hand on her belly again.

Jessica stared at him.

"Baby."

She shook her head, gasped at the pain this caused.

"Oh God," she whispered. She pressed her hands into her waist and screwed up her face.

"Now rest. You drink this lady give you." He squatted beside his box with the young woman and they conferred over a jar of dried fungi and a plate of tea leaves.

She thought of the stock cupboard beside the rainbow office, where Moses had taken her virginity amongst the crystal angels and the fertility symbols. How could she have thought that was wonderful? How could her body and her mind have reached such ecstasy when this was where it ended? Lying in a shack wishing she was face down in the mud at the bottom of the khlong.

~

"Gone? Since when has she gone? For fuck's sake, Sam."

Sam's hand was sweaty on the receiver.

"In fact I tried very hard to stop her." His voice was level. He could not take this on. Jessica was not Anna. He couldn't start again, sliding backwards when he had just begun to 'function' – to shower, to eat, to hold his children, attempt to drink less.

"Did she have any money with her?" Bristol steadied his breathing. Linda was mouthing at him, 'What's happened? Who's gone?' but he pressed the phone to his ear and turned away.

"This girl is from Surrey," said Sam. "It's a very English, very posh part of London. She'll have daddy's credit card on her." Sam crossed his fingers and shut his eyes. "She chose to go. Short of getting her in a headlock or tying her down, I had to let her."

Bristol tore one of his square fingernails with his teeth. Behind him, Linda cursed as the baby latched his mouth to her nipple.

"I didn't mean this to happen." His voice was so tense he sounded as if his internal organs had been knotted together.

"Didn't mean for what to happen?" Sam tried to picture the scene at Linda's parents' house.

"All this. She could have stayed, we could have – I don't know. I have to go. Think. Try to remember what she said when she left. You're sure you've asked everyone?"

"I've got people looking out for her in Ko San. I've paid several hundred hotel staff to look up names. Bangkok is not a small place, Bristol."

"Do we have a photo? Could we get a poster round?"

Linda huffed as she shifted the baby to her other breast.

"She isn't missing, because she left of her own accord," said Sam. "Do you know, I really think she'll turn up. I feel it. She'll think things through and come back. She thinks she was set on this mercy mission in the slums and she needs the support of Eastern Vision to do that. Give her time."

~

In Jessica's mind, she had a clear image of her insides. The pink moon surface, shot through with red. White lumps of fat like the gristle on a joint of lamb. The foul sewer of her intestines where everything she'd ever eaten rotted away. And now a creature, half-human, half-fish, chewing on the fat and swelling. She wanted to ask the medicine man to give her something to finish the absurd pregnancy, to end her own life and the one eating her from inside.

She dug her nails hard into her stomach and twisted from side to side faster and faster, more and more violently.

The little boy dropped the fan and dived out of the shack.

Jessica banged her head on the mat where she'd lain for longer than she knew. She flung her neck back and forth, slamming her head harder and harder.

"I-want-to-drown," she repeated through clenched teeth. "I-want-to-drown."

The mat was thin and the ground was hard. But no pain was enough; her face was scrunched as tight as a boxer's fist, her body thrashed and her head banged and she tore at the skin on her stomach.

The creature inside her would kill her but too slowly. She had to do it now. If she could turn her body inside out it would be easier, she could scrape away the gristle, the festering waste and the monster and throw it all in the khlong. Then she would be so light – featherlight, flimsy, transparent and she'd slip blissfully into oblivion.

People filled the shack. It seemed to Jessica that they fought her, that they scratched her wrists and ankles, submerged her head in water, smothered her face with a wet towel. They taunted her in nonsense words.

"I have to die. I have to slide into the blackness. You don't understand! Let go of me!"

Her speech slowed down, grew quieter and less distinct. And the little boy who held the fan squatted cautiously beside her, glancing every minute at his aunt who sat rubbing oil gently over Jessica's belly. She murmured as she rubbed, humming soft little prayers.

~

A serviced apartment on the fourteenth floor. A swimming pool on the ground floor. And space for the new furniture that had already been delivered. Two leather sofas, a carved antique Chinese day bed and a mat woven by a craft community in Chiang Mai.

A room for the baby. A little room off the kitchen for the nanny. And a balcony where you could look down on the traffic jams or up past the endless towers to the sky, wondering what the hell was happening to you.

When Linda was asleep and the nanny had been briefed, Bristol returned to his old home to collect what was left of his life.

Tutu was cleaning the kitchen window.

"Hey, Tutu one-two."

She wouldn't look at him.

"Hello, Mister Bristol. You back safe."

"What's up?" He took the cloth from her hand and dropped it in the sink.

Tutu stared at her feet.

"You go," she whispered. "New mister coming. And madam. No like. Lady gone."

"Tutu, I'm sorry. I've been–" he opened the fridge and grabbed a beer. Tutu passed him a glass. "My life has been hijacked. I haven't even had a chance to think about phoning you. My major investor has morphed into the father-in-law from hell." He sat down and stretched out his legs. "And he has installed me in a new apartment with what might be described as a family."

Tutu smiled. She was glad to have Bristol back talking at her.

"New mister madam not come." She hoped the guard on the gate had got it wrong. Maybe it was another apartment that was changing hands.

"Yes. I have a new place. We must pack my things." He gestured round the room.

Tutu turned away to wring out her cloth.

"I like working you, Mister Bristol," she whispered. "You kind mister."

Bristol finished his beer. Why the hell should Linda's parents tell him who to employ? Some contact of theirs had sorted the apartment and taken on nanny Pepsi, and Bristol had felt that both his arms were held fast behind his back. He couldn't lose the money, not when the diggers had begun to clear the land. And there was no way he was going to accept his own father's graceless, sneering offers to bail him out. So he'd gritted his teeth and been led like a hostage to a cell.

"Tutu, would I leave you?" he said suddenly, standing. "You come with me, yes? To new place."

Tutu nodded.

"Can you share a room?"

"Share-share good."

"Then let's pack. There's a van coming."

All trace of Jessica had been swept and polished away. The sheets on the bed were clean. Only Bristol's things sat neatly on the bedside table.

Maybe Sam would have agreed to rent this place for Jessica, and Tutu could have stayed. But it was too late. He'd find her a place when, if, Jessica came back. Had she gone home? Moses said her parents had moved. He'd been damn vague, but it seemed nobody had an address for her. Pippa would only shrug if he said Jessica's name: "This rich girl cannot clean her arse. She knows only a big house and what she likes."

In the bathroom, Bristol scooped the contents of the cabinet into a plastic bag. He couldn't remember buying all these packets of tablets. Six identical white boxes. He caught one as it fell and his mind ticked over.

His fingers felt too fat to open the box. He fumbled and swore, pulling out a slip of paper. Lithium. Jessica took lithium. There was an address on the packets, too. He could try it on Moses, maybe he could go there. See if she'd been in touch with her parents.

He checked his watch, subtracted the hours and rang his mother at the clinic.

"Lithium?" she said. "Who's on lithium? Not Linda? She shouldn't be breastfeeding–"

"No, mom. Linda is not on lithium. I just need to know what it's for. Why would someone take it?"

"Manic depression. It's—"

"Depression? That's not—"

"*Manic* depression. Bursting with ideas and energy or slumped in gloom. Out of touch with reality at both ends."

"Could you go quickly from one to the other?" Bristol's heart began to thud. "What do you mean 'out of touch'?"

"Bristol, sweetheart, we're talking about someone you're close to, aren't we?"

"I don't know. Maybe. Please just tell me. Does it make you do anything dangerous?"

"Yes. But cool it a minute, sweetheart. If this hypothetical patient is taking lithium, he or she may be very stable. They might have been well for years. It's patients who abandon their lithium that cause a problem. Because the mania, or the depression or the mixed state, can be dangerous."

Bristol's hand was so tight around the packet, he crushed it.

"Is there anything I can do?"

His mother's voice was so calm, so in control, he wanted to be with her. He wished he'd communicated better with her over what his father referred to as his 'shotgun' wedding. He'd shut her out because he couldn't bear his father's voice, but phoning her at work was good. It felt comforting and unsettling at the same time.

"Thanks for the information."

"Your friend is probably fine." A pause. "Bristol, are we talking about Anna? You don't have to tell me."

"Anna? Oh, I see. No, no I don't think she had manic depression. She always seemed quite steady. Until."

"Sorry. I shouldn't have brought that up. I just thought, you know. Well, it can be a cause of suicide. Bristol, I realise things are really hard for you right now. Having a new baby to take care of is pretty hard even when you're prepared for it. But you didn't know, did you? Your dad was right when he said 'shotgun', however crass he was being."

He sighed. "No, I didn't know. Linda sprung this one on me." He felt oddly naked talking so openly with his mother.

"And you decided to make the best of it. You are an honourable young man, Bristol, and I'm proud of that. But are you sure you're in love, sweetheart? It matters, in the long run." Her voice was different; she wasn't used to this either.

"There's no doubting I'm in love, Mom," he said.

"That's good. And I love you, you know that, don't you?"

When he put the phone down, he could still hear her voice telling him she loved him. He was sure he'd never heard her say it before. And his own voice, 'There's no doubting I'm in love.' *It's not Linda, Mom. I'm not in love with my wife or even this son I've gotten. My head is full of someone else.*

~

The pavement was warm under Moses' feet. He was thinking about growing his hair; he could have a moustache or a beard perhaps. There was more to shave recently, it wouldn't be so patchy.

Number twenty-eight Sycamore Tree Close. He felt good to have liberated Jessica from such a stifling address. Now Bristol had him playing nanny, checking up on her because she'd gone walkabout. In his experience, someone who stormed off in a huff should be allowed to come back when they'd simmered down. Chasing people turned up the heat. But Bristol was adamant, even when Moses told him Jessica had turned her back on her parents. He thought she said they were moving and she had no UK address. But he'd been heady with something a client had given him and her incessant rambling had floated over him that day.

"Hari bloomin' Krishnas!" A man pruning his hedge dropped his secateurs. "Be out." He disappeared, hurrying his wife ahead of him and slamming the front door.

Moses was tempted to ring their doorbell but he had a lady visitor to get back to the rainbow office for, and it wasn't beyond the bounds of possibility she'd be ready for the virgin monastic semen. He could sometimes tell these things from a first meeting, how long it would take a woman to ask him.

Number twenty-eight had a car outside it. A brown saloon that had recently seen a hose. It was parked in front of a mirror mosaic cone surrounded by pebbles, which Moses suspected of being a 'water feature'.

He cleared his throat at length, stretched out a hand and poked the doorbell with a long finger.

Through the obscure glass pane in the door, he could see movement. A chain rattled. The door opened a little and the man behind it pursed his lips when he saw Moses.

Moses looked down at the man and held his hands up in surrender.

"Please, do not be alarmed," he said.

"Are you trying to sell me something?" The man held the door like a shield.

"Not at all," said Moses. "I'm not sure that I could."

"Are you here to push religious claptrap?"

Moses shook his head. His mind was back at the rainbow office shaking his head sadly whilst a young woman begged him to open her womb to a miracle.

"I'm a friend of Jessica's. I wondered how she is."

"Who is it?" called a voice from the kitchen.

"Salesman, love. Be there now, hmm?"

"Have you heard from her since she went to Thailand? Only–"

"Listen." The man pressed his head into the gap between the door and the frame. "There is no Jessica here. I don't know who you are or what you want, but I'd like you to go. This is not a good time." He stepped back to shut the door but Moses placed his hand on the glass.

"Do you know where Jessica is? Are you her father, could you just tell me that?"

"Get your hand off my door now." The man's eyes bulged.

"I mean you no harm. I come in peace, old man."

"Old man? How dare you? Good day, sir." He leaned his whole weight on the door to shut it.

~

"We've screwed up here, Sam. She has manic depression."

"*We've* screwed up?! She's the opposite of depressed. She's full of herself. And when she left she was angry."

89

"*Manic* depression. It's dangerous. Crazy highs and lows bad enough to top yourself."

Sam winced.

"God, sorry. I'm not thinking. She could be in danger. She's so young."

"How young?"

"Nineteen. Just. Her date of birth is on the medication she should be taking."

"Nineteen. Shit." Sam leant his elbow on the filing cabinet. "I didn't realise."

She hadn't been admitted to any hospital Bristol could find listed. Moses had come up with nothing. It seemed her parents really had moved away without a forwarding address.

Sam rolled his shoulders back, standing straighter than he had since the bomb fell.

"I have to speak with the Summer Towers contractors this morning," he said. "You get out there and see if you can find her. I'm on the case with the luxury condominiums."

Bristol laid his palms flat on the desk. A patch of dry skin itched under his signet ring. "Ah, the luxury condoms," he said. "Sam, you sound almost like yourself."

~

Pepsi's daughter was six and she lived with Pepsi's mother in a one-room construction in a line of shacks and huts that had grown up around a derelict garage. The garage served as a common room; during the day young men could be found stretched flat on the ground smoking while children drew marks in the dirt and rolled stones. At night new arrivals slept there until they could gather some boxes, canvas, scaffolding, or whatever materials they could to squeeze a new home onto a remaining patch of ground.

Her grandmother shuffled in through the beaded curtain, snorting softly as she heaved a bag of shopping over the threshold.

"Here, take a knife and cut this fruit."

The little girl stood, wiping her hands on her dress. They didn't speak as they sliced the orange and the banana, popping bits into their mouths and sucking the juice from their fingers. Then suddenly the little girl said, "Mamma!"

The grandmother looked up as the beaded curtain parted and Pepsi appeared.

"Toi," said Pepsi, and her daughter clasped her round the middle. Pepsi combed the girl's hair with her fingers.

"Is she well?" she asked. "Are you well?"

"Yes, yes. Eat." Her mother prised the lid from a tin and offered her crackers.

Pepsi ate, cross-legged on the floor, the little girl's head in her lap.

"There is a farang girl, lost in the city," she told her mother. "Mister Bristol is looking for her. She might be sick."

"In what way, lost?" The mother lit the little gas stove and began to crush ginger with the side of a bowl.

Pepsi grinned. "Khun Tutu says the farang's heart broke when Mister Bristol married Madam."

"Is Mister Bristol such a prize?" The mother's eyes twinkled as she rolled balls of rice with chillies and ginger in her palms and dropped them into the sizzling oil.

"I feel good in my heart to think of your work now. Will you stay with this work, Pepsi?"

"Yes, Mamma," said Pepsi. "I will stay with this work."

~

"Ah Moses," said Pippa, "you are well?"

She wore jeans and a green T-shirt embellished with sequins. Her hair had been cut into a swinging bob with streaks of yellow through it.

Moses tried not to stare. She was Pippa, but she wasn't Pippa. He cleared his throat and searched for an answer.

Pippa sat on the desk and crossed her legs, dangling gold shoes from manicured toes.

"You have not some words today?"

"There are times," intoned Moses, "when words are so clumsy as to be – well, clumsy."

Pippa covered her nose with her hand and pretended her snigger was a sneeze.

"Please to make some signature," she said, reaching behind her.

Moses held out his hand. He sank onto the rug. With one foot in place, he put the papers down and pulled his other foot into position. He breathed out slowly. He'd been trying to work out if it was easier with one leg on top but neither would last for long yet.

Applying a monastic mindfulness to the discomfort in his knees, he perused the documents Pippa required him to sign.

She hooked one side of her bob behind her ear and waited.

"Pippa, I sense anger in this paper."

"No anger, Moses. I feel calmly, thank you."

His left foot slid off his right thigh and he stretched both legs out in a wide V. Pippa looked away in case his robes fell open in the wrong place.

"You want Eastern Vision to pay the rent on a flat in Twickenham?"

Pippa hooked her hair behind the other ear.

"And you have constructed yourself a salaried position." He spread the papers in the space between his legs.

"I am now making true value of my weight," said Pippa lightly. She tossed him a pen.

"So you are. I am impressed. Of course you understand that I need to consult with Bangkok on certain aspects of London finance before I can–"

"This is some rubbish. What they do in Bangkok keeps those Americans busy. Eastern Vision London is you and me and this actor Alexis. And we make for them a lot of money now. They can be thankful to us."

"Indeed they are." Moses lay back on the rug in an enormous star.

"So please to signing now. I like to go home."

"And home is now this address in Twickenham?"

"I rent from Hypnogem lady. Is nice. Moses," Pippa sprang off the desk. She stood over his spread-eagled body with her hands on her hips. "Thank you to sign." He rolled onto his front and scratched his balls, then rested his chin on his fist while he looked without focussing at the papers. "You do not know my story, Moses. You never have ask. But I know your story and I know what you do."

Moses' eyes blurred even more. "Are you blackmailing me?" he said, oddly aroused.

"I do not know this word. I tell you is better to make signature. We have many many customer after Alexis came to you. And I think is good that way. I am a quiet person, I do not telling newspapers what I know."

"Well," said Moses, clicking the pen, "certainly not now that you are Associate Director of Eastern Vision London."

"Is good name. I like it."

"Will you sleep with me now, Pippa? It would do us both good. Like a bond on the new arrangement."

"No, thank you," she said, stepping over him to retrieve her bag. "I do not like to do that with a virgin monk. Maybe it will open the womb and I am not looking for a baby."

13

The little boy who held the fan let go a blast of wind from his backside. Jessica turned to him, wide-eyed, and they burst out laughing.

"Big fart," she said.

"Bi' far'," repeated the boy and mimed another one.

"No, no more!" Jessica took the fan from him and stood it on the floor. "What's your name?"

He giggled. "Bi' far'."

"If you're not careful, I'll start calling you that."

The medicine man came in and Jessica wiped her hair away from her face.

"Happiness," said the medicine man.

"What is your name?" asked Jessica.

"Noah," he said. "I choose from Bible."

"Mine is Jessica," said Jessica. She wai-ed, blushing a little. "I don't know who chose that."

"Khun Jess'cah." He seemed to like the sound of her name.

"You have made me well, Khun Noah. I have a lot to thank you for."

Noah took her hand and rested two fingers on her pulse.

"Bi' far'," said the little boy and Jessica began to laugh again.

"Happiness. So good to laugh," said Noah. "Baby also happy."

Jessica laid her hands on her middle. The laugh vanished from her face. She rubbed a circle, wondering what the creature looked like now and whether it really was there.

"Are you sure there is a baby?" she whispered, looking down at her hands.

Noah said nothing. He sat quietly watching the fan, enjoying the movement of the air.

"You are sure. Sorry, I didn't mean to question you – it's just I can't get my head round it."

"Where your home?" asked Noah softly.

Jessica drew her knees up to her chest. "I don't know," she whispered. "I was going to make a new one."

"What you make in Bangkok?"

Jessica began to laugh again. Noah smiled. The little boy giggled.

"I came to help the poor people," she said.

~

"A year. I can hardly bear to say it, it sounds so long. But I will stay here for a year and then we are going home."

Bristol wondered if Linda had got dressed at all; she was asleep when he left and now she wore a cotton robe.

"You'll settle, Lind. It's tough for you right now. Andrew is pretty demanding and you've left everything you know."

Linda looked as though she might scream, but instead she swigged from her glass of wine and stared at a fixed point on the polished floor.

Andrew started to cry. The sound came from the kitchen, where Tutu was cooking and Pepsi was ironing sheets.

"Did you swim today?" asked Bristol.

Linda grunted.

Tutu brought in a carved wooden bowl of salad.

"Ah, Mister Bristol home. Speak Pepsi."

She went back to the kitchen and Pepsi came out, feeding Andrew a bottle of milk.

"Mister," she murmured, "Madam."

"How's this little monkey?" In his effort to be ebullient, Bristol succeeded only in sounding like his father and feeling even more miserable. "No, no, I won't disturb a man while he's having his milk."

"Mummy see farang," said Pepsi, jiggling the teat gently in the baby's mouth.

"Jessica?" Bristol's nerve endings were alive. "Your mother? Where is she?"

"Is not nice place." Pepsi put the bottle down and draped Andrew over her shoulder, rubbing his back. She wouldn't look at Bristol.

"Is that where Jessica is?"

"Mummy say very near. Farang play game children. My little girl."

"You have a little girl?"

"Like this," Pepsi stuck out a hand level with her waist, where Toi's head rested when she clasped her round the middle.

Linda looked up.

"She stay mummy. Husban' gone." Pepsi giggled and rolled her eyes.

"Will you take me there now?" Bristol grabbed his keys. "Lind, listen, I'm sorry, can you – I'll be back. Take Andrew."

"Is dark. No good place farang." Pepsi looked from Bristol to Linda, unsure.

"It's fine. I'd like to go now. It could well be Jessica." He took Andrew from Pepsi's arms and put him on Linda's lap. Linda didn't move.

As the door shut behind Bristol and Pepsi, she whispered, "This is what Sam's wife died of."

Pepsi told the taxi driver where to go and he sucked his teeth.

"He stop near. No like."

"OK. That's fine."

The streets were still jammed. Bristol drummed his fingertips on the seat.

They passed a night market that sliced the edge off the road at the corner so that vehicles came at each other head on, hooting and jostling. The lights rigged over the stalls were glaring bright. Children shuttled like chickens around people's feet. A little boy wearing only a vest stared at the taxi, scratching his stomach.

The driver pulled up outside an Indian tailor's shop. A man lay on the front step, staring at the sky.

"Kop khun kop," said Bristol, *thank you,* pushing the fare through the window. The air smelt of petrol.

"Come me," said Pepsi. She ducked down an alley, invisible from the street. The light came from candles, cigarettes and torches, so that Bristol could see only small glimpses of what they passed.

On a table covered in a wipe-clean cloth sat three buckets of soapy water. There was a stack of plastic stools and a wheelbarrow. Behind it, an open-fronted hut was lit by a small bulb. A gutter stuck along the top was draped with mobiles of birds and butterflies, and a gold foil banner that said 'Happy Christmas'. Inside, a young man watched television. A woman wiped bowls with a cloth.

Bristol raised a hand in greeting and the woman giggled. Further up, past a bicycle and a rail of clothes, was a girl with no hair washing out the intestines of some animal in a tin basin. A fan was attached to a lead trailed out of the window.

"Some electric have," said Pepsi.

"Yes," said Bristol, following her closely, not wanting to trip on ground he couldn't see.

"This my home here." Pepsi glanced back at him.

"Right."

A woman squatted by a beaded curtain, a candle almost melted on the ground beside her.

"Pepsi," she said, nodding.

They spoke in Thai. Bristol felt like Gulliver; his head was the height of the roofs around him.

"Mister Bristol," said Pepsi's mother, heaving herself to her feet and wai-ing him.

"It's good to meet you," said Bristol, approximating a wai in return.

"Come. Eat," she said, parting the curtain.

Bristol looked at Pepsi. He was anxious to find Jessica. But Pepsi nodded and smiled at him, holding her hand out to show him in.

He stooped under the threshold and couldn't straighten up again. Pepsi laughed.

"Very small here."

A little girl slept on a mat in one corner. Pepsi crouched beside her and stroked her hair.

Pepsi's mother offered Bristol a plate of deep-fried meatballs. He reached to take one but she laughed.

"No, take."

He held the plate, eating one, wondering how close he was to Jessica, wondering what went through Pepsi's head as she cared for his child instead of her own.

Pepsi's mother wrapped green candyfloss in pancakes and stacked them on Bristol's plate.

"Eat. Good." She smiled.

"Yummy?" asked Pepsi.

"Yummy," said Bristol. "Kop khun kop."

The women giggled.

"Thank you. You are very kind. Where is the farang girl you saw?"

They conferred in Thai.

"Mummy show you. I stay here Toi." Pepsi smiled.

The grandmother wheezed and waddled, though she was probably only forty-five. He followed her down a narrower path, where a wolf-dog guarded the severed bonnet of a car. The dog's eyes were yellow-green. Bristol took small steps, trying not to breathe too deeply. The nearer they got to the khlong, the more sewage and fish overlaid the smell of petrol.

The dark was less intense as they reached the edge of the maze. An oblong bulb was suspended from a wire above their heads and streetlights shone on the other side of the khlong. A rail of skirts and dresses stood in their way. Pepsi's mother shunted it aside and they stepped onto the boards that separated the water from the shacks built along it. On the other side, behind a building site, was a gleaming tower maybe fifty storeys high.

"Here," said Pepsi's mother, indicating a cardboard wall. "You go?"

Bristol looked for something solid enough to knock on. How did flattened cardboard boxes survive rain?

"Hello," he called. "Sawadee kop."

He waited.

"Hello?"

Pepsi's mother stood behind him. She said something in Thai.

There was whispering from inside and then the sheet that hung in the doorway was pulled back.

Bristol didn't recognise the feelings that shot down his spine when he saw her standing in the doorway. They were chemical, raw.

"Jessica."

Her clothes had the faded look of the slum about them. She was thin; it made her look very young.

They looked at each other. Pepsi's mother looked at her feet.

Bristol's arms twitched to reach out.

"Hey," said Jessica, smiling.

"Hey," he said, and the chemicals that were filling his blood fizzed. "Are you OK?" Damn stupid question.

"I'm good."

A small boy emerged, rubbing his eyes, and clutched Jessica's hand. He stared up at the giant on the doorstep.

"I found the lithium. I was worried you'd left it behind."

Jessica shrugged. "Don't be. You can't take lithium when you're pregnant. And Noah's medicines are a thousand times better than that sort. He picks jasmine in the moonlight."

"You're pregnant." Bristol felt that he might be dreaming. He wasn't having this conversation.

"You're not the only one with secrets."

"Jess, listen." Bristol decided to ignore the fact that Pepsi's mother and the small boy were there. He had to make her understand. It struck him that she'd got pregnant as some sort of crazy revenge. "I didn't know about Linda and the baby. She sprang it on me in London when she was about to pop. I thought she and I were–" He stopped himself. He was married to Linda. Every morning when he woke up before the light, he knew it all over again. And saying things out loud was not a good idea.

"How is fatherhood?" Jessica squeezed the little boy's hand. He leant his head on her thigh.

"Weird. I didn't exactly have time to get used to the idea."

Bristol smacked a mosquito on his wrist, splashing himself with his own blood.

"They're bastards," said Jessica. "But your body acclimatises."

He remembered her saying this in his old apartment, in his old life, when he watched her with amusement and another feeling that was altogether new to him. He wiped his wrist with a tissue.

"How long have you been pregnant?"

"Does it matter?"

"Of course it fucking matters." The shuddering in Bristol's spine started up again. "Jessica, this happened in the UK, right? You haven't got yourself pregnant since you came out?"

"I didn't know it, but I was pregnant when I came to Bangkok."

Bristol sighed. "There's some poor guy going blindly about his business in London without any idea."

"You don't know that. You don't know me at all." She set her jaw. The little boy looked up at her.

Pepsi's mother stood still, the only reminder that she was there a faint intermittent wheeze.

"Will you come back with me? I'll put you up. We'll find you a place. We can sort this. You can go home for a while, or stay in Bangkok. I wanted you to be part of Eastern Vision and I still do."

The little boy stared up at the giant's face. He thought giants were supposed to be scary but this one looked scared himself.

"I have somewhere already. And I don't know that your new wife would be keen on you bringing home a pregnant teenager." Jessica laughed. "So thanks."

"Linda would be fine with you coming."

"Liar." She was still laughing.

"Listen. Anything you need, Jess, you know where to find me."

"Actually I don't. Word on the street is Linda's daddy has got you a nice new apartment."

Bristol nodded grimly. He reached into his pocket in a practised gesture and produced an Eastern Vision card.

"I'll come by the office then," said Jessica, tossing her head.

"Do that," said Bristol. He held her in an eye lock until she nodded.

When he left, Jessica crouched down so that her face was level with the little boy's ear.

"Big fart," she whispered and they both laughed until they couldn't breathe.

14

Sam sat on a corner sofa, drinking beer from the bottle. Number Eight flirted with her eyes, dancing especially for him. He was tired. He raised a hand and a half smile.

She put a finger in her mouth and winked at him. Number Seven glanced at her, at Sam, and at the man in the other corner. Unnoticed by anyone else, the heel of her shiny black boot struck Number Eight's shin as she moved round her pole. Number Eight bit her lip and smiled at Sam again. Number Seven resigned herself to the unwashed German in the corner.

When they swapped with the others, Number Eight slid into the seat beside Sam. Her bikini was tiny, the big round number badge fixed to the string on her hip. Her naked flesh was right up close.

"Hi, Mister," she said loudly, over the beat of the music.

"Hi," said Sam, nodding at the matron to bring drinks.

"You so lonesome tonight?" she purred into his ear.

Sam's throat constricted. "More lonesome than my worst nightmare," he said.

She giggled, taking her drink from the tray and slurping it through the straw.

"You America?" she said, when her glass was nearly empty.

"I am. But I live in Bangkok."

She nodded, edging closer still, tapping her foot in time to the music.

"What's your name?" he asked.

"Lula."

"Really? Lula?"

"My daddy America."

Sam smiled. "Of course he is."

"How old Mister?"

"Twenty-five," he said, thoughtfully, as though this were news also to himself.

"You so young so hangsong."

"And how about you, Lula? How old are you?" He wasn't even going to consider paying her bar fine if she was a day under twenty.

"Twenty year," she said, flashing all ten fingers up twice.

Her boot nudged the hem of his trouser leg. He didn't move. The part of him that was furious with Anna wanted to spend every night in Patpong, smoking whatever he chose, doing whatever his body told him to. The part of him that blamed himself for her death was tortured by it all. *How is this so different to sleeping with Gina?* He challenged himself. *Who is there to care what I do?*

"We go short-time?" suggested Lula, anxious not to lose him when the dance shift changed. "You so sexy Mister."

Sam took her hand and looked at her. "Come home with me," he said.

Gina heard the door. She couldn't sleep because her head ached. She began to fantasise that Sam would come into her room and rub her shoulders. Maybe bring ice for her head. Take her in his arms until she fell asleep.

But he wasn't alone. There was a woman with him. A Thai woman. They were laughing, something to do with her shoes. He was pulling her boots off.

Gina closed her eyes tightly.

Sam said, "Ssh, the maid's asleep," and they went into the bedroom. The girl was still laughing.

~

Noah took Jessica to his home, about half a mile from the slum where she had been taken in and cared for. Early pregnancy was sapping her energy and the walk tired her. They stopped outside a shop selling temple offerings, plastic garlands and second hand clothes. To one side was an entrance leading to a flight of concrete steps which they climbed slowly until they reached Noah's apartment on the third floor.

He opened his door, revealing a huge dark wooden cabinet that took up the widest stretch of wall. At the top were drawers just a few inches deep. Lower down, shelves and cupboards were stacked with jars of tablets. A row of thermos flasks stood along the bottom shelf, all the handles turned the same way.

Noah opened a drawer and Jessica saw tiny pots of leaves and powders and vials of syrupy liquid in miniature racks. She watched him weigh a lump of something the texture of oasis. He scraped at the edges, his nails scything through it, until the scales balanced exactly. Then he crushed it in a tin bowl and added six drops of purple oil from a flask.

"Must wait mixing," he said, and smiled.

"How did you know what was wrong with me?" she asked, gazing at the display.

Noah's arms hung loosely by his side, his weight even on his feet. "I ask not what is wrong. I ask what is at the—" His hand hovered over his chest.

"At the heart?"

"What is at the heart of this person? What – colour – is this person? Is hard say in English." He laughed.

"I understand." Jessica's eyes fell on the tin bowl, where the oil was gradually turning the oasis to black ice cream.

"I see you have big yin-yang battle." He made fists and mimed little punches. "Yes?"

"Yes. I have a yin-yang battle. I have more life in me than I can hold and I have death-sleeps. Times when I want only to slide into the blackness and die." She shook her head. "I look at other people. And their yin and yang are balanced." She laughed and wiped her face on a piece of toilet roll she'd stuffed in the waistband of her skirt. "People are so strong, so consistent. They work every day. And I am so weak. So temporary."

Noah blew gently across the surface of his fragrant potion. He left a silence and then he said, "I think no weak. I think Jess'cah strong. Can work me now. Learn medicine."

"That's what I'd love. Noah, can I? Can I work with you in the slum?"

"I work many people." He crossed to the window and she followed him. He pointed at a lady hailing a taxi. She had delicate heeled shoes and she wore a neat cream dress and a tailored jacket. They watched her disappear into the taxi, clutching a patent white handbag.

"I work such people," said Noah. "They pay me good money for keep well. I work also such poor people in camp by khlong and under road bridge. They give me gift and good prayer."

Jessica looked down at the street; at the charms and garlands strung in front of the shop below them, at the traffic and the people and the rubbish. They were so near the edge of the slum, and yet it was possible to walk right past and not see that squeezed alongside the canal and in the stinking corner of a road were so many hundred lives.

"I had this idea. I was going to collect clothes, food and money and distribute it to people who needed it. It seemed so simple. But I always fall flat on my face."

Noah nodded. "You fall and lady find you. Good luck for you."

Jessica smiled. A woman spread a mat on the pavement next to the shop and set out her wares. It was second-hand stuff. The kind of thing that made Jessica wonder if anyone ever stopped to look, let alone buy.

She laughed suddenly.

"I don't believe it!"

"What happen?"

"That lady selling things on the mat. She's got my dress."

Noah peered out of the window. "This your dress?"

"Yes! I tore the hem because I didn't like the bottom. It's definitely mine."

Noah looked thoughtful.

"Don't worry," she said. "I don't want it back. I like having nothing. I hated all that luggage."

"You know, Jess'cah, I cannot give you money. I can give you place sleep."

Jessica's thoughts sped up a little. She tried to breathe them apart. Did Noah expect her to share his bed? What did she owe him for saving her life? Bristol and Sam could pay him for the medicine. It was them who had messed her around. But she'd run away. She'd been her own worst enemy.

"Jess'cah?"

She liked Noah. She liked it when he came into a room, when he spoke to her, when he took her pulse and nodded. She looked out for him in the alleys when she played with the children. But it hadn't occurred to her that they might have a physical relationship. She was pregnant. With the child of a pseudo-Buddhist monk. She wished she'd never even heard of sex.

"Jess'cah? I sorry. You no like stay here." Noah crossed to his apothecary's cabinet and stared into his potion.

"Noah, I really want to work with you in the slums. And I would love to learn about medicine. Not that I could ever understand more than a fraction of–"

Noah held up his hand. "There is problem. No more speak."

"I only meant. Well, where would I sleep?"

"You have room. I sleep here to window. Look." He pulled aside a curtain in the wall opposite the cabinet to reveal a tiny room. Jessica turned to see a futon mattress with pale green sheets. There was also a chair on which Noah had draped his spare clothes. Against the wall was a folded screen with a sunbird painted on the fabric. Noah lifted it and took it into the main room, where he set it up to create a private corner by the window.

"I sleep here. You have room."

"I couldn't take your bedroom. You're so kind. Too kind."

"I am happy give you room."

Jessica ran her finger along a silver branch above the sunbird's head.

"Noah," she said quietly. "You and me, we're not–" She closed her eyes. "I like you very much. But I don't want to have sex with you." She was almost whispering now. She opened her eyes and looked at a tiny leaf on the branch.

Noah wove his hands together.

"I want only give you place. Nothing more. Please understand I am not that man."

Jessica's face felt very hot.

"Sorry. I'm so sorry. I didn't even say that. Can we forget all that?"

Noah tapped a pot of shrivelled leaves. He pinched two tiny scraps and crumbled them into the tin bowl. "Look," he said, "jasmine. Very good helping."

Jessica watched him work, wondering if in that cabinet there might be some medicine that would magic away what grew inside her. But she could never ask Noah. And as he opened drawers and cupboards, collecting bottles and jars for his concoction, she saw that amongst the powders, oils and tablets there was not one sheet of paper. No books, no notes, no leaflets or instructions. No lists or invoices. Nothing was written down because everything was safe in Noah's memory.

~

Pippa blew her nose and dropped the tissue in a puddle. She had seriously considered staying in bed. The days when travelling on the underground was a novelty were long gone; she could even walk past shop windows now without staring. But these were gains rather than losses, she decided, lifting her face as a faint wash of sunlight lit a cloud from behind. It was simply that her standards were higher. Admittedly she didn't look the part this morning; after a night of mopping her streaming nose, she hadn't had the energy to put make-up on. But she was no longer a grubby immigrant sleeping on a friend's floor. She had a double bed in a bright little flat in Twickenham with clean kitchen surfaces and an incredible shower. So really, if a cold and a commute were the worst of her troubles, she could feel quite smug.

She stopped at an open shop front selling freshly-squeezed juice and bought a Health and Vitality Special.

"Have a nice day," she told the student in the ridiculous uniform. He gave her her change and smiled but she suspected his English of being poorer than her own.

By the time she arrived at the rainbow office, sucking the dregs of the smoothie noisily through a straw, she had talked herself into a much improved mood. Even finding Alexis sitting at her desk was not so irritating as it might have been. She merely waited while he blushed and turned over what he'd been writing.

"Good morning," she said.

"Hi."

Alexis stretched his arms above his head and yawned self-consciously as if to show how long he'd been working.

"You are well?" asked Pippa, hanging her jacket on the back of the chair behind him.

"Yes. Good, thanks. You want to sit here?"

Pippa smiled and stepped back to let him past. He clutched his papers to his chest and sat on the other chair, across the room.

"That is very far away," said Pippa, "is it my cold you keep at distance?"

"No, not at all. You can't get away from these damn British colds. They seek you out whatever you do."

Alexis pulled his chair awkwardly across the rug, still half-sitting, and rested an arm on the desk.

"Anything so interesting?" Pippa indicated the papers he held on his lap.

"Possibly," he said, and nodded significantly.

She smiled. He had the face of a cherub with thick black eyelashes. Booting up the computer, she blew her nose and tried to decide whether she'd blast the shower over her back when she got home or run a bath instead.

"Actually," said Alexis, stroking the papers on his lap, "I'd value your opinion."

"Oh?"

"The thing is, I've been thinking a bit about my role here at Eastern Vision and–"

The buzzer from the street sounded long and hard.

"Eastern Vision London?"

"Pippa, Mick here."

"Mick! So many weeks!"

Pippa ran down the stairs and met her brother halfway, flinging her arms round him.

106

"It's good to see you," he said. "Don't come so close, I'm soaking wet."

"And you'll catch my cold," said Pippa, "but I am so happy to see you."

She held open the door and he looked around, dripping water onto the rug. He was taller than Alexis and broader across the chest. He shook himself like a dog and laughed.

"Alexis, this my brother, Mick."

"Pleased to meet you, buddy."

Alexis' accent came out a touch comic when he tried too hard, but he took Mick's hand firmly and shook it like a man.

"Have my chair," said Pippa.

"No, I want to see my sister *Director* in her desk."

Pippa giggled. "*Associate* Director," she said, sitting down and wagging her finger. "Now tell me, what is happening so long you are away? Delivering?"

Mick shook his head. "No more delivering. This boring job."

"It's a job, Mick. It's paid in pounds."

He scowled.

Alexis pulled back his chair and stood.

"Well, I'll–"

"It's OK, Alexis. No worries to stay here."

"Thanks buddy," said Mick, raising his eyebrows. "I like to speak my sister."

Alexis cleared his throat. "Of course, good to meet you. Briefly."

As he left the room, Pippa caught Mick's eye and sniggered.

"Sit down. Or shall we go out and drink coffee?"

"No, I don't have time. I just needed to ask – for your advice."

Pippa smiled. "Is my advice so valuable? Suddenly everyone wants my opinion."

"You are a very clever girl. So tell me, little sister, should I register with an employment agency?"

"A government agency?" Pippa wiped her nose on the back of her hand and shivered.

"No. A private business. They find jobs for people and people for jobs."

The rain hammered faster against the window.

"What sort of jobs?"

"Offices. Businesses. Managing." Mick made a dismissive gesture.

"They would take you?"

"I have already been for interview."

Pippa grinned across the desk, feeling a release of long-held tension in her gut.

"We have refused to be beaten, you and I. We can be proud."

The telephone rang.

"Eastern Vision London. Have a nice day."

"It's Moses, and I probably shall. Is Little Mr Boyband there or am I safe to come in?"

"Speak that again?"

"Alexis – is – there?"

"Don't speak so slowly, I am not idiot. He is out now but I can take a message."

"Thank you, Pippa, that won't be necessary. I will see you anon."

Pippa reached for her brother's hand.

"I feel strong," she said. "I love you my brother."

"And I love you."

Mick's eyes looked wet.

"Pippa, I must go now. Do you have some money for me to register at the agency? It all gets paid back after the first week's wages."

"Of course. How much do they want?"

"A hundred pounds."

Pippa coughed.

"It's not much," said Mick, "for the type of jobs they find."

"That's fine, of course it's fine. We can organise that."

"Today?" he said, standing.

"Today. And very soon you too will be an Associate Director."

"*Director*," he said, and winked.

15

The doorman saluted. Jessica smiled. Her insides were scrambled and her nose itched, but as the air conditioning cradled her, her breathing slowed a little.

She stood by a laminated board that listed the companies and their office numbers, but the words refused to make sense.

"Escu' me. Easter' Vision?"

A young woman in a uniform pointed along the corridor.

"This floor. Number six."

"Kop khun ka."

Jessica walked past the doors, cross with herself for feeling nervous. Anyway, he probably wasn't there. Maybe he was out inspecting some tower block he was ruining the place with. Luxury for the rich. How naïve she had been to think that Eastern Vision was about anything except turning money into more money. Bristol was the most arrogant, self-centred person she had ever met. But she was about to tell him that the slum project was going ahead as planned. And that he was going to finance it.

She half expected number six to have a rainbow on the door, but of course it didn't. It had a modest sign with 'Eastern Vision, London-Bangkok' and a Thai translation.

She rolled her shoulders back and swallowed, rubbed her nose and wet her lips. He's probably not here. Her head was aching. Her stomach knotted.

She knocked.

"Yes."

It was Bristol. She was sure. She shook her head, set her jaw and went in.

Bristol was at a desk. It was polished and neat, as were the shelves and cabinets around him, and even the floor under her filthy feet. He leaned back in his chair.

"Hey," he said, twirling a pencil. His shirtsleeves were rolled up. His hair was spiky at the front where he'd rubbed it.

"Hey," said Jessica. There was another chair but it was right up against the whiteboard where sets of dates and figures were written under the headings *Summer Towers* and *Tranquillity Place*.

Bristol pointed at it. "Sit down."

She pulled the chair away from the wall and sat.

"That's a long way off."

She flushed and dragged it closer to the desk.

He glanced at the door.

"It's good to see you, Jess."

There was a patch of inflamed skin on his neck, just visible over his collar. She tried not to look at it. He laid his hands flat on the desk and sighed. She remembered the feel of those hands. She shifted in her chair.

"I've come to talk about the slum project."

"You look like a slum dweller yourself, Jess."

"Thank you."

"Are you still pregnant?"

"What do you think?"

The pencil snapped in his hands and one end rolled onto the floor. He leaned on the desk and looked at her. "I think," he said, "that you have had a very difficult time. Most kids would have run home."

"I'm a kid now, am I? As well as a slum dweller?"

"I'm joking." He smiled. "Are you OK? Are you taking lithium again?"

"Yes to the first and no to the second. Noah's medicine is more powerful and so much more gentle than lithium. He's an incredible man."

Bristol raised his eyebrows. "I'm sure he is."

"I don't mean like that. We don't have that sort of relationship."

"But you're living with him."

"How do you know?"

"Bangkok telegraph." His fingers found the rough patch on his neck before he could stop himself.

"Well, yes I am. He does a lot for the people in the slums and I'm going to help him. I'm going to collect aid and distribute it, and make sure families don't suffer when someone's ill."

"That's very admirable. And you are very beautiful." Bristol came round to lean against the desk, looking down at her. He smelt like home. She rubbed at her nose. "Very beautiful and very grubby. Come back with me and have a shower."

"We're talking about the slum project. You said you wanted Eastern Vision to have a benevolent face."

Bristol nodded. "I do."

"I need living expenses. Noah's apartment is small but it still costs money and he only charges people who can afford to pay. So if we are to develop this work, I need the rent paying and a small wage."

"Interesting pitch. Lucky old Noah."

"Noah is a thoroughly good person." Jessica sat up very straight, looking Bristol in the eye.

"Unlike me, you mean? You're blushing."

Jessica wished her nose didn't itch and her bowel was less bubbly.

"I'm thirsty," she said.

He let go of the desk. "We'll go out. I need a break from the luxury condoms."

She smiled. As she stood and turned to the door, she felt his hand on the small of her back. She stopped. He didn't move. The air conditioning seemed to grow louder.

"Jessica?" He came closer, so that the air between them vibrated where they almost touched.

"Hm," said Jessica carefully.

His lips brushed the top of her head.

"I've decided to be celibate whilst I'm pregnant. I'm not interested in sex." She shook her curls out and reached for the door. "I do need a cold drink though. And some chocolate."

~

Alexis was wearing a suit and battered trainers. He fiddled with the top of the pocket where it was stitched together. How ridiculous not to be able to put anything in a pocket.

"Right," he said, "I'd better ring Bangkok before they all go to bed."

Pippa looked up from the proof of a brochure she was designing.

"Go ahead my guest," she said, turning the telephone to face him.

"Right," said Alexis.

111

Pippa circled a photograph of a string of beads. *Middle this one,* she wrote.

"There is problem?"

"No connection. I'll try again."

Alexis checked the number he'd written on his hand and dialled.

"Still nothing."

"You need zero zero," said Pippa. "For exit UK."

He slapped his forehead and laughed.

"The lines must all be full, still dead."

"And six six. For enter Thailand."

This time he said nothing.

Pippa held the brochure up and made a face.

"So many purple," she murmured, "need some more yellow."

"Ah! Sam, how are things in the City of Angels, mate?"

Alexis winked at Pippa.

"Damn. Sorry. Did the math wrong." He grimaced, reddening. "Just checking up on progress, really."

Pippa pretended to survey the back cover, her head on one side.

"Marketing. Yes. Pivotal. Well, in fact I've begun on a book, autobiography in a – no? Right. Not yet, anyway." His fingernail snapped on the tight thread holding his pocket shut. "Understood. I did wonder if you'd thought any more about me coming out. To Thailand." He screwed his face up, held his breath. "Here. Absolutely. This is it. Yes, on the spot so to speak. And Bristol – I know, communicate. Yes. I'll leave you to go back to sleep. Righto."

Putting the phone down carefully, as though this would help Sam drift off again, Alexis sighed.

"You stay here, yes? Is not so bad."

"It's not just not bad, it's great. Interviews everywhere I look. I haven't been this popular for years!"

"You are – what is word? I hear Bristol saying Moses you are indispersable."

"Indispensable? Oh! Well."

Pippa smiled and showed him the brochure.

"What you think this one?"

"Great," said Alexis.

"Of course I need someone the marketing for check the words…"

He grinned. "I'm your man," he said.

~

"How many people live here?" asked Jessica.

"In Phetbin? Maybe one thousand," Noah made a gesture with his hands as if to say it was hard to know.

A little boy stepped out of a hut in front of them and, seeing Noah, came bouncing up to them.

"This is Yim Sao," said Noah, ruffling the boy's hair.

"Hello," said Jessica, and he took hold of her hand. She was taken aback, scared almost by his trust.

"You have a new friend," said Noah.

Jessica stopped; they had walked past Yim Sao's home.

"His mother won't know where he's gone," she said.

Noah walked slowly on, nodding at her to follow.

"His mother will be home when it is dark," he said. "Let him come with us."

Yim Sao clutched Jessica's hand, staring at her with wide eyes. She smiled at him and he laughed.

"He is a bright child," said Noah. "You might teach him, perhaps."

Jessica looked at the little face laughing up at her and felt elation spread through her veins. She stopped where a mound of spilt concrete made a good seat.

"Jessica," she said, pointing at herself.

"Jess'cah," said the boy. "Khun Jess'cah."

"My name is Khun Jessica."

"My name is Khun Jess'cah."

She laughed, shaking her head, "*Your* name is Yim Sao."

"*Your* name is Yim Sao," he repeated.

Noah watched them laughing and nodded.

~

113

Sam sat Jack and Tilly on his lap and looked into the camera.

Bristol swigged from his wine glass, watching. He wondered how late these people would stay. Linda looked tired already, saying little, frowning slightly. She'd tried even after she was dressed and ready to get out of it. But Bristol told her Sam needed them there and it was time she stopped using Andrew as an excuse to stay in all the time.

"Tutu and Pepsi manage fine. And he'll be asleep."

"You think Tutu and Pepsi do bloody everything. You've no idea what I do because you're never here."

They'd said nothing in the taxi.

Now Gina took Jack from Sam, leaving Tilly on his lap staring at all the strangers.

"I should lend you Tutu," said Bristol. "Gina has a lot on her hands with two kids. She might throw the towel in."

"Bet she needs the money, poor wretch." The guests were new arrivals – solicitors from Manchester. The wife was looking rather accusingly at Sam. "I've heard they usually give their own children to relatives so they can work."

"Yes," murmured Bristol, "I believe they do."

Gina returned for Tilly.

"Thank you," said Sam.

"I'm going to have hundreds of children," announced the English girl. "Whilst we can just pay other people to do the dirty work."

Her husband pushed out a short laugh, glancing at her glass.

Bristol caught Sam's eye for half a second.

The English girl sat herself beside Linda at the table.

"I should grill you," she said, "on shops and so forth."

Linda nodded.

The husband groaned. "This sounds dangerous."

Bristol poured more wine into the girl's glass. "In fact Linda's not been here that long herself. And we have a new addition to our own family."

"Oh! Congratulations!" The girl spilt some wine on her chest.

"His name is Andrew," continued Bristol, as though he hadn't noticed the spreading stain.

"What do you all do for Christmas out here?" asked the husband, shunting a napkin across the table.

Bristol didn't need to look at Sam. He sensed him flinch. His first Anna-less Christmas.

"Parties," said Bristol, "holidays. Phuket maybe."

"Now you're talking," said the English girl. "Christmas in a spa. With no in-laws."

Her husband smiled. "Here's to that."

"It makes you wonder why the whole world isn't out here living in luxury." The top of her blouse slipped so that too much of her breast showed. "We are going to have the time of our lives."

"How long did you say you were here for?" Linda's voice seemed to stop the table in its tracks for a second. She had sunk so far into the background she was almost invisible.

"Five years, probably," said the husband.

"And then we're going home and we're going to race to make partner."

"Well," he sipped from his glass. "Something like that."

"We're here for a year," said Linda quietly.

Bristol felt Sam look at him but he kept his face blank as though he hadn't heard.

"Do you work for Eastern Vision?" asked the English girl, looking sideways at Linda.

Linda gave a soft snort.

"Linda was in PR in the UK," said Bristol.

"Oh?"

When Linda didn't elaborate, the husband asked quickly, "And is Eastern Vision primarily about investment capital or real estate?"

"Interesting question. I think I'll let my cousin answer that one. Sam?"

The English couple laughed.

Sam shook his head, grinning. "Bristol and I are open to diversification when opportunities present themselves."

"Opportunities to make money, this is?" The English girl leant back in her chair. "Oh God! Why didn't anyone tell me I was flashing my tits?"

"We simply didn't notice," said Sam. "And we are in fact an ethical business. We put back into the city. We support–"

Bristol picked up an empty bottle in front of him. "Sam," he said, "stop bullshitting and come and show me where your wine cellar is."

They stood outside the bathroom, Sam with his arms folded and Bristol running his hands through his hair.

"Linda doesn't know about Jessica, does she?"

"No. And no need." Bristol found a little scab on his scalp.

"Don't pick it," said Sam.

Bristol folded his arms.

16

"You rest, Jess'cah. Too heavy."

Noah was sweating and his skin was translucent, strained.

"I'm fine. Thank you." Jessica dragged the sack up the steps behind her, gritting her teeth.

Noah followed, carrying a box of tins and packets. They sat on the floor beside the apothecary cabinet, neither of them speaking, letting their breath settle.

After a few minutes, Noah got to his feet and began to prepare a syrup.

Jessica unscrewed a bottle of water. She looked down at her spreading middle. What if nothing happened to stop the pregnancy? What if, however hard she ignored it, this baby grew and was born?

She drank the whole bottle and wondered if she had the energy to go back down to the street and buy a plate of noodles. Eating was the only way to stop herself being sick.

Noah divided the syrup into two small bowls and handed one to Jessica.

"For get strong," he said. He slurped his bowl straight back.

Jessica looked at the purple goo, which smelt of berries, disinfectant and coal. She imagined it sliding down the pipes that were her insides and through to the tube that fed the baby.

"Snake blood. Long life."

"Snake's blood?"

"For – get – strong." Noah crawled to his mattress in the corner.

"For get strong," she murmured, and drank it. A connection in her brain spotlit an old memory of downing a cocktail with a school friend. They made it when the friend's parents were out and dared each other to drink it.

~

Maureen's head itched but she daren't touch it for fear of dying her fingers black in the process. She glanced at the clock in the corner.

"Nearly cooked, Mrs Cotton." The hairdresser spoke as if Maureen were ninety-six and in the final stages of dementia.

Maureen smiled tightly and tried not to look in the mirror. With her hair slicked tar-like away from her face, every crinkled, blotchy inch of skin was exposed. She wasn't sure she'd recognise her face without the hair if she had to pick it out from any other. It was an unsettling thought and she dismissed it, flicking a page in the ridiculous magazine she'd been left with.

She had intended to let the grey grow through. But Geoff had peered at her one morning, before she'd had a chance to do anything with it, and asked if she needed money to go to the salon.

"No, it's fine," she'd said. "I've plenty left."

"Well what are you waiting for, girl? Hm? Christmas?" He laughed loudly.

And here she was, being painted in again when she'd all but faded away.

He wanted to take her to a restaurant. Just the two of them.

"Geoff," she said. "What on earth would we talk about?"

He grabbed her then, by the wrists.

"Exactly, woman. Hmm?" He shook her arms so that her hands flapped idiotically. "Stop looking at the floor. Look at me for once, hmm?"

As the girl rinsed her hair, Maureen went through what she was going to talk about. She had one or two ideas of things she hadn't mentioned – her cousin was thinking of emigrating to Spain, and there was talk of the Theatre Royal closing. That actor, Alexis George from the television, had been in the paper talking about it, with some other names she didn't know.

But these were only remarks, really. Where would they go from there? She imagined Geoff scoffing at the cousin. And he'd have nothing at all to say about a theatre where he'd only ever been once, many years ago. He'd have forgotten he'd ever been. But Maureen remembered. They'd taken Jessica the Christmas she was five. Jessica's eyes reflected the glittering lights above the stage and she bounced on her seat when the villagers danced.

"That water all right for you, Mrs Cotton?"

"Fine. Thank you."

"I'll rinse this conditioner off and then Penny will do your set. OK?"

The girl washing her hair was Jessica's age. Maureen was pretty sure they'd been in primary school together. Probably didn't get into the grammar. And now she was working happily down the road from where she'd always lived and no doubt visited her mother at the weekends.

"There you are." The girl wrapped Maureen's head in a turban and steered her back to the mirror.

"Penny will be with you now. Can I get you anything? Another magazine?"

Maureen shook her head, holding the turban in place. She could go back to that rainbow office. When Geoffrey was at work. She'd find the gangly monk boy and ask him what Jessica was doing, whether she needed anything. Maybe he'd send her a letter. Jessica could write back, using the office address so that Geoff needn't know. She smiled at Penny in the mirror as she approached.

~

Noah shook his head.

"Drink ginger tea," he scolded, "not Coke. Why must you poison yourself?"

Jessica drank half the can in one go and sighed.

"Lost cause," she said. "Is that for Khun Dha?"

"Yes. Good. You remember well." Noah counted eight pellets into a tissue and fastened it with an elastic band. "You take to her later?"

Jessica nodded and glugged more Coke. She burped.

"Oh! Sorry!"

Noah grinned.

"I am revolting," she said. "Burping away, fat and—"

"Not fat. *Pregnant*."

"Well, that too." She hiccupped. "I used to be quite pretty." She lay on her side on the floor, hugging a blanket she'd punched into a ball. "But I don't care. It's awful how much of my life I've wasted fussing about how I look. I'm putting all that behind me now." She pinched the top of one of her arms, which had softened and spread in sympathy with her middle. "Good thing, really, or I'd be in tears every time I looked in the mirror."

Noah sieved some earth into a tin jug and said nothing. Jessica stifled another hiccup.

"I drank that Coke too fast," she said. "I'm glad I don't have any photos. To remind me what I looked like when I gave a toss."

She let her eyes fall shut. In the backpack she'd lost when she fell by the khlong had been just one photo. Golden syrup-coloured hair twisted in a little lace band so that her curls fell softly, carelessly around her face. A cornflower blue dress. Sleeveless, with a pinched waist and a full skirt.

Geoff had said, "Hm, you scrub up well. You wouldn't know, to look at you," and patted her shoulder briskly. Maureen had taken the photograph at the door when her friends had picked her up. As she walked down the path, she heard her mother's sigh.

"She's lovely."

"Intermittently," muttered Geoff, and Jessica pretended not to hear.

The friends were worlds away now. She felt her face tremble a little. They'd been baffled by her, at school. The times when she talked all the time to everyone. Without thinking about it. Words just came and she spoke them and people spoke back and she felt – whole. And then, when her pilot light went out, when words were out of reach and everything was frightening, she was a stranger. A cold, weird stranger who repelled anyone who came near. The bleakness inside ate away at her sense of self until she felt she was nothing at all.

Burying her face in the balled up blanket, she gritted her teeth together in defiance. She could shake that shit off. She could grow up. She had to. She was going to be a *mother* for God's sake.

~

"I have learned a word today," said Pippa, sitting on a table in the empty exhibition space.

Alexis rubbed his eyes.

"Long day," he said. "That was one hell of a crowd."

Pippa shrugged. "Good marketing. You want know this new word?"

"OK."

"Cute. You know what means cute?"

"The pigs are cute, and the baby Buddhas. It's like 'sweet,' like you want to hug it."

Pippa looked at his face until he looked back.

"You're cute," she said.

"I wish."

"Sweet."

Alexis flushed and straightened his back a little. "You're teasing me, Pips."

"So cute when you feel shy like now."

Alexis drew in a long, slow breath.

Pippa stretched out her arms. "Long day," she said.

He moved nearer her table, fighting a smile.

"Feel nerves?" she whispered. She put her hand on the back of his neck and kneaded a little. He purred.

"That massage lady tell me massage so good for nerve. For long day." She drew him closer and rolled her knuckles between his shoulder blades.

"That — is — delicious."

"Ssh, not saying nothing."

"Mmm, so yummy."

She laughed. "Food is yummy."

"So is that. Don't stop."

She put her hands on his shoulders and turned his back to her, chopping her hands up and down. He reached behind him and pulled her feet so that her legs were round his waist.

"I happy for you come Eastern Vision," breathed Pippa into his ear. "We are team, you and me."

17

The baby took up so much room that Jessica's lungs were crushed. She had to gulp and gasp for air. She thought she would stop breathing altogether.

She heaved herself onto her right side, wedging her shoulder into the cushion, but her back pulled in that position. Using her right arm as a lever, she yanked herself over so that she was lying on her left and brought her knee up to stop herself rolling forward.

Inside her, the baby fought back, wrestling its own life cord, flinging its limbs in every direction as Jessica twisted and turned.

She clutched her mother's letter, begging her to come home. But she was too far gone to get on a plane, and the letter said not to ring the house in the evening or at weekends, so it was clear that even if she could go back in shame, she wouldn't really have a home to go to.

Bristol's knock. No one else knocked like that. Mostly they called out or stepped in if the door was ajar. Jessica's stomach lurched. She couldn't see him. She'd decided that weeks ago.

"Jess? Open the door."

"I can't get up."

"Are you really that fat?"

"I'm not here."

"I can see that."

A little bubble of a smile escaped her lips. Despite herself, knowing he could only be revolted, she was excited.

"OK, I'm going. I'll leave this stuff outside the door. Don't let the chocolate melt."

She opened the door.

"Hey."

"Hey."

"You look like a lioness about to have cubs." He scrunched a curl in his hand. "Do you bite?"

"Yes," she said, scraping her hair as flat as she could.

"That sounds fun. Can I come in?"

She stepped back.

He put down a large paper bag on the apothecary cabinet.

"Where's Noah? Out building his ark?"

"I'm not even going to answer that. What's in the bag?"

Bristol pushed it towards her. There were bars of chocolates and bags of sweets, flavoured UHT milk in little cartons with straws, a bottle of Coke.

Jessica smiled at him.

"I'm sorry," she said. "I have to sit. I can't stand for long."

"Go back to bed," he told her, bringing the paper bag.

He sat on the mattress by her feet and looked at her.

Jessica found an elastic band and forced her hair into it.

"I'm a mess." She wanted to cry. She wanted him to take her in his arms and rock her.

"A delicious mess. You're cute even when you're fat."

She kicked him in the side.

"Jess. Linda wants to go away, sometime in the New Year. She says I'm always telling her to get out and now she wants to."

"Excellent. Take her."

All Jessica knew for certain about Linda was that she was older than Bristol. She tended to picture a tall woman with a pinched face and very short hair. The image didn't fit with Bristol at all.

"You know I don't want to go. I want to be here when you–"

"Explode."

"How graphic."

"I still can't believe there's actually a baby in there. Even looking like this." Jessica belched delicately, tearing at a straw that was firmly stuck to its carton.

"I'm going to book you into Samitivej hospital. Will you come and book in?"

Jessica sucked the fruit milk, looking at him. "Noah's medicines work fine for the woman in Phetbin."

He took hold of her feet, rubbing her toes. She wanted to close her eyes and lose herself in his touch.

"Sure they do. But I would sleep better in my bed at night knowing you were in a proper hospital."

"What's proper about it? I've seen what 'proper' medicine does and I've seen what Noah's ancient medicine does, and I know which is–"

"Jess, do it for me. I need to know you're somewhere safe, somewhere hygienic for God's sake. And Linda was climbing the walls until she had an epidural."

At the thought of Bristol holding his wife's hand while she scowled and cursed her way through labour, Jessica's breathing grew tighter. In another life, in a path that hadn't been taken, it would be her holding Bristol's hand, going on holiday with him, sharing his bed when he came home at night.

"Jess, I want to look after you. Let me. I'm going to have you cared for at Samitivej." He straightened his back and swallowed. "And we should talk some more about contacting either your parents or this baby's father." Jessica bit open a bag of chocolate drops, spilling some onto her expanded chest. "Don't be so damn stubborn, Jess. Grow up." She began to cry. Fat tears running into the little packet of drops that didn't really taste much of chocolate. She wished things were different, sometimes so hard that when she knew they couldn't be, she returned to the old fantasy of drowning herself in the khlong. *But*, said the voice inside her head, *that would be murder, not just suicide.*

Bristol rubbed her feet and sighed. "If things were different," he said very quietly, "I would never leave your side."

He rubbed further up her shins and in some distant part of her mind she thought how hairy her legs were and that his hands would feel every prickle.

"How old is the shit who did this to you?" Bristol was looking at her feet and at his hands massaging her gently as he spoke.

"Older than me," she said, "younger than you."

"Oh?"

Jessica's head felt eased by the crying. She let it fall heavily against the pillow and said, "Do you know I've only ever had sex once? You would have been the second."

Bristol's grip tightened on her puffy ankles. "Jess. Let me help you. Tell me who to ring. Who is the bastard who did this to you?"

She waved him away.

He stood, as if he were about to stride all the way to Surrey and find out for himself. "The first time you had sex and you didn't even use contraception for God's sake!"

"You," murmured Jessica, "are a fine one to talk." She let her eyes fall shut.

Bristol ran his hands through his hair. "Linda was on the pill," he said through gritted teeth.

"That's what she told you anyway. But I'm not about to go telling someone I need a wedding ring and a new apartment." Jessica opened her eyes long enough to see Bristol nod. "I have to sleep now."

He looked out of the window and then down at Jessica's bulk amongst the sweet wrappers.

"I'll stay until you're asleep," he said hoarsely. "And I'm sorting the hospital. I won't take no for an answer."

~

Pippa had her head on Alexis' lap. The box of chocolates on the poof beside them had only the coffee and hard ones left. She'd eaten everything nutty and he'd eaten the strawberry creams and turkish delights.

His hand slid idly under her T-shirt, fondling a braless breast.

"Leave it," she said, her eyes on the television.

He whined like a kitten and tickled her armpit.

"No, really." She sat up, hooking her hair behind her ears and leaning her elbows on her knees.

"Wh–?"

"Ssh," she told him, "watch. Listen."

Pippa didn't notice that tears were streaming down her tightly set face.

Tanks. An empty street. A crowd. An elderly couple hurrying from the scene.

Pippa gaped at the montage of footage, scrambled together from freelancers and explained patchily by the correspondent.

"Pips?" Alexis glanced about for a box of tissues.

Pippa could hear only her brother's voice from years ago. *It can't last.*

"That is my country," she said, looking straight ahead still even though the piece had finished. "This wicked man he is dead. Shooted. And his bitch wife. It did not last."

"They were the King and Queen, right?"

Pippa looked at her celebrity boyfriend and then down at the floor.

"Your word is dictator." Her shoulders shook. Where were her parents? There'd been bullet holes in the walls of those empty streets.

"So he was really unpopular?" Alexis stroked her hair nervously, taking a coffee chocolate with his other hand. "Yuk. We'll need to open the other box now to take the taste away."

She put her hands over her face. "Mama, Papa," she whispered.

"You could go and see them, sweetheart. Put your mind at rest."

Pippa turned to him, her face witheringly hard. "I cannot have passport," she spat. "I am prisoner in this country because I runned away from my own."

18

"Ooohh."

"Breathing this oil, Jess'cah. Good pain."

Jessica pointed her toes and clenched her fists as the contraction reached its height. "Ooh fuck."

"Breathing," murmured Noah, massaging oil into her temples.

She flopped back, the oil mingling with the sweat and stinging her eyes.

"I make more syrup," said Noah, easing himself upright.

"I don't want any more syrup," she wailed. She yanked herself onto her hands and knees, biting the sheet.

"I find sleeping syrup," said Noah.

"No, the baby might sleep. That's not good."

"Jess'cah. I bring many baby. Many. Can trust. Best quality syrup."

"Nooo-ahhh!" Jessica sank her face into the mattress and screamed until she had no breath left.

When the contraction released her, she twisted her neck to one side so that she could speak. "Bristol. Booked. A bed at. Samitivej."

"I know this. We talked about it. You say no hospital."

"Please. Get me to Samitivej. Money. There. In envelope. Fuck nooo, not again, not yet." She thumped her fists and ground her teeth.

"I find taxi," said Noah. He laid a hand lightly on the small of her back and pressed a scented cloth to her face.

"Quickly, Noah. This baby isn't ready. It's not supposed to come yet. We have to stop it coming out. We have to get it out. Quickly."

A part of Jessica, so deeply hidden it felt like vomiting when it forced itself to the surface, was thinking of Maureen. Imagining her mother walking through the door and sighing. Soothing her, taking her to hospital. The imaginary Maureen said, *You've really done it now. You silly, silly girl,* but she was holding her hand.

And then Bristol took her mother's place. He rocked her in his arms, pressing his lips to her hair, rubbing her aching back.

"Bristol," she said. "Tell them to get rid of it. It won't be ready. It's too early."

"OK, Jessica. I'm going to give you something for the pain now. Just try to relax."

"Bristol?"

"No, we're in Bangkok. You're in the hospital. You're doing really well."

Jessica was hypnotised by the regular beep and the soft, continuous buzz. She looked down a kaleidoscope at a shifting pattern of brightly coloured glass and wondered if they'd use the sharp edges to cut her open.

Then she realised it was the gemstones from the glass jar in the rainbow office cupboard. She delved her hand into the jar and it swallowed her whole and she was swimming in translucent rubies, sapphires and emeralds, the rainbow lights rippling across her body. The relief of weightlessness after the burden of her own bulk made her smile. She let out a long breath and turned onto her back. Then her hand found a piece of glass that had broken and the shards sliced through the back of her hand. It hit another piece, shattering it so that more splinters pricked her all over. Each one split another crystal until a thousand tiny daggers were cutting at her skin.

"Get me out," she tried to say, but her mouth filled with glass shards and bled until she gagged.

"Good girl. Not long now."

"I didn't mean to fall in. I'm sorry. I'm my own worst enemy."

"What's that, sweetheart? Try to keep still."

With a huge effort, Jessica swallowed the glass in her mouth and then clamped her lips shut.

~

When the phone rang, Pippa was struggling with the cardboard box. It was so tightly bound and with such tough tape that her scissors were useless. She ruined her fresh manicure trying to tear into it with her fingernails.

"Eastern Vision London, Pippa speaking. HowmayIhelpyou?"

Pippa kicked the box. She had just shut down the computer. It would take forever to start up again. She grabbed a sheet of paper and decided she'd book whatever it was tomorrow.

"Good afternoon."

"The same thing to you," said Pippa, drawing a house with four windows and a triangle roof.

"I wondered — is that the rainbow office?"

"Is Eastern Vision London. Pippa speaking. HowmayIhelpyou?"

There was a little cough on the other end and then the voice asked, "Is — Moses — available?"

"Moses he is teaching such a course right now. Who is here?"

"My name is Maureen," whispered the caller. "I am Jessica Cotton's mother. She went to work for Eastern Vision in Bangkok."

"Ah! Yes I see now." Pippa drew fat flowers down the path.

"I wondered how she is. Perhaps you have a letter for me somewhere?" She sounded tearful. "Could you check with Moses that there's nothing he's forgotten to pass on?"

"I think Jessica is very busy with the charitable arm. We have here no letters."

"Have you spoken to her? Is she well?"

Pippa drew a plane in the sky above her house and a fluffy cloud.

"I'm afraid not. Do you know a telephone number in Bangkok?"

From the other end came a sound halfway between a choke and a moan.

"Hello?" said Pippa.

"Thank you," said Maureen. "I'm sorry to have bothered you."

Pippa waited but after a moment the call cut off and she put the receiver down. She drew a boat with waves and fish underneath. Then she began to scrawl lines across the picture in all directions, through the house, the flowers, the plane and the boat, until she was scribbling furiously all over it. Her hands were covered in ink. When the pen made a hole and went through to the desk, she crumpled the paper and threw it across the room.

~

She could drop the baby from a great height; out of the window or down the stairwell. She could wrap it tightly, including its head, so it would stop breathing. Inject it with poison.

A nurse pulled the curtain aside and looked in. Jessica put her hand on the perspex cot beside her.

"Don't take it away," she said, squaring her jaw.

"No take baby," said the nurse. "You sleep."

Jessica kept very still. It was important not to move until the nurse had gone. But she stayed where she was, just looking.

She knew that some of the nurses were monsters in disguise; paedophiles, child slave traders, killers – they bought uniforms and infiltrated the hospital – and the real nurses were so stupid they didn't realise. She couldn't tell for sure who was real and who was fake, though she had suspicions. Surely she couldn't be the only person who could see what was going on? They were probably paying the doctors huge sums of what Bristol called 'under-the-table' money to keep quiet.

She had to get out. But first she had to destroy the baby before it was stolen.

The nurse let the curtain go and disappeared.

A hand seized her ankle. She kicked but it gripped tight. She kept hold of the cot, a scream hovering on her lips. Then another hand grabbed her shoulder and pulled her back into the bed.

"Get off," she said, "I'm capable of killing."

The bed grew hand after hand, grasping at her arms and legs, the friction of skin on skin painful.

"Let go of me. I'm going to scream. I'm going to set fire to this whole fucking hospital."

More hands seized her throat and twisted her ears. She bucked her body, freeing herself of some of the hands, and tried to rock violently enough to throw off more. She managed to get hold of the cot again. The baby began to cry.

A nurse and a doctor stood over her, but they did nothing about the hundred grabbing hands.

"Be calm now. There is no problem."

"How do I know if you're real or not?" shouted Jessica.

The doctor touched her forehead.

"You're one of them! Back off or I'll bite." The doctor wasn't real. Even his badge was different. Stupid man, you'd have thought he'd have checked something like that if he was going to fool people. He came closer.

"Leave the baby where it is! I'll scream the place down if you touch it!"

"I think you already scream." The nurse held the baby to her shoulder, rubbing its back. "I find milk."

"Miss Cotton," said the doctor. "I need you to look at me. Try to be still. We are not going to hurt you or your baby."

Jessica shut her eyes tightly. He'd mistaken her for someone else. He'd see his mistake and leave her alone. She clenched her fists and gritted her teeth, rocking to keep the hands off.

~

As the dark closed in outside, Lazuli drew the purple velvet curtains across the french doors. She stood by the light switch that would illuminate her chandelier; a vast inverted pyramid of crystals the colour of the ocean. She had strung each one herself from gold-coloured chains and beaded ribbons, twists of silk and gauze, and the construction hung so low that her ex-husband would have had to duck to pass underneath. She flicked the switch and tapped the chandelier to make the light dance on the curtains, the ceiling, the walls, the floor and the mirror so that she might have been under water watching rays of sun on tropical fish.

She stretched herself out on one of the daybeds that bordered the room. They were built into the wall all around, with a soft undulating edge and a valance of beads. In her mind, she imagined what the journalist might write. *Acclaimed Hypnogem Therapist Lazuli takes a break in her jewel-decked lounge, prisms of aquamarine light spraying forth from the chandelier she designed herself.* She grinned, thinking maybe her ex might stumble upon the article as he tripped over the clutter of his stepchildren and his rather consistent new wife.

A car drew up outside. Lazuli replaced her grin with a look of serenity and went to the door.

The journalist was very young. Skinny, blonde, wearing jeans.

"Welcome," said Lazuli, taking both the girl's hands and looking deeply into her eyes.

"Thanks. Eve Sanderson. May I call you Lazuli?" The girl seemed already to be looking past her into the house.

"Come. I have prepared some mauve tea."

Lazuli led the way to the lounge. She heard the click of a handbag latch as the girl grabbed her notebook. Maybe mauve tea was going too far.

"Wow," said Eve as Lazuli shut the door and the full effect of her under-the-sea lighting was revealed. "I hope you don't mind if I scribble. My dictaphone needs replacing."

"Do," said Lazuli, pouring an infusion of home-grown lavender into two ceramic vessels.

"Maybe you can tell me about what Hypnogem Therapy actually involves?" Eve settled herself onto a daybed, knees drawn up to rest her notebook on.

"I think," said Lazuli, "the best way to understand the process is to experience it for yourself."

"Oh, wow, yeah. Can we do some?"

Lazuli frowned into her lavender. She hoped she hadn't been sent the work experience girl.

When Eve was lying on the mat with gemstones in an outline around her body, Lazuli placed a warm flannel over her eyes. The girl's breathing deepened.

"God, this is so relaxing."

130

"Try not to speak." Lazuli moved round her. She glanced at the notebook on the daybed. "Now, no pressure and no rush, just very relaxed, you'll find one of the gems·is drawing you. Don't try, just let your mind float and the right one will speak to you."

Very slowly, Lazuli turned the notebook over to see what the child had written. Fortunately it was not full of shorthand, but a rather scruffier note-taking system.

"Shall I pick it up?"

Lazuli dropped the notebook, her eyes on the flannel over the girl's face.

"Yes," she murmured. "Let your hand reach out and take the stone that calls to you."

A little hand with chipped nail polish took a stone the colour of brown blood from just above her right ear.

"Now cup it in your hands," instructed Lazuli. "Breathe on it if you like. Fill it with yourself."

Lazuli had the girl focus on each part of her body in turn, letting the energy from the stone fill her from head to foot. She had a way of lengthening the word 'vulva' so that it sounded much longer than two syllables, and she saw the girl's face contract. She said 'buttock' in a clipped, precise way that made it sound like something nice to eat.

"You can hear my voice and only my voice." Lazuli flipped a page silently. "We're standing at the top of a staircase," she murmured. *False claims?* she read, *Illegal immigrants or exploitation? Poss financial inconsistencies.* "We're heading down the steps one at a time. Keep the gemstone held close."

Lazuli had to stop. She couldn't keep her voice serene. She had actually believed that *Tomorrow* magazine wanted a feature on her. She'd planned photographs of herself in her garden, close to nature; in her lounge, sprinkled with glittering light; in her kitchen, maybe doing something with a pestle and mortar. But all they wanted was to dig for dirt. She'd had suspicions about Pippa's citizenship, but she hadn't given it much thought.

"At the very bottom of the steps, there is a door."

She had considered breaking her contract with Eastern Vision, but she wanted the logo on her cards because it was this connection that had made her and she wasn't sure she had the nerve to let go. If she upset Eastern Vision, they might publicly discount her as a fraud and she'd be lost.

"Explore the safe haven you have found at the foot of the steps."

But if Eastern Vision was going down, perhaps she'd be better to get out first. She'd assumed the Alexis George success was luck – maybe he'd never even been tested for HIV– but if he'd been bought and it came out, could they be sued? God, if she had to refund all her clients, let alone pay compensation, she'd be back in the flat she was renting to Pippa – or worse. People couldn't sue Hypnogem Therapists, could they? What did her contract with Eastern Vision say? Could she get out in time?

"You may find you are alone or you may be in company."

In her mind's eye, Lazuli could see the walls around her being dismantled brick by brick. The chandelier crashing to the ground.

"Use all your senses," she said, her voice hoarse. "See what you see, hear what you hear, feel what you feel."

She was renting a flat to an illegal immigrant. Becoming rich on the back of fraudulent claims. And this stupid little girl on the floor was going to ruin her.

19

Jessica floated in a pool of sunlight, lapping at the sweetness with her tongue. The metal chains they'd used to control her head were unbolted and as they slid away, every pore on her scalp exhaled. Her brain sighed as it stretched out at last. *I have never felt so peaceful.* She smiled. *I never knew what it was like to have a head so light you couldn't feel it. I didn't know until now but it's all so easy, so beautiful.*

~

Pippa dropped onto the sofa, letting go of her shopping bags. Her arms felt longer for carrying their weight.

"Hello, I am home," she called out, wiping her hair away from her face. "You can bring me nice drink?"

Alexis appeared in the doorway.

"God, Pippa. What have you bought now? You must have more clothes than you could ever wear."

"Don't be a bitchy," she said, rummaging in one of the bags. "I have buyed you a present so be nice to me."

Alexis sighed and sat down.

"Please to get me drink," she said, her head on one side. "Then I give you present."

He went to the kitchen and she lolled her head back and shut her eyes for a moment. In bed, Alexis had managed to push the memory of the smelly border guard far to the back of her mind. He had a beautiful body, which he worked hard at, and he gave as much as he took. But she could not get away from the growing irritation she felt at his stupidity, his pettiness. She wondered every day whether to tell him it was over. To ask him to move out. There had been a lot of shopping. As if the credit card he'd leant her when they were first wrapped around each other knew that it might soon be handed over.

"Here." He handed her a tall glass of fresh orange juice.

"Your little present," she said, trying to smile.

He took the little box she gave him.

"Open that, what you wait for?"

Picking off a piece of Sellotape, he lifted the lid and frowned.

"You not to like that?" Pippa drained her juice.

"Yes I like it. But you can't buy everything you like."

"And why?" Pippa hooked a leg between his and rested her elbow on his shoulder.

"Because, Pips, if you hadn't noticed, I don't in fact have a job. I was kidding myself they wanted me at Eastern Vision; it was never going to go anywhere. And now I'm just a goddamn unemployed actor again." He shrugged her off.

"A goddamn unemployed actor. What is this?"

"Don't take the piss. Your English is better than that."

"Sorry," she said, folding her arms.

He put the boxed watch on the floor. They sat for a moment with their feet amongst the shopping bags.

"So you don't want to see my nice shopping?"

Alexis said nothing. He tore at a piece of skin hanging off near his thumbnail.

"Listen, Alex. You are needing money, you go to Eastern Vision. They buyed your story and now they must to buy it again."

"They don't need me, Pippa. They're massive now. I've been shat on."

"You have not been sat on. You are being stupid. You can have so much money if you just ask."

Alexis frowned at her. He picked up the watch and looked at it as if he'd never seen one before.

"You can say to newspaper you made a story. You can tell them it is all not true. And Eastern Vision make up some rubbish for people who pay so much money. This Hypnogem Therapy and Wisdom Meditating, they know nothing. You can just tell the newspaper this. And the little statues with big willies, they are made in factories far away from Thailand."

"I don't understand what you're saying. I haven't lied to anyone. What I said was true. Moses has got powers of divination."

Pippa bent down and opened a bag. She pulled out a pair of silver shoes with green stripes down the sides. Prising off a trainer, she tried it on.

"Pippa? I'd look ridiculous if I went telling people it was all a story. And anyway, it's not."

"You like my shoe?"

"No I don't like your bloody shoe."

Pippa laughed. "You don't have to wear it. I will keep it."

"You can't go telling people I made it up. It was all true. Pippa, look at me." She looked at him. "You cannot start telling people I lied. I didn't lie. I'd look stupid."

"Alex. I not say nothing to nobody. You made a story and Bristol gave you money. But he gets a lot of money, much more than he gave to you. And you can have some more of this money."

Alexis screwed up his face. Pippa watched him trying to think and didn't know whether it was funny or maddening.

"What you're saying is, I threaten him. Right? I threaten to take back my claims and he has to pay me to keep me quiet." Pippa put the other shoe on. "Buy my silence." She pointed her toes and examined the green stripes. "Blackmail."

"It is sharing. He makes money from your story and he must share that."

Alexis broke wind quietly. "How long have you known I lied when I made those claims?"

"Alex. Nothing happens at Eastern Vision without I know."

He laughed. "Do you really think I could–?"

"What you think?" she snapped, tired suddenly and hungry.

"I think I want to take you to bed. You're bloody fantastic, you are."

Pippa grabbed the bags and left the room. "I go to eat," she said. "You have to rub your willy in the shower."

~

Jessica saw a spiralling blade, a food mixer so mammoth it would slice her to pieces in a second, the blade whirling faster and faster.

"Look. Here is baby to see you."

She wanted to break her own arms with a hammer. It bothered her that, having smashed the first arm, she wouldn't then be able to lift the hammer for the second.

"You want give baby milk? I show you."

The child's eyes were monstrous. They told her they would follow her wherever she ran. Blue eyes, wild eyes. Eyes that didn't belong in a baby's face.

"Up bottle little bit. Like that. Very good."

Jessica's arms felt like steel. She looked at the doll in the white hospital pinafore, sucking milk and staring at her as if it could see inside her head.

It coughed and milk dribbled from its mouth. Jessica didn't move.

"Now wind baby. Make burp, yes?"

Jessica leant her head back and closed her eyes. She let tears slide down her cheeks.

"Sleep now. Good girl."

She thumped her head on the wall behind her. As she thumped harder and harder, she saw it shatter and explode. The skin would split, her skull would crack and she'd know nothing.

~

"Alexis, what is 'gay'?"

"Gay?"

"Yes, in this folder of yours one article states 'a contact claims ex-soap actor Alexis George is gay, but he won't admit it, even to himself.' Look."

Alexis took the folder from Pippa's hands.

"Do you often go round reading people's stuff?"

"I feel interesting this. Your articles. I like see those photos when you were on TV." She shrugged. "I ring for some takeout?"

Alexis pursed his lips.

"You look as the arse of a dog like that. Don't say me takeout is too much money. When you call Bristol, we do not have to thinking of money."

Alexis stamped his foot and hugged the folder to him.

"Spice Palace or Pizza Pronto?"

"Pippa! Stop it and listen for once. I've thought about it and it won't work. Bristol knows I wouldn't make a fool of myself. To bring him down I'd have to stand up and say I'm a liar. I'm a desperate out-of-work actor prepared to do anything to get in a magazine."

"Make use of your head, Alex. Or is it so stupid? Tell them Bristol made you say it. He was the person backmailing."

"*Black*mailing. You've been in this country God knows how long and you can't even speak the language."

"You can speak to me some Romanian? Hungarian? Any language?"

Alexis sat on the arm of the sofa and bit the top of the folder.

There was a loud knock and someone rattled the letterbox.

They looked at each other and Pippa went to open the door.

A young woman stood on the doorstep.

"Hello," said Pippa.

"Eve Sanderson," said the woman, holding out her hand, "*Tomorrow Magazine*. I rang the bell several times but–"

"That battery is finished."

"Oh, I see! I'm sorry to disturb your evening, but I'm doing a piece on Eastern Vision and I wondered if you could give me a few quick quotes. I've had a good chat with Lazuli, your Hypnogem Therapist, and the people at Wisdom of the Orient. I've not got the–"

"You are speaking very fast," said Pippa. "Please to wait a moment."

Eve Sanderson's eyes lit up. She licked her lips. Pippa thought this was odd, it was as if she'd been offered a piece of fudge cake.

"Who is it?"

"A lady. Alexis, please to come. I don't understand."

Alexis came to the door and Eve thrust out her hand.

"It's such a pleasure, Mr George. Eve Sanderson. *Tomorrow Magazine*."

"Hi," he said, dropping the folder into a pile of shoes, bags and jackets by the door and using his foot to bury it underneath.

"May I come in?"

"Yeah. Sure. Did my agent–?"

"All very last minute but they've said it's fine and they'd sort…"

As she followed them into the sitting room, Eve Sanderson's eyes swivelled to take in walls, furniture, clutter, even floor and ceiling. Her fingers twitched at her bag.

"What's the article?" said Alexis, gesturing for her to sit on the sofa and then reclining on the beanbag.

Pippa smiled. It would buy a few takeouts, whatever it was. She picked up a menu from the side and went to phone Pizza Pronto.

When she came back, Alexis was sitting upright, looking pale. He wouldn't meet her eye.

"You like some coffee?"

Alexis looked at her quickly, mouthing, "No."

Eve Sanderson was making notes. She smiled at Pippa.

"I've not met many Pippas. Is it your given name or did you adopt it when you came to this country?"

"Pardon me?"

Alexis clenched his fists.

"You've been in England a while now, have you?"

"For some time," said Pippa, still standing.

"And do you have full residency?" She giggled a little. "I suppose if you marry the gorgeous Alexis you might get American citizenship." She winked.

"Alexis and me are not marrying."

"No wedding bells yet?"

"Look," said Alexis, getting to his feet. "One minute you're telling me I'm a liar and the next you want to know if I'm getting married. What are you after exactly?" He folded his arms and looked down at the journalist, who flushed and shut her notebook.

"Sorry," she said. "I'm new to this. Shall we have that coffee?"

"No, we're not having coffee. What are you getting at? I want to speak to my agent before I–"

Eve coughed. "Here's the problem," she said. "There are rumours flying around about Eastern Vision and I've been told to investigate. People are saying their success is based on false claims. That–" she clicked her pen. "I'll be straight with you. I've heard it said that you lied about being HIV positive in the first place, and then said Eastern Vision cured you."

Alexis closed his eyes. "I took a test," he said. "I was scared. But after I went to Eastern Vision I was cleared."

"So you never actually were confirmed as–"

"This is very difficult for Alexis to discuss, Miss Eve." Pippa put a hand on his shoulder. "And I do not think it is interesting story."

"Oh really? Well let me ask you a few questions, Miss Pippa." She opened the notebook. Her hands were trembling but her face was set. "Under what authority are you in this country?"

Pippa could feel Alexis' tension through his shoulder. But she didn't panic. A part of her mind had rehearsed for this, as she lay awake in the early morning or sat on a bus watching people who moved as though the streets belonged to them.

"Turn to a new page in your book."

"I'm sorry?"

When Pippa just stood staring at her, Eve twisted her earring and looked away.

"If you want, you can make another article about an actor who believed he was cured of terrible disease. You can say was this some lies. And you can announce that some people are living in London without authority. But I think this is not so interesting. I can tell you better story. True story. Your director will be very pleased."

"Oh? How will I know it's true?"

"For good price I give you some name and number. First you promise you leave us alone."

Eve bit her lip and turned to a new page in her notebook.

When she'd gone, Pippa leaned against the door and looked at Alexis.

"Bloody hell," he said. "How did you think of all that?"

"Is absolute true. Because Eastern Vision sells stupid statue and some piece of coloured glass, those people think they can buy their dreams. With so much money they can learn some secret of rainbows."

Alexis came up close to her and, when she didn't move, he pressed himself up against her. He kissed her hard, plunging his hands under her T-shirt. Pippa let him fight her tongue with his and squeeze her breasts. But when he unzipped her jeans and tried to edge his fingers into her knickers, she prised him away. Holding him at arm's length, she looked him in the eye and said, "Now you explain me what is 'gay'."

20

Bristol slid into the telephone booth in reception, his diary open where he'd written the hospital number. He'd waited in case Linda's clay-wrap appointment was delayed and she came looking for him. But it seemed she was safely in the spa, and Tutu was dipping Andrew in the shallow end of the pool.

"Could I speak to someone on Maternity please?"

"Is your wife having baby now?"

"I'm sorry?"

"You want antenatal, labour or postnatal?"

"Oh, I see. Postnatal. Thanks."

Bristol was wearing shorts. He looked at his knees. Patches of chalky psoriasis on both. He twisted an arm to see his elbow, and sure enough it had started there too. He'd have to sit in the sun. That would help. The tinkling music in his ear paused for a second and he took a breath to speak, but it began again. He shut his eyes and scratched a kneecap.

"Jessica Cotton. Is she on the ward? Can you tell me how she is?"

"Your name, sir?"

"Bristol Chambers. I came in with her before, when you booked her in."

"Ah, Mister Bristol. It is good you are calling. Jessica has unfortunately some puerperal psychosis. Now she is getting better, making some sense. But we are concerned that she cannot care for her baby."

Bristol's hand shook a little. He stretched it, flexing his fingers, and cleared his throat.

"Can you keep her with you? Don't move her. I'll pay when I get there. But I don't know how long it will take me."

"This is a postnatal ward. Really if we need that bed, she must go to Psychiatry."

"I'll be there tomorrow. Please keep her where she is. And keep the baby there."

"Yes Mister Bristol. We will discuss tomorrow."

Shit. Psychosis. He didn't know the first word, but psychosis said enough. He hoped they'd started her back on the lithium, although she'd insisted she wouldn't take it because she wanted to breastfeed the baby.

He hung up, but his hand still clutched the receiver as he bit his lip and gazed at his knees.

He'd have to invent a business trip. Linda would be furious. But he couldn't risk leaving Jessica there. They might lock her up, take the baby off her. She might run away again, disappear into the slums.

"Excuse me, are you done telephoning?"

Bristol jumped. He stepped aside, looking at his wrist but there was just a white patch where he usually wore his watch. Linda had taken it off him, telling him he shouldn't wear a watch on holiday.

~

Marina walked backwards up the stairs with the pushchair and Pippa lifted the front.

"You have no phone call or letter?" asked Pippa, blinking as the strip light turned itself on.

"Nothing," said Marina. "Good riddance."

"What is 'riddance'?"

"Sorry. He is your brother. But I am not sorry to see him gone."

They reached the landing for the rainbow office and put the pushchair down. Pippa tucked her hair behind her ears.

"My brother bringed me to this country. We were in the beginning just him and me." Pippa took the key from her bag but she didn't move to unlock the door.

"It is not my fault he is gone," said Marina. "Please do not be cross with me."

"I am not cross with you! You gave us home. You are my friend. My only friend."

The child chewed at a frayed stuffed animal. Pippa put the key in the lock.

"He will come again. He always come again."

"When he runs out of money," muttered Marina.

"This key is wrong?"

Pippa yanked at the key but it wouldn't turn. The strip light clicked off. Marina jumped on the top step and waved until it flickered on again.

"It's open. Unlocked." Moses opened the door and made a sweeping gesture. "Come in, ladies."

"You are so early today." Pippa frowned at him as Marina brought the pushchair in and shrugged off her jacket.

"I have been meditating. The rainbow office at night is a place of great silence."

"At night?"

141

"You are sleeping here?"

Moses put his palms together. He looked awful. Grey-faced, the stubble shorter on his head than on his chin.

Pippa sat at the desk and produced biscuits from a drawer. Marina had bought her a floral-patterned tool kit for her birthday, to stop her ruining her manicures. Scrabbling amongst the detritus, she found the Stanley knife and slit the packet neatly. She gave a biscuit to little Sasha, who stood examining a broken fertility god and spreading crumbs on the floor.

"I have been thinking," said Moses. "We should insert charms or predictions into the middle before they set. Then when they break people will feel blessed instead of pissed off."

Marina sat on the floor and took the lid off a toy box.

Pippa's stomach fluttered as she switched on the computer. She tried not to look at Moses.

"It is cold in here today," said Marina, peering into the child's nappy and sniffing. "You need the potty?"

"It is time for me to travel East." Moses stretched his arms high above his head. He wasn't far off the ceiling.

Pippa looked up. "You're going to Bangkok?" She hadn't thought of that. Would the journalist keep her promise even if her story ran away?

"Not Bangkok, no. Somewhere more rural altogether. But I have for some time now felt the call of the East. And last night I kept a vigil here. I opened myself to the abundance the universe has to offer. And I saw clearly that I must go to Thailand."

"You have pooed in your nappy. That is like a baby. You are a big boy now."

Sasha whined and batted at Marina as she wrestled him to the floor. Pippa threw her a tub of wipes.

Moses came round to where Pippa sat and perched himself on the desk. He tucked his robes modestly across him.

"Pippa," he said.

"Yes, Moses?"

"There may be clients who ask for me by name. There are some services I prefer not to contract out. These clients should be referred to me personally."

Pippa kept her face blank. "We have many freelancers for the predictions, meditating, charms, all the services. We find out more if this is not enough."

"Pippa." Moses took her hands between his. "I think you know what I refer to. There is a gift with which I particularly am endowed. It is not something any freelancer can do in my place. Do you understand?"

"OK. If you want."

Marina set the child on his feet and stood up, rubbing her knees. "I go to put this outside," she said. "Can you watch him?"

"Sure," said Pippa.

"It's the fertility treatments," murmured Moses, "as well you know. I have particular success. It's me the clients will want to see. And I think they will travel East if they know where to find me."

"OK." Pippa looked at their hands. Moses' grip was tight and his palms were sweating. "You make me wet."

Moses stared at her.

"Your hands are wet. Please."

"Oh. Yes. Of course." He let go and wiped his hands on his robes.

"When you will go to Thailand?"

"Today perhaps. I have spoken to Sam."

"So quickly?"

"He has released me from my more worldly duties so that I can focus my energies on the incorporeal. It is best that I travel to Thailand. This country has a poor understanding of my skills and an intolerance of different approaches to life." He glanced over his shoulder. Sasha was pushing a crystal through a hole in his shape-sorter.

"Pippa, I suspect a client who I failed to satisfy has not been able to accept her fate. There may be some media rubbish. It is simply an illustration of how cultural artifice presides over universal truths in this ignorant country. Do not be alarmed by what you hear. Those who need me will seek me out."

"And I will send them to you."

"Exactly. I am grateful for your understanding. I feel that you too are—"

"For a good price."

Suddenly, Pippa sprang out of her chair and ran to the little boy. "Give," she said, hitting him on the back. "My the God, he has a little stone in his mouth. He can swallow that." She took the stone and held the boy's chin. "No eat that. Dangerous. Understand?"

Marina opened the door.

"Is fine now. He has a stone in the mouth." Pippa gave her the stone and breathed out. Slowly, she turned to look at Moses. He was still perched on the edge of the desk, contemplating his hands. "Come, we look at enrolment for courses."

"Ladies," said Moses. He cleared his throat and made for the door. "I will leave you. I wish you well. You will naturally be remunerated for the specialist referrals you make." He looked at Pippa and she gave a tiny nod.

When the door shut behind him, Pippa said, "I am thinking. About this word 'Eastern' with 'Vision'.

"Oh?" Marina yawned, stroking Sasha's head.

"Eastern where?" said Pippa. She sliced neatly through the tape on a box. "East of London? East of UK? What means East is also Eastern Europe. The countries behind the steel curtain."

"Iron. But it has gone."

"Exactly. The wisdom of the Eastern countries can now cross the borders. I can work with gypsy magic from Romania. Use this company name that is so popular to sell, and make from it some money for ourselves. We work good for this company and we are deserving of something."

"You are such a pretty face," grinned Marina, and Pippa tossed her sleek little bob.

~

"She is sleeping a lot. We have to sedate her because of the hallucinating that poses some danger to herself and others."

"She has manic depression. She's supposed to take lithium."

The doctor folded his arms and nodded. "For such a person, the hormonal changes of this time are a danger."

Bristol swallowed. "Can I see her?"

The doctor spoke in Chinese to a nurse, who put a hand on Bristol's elbow and smiled gently.

"Your little baby very nice," she said.

Bristol coughed. "Oh–"

"Good baby. So happy."

He nodded and said nothing.

Jessica was sitting cross-legged in the middle of her bed, shredding paper. Confetti lay on her lap and her sheets and fluttered from her hands as they tore the paper into precise lines and then tiny squares.

Bristol stood at the foot of the bed. Without looking up, she stopped. Her hands froze on a half-torn sheet of paper. Her hair had been brushed and fastened in a ponytail. Her arms were bruised.

She stared at the paper.

"Hey," he said.

Jessica blinked, but she still didn't look up.

"I could just go away again if you like. I have a stampeding wife to deal with in Phuket."

She shook her head a little.

He took a bar of chocolate from his pocket and put it on the bed.

"That's chocolate," she said, still not moving.

"Where's the baby?"

"Come here so I can whisper."

He moved the chocolate and sat close to her, his knee touching hers.

She whispered but he couldn't make out the words.

"Try looking at me, Jess. You're acting like something out of the cuckoo's nest."

"It's a different one each time. They bring a baby and say it's mine then they take it away and change it. I need you to find out which one's mine. Then we can put it back because they took it out too early. It's not ready."

Bristol scratched his scalp. The chlorine in the hotel pool had been a disaster for his skin.

"Jessica," he said, "would you get a grip? You're mumbling rubbish and you'll get yourself locked up."

She grabbed his wrist and fixed her eyes on his.

"Don't tell anyone but I know where the poison is. I'm going to drink it."

Bristol took a long breath in through his nose. "Now why would you want to do that?"

"I have to get away from my head. I can't stay inside myself. So I'm going to have to kill myself."

Bristol raised his eyebrows. "That is certainly an option. Sam's wife did it. And she left her children without a mother. You could do the same."

Jessica looked down at her hand clinging to his wrist. "I wouldn't leave a very big hole in the world. It would close over soon enough."

"You sound quite rational now, if massively self-pitying. Maybe they won't lock you up."

"I could throw myself out of the window."

"Indeed."

"Or get a razor blade."

"Messy."

"Poison."

"Probably best."

"Will you get it for me?"

"Jessica stop it. Pull yourself together, for God's sake. If you're going to kill yourself, go ahead. But I'd be – disappointed. It's not who I thought you were. I had you down as something special."

She looked up.

"I was hoping we'd see more of each other. We've got your slum project to sort out. Remember? And Linda knows I have to work late, so you and I needn't be strangers." He looked at his watch. "Maybe I was wrong. I was just mesmerised by your golden curls and your smile."

He made to stand up.

She kept hold of his wrist.

"Stay," she whispered. "Please."

"I was going to leave you in peace to end it all."

She shook her head.

"You've changed your mind?"

She shrugged. "I remember the promise kiss," she said, crying.

"Now that seems like a hell of a long time ago. Two babies ago."

"Hold me."

He drew her shoulders towards his and held her ponytail in his fist. Her head dropped into his neck. He looked up at the ceiling and wondered how he had got himself caught between these two demanding young women and what on earth he was going to do about them.

~

Marina looked at the card and then up at Pippa.

"You have made these very well," she said. "And you are a clever woman."

"I saw some words in a magazine," Pippa told her, "*To make money find gap in market. Niche.*"

"Niche?" Marina handed the card back and stretched blissfully, catching a glimpse of the crack in the office ceiling.

"I looked in the dictionary book. *Particular range of product or service.* And Moses he is too sacred to handle moneys, so of course I am handling that."

'*Did you know? The seed of a virgin monk can open your womb. If a bundle of baby joy means the world for you, come at Bamboo Grove where is waiting your miracle. www.bamboogrove.com.*'

Marina laughed. "Are people so stupid they think Moses is saving it for them personally?" She put her bag over her shoulder and applied a touch of lip gloss. "I am going to pick up Sasha."

Pippa spread her arms wide. "Maybe I have a long queue of virgin monks!"

"What a thought. I think I'll stay with builders who don't claim to be virgins. I'm not that thrilled about orange robes. Yuk."

Pippa made a face and shook her head. "I am waiting still," she said, "for a friend of your builder I can have for myself."

Marina winked. "See you later, Pips."

Pippa sat at the desk and wiggled the mouse. Rolling to favourites, she clicked on the Bamboo Grove mailbox. 'Hi, I'm a 41-yr-old PR manager and have tried IVF 4 times. Do you have an age limit? Give me a ring. *Please.*'

'Dear Sir or Madam, my wife and I found your card when it fell from a leaflet at the fertility clinic. Forgive the ridiculous phrase, but it felt like a sign. I'd be grateful for a call or an email.'

'Virgin monks?! Bring 'em on. Let me at 'em. Yours deliciously, Graham.'

Pippa deleted the last message though she imagined Alexis or Moses might have liked to meet Graham. She wrote down the other two telephone numbers and sat up very straight, clearing her throat.

As she reached for the telephone, it rang, making her jump.

"Hello, Eastern Vision London?"

"Pippa, it's Eve."

"Hi, how's life?" Pippa leant back in the new office chair, her head cradled in the cushioned leather.

"Fine. I have a cracker of an interview with what's-her-name."

"She's back?"

"She's back and she's pregnant."

"Bingo!"

Eve laughed.

"He is remarkable," sighed Pippa. "Revolting. But also remarkable."

"I'm working on deals with three celeb mags and a glossy. *Tomorrow* want an exclusive but they'll have to get their bid up sharp or I'm going with the others in one go."

"I leave this in your hands. It's nice doing the business with you."

They giggled.

"Look," said Eve, "do you want to come to a party? It will mostly be pretentious arseholes but I do also have some proper friends."

"Thank you," said Pippa. "I would like that very much."

21

"Noah." Jessica sat up in bed. "I thought you couldn't stand these places."

"For you, I am here. I bring good medicine. We balance Yin and Yang. You good."

Jessica smiled. "Thank you, Noah. I don't know what they're filling me with here. Some rubbish to make me behave."

Noah pulled the curtain shut behind him. He sat on the edge of the bed.

"Where is the baby?"

"They keep taking her away. They don't trust me."

Noah looked thinner than ever. The bulge in his throat was solid, shifting stiffly as he spoke. And his skin was yellow-green.

"Noah, are you unwell?" Jessica took his hand.

He sat up very straight and put his hand in the pocket of his threadbare collarless shirt.

"I am good. I have many medicines for keep strong. Look here." He glanced at the curtain and produced a miniature jar of thick black syrup.

"It looks like tar."

He took out the tiny cork and whispered, "Drink?"

She sniffed. "All of it?"

"Fast. Maybe nurse come."

Jessica smiled again and tipped back the syrup. It tasted of ash.

"Have you come to rescue me?"

"You want to leave?"

She handed back the little jar without looking at him. Twisting her fingers together, she fixed her eyes on the empty cot.

Noah sat silently, still very straight and as tall as his small body would stretch. He breathed carefully, looking neither at her nor away from her.

"I need to know," she said, "if—"

He continued to breathe and to wait.

"Noah, you've been so—"

There were voices just outside the curtain. Their eyes met and Jessica folded her arms.

The curtains parted and Bristol stood framed by the wipe-clean jasmine print.

Jessica felt her heart reach out. She shut her eyes.

"Am I interrupting?"

Noah stood, pressing his palms together.

"Yes," said Jessica. "You are."

Bristol grinned. "You look better. Your eyes are less mad."

"Noah brought me some medicine. To balance my Yin and my Yang."

"Jesus."

A cloud passed across Noah's face.

"Noah's offended by your blasphemy," said Jessica quietly.

Bristol looked at her. She found herself biting back a smile.

A nurse pulled aside the curtain now, cradling the baby in the crook of her arm. She kept her head bowed but her eyes flicked up to take in the two men standing by the bed. She eased the baby into her transparent box and arranged the blanket in a rapid form of origami.

Bristol squared his shoulders. "I've come to take them home," he told the nurse.

Jessica opened her mouth. Noah pressed his palms together so firmly they trembled.

"Of course, Mister Bristol," said the nurse.

Bristol winked at her and she dipped her head, reddening.

"The paper is ready for signature. I talk doctor. Bring now."

"Good girl," said Bristol. As she disappeared, he took her place beside the sleeping baby. Without looking up, he said, "They think you're my wife."

Jessica bit her lip. "I'm not coming to your apartment. It's a bloody stupid idea." She shut her eyes.

"Just while you get yourself together. It's not easy. Linda fell apart."

Through her teeth, Jessica said, "I can't be there with your wife. You share a bed with her."

"It's conventional, I believe, at least in the early years."

She opened her eyes. "You're staying with her then?"

"Jesus, Jessica. Sorry, Noah."

A giggle rose in Jessica's throat. "Bastard," she muttered.

Bristol began to laugh.

Noah smiled gently and nodded.

"Noah," said Jessica. "Could I maybe come back with you? Just for a while?" She looked down at her fingers, her throat strangling halfway between a laugh and a sob.

"My home for you," he said, dipping his head in a chivalrous wai.

Her lips formed the words, "Kop khun ka," but the sound got stuck before it reached them.

Bristol screwed up his face and then stretched it wide. "The arrangement works well," he said. "If you will excuse me." He made a wai greeting with his eyebrows raised and swept aside the curtain.

Noah vanished behind him.

Jessica heard the nurse return as she stumbled out of bed.

"You can make signature here?"

"Baby Cotton?" Bristol's voice. "Yuk. Hasn't she got a name?"

"Baby will show us name when ready." Noah's voice; soft, calm.

"It will show you vomit, writhing and wailing. In English, those won't work. Maybe they're better in translation."

"Sorry, I don't understand."

"Forget it. The cynicism of the new father. You might understand by next week."

Jessica stepped through the curtains, dressed and holding the baby. She stood straight and her pale face was set.

"If you'd asked," she said. "I'd have told you what my daughter is called. Her name is Yingyang."

PART THREE

22

Pippa thinks my childhood was more traumatic than hers. She says she'd choose a violent dictatorship over life with Jessica any day.

"She is crazy, your mother. Like a wind-up toy that spins around until it crashes into something."

"And she crashed into Eastern Vision."

"Yes. Or perhaps Moses crashed into her. He was pretty crazy too."

I feel my throat constrict as if I'm a silent child again.

"But you are not crazy, Yingyang." She is suddenly serious, watching my face. "You are yourself. You are unique. Remember that – please."

I nod. She's good for me, Pippa. She is of course old enough to be my mother but she treats me as a friend, a partner, an equal. And I respect her. I laugh at her sometimes, and call her the Gypsy Tycoon, but really I'm in awe of what she's done. Nothing floors her. She'd find a way out of anything. She never speaks about her brother anymore. He doesn't exist; he never existed. Her secrets are safe with me. If I can remain silent for three years, then I can certainly keep a secret.

I don't feel bitterness towards my mother. She is who she is and she never ever meant any harm to anyone. I know Pippa felt a sort of furious jealousy when they first met in London. There she was, doing the jobs no one else wanted to do, and Jessica swanned in one day and was handed Eastern Vision on a plate. The men all fell at her feet; Moses, Bristol and Sam, ready to rescue her again and again. I tell Pippa that Jessica is jealous of her adventures. It would have suited Jessica to be an illegal refugee. Bristol asks her sometimes if she wants to look for her birth mother. He says it's uncharacteristic of her not to take on a battle. But Jessica always preferred fantasy to her real life. She can dream up a tragi-comic romance to rival even Pippa's story; she can see her birth mother in a ruby or in the face of a cinema heroine, she can pick a story to suit her mood. She would be furious to find a boring birth mother.

"And," I tell Pippa, "if it weren't for Jessica, you might never have been so ambitious. You saw in her what you wanted for yourself."

When I say this, Pippa snorts.

"I never wanted to be like Jessica! God forbid! No offence, Yingyang," she adds quickly. "But you understand."

"Better than anyone," I say. "I lived with her for sixteen years."

~

I was weird. The children at school were from all over the world. They had Australian mothers and British fathers, or Thai mothers and German fathers, they were Chinese-American, French-Canadian, Indian, Indonesian. But somehow, in the middle of all this difference, I stood out. The others lived in the white houses with maids and swimming pools, televisions and computers. I lived in a tiny apartment on the edge of a slum that was filled with their second-hand clothes, and my mother caused scenes in public. Girls would look at me and glance away, their eyes flicking towards each other, making little faces. So it wasn't so strange that I should decide eventually to lock my real life inside my head and keep my words safely hidden in notebooks tied with ribbons.

There was quite a rapid turnover of staff and students in the school, and it wasn't long before it was generally accepted that something regrettable but irreparable was wrong with me. But silence was my defence, my protective layer, just as some people cope with their own awkwardness by talking endlessly, emptily, falling over words in an attempt to fit in. And the more they talk, the less they seem to say, until in the end they're all saying the same thing. I was surrounded by words, most of them so insubstantial they popped soundlessly like bubbles in the air and vanished. Perhaps it was the permanence of the written word I sought, its power to channel my thoughts through my right hand. Or perhaps it was my feeble attempt at protest against the chaos that was my upbringing.

Jessica was adamant she wouldn't drag me in front of doctors.

"They'll make things worse," she said. "They'll invent problems she hasn't got!"

She hated doctors. Bristol held them over her as a threat; they were his trump card when she was being more difficult than usual. So I have her to thank that I didn't spend years on some medical specialist roundabout but was left in peace much of the time to write.

I'd sit by the river, the weird white girl with the diaries, writing stories and strange narrative poems, scenes full of dialogue and descriptions of the people who ignored me as they passed. I could write whilst I was walking along the sidewalk that was crammed with barbecue chicken stalls, dusty children, immaculate women with manicures and set hair, tuk-tuks, mopeds, bicycles, animals. I stopped squeezing past and edging round and I kept my head in my notebook, writing as I walked. People moved out of my way as they never would have done if I'd been looking where I was going.

Jessica continued to redistribute the world's wealth, or at least that of our corner of Bangkok, and I was enlisted as soon as I could walk. As I grew up, I saw how my mother's intermittent but determined altruism was part of her mood swings. She was like a child in the way she saw the world and in the way she wanted to put it right. She was an angel as well as a demon, a virgin as well as a whore. Bristol and Sam were addicted to her. And, as far as I know, (not counting the three city officials, and that was an act of altruism) there was never really anyone else. She was faithful, in her way.

~

Pippa has told me her story, which begins long before she started work spraying plaster cast Buddhas and photocopying leaflets in the rainbow office. We were stranded all night once at Heathrow airport, while the rain was too thick for planes to take off, and she lay on the floor with her head on an inflatable pillow and told me how she came to England.

She lived in a cramped apartment block in Romania, where her brother whispered to her that it was different in the West. He spoke in Hungarian, the secret language they couldn't speak in the street. He said there were shops that sold everything you could think of. That there were films and denim jackets and chocolate, Coca-Cola and magazines. He said there were real jobs to pay for all this and that no one over twenty lived with their parents. He said people had everything but they still wanted more.

At school, Pippa was taught that Romania was a country in boom. But Mick made sure she was looking at him and said silently, "It's the

Communists. They're wringing us out. And it can't last."

She understood that she was not to trust anyone with what her brother told her when they were alone. He told her to study hard, to learn English. He made her practise with him.

And, when he said it was time to go, she knew she couldn't even tell her parents. She embraced her mother when she went to bed and looked into her face. She whispered, "La revedere," which translates as *goodbye* but means *to see again*. Her mother swallowed and said "Good night, beloved daughter of mine."

Mick told her, "They won't tell anyone that we have vanished in the morning."

He had typed a letter inviting them to stay for a brief visit in Hungary. He rolled some notes in it and handed it to the border guard. The guard pocketed the money without looking at it and peered at the letter.

Pippa became very aware of her own breathing. She glanced at her brother. He produced the little sack of treats he had gathered. The guard grinned at him and swung it over his shoulder.

"You want to get through the border," he slurred, in the voice of a delinquent drunk. He swaggered when he moved. He beckoned to Pippa to follow him into a cabin.

Mick put his hand out to stop her.

"You've done everything. It's my turn to help us now," she whispered, and went in.

Mick clenched his teeth and smashed his fist on a concrete post.

That night, he couldn't sleep. This man, who lay on the hotel floor so that they could have his bed, what if he were not to be trusted? What if he were questioned and he admitted that amongst his little party were two young Romanians matching the descriptions given?

'I have to be strong,' he thought . 'I have brought my sister this far and I cannot waver now. She will look back and know that freedom is worth all this and more.'

The man appeared the second evening with news.

"I have found a coach going to England. It will leave at half past five tomorrow morning, so you need to hide there during the night."

"You have been so kind to us," whispered Pippa. She stood at the window, staring as if she could see through the drawn curtains.

"Your parents have done more for me than I can ever repay them," the man told her. "They are brave people who know their own hearts."

Pippa folded her arms across her chest. Her face grew flushed.

"No need for fear," said the man. "Go in the bathroom now and then I will show you this coach."

The parking lot was a strip of waste ground near the hotel. There were a few cars, a smashed up motorbike, a lorry and three coaches.

Pippa walked beside the man, pretending to discuss a paper they were looking at. Her brother followed a while behind.

"We are coming near. When I fold the paper, the coach we are passing is the one."

Pippa looked down at her standard-issue shoes and thought that they were enough to give her away, despite the suit and the glasses. They were the same brown shoes as every girl in her school had worn and she was lucky her feet hadn't grown too much since.

Her companion folded the paper and said, "I think the programme is all arranged then."

"Yes. And thank you for your time," she said. She slid into the shadow of the lorry at the edge of the lot and waited for her brother.

They lay underneath the lorry until after two in the morning. Pippa fell asleep and woke up with her bladder full and cold. She had to hitch and twist her clothing to relieve herself, banging her head and gasping with the pain.

When the lot had been still for a long time and the nearby roads had gone quiet, they pulled themselves out on their elbows and her brother picked up a broken brick.

The driver arrived and drove the coach to the front of a hostel, leaving the lights blinking, then sat back in his seat chewing gum.

Twenty-six sleepy English teenagers emerged dragging cases. The driver broke wind and eased himself out of his seat to load up.

"Move. How can I get to the luggage racks if you're all stampeding?"

"One by one, you're used to this by now for goodness' sake."

Pippa held her breath. Across the aisle, Mick shifted slightly and hit his knee.

"Miss! The window's broken. There's glass on the seat."

"What? Don't touch it. Move away from it. Let me through."

She could see feet now. Trainers with laces untied. Sandals. Boots. A pair of socked feet, one striped, one plain. And all the feet turned to face the broken window.

"Nobody needs to sit there. Those can be the spare seats."

"Driver! Did you know you've got a window smashed?"

The feet shuffled out of the aisle as the driver's shoes stamped towards the window.

"Bloody foreigners," he muttered. "Bloody-minded vandalism."

"Can we tape something across it?" The teacher's shoes had buckles. "We really can't risk losing any time this morning."

Behind Pippa, almost touching her, bags were plonked down in the footwell. The seat above her sagged, giving her even less space. She was alternately breathing through her mouth and her nose, trying to find the quietest way.

The shoes were wide but the feet inside them spilt over the edges. They were planted squarely on the floor and when the engine finally stopped ticking over and fired up, there were still no feet beside them.

On the motorway, the plastic bag across the broken window sucked and puffed until it tore its tape and flapped free. Half a biscuit fell between the fat feet.

It had two layers, with a filling to stick them together, so really it was a whole biscuit. And the feet didn't move.

Even if Pippa shut her eyes, she could see the biscuit on the back of her eyelids. If they went up a hill, maybe it would slide towards her. Her left arm was crushed beneath her but she might be able to edge her right hand forward just enough to reach the biscuit. She pictured the action, calculating how little movement she could get away with.

The coach was quiet. Some of the children had gone to sleep. The faint beat of music drifted down to her ears. When her daring matched her hunger, she began to move her hand. She had been still for so long she felt her shoulder would groan out loud. Her hand touched the floor just short of the feet.

"Miss, when are we stopping?"

159

"Not yet. Sit down."

She stretched her fingers as long as they would go and just touched the biscuit. If she was going to get hold of it, she'd have to roll her shoulder very slightly.

She swallowed. The sound was loud in her ears.

The fat feet jolted together, trapping the biscuit. Her face crumpled silently.

And then the feet were drawn up onto the seat and a plump, upside-down head and shoulders appeared, staring.

Pippa snapped her hand back and pressed her finger to her lips. For several seconds, they stared frozen at each other.

The English girl sat up.

Pippa's heart thudded. If they were found now because of a *biscuit*.

A slip of paper dropped to the floor and one foot pushed it towards her. It was followed by a pen.

Who are you?

She took the pen and wrote with difficulty, because she couldn't hold the paper down, *From Romania. Please not saying nothing.*

The English girl wrote, *Are you running away?*

No understand. Please to not saying nothing.

In place of the paper the third time, there was a stick of chocolate.

~

Not far from our apartment, by the edge of the river, there used to be an upturned wheelbarrow without a wheel which made a good seat. I would lean against the rusty metal with my notebook on the slope of my thighs and fill the pages with secrets.

"Yingyang." Jessica found me there one day. Her red shoes were coated with riverside muck. "Can I see? Is this a story for me?"

She crouched beside me. I held the cover shut and shook my head.

"Why do you never let me see your stories?" Jessica reached out for the notebook but I snatched it away. She sighed. "Maybe I'll write a story," she said. "Would you want to read it, if I wrote a story?"

My knuckles quivered, I was gripping my notebook so tightly.

"It's a boyfriend! You're writing about a boyfriend. And I thought you were still writing fairy stories. No wonder you're keeping it so secret."

Jessica sat down and looked at the river.

"You and me, we are so different," she said. "You like to be alone. You don't need people the way I do. You're lucky, I suppose."

I counted the hard-shelled beetles shuttling around in the mud.

"You know your father was—"

I put my hands over my ears.

"But he's dead now. We won't speak of him. Are you happy?"

I shrugged and blinked.

Jessica's face flickered.

"You're not, are you? Are you really unhappy?" The creases appeared between her eyebrows.

I smiled and shook my head. If I said I was unhappy, Jessica would chew the inside of her mouth until it bled and tear skin from around her fingernails. I had always been as helpful, as unobtrusive, as compliant as it was possible for a child to be, but if the pendulum had begun its mighty swing, there was nothing that could be done. And that question, *are you happy, Yingyang?* It was as if that was what held us together; if I too began to cry we would both be swept away in the monsoon. The rise and fall of my own spirits were like a ripple at the edge of the khlong in the wake of Jessica's moods. And I could write myself through a grey cloud or a spiky sea, whereas Jessica didn't seem to have any defence at all against the darkness inside.

The story of our lives is inextricably, messily entwined with that of Eastern Vision. I'm piecing together the fragments of the jigsaw, and there are many parts where I've had to rely on what I've been told or to imagine how it might have been. But I come into the story as a character in my own right here – just before it all begins to fall apart.

23

On her sixteenth birthday, Bristol gave Yingyang some money to buy new clothes. Jessica took her to the Emporium.

It was a vast glass-fronted building where thousands of tiny spotlights made the displays glow. Little white boxes sat on make-up counters behind rows of nail polish in deepest indigo, wine, salmon, copper, silver. She imagined coating each nail with a different shade.

She read the labels. There were creams, serums and oils for endless complaints. A lotion to whiten skin. A gel to bronze skin. A powder to calm redness. You could erase any trace of your own colour and paint yourself with stripes if you liked. She looked at Jessica, who was puffing a perfume tester onto her wrists, wafting away an assistant trying to show her a compact.

There was a spiral of eye shadow testers that started soft gold in the centre, then pale yellow, green and pink to bright tropical fuchsia and electric blue. Yingyang spread her fingers so that each one hovered above a different pot. One by one, she rubbed the pads of her fingers onto the circles of make-up, then turned her palms upwards. She wriggled her fingers in the air to make the rainbow dance. The assistant looked at Jessica.

"Thank you," said Jessica, "kop khun ka."

Yingyang wiped her hands on her clothes as they moved through the shoppers and away from the make-up. Jessica smiled a little and sniffed the inside of her wrist.

They got out of the lift on the fifth floor. Pastel blue taffeta dresses sheathed in plastic hung on a rail where the doors slid open. Yingyang ran her hand down a transparent cover. She wanted to feel the fabric underneath. Jessica stopped beside a snowy wedding dress with silk roses cascading down the skirt. Yingyang lifted the plastic and stroked the ruffle on the pastel blue taffeta.

A security guard marched towards them. Yingyang let go quickly. His radio buzzed and he held it to his ear. She looked at a rack of crimson bridesmaid dresses with puff sleeves.

In the Young Fashion section, Yingyang's frame was a problem.

Her shoulders were too wide for the T-shirts and her hips too broad for the frilled skirts. She had to reach to the back on every rail for the very largest size.

Jessica liked clothes to cling. Even though Bristol's money was for Yingyang, she piled her arm with dresses just to try. She kept one of them on for ten minutes; a fitted white bodice that flared into swirls of pink and red on the skirt. The red was nearly the same as her shoes, they might have been bought for it. She twirled in front of the mirror, admiring the swish of the skirt and the way the bodice held her breasts.

Yingyang found a silky-smooth peach cardigan and slid it over her grubby shirt. Tiny mother-of-pearl buttons ran all the way down, three times more than were necessary but there was something about there being so many that made it special. The sleeves were close-fitting and stretchy, they came right down over her fingertips.

"That's pretty," said Jessica, fastening a silver belt around her own waist and frowning at it. "Now you need a bottom half."

Still wearing the cardigan, Yingyang wandered back out onto the shop floor. An assistant appeared, tracking her as she moved. She watched her take a full white skirt from the rail and hold it against her legs.

"Very good," she said. "You wan' try?"

Yingyang nodded.

"What size?"

She nodded again. She had picked the biggest. The assistant shrugged and took the skirt, went to the changing room and held it out. Yingyang took it back and stood beside Jessica.

Jessica was back in her own clothes, applying red lipstick in the mirror. Yingyang wrestled herself out of the denim sawn-offs that were so uncomfortable they gave her wind and put the white skirt on.

"Yingyang!" said Jessica, catching sight of her in the mirror and turning round. "That's lovely. We'll buy them."

Yingyang didn't want to take the clothes off. She had never seen her reflection like this. The air-conditioning had softened the pink in her face and the drape of the clothes gave her bulk a smooth, rounded outline.

At the till, they needed all Bristol's money for the peach cardigan and the white skirt.

~

Jessica sat on the log bench by the tap in Phetbin and looked up into the branches above, chewing her lip. It felt as if the slum had doubled in size since she had first seen it. It was, like all the slums in Bangkok, built illegally, spreading gradually as more families built their shacks from whatever they could find.

Next to the bench was a little spirit house on stilts. It was well cared for; its wood was intricately carved and varnished, its frame edged with fresh red paint. On the rim sat ripe fruit, flowers, and the hopes and dreams of people whose prayers were rarely answered.

Little Mai sat beside her and looked up into her face. Jessica smiled.

"Hello, Mai. What are you up to?"

Mai mimed tears and pointed to a shack at the end of the terrace.

"Poey? She's crying?"

Mai nodded.

"OK, I'm going to see her now. You stay here and play."

Three children were jumping in a line while two others turned the rope. Mai tried to jump in but her foot caught and she tripped.

"Mai pen rai," said Jessica, *Never mind*.

She called to Poey through the little window.

"Can I come in to see you? It's Jessica."

She opened the wooden door that would never quite shut and found Poey curled up on her blanket.

"Is everyone out working?"

Poey nodded. She rubbed the tears away with a teatowel and sat up.

"Please sit," she croaked.

Jessica sat cross-legged on the ground, smiling gently. Poey's name meant 'plump'. She had a lovely round face and curves where her friends were straight.

"They're skipping outside," said Jessica. "I don't know that word in Thai."

Poey looked at her urgently, opening her mouth to speak, but all she did was cry a little more.

Jessica waited. She wiped the sweat from her face. She could feel it pooling beneath her breasts, under her arms, between her legs.

"Poey, what's happened to the fan?"

The girl shrugged and looked at the floor.

"Did your brothers fight again?"

Poey hugged herself, rocking. The children outside burst out laughing.

In English, Poey whispered, "Mummy say me work. I go short time," and she covered her face with her hands.

Jessica sighed. "She ran out of whisky, right?"

"No understand."

"Come here."

She wrapped the girl in her arms and kissed her head. Poey's body sagged against hers.

A child shrieked. The others laughed and scattered.

"Tell mummy no more short time. I'll bring her whisky."

"Kop khun ka," said Poey softly.

Jessica searched in her bag.

"If they make you work again, you must give the guy one of these, OK? You know what they are, yes? So you don't get sick. And you don't want babies. No babies, OK?"

Poey took the condoms, nodding slowly. "I understand."

"Tell me if you need more."

"Thank you, Khun Jess'cah."

~

Pippa's priority was the light fittings. The stainless steel twisty ones were getting on for five years old and they were completely wrong for the new bed. She ran her hand over the voluptuous contours of the mahogany board that enclosed the mattress on every side. At either end, it swept up and down in an undulating wave. With her sleeve, she rubbed at a smudge on the sheen of the wood.

Her mobile rang, and she bounced onto the bed, resting her fleece-socked feet on the wave.

"Gypsy Magic. A privilege to take your call."

"Pippa?"

"Yes. To whom do I have the pleasure of speaking?"

"You're overdoing it, Pippa. Gypsies don't speak like that."

"Moses."

Pippa caressed the curve of wood with her toes and stared at the bare light bulbs. She was pretty sure you couldn't get mahogany lampshades.

"You sound as though your soul is brimming with happiness."

"Thank you." A big round one. White but not white. What had the decorator said? 'Off-white.'

"I'm in an internet café but everything's crashed."

"I am sorry to hear this." She'd seen a duvet cover in bright pink with a sky-blue border. If she got that, maybe the lampshade could be blue.

"I just wondered if you'd maybe check the hits for me?"

"I am on the case," said Pippa, tapping her finger on the headboard.

"Thanks, my Gypsy Princess."

Pippa made a face. "Mmm," she said, "there have been some visitors. I feel sure we will soon have another client."

"Where are you? I'm getting bed more than desk."

"God, Moses, sometimes I think you do have second wisdom."

"Of course I bloody do. And a magic wand I haven't had a chance to wave for a while. Isn't there anyone?"

Pippa stood up. "I will make some follow-up calls," she said, "later. I will get back to you."

"Ah, hang on, I think we've managed to reenergise the terminals."

Pippa clicked the red button and wondered about trying her parents. But she wanted to get the other room sorted before they came and if she didn't return the curtains to the shop, she wouldn't get replacements in time. Admittedly, she couldn't be sure she'd measured in inches and not centimetres. But they weren't even three-quarter length and she wanted them swishing on the new carpet.

~

The bowls were plastic. The forks were plastic. The table. The bucket full of soapy water for washing all these. Along the centre of the table, tiny dishes held extra chillies – whole and diced, green and red – and each flanked by bottles of soy sauce.

Jessica waved as Bristol approached, but he couldn't see her through the cloud of steam that burst from the wok and merged with the thick exhaust of a passing car.

"Bristol!"

He stopped to admire her for a moment before sliding onto the bench beside her.

"Nice choice of venue."

"Better than that arsey bar. How's life?"

"Good. Thanks. Good."

"You look naked without your laptop. Do you have a twenty?"

An obese woman in a splattered Betty Boop apron presented Bristol with a bowl of mince and noodles.

"Kop khun kop," said Bristol, handing her fifty.

Jessica moved closer as a girl sat down next to her, talking into her phone in Mandarin and laughing.

"Is this a social get-together or a business meeting?" Bristol slurped his noodles, pressing his tie out of the way.

"Both," said Jessica. She took a red chilli between her finger and thumb and turned to face him, looking into his eyes. Then she bit the chilli in half and chewed.

"Ow," said Bristol.

"You do it."

He crammed a huge forkful of mince and vegetables into his mouth.

"Do you think this is pork?"

"Go on, I dare you."

She tickled him and he grabbed her wrists, laughing. The waitress looked at them with hazy eyes and wiped her hands on Betty Boop's breasts.

"Now then," said Bristol, checking his watch. "What are your ulterior motives?"

"Water," said Jessica. "It's a basic human right."

"Indeed, beautiful."

"The tap at Phetbin has been disconnected. I need money for bribes."

Bristol nodded.

"Quite urgently," said Jessica, her head on one side.

"And I wonder how often this tap will run dry once it's seen to be a money-spinner."

Jessica shrugged and rubbed her eyes.

"Ow."

Bristol grinned. "Common complaint, chillies in the eye."

A tall white man and a young Thai woman climbed out of a tuk-tuk and rummaged in their pockets for change. Taxis began to hoot and edge round the tuk-tuk.

"It would suit you," said Jessica. "Bristol Chambers, god of water."

Bristol sighed and held up his hands.

"Of course I'll sort it," he said. "Now give me a kiss, I have to go."

24

"Mama! Papa!"

Pippa squeezed them, blocking the exit where people were trying to get their trolleys through.

Her mother began to cry and her father couldn't take his eyes off his daughter.

"A year is too long, Mama, we won't leave it so long again."

"We're in the way, my love." Her father steered her mother gently to the side.

"I only got half an hour on the car, we'd better hurry." Pippa grabbed the trolley and strode towards the lift.

At the flat, her parents were deeply impressed.

"It's like a different place," breathed her mother. She took off her shoes and set them neatly to one side.

"I've done up your room," Pippa said. "Look."

"Zoli, have you ever seen anything like it? It's like a – hotel."

"It's better than a hotel, it is a true home. Nearly as beautiful as its owner."

"I had forgotten," sighed her mother, "how *colourful* this country is. It makes me feel grey."

Pippa kissed her. "Not grey, Mama. Silver. Shining like a star."

In the cases, alongside a few changes of clothes and some soap, was a gathered, traditionally-embroidered blouse.

"It's perfect, Mama." Pippa held it up to the window and inspected the stitching. "Did you do this one?"

"I did. And the ladies want you to see their other new ideas."

She smoothed the Laura Ashley bedspread and set out a bookmark, a cotton bag that rolled up like an umbrella and a wide belt.

Pippa nodded at the bookmark and the belt. She rolled and unrolled the bag and hung it over her shoulder.

"These will sell," she said. "How fast can they be turned out?"

"We have eight new women asking to join, they are happy to start on the old pay and move to the higher wage if they stay a year," said Zoli, loosening his tie. "The bookmarks are really quick, the belts take longest."

"Well," said Pippa, "you certainly don't sound like a Romanian Gypsy farmer."

Her mother shook out her spare dress and hung it on a hanger behind the door. Pippa decided she'd need at least one extra case for the new clothes she was going to send her back with.

"And Marina is well?" asked her mother, absorbed in a skirt and a hanger.

"Yes. Very well. Maybe getting married." Pippa searched quickly for something else to say. About the blouse, the curtains, the food she'd put in the oven.

"And your brother?" It was a whisper, directed at the hook on the door.

Zoli gripped the windowsill and examined the view of the zebra crossing. Pippa laid the bookmark and the blouse carefully on top of the bag.

~

169

The dress was perfect. Toi would love it. She'd twirl so the skirt fanned out and her grandmother would be so happy. They lived in a proper room now which opened onto the street, though the back window looked over the alleys. They had mattresses with sheets, lamps and fans.

Jessica trotted up the steps, humming, the dress draped over her arm.

"Hello! Toi! It's Jessica."

Toi opened the door, dressed in the pleated navy skirt that skimmed her knees and the crisp white shirt with the navy bow.

"Khun Jessica. It is good to see you. How are you? Come in please." She shut the door behind Jessica and smiled.

Jessica bowed a wai greeting to Toi's grandmother.

"Come. Eat," said the old woman, producing a spring roll on a sheet of kitchen paper.

"Kop khun ka," said Jessica. "Toi, this is for you."

Toi took the dress, her eyes sparkling. She held it up against herself.

Her grandmother told her to try it on and they looked away and ate spring rolls while she changed.

"Look, this is a beautiful dress," said Toi. She twirled exactly as Jessica imagined and her grandmother beamed. "Thank you, Khun Jessica. You are very kind."

"Hey, I'm just the postman."

Toi sat down suddenly on a cushion.

"I must tell you my news."

Her eyes sparkled still, she radiated light. She reached out for Jessica's hand.

"I am to have further educations," said Toi.

Her grandmother nodded and wiped a flake of crispy pastry from her mouth.

"Toi, that's wonderful. You'll go far." Jessica's eyes began to water and she gave a row of tiny sneezes.

"I plan to become a nurse or a doctor. Or a teacher. Imagine that!"

"Toi, you will become whatever you choose. And your English is immaculate. You put me to shame."

"Since my mother becomes – became – a nanny, everything is good for us. When I was a little girl, you would have laughed if they said I was to be a teacher. Teachers are not born below the expressway."

Toi leant across to one of the fans and turned it to face them. Jessica closed her eyes and put her face in the cool air. She heard her mother's sigh and her father's voice, *You, Jessica Jane, are your own worst enemy, hmm?*

~

"Rather 'bijou' darling. I love it."

"Thank you, Lazuli. We feel proud."

The cash desk, the little step up to the back of the shop, every shelf and every display unit was made of pine and painted with a different colourwash that let the knots show through. A clematis in a blue flowerpot spread over the back wall, around the mirror and into the far corners.

Marina was talking into her mobile, smoothing blouses on a rail with her other hand.

"What happened to the bus? Oh, Sasha, I'm at the new shop - you didn't tell me this morning about a rehearsal."

Pippa waved at her. "Go," she mouthed, "I'm OK here."

Marina shook her head. "I will pick you up at five. Wait inside the door. I love you."

Lazuli peered at the jewellery.

"It looks six times the price displayed like this!"

Pippa nodded, smiling. Marina scratched at the edge of a label on the glass panel in the door, cursing as she chipped her nail varnish.

"Olive oil," suggested Lazuli.

"For my nails?" Marina frowned at the bare patch in the red.

"For the window. Olive oil is brilliant for cleaning." Suddenly, Lazuli picked up her knitted bag, said, "Girls, I'll be in to see you soon, kisses all round," and rushed out into the street.

"I did something?" said Marina.

"No idea," said Pippa. "She has told me over the years that olive oil is good for washing hair, massage, skin, wax in the ears, and now for cleaning a window."

171

Eve swung open the door and waved both hands.

"Hi! I couldn't wait."

"Eve, welcome."

"It's bloody fabulous."

"Thank you."

"It's incredible how Lazuli and I always seem to miss each other." Eve looked out of the window and shrugged. "Anyway, fabulous. Gypsy Magic hits the high street."

"Not the high street," said Pippa. "This is a delicate little alley of boutiques. *Bijou.*"

"Sorry. I'll be sure to emphasise that. Is that really where you lived, in that caravan?"

She pointed at the poster, a blown-up sepia photograph from the back of the brochure. Pippa's mother on the step of a painted caravan beside a little fire, stitching a length of fabric.

"Yes," said Pippa. "Nearly all my life."

"Wow."

Marina hit a key on the cash register and the drawer sprang open.

Eve took out her dictaphone. "I've got Pete coming to do the photos between ten and twelve tomorrow. OK?"

Pippa nodded.

"So all the products are made in Romania?"

"Made in a collective cooperative by gypsy women."

Eve scanned the shelves. "Belts and other accessories," she muttered, "plus jewellery, blouses, skirts. And some of the profits go back into the community, yes?"

"We pay those ladies a fair price. This is ethical business. Eastern Vision has ever been like this."

~

The minibus had seatbelts but no buckles to secure them. Alexis watched the Japanese man struggling to strap himself in and summoned the energy to explain. Slowly. With hand gestures. And magnified facial expressions.

"No work, sorry," he said, giving a pantomime shrug and jiggling the strap in the air.

The Japanese passenger nodded, smiled and continued to try. Alexis jumped down onto the tarmac to herd the others.

Under the concrete roof of the airport pick-up, it was dark and hot. It was always a stressful time, between emerging from the building and pulling away in the bus. The drivers left their engines running while the passengers, dazed from the plane and stunned by the sudden heat, were distributed amongst taxis and minibuses.

"How far away is Bamboo Grove?" asked the prettier of the two Australian girls.

Behind them, a coach driver slammed his horn and accelerated. They pressed themselves up against the sliding door, choking on the diesel fumes.

"Five hours." Alexis yawned. The travel sickness tablets made him drowsy every time. "But the air-con will work once the engine starts running."

Five hours with five passengers. The identikit Japanese businessman, two Australians – one pointy-nosed, one pretty, and a retired couple from Sussex who had apparently done every other continent. Alexis went to heave the doors shut but the Sussex woman hadn't quite squeezed her backside in and he stared up at it whilst her husband tugged her inside. He resisted the urge to shove from behind. Wiping sweat from his face, he passed round the itinerary and sat back in the front seat. The driver was his regular and would wake him if he needed him.

He didn't mind Bamboo Grove. People made fewer demands with sand and sea to lull them; it was easy money compared to Chang Mai or Luam Prabang. One minute he was gazing out at the asphalt desert of the expressway and the next he was bumping to a halt at a roadside café for the halfway stop.

"Thanks, Khun Ta," he said, patting the driver's shoulder. "Twenty minutes, ladies and gentlemen." He flashed up all his fingers twice and tapped his watch, aware that his breath stank. "Is everyone OK with baht?"

Stepping down onto the stony roadside, Alexis helped the ladies out and stood back for the gentlemen. He rubbed his eyes and rolled his shoulders.

"Is good cup tea?" said the Japanese man, showing him a five hundred baht note.

"I'll come and help you," Alexis told him and hurled the door into position.

The boat pulled into Bamboo Grove at twilight. The Sussex contingent were disappointed that the stars were obliterated by cloud, but Alexis ignored them. He was waving at a man he'd seen on the beach adorned by what appeared to be a spectacular example of tribal headwear.

"Buddy! It's me! Alexis!"

He clambered over the side of the boat into the shallows before the boat had stopped and called out to the man's retreating back.

The man turned serenely, if a little resignedly, to face him.

"I thought I sensed your vibes," he said.

His turban was loosely bound and sported charms including one that said 'Long live the King,' a Hello Kitty face, a Union Jack and the ancient symbol for OM. He wore a long-sleeved collarless shirt, a yellow sarong and bracelets to his elbows.

"It's been a while," said Alexis, wading in. "Have you been on your travels again?"

"I head where the wind blows me," said Moses.

The Japanese man was sitting on the edge of the boat taking a photograph of Moses, and the Sussex contingent were refusing to get off.

"Is there a problem, Mrs Smith-Hamilton?" asked Alexis, remembering his role.

Mrs Smith-Hamilton began to cry. Her husband stuffed a wodge of notes into the boat boy's fist and looked desperately at him.

"Hail, travellers," said Moses.

"That camera bag has almost six hundred digital photographs in it," sobbed Mrs Smith-Hamilton. "Australia. Oh God, it's got Australia on it."

"We renewed our vows in Australia," said her husband, shouldering a backpack and holding a hand out to his wife.

Alexis took out his phone.

"I'll ring my driver," he said. "See what I can do. Wink and a nudge."

Moses had gone on ahead with the girls.

~

Pippa dragged a box of tablecloths away from the wall, sniffing them tentatively. She wondered if the rainbow office had always been damp, if she'd simply not noticed. Perhaps it was fusty now from lack of use.

She adjusted a star-shaped earring and rifled through her desk. Faded receipts, bent paperclips, biros. The floral tool kit Marina had given her. And just when she despaired of finding it, a torn envelope with a telephone number on it.

She was at once revolted and comforted by the scent of mildew in the air. It reminded her of buildings back home, where rapid construction hadn't allowed for cavity walls or ventilation. But she was worried about the stock. If she was going to keep stuff in here, she'd have to have sealed storage of some kind. The beads would be all right, and the charms, but the textiles would have to come straight to the shop.

She locked the door and the landing light struggled into life. The rest of the building echoed with silence. Feeling in her pocket for her phone, the envelope held tightly in her other hand, she trod on a biscuit someone had dropped. It crumbled soggily, sticking to the sole of her tan ballet pump, and she brushed it off with the edge of the envelope. A flash of memory was triggered: a broken biscuit, just out of reach. And Mick under the seats across the aisle, so much more of him to fold up and keep still.

The lights clicked off on the stairs and Pippa performed a long-practised dance to wake them up. She hadn't heard from Mick in too long. His mobile number was disconnected. She bit her lip. She wanted to see him even if he only came to ask for money. He could work in the shop. Sort the stock.

Her phone rang as she stepped into the street. Cyndi Lauper, 'True Colours.'

"Hi, Pippa speaking, Gypsy Magic Eastern Vision."

"Three guesses."

"Alexis."

"How's the London side of things?"

"London is fine thank you. Not raining today." Pippa stuffed the biscuity envelope into her handbag.

"With you in control, I'm sure it's thriving. Listen, scrumptious, wink and a nudge, I'm supposed to do a review of EV London. I need your figures for this financial year and a forecast, yawn yawn."

Pippa pressed the button on the crossing and waited for the green man.

"What is forecast?" she said vaguely. "And final year?"

Alexis' voice took on a new depth.

"I planned to fly over and sort it myself," he said, "but Sam – well, the tours side of things is busy of course."

"Of course. Alexis, we can maybe leave for now? Time is after midnight yesterday and I am very sleepy."

"Oh shit. Shit. Sorry. I thought I'd got this cracked."

"No worries. Good night."

"It's very noisy, Pippa. Are you watching television?"

"At this hour of day? That is ridiculous statement."

Pippa locked her keypad and grinned, catching the eye of a woman with a double buggy who smiled but looked like she might cry. It wasn't a lie. It was most definitely after midnight yesterday.

25

Bulk (42). Inbox (26).

Sam's stomach clenched and knotted as it always did when he opened his inbox. He scrolled down the messages, tapping the desk with his other hand.

A second row of huts had been constructed on Bamboo Grove. His utility bills were available to view online. Attawa Transportation required another frighteningly large injection of cash before the crude oil storage project could begin to pay off.

"Bristol," he muttered, "we have to meet with Attawa. This was not a wise move."

Bristol raised a hand and nodded. He was on the landline, listening to a lengthy explanation as to why one third of the apartments in Tranquillity Place would have to be vacant before maintenance work could be resumed. Sam continued skim-reading his emails.

Construction work was miraculously running ahead of time on the new apartment block they had christened Emerald City. The twins' maternal grandparents had sent a huge attachment of photographs they wanted Sam to print for the children. Negotiations regarding the hotel in Vientiane had stalled. And Alexis had had an idea.

"Why the hell is Alexis emailing me when he's in the office this week?"

"Maybe he feels you give your inbox more attention than—"

He says he has a lucrative project idea. Exportation."

Bristol returned his attention to the phone. "I need some sort of guarantee, however. This is getting more than a little out of hand." He laughed politely, gritting his teeth. "Two months. Two. Ha ha, I know. Kop khun kop."

Alexis strode in, smiling. He had a sunburnt nose.

"Greetings!" he said and sat on the sofa.

"You look even cuter with a red nose," said Bristol, scribbling a date on the wall planner.

Alexis blushed and cleared his throat.

"Did you get my email?"

"I did." Sam swivelled his chair to face him.

"Well—"

"Hang on," said Bristol, "I have to get on to the agent about Tranquillity Place. Can you just fill me in quickly on Bamboo Grove?"

Alexis flicked his hair. He'd let it grow a bit so that it curled round his neck. He'd experimented with stubble on the tours too, which had left his chin slightly paler than the rest of his face. Particularly his nose.

"All in order," he said. "Staff sorted. Two rows of huts. We've begun on the shop."

He wasn't sure about the 'we', it could have been a mistake.

"Excellent," said Bristol, hooking his jacket over one shoulder.

"Actually, Bristol. Before you go. If I could just run this – concept – by you both."

"Naturally," said Bristol, leaning against the bookcase.

Alexis sat up straighter.

"Right. Exportation. Massive returns within a short time period. And I can action it as soon as you two are on board."

Bristol put his hand on the door handle.

"Not strictly speaking a kosher product, but it's..." continued Alexis, with less conviction.

"Thanks but no thanks. Good to hear your ideas, though."

Alexis stood up as he left; he had to stop himself stamping his foot.

Sam sighed and put a hand on his shoulder.

"Alexis. Buddy. Unless you're up for a stay in Bang Kwang, I suggest we drop this one. Some ideas just aren't–"

"I could arrange it on a very small scale. I thought we were into diversification."

"If you give this idea one second's more thought, I will have to sever all ties with you. Eastern Vision cannot have any connections with such things."

Sam's grip on Alexis' shoulder tightened and then he went back to his desk.

~

Jessica had no umbrella with her and no money to buy one. She had no bag and no pocket. She had left the apartment unsure where she was going. She just knew she must walk.

And then the rain began. Suddenly, like a thousand hoses turned on in the sky. Her hair was flat to her head and her clothes stuck to her.

Within minutes, the streets were flooded. Traffic came to a standstill. Passengers abandoned taxis and tuk-tuks to wade through the water, sharing umbrellas or holding plastic bags over their heads. And when the hoses in the sky came on, the lights went out. Darkness fell instantly around the scuttling people and the stationary traffic.

Jessica headed for the slum. Toi's grandmother had told her that days were numbered for the slum at Phetbin. The land belonged to the authorities and they wanted now to make it pay. Jessica had exploded.

178

"That's ridiculous," she'd said. "They'll just go somewhere else and then what will happen when the arseholes decide they want to build luxury condominiums on that land?"

"It is the way of things," said Toi's grandmother.

"We should write letters."

The old woman had put her head on one side and smiled.

As Jessica approached the slum, she felt stupid. Of course Phetbin was temporary; she was the only one who refused to see it. The people who lived there knew it was only borrowed, that one day they'd have to move on. She'd dropped anchor in shifting sand.

And now the rain was doing its best to wash the place away. The alleys were stagnant rivers, flooding the shacks. Her head wouldn't settle. Her thoughts scribbled and scrambled for space. She lifted her face to the sky, letting the rain gush into her mouth and slide down her top. She was angry that no one came to greet her and at the same time anxious not to see anyone. She wasn't sure she'd be able to speak without crying or shaking, her silence was holding her in.

By the bench was a pool of floating rubbish. Plastic bottles, drink cans, empty cigarette butts. The spirit house stood stoutly above the swamp. And in the darkness beside it a tiny figure. Jessica heard a little gasp as she approached.

"Who's that?" she said.

The child turned away and hunched its shoulders. Jessica stepped nearer, skirting the edge of the rubbish pool.

"Mai? What are you doing?"

Little Mai shook her head. Jessica reached out to her and stroked her soaking hair. The scribble thoughts were holding their breath.

Mai trembled. The rain stopped as abruptly as it had begun.

"I wait," whispered the girl. Her eyes pleaded with Jessica to understand, to leave her.

Jessica took her in her arms and squeezed some of the water from her hair.

Mai sniffed.

"Mister come."

Jessica stiffened.

"What for? Mai, you have to hide."

"Must pay baht. Poey want pill."

Jessica sighed.

"Thank God. Look, Poey should be doing this herself. Go home. I'll tell her."

Mai shook her head.

"Give me also baht. Buy sticky rice chicken." The sound of a motorbike stopping at the end of the alley. Jessica glanced at Little Mai. "Come now." Mai's eyes pleaded more urgently.

Jessica folded her arms.

The man came straight through the rubbish pool as if he hadn't noticed it. He glared at Jessica.

"You nothing here, farang," he said. "You wan' live good?"

Jessica felt the blood rush through her. She heard her voice inside her head. *I don't know. Do I want to live? I'm not sure. Make up my mind for me, arsehole.* She said, "Go ahead. I'm not looking," and, edging back round the rubbish pool, she disappeared into the alley.

He was gone within seconds. Heading for his motorbike.

"Mai?" Jessica came out of the shadows to find Little Mai triumphant. She flashed the tablet at Jessica and hid it again in her fist.

"Please don't do this again. Someone will find you with the tablet and there will be trouble."

Little Mai shrugged and waded into the alley.

Jessica slumped on the bench, staring at the rubbish. She imagined herself taking the rap for Mai. *The drugs are mine, take me to the Bangkok Hilton.* There was a part of her that dared herself to do it. To suffer the prison that should be so unthinkable. Would they shoot her? How long would they keep her there? She'd go into a trance and never have to move again. Something in her mind said, *And Yingyang? What would she do without a mother to care for her?* But Jessica felt so far from motherhood that she couldn't imagine Yingyang's life would be any different without her.

~

Marina slid the tiny satin flowers into a paper bag.

"Nineteen ninety-nine, please," she said, and as she took the twenty pound note from the girl in the tie-dyed clothes, she leant forward and whispered, "Use them with care. They're very potent."

"Goodbye, see you again and good fortune to you," said Pippa.

As the customer left, Pippa took out the crumpled envelope with the number on it.

"OK?" said Marina, sitting on the high painted stool behind the counter.

"You are not wearing your ring." Pippa frowned.

"It's tight," said Marina. "I might get it stretched. Whose number is that?"

The door tinkled open and a young man came in. He began to browse without looking at them.

"Good morning," said Marina.

He looked just to the side of her face for a moment and gave a half-smile. As he peered into a sky-blue crystal ball, Pippa tapped the envelope.

"This is the number of a stylist. She takes fashion pictures. She gave me this number years ago and she said that if Eastern Vision ever did clothing, she'd be pleased to hear about it. And now we do clothing."

She sashayed across to a rail of individually designed maxi-skirts. Narrow stripes, flowers, printed, appliquéd, embroidered. Her parents' cooperative was churning them out.

"How much are those?" asked the young man, nodding at the skirts.

"We have a discount today only, forty-two ninety-nine," said Pippa.

He sucked his lips and twitched his nose.

"Thank you. Yes."

"Would you like to take one?"

"Ah, yes."

"Which one?"

Pippa swung a green skirt off its hanger and held it against him. He turned scarlet and his nose twitched again.

"My wife," he muttered. "Somewhat smaller than me."

"Such pretty sparkling threads," purred Pippa. "You'll take this one?"

When he'd gone, his skirt interwoven with tissue paper in a plastic bag, Pippa surveyed her shop. You could dress from head to foot in Gypsy Magic clothes, now they were trialling the slippers. Crochet flowers in your hair, embroidered blouse, skirts that flared and swirled and slippers like fabric clogs. These were a unique design and Pippa was yet to be convinced, but she'd taken a few for a quirky little display using real daisies that needed constantly replacing.

"You are up to something," said Marina, rubbing her ringless finger.

"I certainly am," said Pippa.

~

Their father had sold sweeping brushes and dusters from a cart. They'd slept on the cart when they were babies and pushed it for him as his strength petered out. And now it belonged to them.

But, while the brother and sister were more than capable of running the family business, they had no idea how to dispose of their father's body. The sister suggested cremation, though she didn't know to call it that. The brother wanted to dig; he said streets like theirs could burn to the ground in minutes and they mustn't risk it.

On the second night, they unloaded the sweeping brushes and dragged their father up onto his cart. As their neighbours slept, they pushed and pulled him to the edge of the khlong and filled his clothes with stones. The sister cried, she said he'd looked directly at her as he sank, but her brother was silent.

When Jessica came with their father's medicine, she found them crouched in the corner of their shack. She looked at the rug where he'd slept and bowed her head. Then she knelt between the two of them.

"Peaceful now," she murmured.

The girl began to sob.

"No, not peace," she said, covering her face with her hands. "So dirty."

Jessica stroked her hair. It was crawling with lice.

"Where is he?" she asked gently.

"Khlong," said the boy, a challenge in his voice.

182

"No peace," cried the girl.

Jessica thought.

"We will bring him peace," she said. "Wait here for me."

As she left, the brother looked at her with narrowed eyes. But when she returned with garlands, oil, limes and paper, he stood to greet her.

They stood by the khlong, pouring oil in circles and throwing limes they'd kissed. They made boats from the paper and tied the garlands to them, watching them glide for a moment before sinking gracefully under the brown water.

"Peace now," said Jessica, and the children walked back home along the boards. Jessica gazed into the depths of the khlong and saw her mother's face.

When she got home, she curled up on the futon in her underwear, her face pressed into her knees, and shook. When Yingyang tried to knead her shoulders with her knuckles, she jerked herself away from her touch and howled.

Yingyang took her some water and some crackers but she wouldn't come out of the tight little knot she had tied herself in. Rolling so that she was smothered by a silk cushion, she let out a muffled scream that went on and on.

"Leave me alone. I want to die. I can't stand it," she spat, and screamed again.

Sometimes, she lay on her bed like she'd fallen from a great height and couldn't move, arms and legs lifeless and spent. But today there was a mine inside her exploding, shattering her bones as they fought to contain it.

The thirty-storey tower where the Americans made their money was down Nana Nua towards Ploenchit. Yingyang wanted to get a tuk-tuk but there were no coins in the little jar they kept change in, and she couldn't bring herself to take any from the donations box. So she scuttled along the streets, her white skirt, now grey from the dust, swishing around her ankles. She hooked the end of the peach sleeves in her fists so her hands were completely covered.

A cyclist scraped her elbow with his satchel wheeling past her, then skidded to a halt so that she had to jump to one side. She began to read the signs on the billboards; *if I read all the signs, everything will be OK.* A yellow one with a Coca-Cola sign in Thai and the words 'electric hair cut no pain.' 'Wally house,' dark green capitals on white, 'precious jewels: best price' battling for space above it.

Sniffing, clutching her sleeves, she dodged a skateboard being propelled by a boy with no legs. A crowd at the entrance to the sky train nudged each other aside, ramming themselves forward onto the steps, shouting into their telephones. She had to walk sideways to get past, squinting at the sunlight and the smell of bodies.

At the bottom of the Americans' building was a bar with leather armchairs round carved wooden tables. Jazz music swam from unseen speakers as a backdrop to all the talking. So much talking, so many words. Most of them so insubstantial that they filled the air for only a second then popped like bubbles. Once, years ago, they had met with the Americans in this bar, and now Yingyang pressed her face against the glass front and searched the armchairs and the high stools for them.

When she didn't see them, she edged round to the front of the tower and went through the revolving doors. It was a horrible feeling, trying to keep up with the panel in front and being chased by the one behind. Her foot slipped on its own sweat against her flip-flop as she stepped out.

The centre of the building was hollow, so that if you looked up you saw every one of the thirty floors above, and then the roof which was a mirror looking back at you. It made her dizzy, so that she wanted to hold onto one of the pillars that held the first ceiling up. Every floor had an open wood-panelled balcony overlooking the lobby where she stood. You could have killed yourself jumping from any one.

On the twentieth floor, two ladies sat at a mahogany reception desk, the wall behind them painted orange. Yingyang shut her eyes every time she had an urge to look in the direction of the balcony.

"Hello," sang the ladies softly, "sawadee ka," and they pressed their palms together and nodded. Yingyang put her own palms together and smiled. One of them was wearing a pistachio-coloured version of her cardigan. It had the same mother-of-pearl buttons. It must have been a much smaller size.

"Look!" said the lady, tugging at her sleeve. "Same-same!"

Yingyang smiled again.

"Who Mister you wan' see?" she asked.

"You wan' see Mister Bristol?" said the other lady, raising a plucked eyebrow.

Yingyang nodded. The receptionist picked up a handset and waited. Yingyang twisted the button at the bottom of her cardigan.

Bristol emerged from his office in rolled-up baby pink shirtsleeves. No cufflinks today. He shook hands with a short man with a torn ear who bowed slightly in the direction of the ladies and pushed the lift-call.

"Yingyang?" said Bristol.

She blushed. His voice was so deep it was too rich for everyday, as if it belonged on a stage somewhere.

"Is this your birthday present?"

Without meaning to, she turned in a circle for him. She caught sight of the balcony before she could shut her eyes, and shook her head to cancel it out.

"Look, Mister. Same-same," said the receptionist.

"So it is. Yingyang is a real lady now."

Yingyang felt so far away from Jessica and her whirling despair that she could have stayed away and not gone back. Cancelled her out by shaking her head. But Bristol was looking around for her.

"Where's Jessica, Yingyang?"

The receptionist with the eyebrows tutted. Yingyang frowned at Bristol and touched her cheeks, trailing her fingers in zigzags.

"She's bad, huh? How long's she been down?"

She bit her lip and sniffed, meeting his turquoise eyes for a moment. His lashes were thick and deep black. He looked at his watch.

"You want me to come, right?"

He sounded cross. She worried that he had read her stories and was angry that she'd borrowed him without asking. But he'd have had to have gone behind the screen to find them, and she couldn't imagine him doing that. She chewed her cuff and blinked at him.

When she got back, Jessica's eyes were open. Jessica didn't speak but she gripped Yingyang's hand so tightly it hurt. Her teeth were chattering.

Outside, a car alarm began to wail. Jessica's head twitched with every honk-honk as if the sound came from inside her.

Yingyang strained her ears for Bristol's knock. He'd said he would come just as soon as he made a call. Then she'd run back to the flat, trying not to think in words. Pictures could be bad enough, but words had a way of repeating rhythmically until they took over all the space in her head. Then she needed to write them down, make them into stories to tame them.

The car alarm stopped in mid-wail so that the part of the sound that was lost carried on and on in Yingyang's ears. Jessica's twitching slowed. Her teeth stopped chattering and she dribbled loosely onto her pillow. Yingyang shook her hand free of her grip and went to the little window to watch for Bristol.

A young man sauntered down the street below, carrying a surfboard on his head. He drummed a rhythm where his fingers rested on it. Yingyang smiled, wondering where he'd found it and what he would use it for in the middle of Bangkok.

Finally, Bristol came. He carried a paper bag in one hand and his jacket in the other. Yingyang leant back against the wall by the door to let him in.

"Hi again," he said, so near they were almost touching.

Yingyang blinked, pulling her sleeves right over her hands and looking at her bare feet on the concrete floor. He sighed through his nose.

"Jessica in her room?"

She nodded. He went through the main room to Jessica's bedroom.

"Hey, Jessica," he said. "Yingyang tells me you're not so good."

Jessica's face flinched.

"I got you something." He dropped his jacket on her crumpled sheet and unrolled the top of the paper bag.

Jessica lay still, her whole body listening to the rustling sound the paper made.

"I'm gonna give them to Yingyang," he said. "She can let you have one when you need one."

"Valium?" croaked Jessica. "I need them now."

"OK." He nodded. "You'll have to sit up to swallow it." He took an untouched bottle of water from the floor beside her.

Screwing up her face, Jessica lifted her shoulders a fraction from the bed, resting on her elbow. Tears pooled around her eyes.

Bristol put a little yellow tablet on her tongue with his finger and tipped water into her mouth. She closed her eyes and swallowed hard, water oozing down her chin. Then she fell back onto the bed, panting softly.

Jerking his head toward the door, Bristol picked up his jacket. In the main room, he said, "Keep these hidden. I don't want her taking them all. They're for when she's really bad. Can you do that?"

Yingyang nodded, taking the paper bag from him. She tried to remember what it felt like when Noah held her in his arms as a small child. She had wished so often that he'd left instructions for making the syrups, the ones he made when Jessica wouldn't move.

~

Through her guest room window, Pippa waved to the lollipop lady and watched three schoolchildren cross the road without thanking her. She didn't actually want the morning off, but when she'd finally got through to someone who understood what she was talking about, she'd discovered that the Urgent Boiler Repair service had to be booked a week in advance. And that they could only specify morning or afternoon.

The lollipop lady raised her lollipop in farewell and Pippa mouthed, "See you." She went into the hallway and looked at the crumpled envelope on the table. Clearing her throat, she picked up the telephone. For the fiftieth time, she dialled the number on the envelope. She could hear the message already in her head; *Emma is currently out of the office. Thank you for your call.*

"Hello, *Froth* magazine, Fashion department?"

Pippa jumped.

"Emma Constant? Is that you?"

"This is Emma's office, yes."

"Are you Emma?" Pippa tugged the phone cable to its full stretch to reach her handbag and find her diary and the little script she'd prepared.

"No. I'm Emma's PA."

Pippa could hear a sharp edge to the caramel custard voice. She straightened up.

"I would very much like to speak with Emma please."

"Can I help? What is it regarding?"

"Is she in the office currently at the moment?"

"Yes." The custard was all but gone.

It sounded to Pippa as if she had hung up on her. She shook the phone.

"Good morning, Emma Constant. To whom am I speaking?"

"Are you Emma?"

"Yes. I am Emma."

"I am Pippa, you remember from Eastern Vision?"

"Eastern Vision…"

"We met some years ago at an Eastern Vision exhibition."

Emma was making exaggerated memory-wracking noises.

"You very much liked our wall hangings and you gave me your number."

"Wall hangings! Lovely. So what can I do for you?"

She was typing, Pippa could hear the keys. Pippa looked at her notes.

"I have developed a beautiful, eclectic and quirky fashion range. I would be delighted to share these with yourself."

"Right. You have a catalogue do you?"

"No, no catalogue. I have a shop, an off-the-beaten-track bijou boutique. Quirky."

"So you said."

Indignation was rising through Pippa's body at the vagueness of the voice, the sense that this woman was waiting for her to go away. She returned to her script.

"I would like to offer you the chance of making the first feature of Gypsy Magic clothing. Perhaps I can bring some examples to your office?"

"Can you get me a cab, Frankie? Thank you *so* much, it's lovely to hear from you. Unfortunately our schedule is full for quite a while. Good luck elsewhere."

The dialling tone sounded before the last word was finished.

"Bitch!"

Pippa kicked the table, stubbing her toes. She crushed the ancient envelope in her fist and threw it at the front door.

The bell rang as it hit the glass pane, and Pippa let the urgent boiler repairer in.

~

The sack was too heavy for one person to carry. Yingyang's wrists hurt holding it. She tried kicking it along the ground and then dragging it behind her. She let go to turn her wrists in circles and ease the strain.

Three young men grouped around a broken bicycle nudged each other. One called out, "Hey, farang, so pretty!" and another whistled.

Yingyang grabbed the sack again, tearing the plastic where it was stretched.

"Fuck," she mouthed, and hardly any sound came out, so nobody would have heard her even if a taxi hadn't started hooting its horn.

The young men wheeled the bicycle alongside Yingyang.

"Where are you taking? We can help you."

She hunched her shoulders away from them, pursing her lips with the effort of shifting the sack.

They took it from her and balanced it on the bicycle, hooking the knot round the handlebars.

"We come," said one, setting off.

She walked beside him. The other two followed.

"English?" they said, "USA?"

Yingyang shook her head, refusing to look at them. She turned sharply down a track beside an Indian tailor's shop. The young men, boys really, stopped talking. They imagined the farang girl must be lost; what could she possibly want here?

An old woman squatted beside a rusting bucket of fish. Her hands were black, thick with fish scales. She scratched her nose, wiped them on a rag saturated with sludge and scooped out a fish.

Round the corner they came to a track where the shelters were made from foraged pieces of fence or old doors, lashed together with rope. The children were naked and the parents had no teeth. It was like a nightmare version of Phetbin, a warning of what might happen to the people who lived there when the slum was cleared and they were forced out.

Yingyang struggled with the knot where the sack was attached to the bike. One of the boys undid it for her, whilst the others hung back, scuffing their feet in the dust.

She had cooking pots in the sack. Woks and saucepans, a thick-bottomed frying pan, a tin opener and some ladles. The sun shot shards of hot light onto the metal.

Taking the frying pan by its thick handle, Yingyang went to the first shelter. The arch of corrugated iron and plastic sheeting provided no place to knock, so Yingyang banged her fist on the frying pan.

An old lady in a housecoat and slippers shuffled out of the arch. Yingyang smiled and handed her the frying pan, dipping her head. The old lady was short and plump and she leant back awkwardly to carry the pan, grimacing but dipping her head in reply, murmuring, "Kop khun ka."

The boys had gone. Yingyang took a saucepan and a ladle, thinking about Bristol. She saw his sandy hair that spiked in every direction, his thick cotton shirt rolled up at the sleeves, the breadth of his chest. She imagined what it would be like if he were to take her in his arms, like he used to when she was a child. She felt his hands on her shoulders, heard him say her name, saw him reach out for her.

She came out of her daydream to find she was holding a wok and the sack was empty. Had she given out all the things? So deep inside her head that she couldn't remember doing so? She scratched at a bite on her arm. She turned to go. *If I count, all the way home, it will stop me going mad. Count, and touch something green, and then you won't end up like Jessica.*

190

26

The office block was well-lit, despite the hour. Bristol pushed the bell at length and broke wind, making an apology there was no one else to hear. He smiled at the guard who saluted and locked the door behind him.

"No rest for the wicked," said Bristol, heading for the lift.

The guard stood to attention.

"Am I so terribly wicked? I guess I must be. For a while there I had myself down as—" He thought about it, stifling a belch. "Nonchalant, maybe. A little irreverent. But nice. Definitely, essentially, at heart – nice."

He wondered about taking the stairs. As a form of penance, perhaps.

"Now I discover that I am, in the words of my wife, *a useless bastard*. Hey-ho."

Revolted, he managed two floors before admitting defeat and calling the lift.

The twentieth floor took him in its arms and rocked him. Tiny lights, blue, red and green, held the fort while the place was empty, emitting faint whirrs and buzzes. On Tina's desk at reception, a neat pile of mail waited for the morning. Smouldering silently.

He sat in Tina's chair. She suffered from pains in her lower back and he'd bought her a padded leather one with cushioned support at the base. He leant back and gazed at the ceiling, at the dim glow of security lights. When he found them obstinately mute, he sat forward and rested his chin in his hands.

"What is it?" he whispered and Tina's monitor blinked at him. "What is it that *actually* matters?"

His father's voice began to answer. He shook his head and grabbed the envelope on the top of the pile.

It was thin and the address was printed in dot matrix. Bristol traced the letters with his finger, smiling. Dot matrix. He was surprised that through the grime in his head he remembered such ancient words.

He opened the envelope and pulled out a sheet of airmail paper with an elaborate letterhead.

Dear Sirs,
With regarding application for Hotel in Laos capital Vientiane main centre,
sorry to regret this is not to be permissive.
In Vientiane we take a long see of future and developments must careful
consideration.
Thank you for patient correspondence regarding this matters.

"Fuck," said Bristol. He saw in the screen before him a murky ditch; dollars, pounds and baht trodden to a pulp in the earth. Architects' fees, consultations with the construction companies, countless gifts to officials on either side of the Mekong. Months of work. Written off, as it were. Put down to experience. His father tried to add his own remarks, but Bristol shook him off again.

"Right." He stood, painfully, his joints clicking and his head foreshadowing his hangover. "We still have Emerald City. It seems we must put our hopes in the Yellow Brick Road."

~

"Bitch!" said Pippa. She put her clutch bag in the cubby hole under the till and perched on the high stool.

Marina stopped polishing bracelets and smiled.

"Oh?"

"That design photograph lady is a cow. She pretended she could not remember me."

"Never mind. It was a long shot."

"Long shot?"

"Long shot. It means we try but we will probably not get what we want." Marina shrugged her shoulders. "Don't worry, Pips. We are a success here. This shop is really fantastic."

Pippa stood.

"What we do is—"

The door tinkled and a pair of buxom women with set hair entered, talking in stage whispers.

"Look," breathed one. "Oh, Joyce, these are super."

"Very ethnic."

"Not ethnic. *Bohemian.*"

"It matters!" roared Bristol, smashing his fist into the arm of the sofa and stamping to his feet. He grabbed his jacket and left, slamming the door.

27

The daily rainstorms had turned the slimy puddle that bordered the khlong into a swamp, where a solitary frog burped his way through the mud. Jessica took off her shoes and tested the depth with her foot. It came up to her knees. Hitching up her skirt, she waded across.

"Poey? Where are you going?"

Poey was going nowhere. She sat with her feet dangling over the khlong, her hands in the swamp. Her head nodded in time to a song of its own.

"Poey. You're very near the edge."

Jessica spoke in Thai-English but Poey seemed not to hear.

"Are you OK? Has something happened?"

She crouched carefully but she still got covered in mud. Poey's eyes rolled towards her.

"Kru Jess'cah," she mumbled, *teacher Jessica*, "I swim khlong."

"Not here, it's not safe. Go up by the steps."

"I swim here khlong."

"Poey, what are you on?"

Poey giggled.

"Mister give me new pill. So small like this."

Jessica chewed the inside of her mouth.

"And this mister is coming back, right? How much for one tablet?"

"No unnerstand."

"You do understand. How many baht?"

Poey hung her head and looked sideways at her.

"Can pay maybe one hundred baht. And make sexy him."

"Shitting hell, Poey. Are you using condoms?"

"Sometime use."

"Sometimes."

"Mister no like."

"You will get ill. Or get a baby. You don't want a baby."

Poey examined her swampy palms.

"I'll get some more condoms," said Jessica. "Use one every time."

~

Pippa watched the back of Marina's head bob up and down as she turned the corners on pages of her wedding magazine.

"Marina, why do you want all this white fluff? If you wear Gypsy Magic you will be a unique bride."

She grabbed a skirt and danced with it, twirling round the central display of scarves.

"Each of them unique!"

Marina looked up, keeping her finger in her page.

"Not absolutely unique. It's hard to see the exact difference between some of them."

Pippa stuck out her tongue.

The door tinkled and she swung round and beamed.

"Good morning, feel at your leisure to browse please."

The woman was older than either Pippa or Marina, and dressed in an interesting selection of clothes. She had a cotton shawl twisted round her neck so many times her chin was thrust forward.

"Are you the proprietor?" she asked Pippa.

"I certainly am."

The woman offered Pippa her hand, heavy with twisted metal rings.

"Maggie," she said. "I'm doing an MA."

Marina tore out a page and circled an advert for custom-made tiaras.

"In Radio Broadcast, Media Design and Fashion Photography."

Pippa swallowed. A bubble swirled and spun in her belly.

The Radio Broadcast, Media Design and Fashion Photography student swept an arm in an expansive arc, narrowing her eyes.

"Would you consider participating in a shoot? For my final piece? I'd like to showcase your range and interview you about your work in bringing fair trade to Eastern Europe."

"Well," said Pippa, the bubble swelling and fizzing.

"Africa's a bit done, if you see what I mean. This," she rubbed the sleeve of a blouse between her fingers, "is new. Fresh."

Marina had closed her catalogue and was sitting on her hands.

~

"Mister! Goo' fortune!"

"Make chanting with lucky charm."

"Mister!"

Plates of offerings were thrust into Bristol's face as he approached the temple; plastic bottles of cooking oil, fruit, narrow candles and little orchid flowers. He bought a candle, squinting to see through the incense and the people into the doorway. Ducking his head, he pushed his way inside.

Gigantic golden beings with multiple limbs and animal noses hushed the sound of the street. He looked up into the face of a fierce-eyed figure with bright green earrings that snaked down his arms. The figure seemed to frown. Bristol swallowed, holding up his offerings defensively.

Further in, people knelt, bowing low as monks chanted.

Bristol stopped by a trough of candles stuck into earth and sand. He lit his candle from another and wedged it in. He stared into the flame and tried to still his mind.

A man with a corrugated face was pouring oil in a circle around a barrel. Seeing Bristol watching, he nodded slowly.

"Make your years," he said.

"My age? In circles?"

The old man smiled softly.

Bristol cleared his throat and began to pour his circles; one, two, three, four… thirty-seven… thirty-eight." *Thirty-nine*, when did that happen? As he moved away, his companion was still counting patiently.

The endless red and gold pulsated around him. He felt dizzy, hypnotised by the chanting and the incense burning in the quiet of each corner. He stared at a figure that sat cross-legged with an altar before him.

"God of peace," murmured a woman selling little slips of paper like post-it notes.

"Kop khun kop," murmured Bristol in return. Then, on an impulse, he asked, "What are you selling?"

She led him to a table where several people were earnestly inscribing characters on the Post-its.

"Make for hope a wish," she said, gesturing at him to sit and write.

He gave her some coins and waied. What did he wish? If this Post-it held the power, what would he hope for? That by some miracle a buyer would appear for the untouchable building site that was Emerald City? Then he considered forgetting money for once in his life and writing down his hopes for the builder's family. It might make him feel better to do that. He put down his pen and scratched his elbows. He couldn't actually bring the dead man back, not with a Post-it, and the family were in luxury they'd never known, living in Tranquillity Place. He wondered about hoping for Linda to leave him for someone else. In the end, he wrote, *Bamboo Grove*, very slowly.

28

Yingyang found Bristol's pocket diary on Jessica's bed. A slim brown leather-bound book that you could hold in one hand. It smelt of him; he carried it in his breast pocket. Yingyang turned it over in her hand, rubbing her thumbs in circles, breathing deeply. The temptation to open it was strong. She flicked to her birthday; there was an arrow pointing to the date. She gazed at the arrow for a long time, wondering when he put it there, thinking about the shopping trip and the make-up counter.

She wanted to wear make-up for him. She would deliver the diary to his office, wearing make-up. She reached for Jessica's little silver purse and pulled out a lipstick without a cap. The base was smeary, it left red on Yingyang's hand. She put it to her bottom lip and drew it across, eyes wide, not breathing.

"Yingyang?" It was Jessica. Come back from buying Coca-Cola in the shop across the street.

Yingyang's hand slipped. She smudged her chin. She crammed the lipstick back in the purse and shoved the diary up her sleeve.

"Are you there? I bought the Coke. Phin said it's still in its date. Yingyang?"

Jessica was in the doorway, smiling. She had the bottle cradled like a baby in her arms. "Is that–? You were putting on my make-up. That's OK, don't look like you've committed a crime or something. Sure, you should wear lipstick."

Yingyang wiped her fist hard across her mouth. She edged past her mother, nodding, and ran down the steps, the diary jumping up and down inside her sleeve. The leather felt different already, gritty and flabby for lying so close to her skin. She tried not to think about it falling out of Bristol's pocket. Maybe he'd leant down to kiss Jessica. Maybe he took the shirt off and that's why he didn't notice it slip out onto the sheets. Don't think about it, rub away the pictures. He doesn't sleep with Jessica, not any more. He only comes to see me. Maybe he got a call when he was round about the apartment or something, put a date in his diary and forgot to put it back in his pocket. Then why was it in Jessica's sheets? Why was he in her room? Stop it, stop it, he left it there for me to find. Or because he knew Jessica would ask me to return it for her.

Yingyang stopped at the glass doorway of the department store, panting. She glanced behind her. Two German women, a mother and a daughter perhaps, pushed past without looking at her. They were both as wide as two people and they clutched shopping bags; a paper box-bag with raffia handles, a dark purple plastic carrier and fake designer handbags. The mother shunted the door with her elbow. A band struck up loudly in the daughter's handbag. She frowned and fished about inside it.

They were wearing eye shadow. Yingyang didn't know why she hadn't noticed people's make-up before. The mother had pencilled-on black eyebrows. The daughter had a mask of beige make-up over her whole face, streaked where she'd been sweating. Her neck was red where it finished.

The tall white stool by the counter was empty. Close up, Yingyang could see that it was tightly covered in plastic that had come loose at the back.

"Yes please?" murmured an assistant in a pink and black nurses' tabard.

Yingyang looked at her, aching to be understood. She sat shyly on the stool and tilted her chin.

"You wan' make-over?"

The assistant laughed. She pushed Yingyang's hair off her face and fastened a white velcro band around it. Then, with the pads of her thumbs, she pressed hard underneath Yingyang's eyes and wiped something invisible away. Yingyang kept as still as she could.

"Ah! One minute!" exclaimed the assistant. She called across to another lady dressed in the same pink and black tabard and was handed a length of thread.

"Eye clo'," she said.

Yingyang shut her eyes.

"No cry!"

The thread was sharp. The assistant's fingers twisted and rolled, making Yingyang gasp as her eyebrows stung.

The assistant dabbed her fingers into a small pot of something cold and magic and pressed under Yingyang's brows, on her temples and around her eye sockets.

A soft cloth was flicked over Yingyang's face, under her chin and through her eyebrows. She dropped it into a basket on the counter.

The face cream stung. Yingyang pushed her nails into her palms and tried not to sneeze.

The pink and black assistant used her fingers as lightly and quickly as an artist or a magician, fluttering them back and forth from the beauty counter to Yingyang's face.

Yingyang wondered if she would look ridiculous. Like the seven-year-olds at the International School who experimented with Mummy's make-up for parties she had never been invited to. As the assistant puffed powder across her nose, Yingyang hoped she would look like an adult. Bristol would laugh if she came in like a child with face paint.

"There. All finish. Same-same princess."

The assistant held up a mirror. Yingyang blinked. Her eyelashes were black. Her cheeks caught the light. Her lips were softly pink. Her skin had turned from crumpled red to smooth white gold.

Yingyang gripped the handle of the mirror, staring at herself. The assistant puffed a tiny squirt of glittering perfume behind Yingyang's ears and ran a comb through the top layer of her hair.

"You like? Which one buy?"

She fanned out the pencils, sticks, brushes and mascara. Yingyang stroked a gold pencil and stood up. She hoped this wasn't theft. It was trying-on, like with the clothes. She pressed her palms together and dipped her head. The assistant smiled.

As she left, Yingyang saw her reflection in the tinted glass of the door. She straightened her shoulders. A smile hovered, quivering. With Bristol's diary still up her sleeve, anticipation squeezing her middle, she swung through the people outside the store, waved to the barbecued chicken sellers and hurried towards the building where the Americans worked.

What if he's not there? He will be. He's always working. He'll be there and I'll walk in and he will stop whatever he is doing; put the telephone down, click his pen, close a file on the computer screen. And he'll shake his head slowly, looking and looking at me. *Yingyang*, he'll say, *you are – delicious*. Delicious, he'll call me, and his voice will sound like twilight. He'll rub his face with his hands and sigh while he realises there's nothing he can do. I'll stand very still and blink at him, maybe I'll very slightly extend my hand for him to take. Then he'll come to stand right up close and he'll put his hands on my face and say, *Yingyang, when did you get so beautiful?* And he'll pull me slowly in until my head is against his chest and he'll have his arms across my back. He'll kiss the top of my head and sigh again.

A skinny dog dashed past Yingyang, wetting her ankle. She righted herself and a man walking behind her sidestepped to overtake.

She breathed right down into her stomach, filling herself with air, daring to think what came next, after Bristol had kissed her head and sighed. Yingyang had never done anything with a man, or a boy. Not kissing, back-rubbing, squeezing, touching naked skin. She knew the basics. She knew he would have a penis hidden beneath the midnight-coloured suit, and the thought that it would harden and strain when she was up close to him made her heavy between her own legs. What would they do? Would he unzip himself and put her hand gently on his penis, murmuring into her hair? Would he push his hands inside the peach cardigan he paid for and hold her breasts the way she held them at night when she thought of him?

She wiped her nose on her knuckle and coughed. She was at the revolving doors. She'd never been inside his office. Never further than the reception desk where the ladies with the telephones sat. In her fantasies, the office had no windows. It was full of books; the walls were lined with them so that it felt like a cave of books. She often imagined Bristol sitting at his desk in the midst of all the books, clicking his computer, frowning. Then, when he saw her, that sigh, and he would stand up and come to her.

She stepped into the revolving doors and went into the foyer, blinking. Sam and Alexis strode towards her, talking. She turned away, biting her lip, hoping they hadn't seen her. She stood still, looking down at the ground, wishing herself invisible. Alexis said, "I'll ring him," and Sam said, "Tell him Monday. I don't want anything under-the-table getting in the way here."

As soon as they dived into the revolving doors, Yingyang hurried over to the lift. On the twentieth floor, she made herself look down. She watched two women wheel a trolley across the entrance foyer below. She turned to face the reception desk.

"Sawadee ka," said the ladies.

Yingyang smiled. She wasn't sure they recognised her.

"Mister Bristol?" asked one, tilting her head to one side.

Yingyang nodded and rubbed her nose with her knuckle again. She hoped she wasn't going red. She could feel her cheeks beginning to heat up.

"Yingyang! Sawadee ka, beautiful." It was Bristol, getting out of the lift. He smelt of whisky and cigars.

She looked into his face.

He cleared his throat. "All OK? What can I do for you?"

She held up the diary, shaking, trying to read his expression. Was it so ridiculous to think he might have left it in the hope that she would come?

"My diary. Thank you."

He bit his lip. She looked at the square, even edge of each tooth.

"You came all this way to give me this?"

Behind her, the telephone began to ring. He winked quickly at her.

"Mister Bristol, you wan' speak Khun Lexis in your office?" asked one of the ladies, her hand hovering over a small switchboard.

Bristol cleared his throat again. "Tell him I'll call him on the way. I'm running late."

The sour hollow of disappointment crept through Yingyang's body. He was running late. She could feel her face twist, tiny knots of dismay and self-ridicule.

Bristol looked at his watch.

Yingyang looked at the lift-call panel.

"I'm–" he said. "Thanks for bringing my diary up for me. Thanks a lot."

The lift doors opened. It was empty. The doors waited for invisible people to go in and out before sliding shut.

"I'm going home for dinner," he said. "I promised."

Yingyang nodded without looking at him. She took a step in the direction of the lift.

"Do you–? Do you want to come?"

To his home? For dinner?

"My cook makes a mean pad Thai."

Yingyang certainly didn't want to go back home. But to his home? To his wife? Surely his wife couldn't know who she was?

"Linda, my wife, she'd love to meet you."

Bristol tucked his diary into his jacket pocket.

"Let me just grab a couple of things," he said, "from my office. I'll be right back."

Yingyang had her back to the receptionists, but she knew they were looking at her. She wondered if she could stay still until Bristol came back and they could call the lift. She wished he would hurry up.

At the base of the apartment block where Bristol lived, to the right of the foyer where uniformed security stood guard, was a long, thin swimming pool. It was lit from inside itself, so that the water shone a velvet-rich turquoise. Yingyang gazed through the glass wall, imagining the feel of the water on her skin.

She felt a long way away from herself. Her head fizzed. Her vision pulsated. She didn't know how to take all this. Was it rejection or invitation? But there was nothing to reject. She'd returned a diary. Nothing more. The rest was still safely in her head.

"OK?" he said. He cupped her elbow with his hand, in full view of the security guard and a tiny woman polishing the leaves of an enormous pot plant.

When the lift door shut on them, Bristol took his hand away. She felt suddenly like a little girl. How could she have dinner here? She looked at him, wanting to read his mind. He stared straight ahead at the silver and bronze of the lift doors. She traced the line of his chin with her eyes, sucking her lipstick off.

"Maybe this isn't …" He blew into his fist and straightened up.

Yingyang cocked her head to one side, still looking into his face. At last he met her eyes.

"Maybe I should have called ahead. But don't worry, it'll be fine."

Bristol's wife, Linda, was a surprise to Yingyang, not because she had imagined her in any particular way, but because she hadn't imagined her at all. Her actuality, her physical presence, was a thud of reality. Vanilla-coffee hair that fell heavy and straight and stopped level with her chin. Thick mascara, gold lipstick. The way her pumps matched her pale blue T-shirt dress. The deep vertical grooves between her eyebrows. The way she looked so much older than Bristol.

"Yingyang?" she said. "Is that a Thai name?"

Yingyang chewed the inside of her mouth and tried not to stare. The Bristol in her head would never be married to this woman.

"And this is Andrew," said Bristol, shaking hands with a younger, narrower version of himself. Yingyang felt as though she'd been hit. Bristol smiled at her, nodded slightly at his son. Now that she looked, Andrew's face had something of his mother's more pinched features and uneasy expression.

"I've seen you somewhere," he said. "Were you ever at the International School?"

Yingyang shook her head, meeting his eye.

"Yingyang's been doing some work for us in the office," said Bristol, loosening his tie. He took off his jacket and undid the top button on his shirt.

When Yingyang was left with Andrew, they both heard Linda hiss, "Doesn't she say anything at all?" but they pretended they hadn't. He squared a pile of paper on the glass table.

"Revision," he muttered.

Yingyang crouched beside the table. She was scared of leaving a mark on the fat white sofa. She read the title on the top sheet. *Tectonic plates.*

"Geography," said Andrew. "And maths."

Yingyang nodded.

In the corridor, Linda said, "You never even think about it, that's why you can't talk about it."

Bristol spoke quietly. "I'm here now. I haven't finished, I'm going back in, but I am here for dinner because I promised."

Andrew pressed his teeth together and scratched his chin. Yingyang looked at the room. The cushions were plump and straight. Books stood in neat lines on shelves built into an alcove. The widest, thinnest television Yingyang had ever seen was mounted on the wall, a pinprick of red light in the corner. A small Buddha and a plate of wooden fruit sat alone on top of the dresser.

Andrew took hold of the wooden apple. He turned it in his palm. When he caught Yingyang looking at him, he pretended to throw it over-arm at the door.

They smiled at each other.

"Sorry," he said, "about my parents. Are yours like this?"

Linda said, not even trying to be quiet, "It's just like you to do this. *Just like you.* Listen to me, don't walk away."

Yingyang stood up. She would go. She shouldn't have come. She felt stupid, wrong. Always doing the wrong thing. Mistaking the life in her head for a life that she could live. She rubbed the remains of her lipstick onto the back of her hand.

"Don't go," said Andrew. She stopped because he sounded like he meant it. "I'm going to get us a drink. Please. Stay there."

He squeezed the top of her arm and left her. She slipped into the corridor. Linda was leaning sideways against the wall, gazing at the front door as if she might make a run for it. Bristol was rubbing her shoulders.

"Go back to the office," said Linda. "That's where you want to be."

Bristol sighed.

"Where I want to be is here. I don't like leaving you in a state."

"I am not in a state. Just go. Come back when you've done whatever it is that is so essential and maybe we'll be able to communicate then. Without your glazed eyes giving away the fact that your mind is still at your desk."

Bristol stopped massaging her shoulders. "I'm sorry," he said. "It's not easy for you. But you'll find another job, a better job."

"I don't want to talk about it."

"I know. I know. OK. I'm going now. And when I come back we'll have dinner and talk properly. I'll see you then. Have a bath, or a lie down. Or something."

Yingyang felt him look at her as she went out of the front door, but she might have imagined it.

When she got home, Yingyang could hear Jessica laughing. She stood with her back to the door, listening for a man's laugh. They were in Jessica's bedroom.

Whispering. More laughing. Sam. Silence for a moment and Yingyang wondered if they'd heard her come in. But then Jessica let out a high-pitched moan and the shuffling, shunting sound of guilty sex replaced the laughter.

Yingyang shut her eyes. She couldn't bear it. Her body was on edge, at a painful peak of anticipation, and now she had to listen to Jessica gorging herself on sex. The sound of Sam's rapid breathing sent waves of disgust and desire up and down her spine. She turned to escape but found herself resting her forehead on the door, daring herself to think, *Where? Where am I going in the dark?* Had Bristol meant her to hear when he said he was going back to the office? Was he waiting for her now?

Just as Sam's breathing came to a loud, shuddering climax, Yingyang slammed the door behind her and ran back down into the street.

Beside the reception desk was a short corridor, at the end of which was a wooden door with a plaque reading 'Samuel Chambers & Bristol Chambers'. Yingyang put her fingers on the smooth, shiny plaque and breathed in. She pushed open the door. Bristol looked up and made a startled face. He was on the telephone. His jacket lay on a leather sofa. His sleeves were rolled up and his top button was undone. As he spoke, he loosened the knot in his tie the way he had when he got home.

The office Bristol shared with Sam was painted the colour of chocolate. It was completely square, with a glass wall looking down on the city. Lights winked from cars, shop signs and windows high and low.

Yingyang closed the door behind her. He waved her to sit on the sofa but she stayed where she was, her breath shallow and shaking. She wondered if she should go. What was she doing here? What had he ever promised her? She still had time to pretend she wanted something else and go before she ruined everything.

He put the phone down, scribbling notes and nodding.

"Yingyang," he said, still writing. "I'm sorry about that. It wasn't fair to drop you into the misery that is my family." He looked at her. "I just thought – I don't know what I thought." He rubbed his face.

The chocolate office was lit by muted bulbs in wall-mounted lamps. She coiled a strand of hair around her finger and looked at his hands. He had a fat signet ring on the little finger of his right hand. He stabbed a full stop onto his notes and leant back in his chair. She smiled.

"It's late," he said. "You shouldn't be out on your own. Where's Jessica?"

Yingyang shrugged. She stepped out of her flip-flops and felt the softness of the caramel carpet. She crossed to his desk and stood opposite him.

"You look lovely," he said, as if he'd only just noticed her.

She smiled and rested her fingertips on the smooth wood of his desk.

They were very close now. Only a desk between them. He cleared his throat. She laughed. She slid her fingers towards him across the desk. He looked at her hand.

In her fantasy, he reached for her. And the desk wasn't in the way. But she couldn't stop now.

She pulled the grubby peach cardigan over her head. She had nothing underneath. Bristol took hold of the edge of his desk and stared hard at the window.

Yingyang walked around to his chair. She was trembling. She took hold of his hands, trying to put them on her waist.

"No," he said, pushing back his chair. "This is—"

She could feel the treacle oozing from her. Moving closer so that his face was level with her breasts, she tugged at his shirt.

"No," he spluttered, trapped against the wall.

He managed to extricate one leg and ease himself sideways out of the way. She was left facing the chocolate wall, shaking.

"Look," he murmured. "It's—" He rested a hand on the chair back, steadying his breath.

Yingyang felt her face seize up and her body grow suddenly cold.

"I think you're beautiful," he said. "I'm – flattered."

She acted deaf.

"Put your clothes on," he whispered. "Please." He grabbed the cardigan from the floor and gave it to her. She watched his face. She didn't move. "I'm not talking to you until you put your clothes on," he said, turning a paperweight over and over in his fist and looking at the door.

Yingyang stood up. She went to the window wall. She could see herself in the glass. Round face, round shoulders, round breasts, rounded stomach pinched in by the long white skirt that wasn't white any more.

She watched her reflection pull the cardigan over her head and push her arms down the long, thin sleeves. Then she rested her forehead on the glass and sighed.

"Yingyang." Bristol's voice sounded more like his own now. He put a hand on her shoulder. "I'm ancient, OK? Far too old. Don't waste time thinking about *me*. Nod your head. Good girl."

She reached out for his hand and he let her touch it briefly before opening the door.

"Go home now," he said. "Go home."

Yingyang shook all night with shame and desire. He thought she was a child, he'd said as much. And she'd shoved her breasts in his face.

At first light, the smell of onions and sweet chillies filtered through. The sunbird wouldn't look at her. He fixed his gaze on the branches above. Yingyang wrapped herself in her sheet and edged round the screen.

Jessica was squatting beside the camping stove.

"You are beautiful," she said. She tipped a bowl of rice into the pan. "Are you hungry?"

Yingyang nodded, staring at the rice.

"Is it so strange that a mother should cook breakfast for her daughter?" Jessica put her hands into the steaming rice and mixed it, sucking in her breath as her fingers burnt. "Don't look at me like that. You should feel blessed with your hot food and your four solid walls. Poey won't have anywhere to live soon, or Little Mai."

Yingyang sat on the floor with her back against the wall.

"You're not wearing any clothes under that sheet," said Jessica. "Why aren't you wearing any clothes?"

Yingyang shrugged.

Jessica looked at her with her head on one side. "You went out. You've been somewhere."

Yingyang started. She hadn't stolen anything. It wasn't as though he had ever *belonged* to Jessica.

"Where did you go?" Jessica put her hand in the pan and snapped it out again, sucking her fingers.

Yingyang took the knife from amongst the onion peel on top of a cardboard box and stirred the rice with the blade.

"Yingyang? I said where did you go?"

Jessica's voice gave Yingyang that thud between the ribs that she got when her mother was about to break.

"You're being shy about it."

Yingyang tried to go back behind the screen to find her clothes, but her mother grabbed hold of her. The sheet came off in her hand, leaving Yingyang naked.

"What the fuck have you been doing?" Jessica seized the knife from the pan, splattering rice at her feet.

Yingyang ran behind the screen, wrestling her clothes on, pressing her lips together hard.

"Come here! What have you done?" Jessica's face was burning. She breathed in heavy snorts, beginning to pace in a circle.

Yingyang clamped her hands around Jessica's wrists and yanked. She bit, drawing blood, until her mother dropped the knife. Then, before Jessica could get her bearings, she picked it up and ran out to the stairs and down into the street.

~

The secretaries looked at Yingyang as if they knew, as if they could see inside her head. She walked past them. She pushed the door open and Bristol jumped up.

Andrew was sitting on the sofa. He stood.

"Hi," he said, "How are you?" He was upset and he wouldn't look at his father.

He brushed Yingyang's arm as he passed.

"Come round again," he mouthed, his back to Bristol.

She blinked at him.

When he'd gone, Bristol said, "He thinks you work here."

Yingyang laughed but it was a short, hard laugh. She stared directly into his eyes.

"I find that very – unnerving," he said softly.

She wanted to reach for him. Her body leant towards him of its own accord.

"You shouldn't be here." He held up his hands in front of him.

Yingyang pulled the knife from her sleeve and gave it to him.

"What?" He jumped back as if it was hot, put it on his desk. "What the hell–?"

She blinked and shrugged.

"Jessica? Shit. You've taken it off Jessica. You didn't tell her, you stupid–? God I don't need this."

He glanced at his watch, his computer screen, the knife, patted his pockets, flexed his fingers. Then he pushed Yingyang ahead of him and slammed out of the office.

"Go anywhere," he said, "but don't go home. Give me time."

Bristol found Jessica exactly where Yingyang had left her. She was staring at her hands, whispering to herself.

"Jessica."

She didn't look at him.

"Will you listen to me? I don't know how this got so out of hand." He checked to see that the door was closed. He swallowed. "I didn't do anything. The whole incident was crazy, and I've made that clear to her."

Jessica moved her head in slow motion to face him. She tightened her grip on the invisible knife.

"I'll stay away. Neither of you will ever see me. Just promise me you'll take care of each other. I can't – leave you in this state. Do you have any medication?"

Jessica let out a howl.

"It was you!" she screeched. "You've ruined her. You've ruined my daughter." She began to hyperventilate. "Why? Why did you have to do that? Am I so ugly that you can't have sex with me anymore and you have to–" She struggled for breath, spiky gasps that made it worse.

"No. Stop that. That's a ridiculous thing to say."

"It's incest. You could be her father."

"That's not true."

"You're like a father to her."

"I have never sought to be like a father to Yingyang. And this was ridiculous, God knows what brought it on. She came to the office and I was – surprised. Maybe I could have – I don't know, run from the room or something. I was tired, I was–" He rubbed his face, exhausted.

"You were tired?" Jessica rocked herself violently from side to side, pulling at her hair. "What the fuck is going on?" she muttered.

"Stop that," he said, grabbing hold of her. "Get a grip."

"Leave me alone! I'm hearing voices! No!"

He shook her. "You are not hearing voices. You are working yourself up into hysteria and for once in your bloody life you're going to deal with this like an adult."

"I'm going to get a knife, a gun, I'm going to throw myself into the road."

Bristol slapped her face. He took hold of her shoulders and wrestled her to the floor.

"I'll tell you what's going on here, it's because I won't sleep with you anymore. But haven't you ever asked yourself why? Jessica, I respect you. God knows why, but I – I like you too much to just have sex with you. You're special."

"Sam still wants me."

Bristol shut his eyes. He'd thought, he'd hoped–

"That is Sam's business," he said. "I love being with you. You know that. But I'm *married*, Jessica." He opened his eyes and met hers. "I'm married. What Sam chooses to do – it's not for me to judge. And I didn't see that Yingyang had developed a – crush – on me."

"I never want to see her again. Get rid of her. I don't know what I'd do if I saw her."

"Calm down. Stop it."

"Get her out of my way. She's old enough now. I wasn't much older than she is when I had her for God's sake."

"Jessica, you don't mean this. You and Yingyang need each other."

Jessica narrowed her eyes and sat up against the wall, panting. "If you don't get rid of her for me, I will find your bitch of a wife and tell her what her husband is really like."

He felt sick, dizzy. Jessica's fury was poisonous. He put his head in his hands and tried to breathe. He wished that he had never met her, never been hypnotised by her otherness, seduced by her need for him.

Jessica began to thump the ground with her fist. She gritted her teeth against the pain, breathing fast. She said, staring at her fist as though her life depended on it, "Get – rid – of - her."

Yingyang didn't know why she went home with Andrew. She found him in the lobby and he seemed grateful for her company. He said he should have been at school but he didn't know what the point was seeing as though they might be moving away.

"It's Mum," he said. "She hates it here. She's never found work she likes and now she says she doesn't like her friends either. She's so miserable and Dad's never home. I'm pretty sure she's going back to London."

They stood on the balcony outside his bedroom. So madly high above the streets that Yingyang should have been keeping her compulsive eye out, but a recklessness had set in since her mother waved the knife at her and she took a furious delight in leaning over the concrete barrier. He gave her a Coke and she drank it down quickly, wanting more. He got another can from the tiny fridge in his room and opened it for her.

"Did you ever talk? Or have you always been silent?"

Yingyang nodded, but he didn't know which question she was answering. He laughed and she smiled. She was glad she'd come with him instead of sitting alone by the river listening to the jumble of her own thoughts.

"It must be peaceful, not talking."

Yingyang shrugged. She didn't feel peaceful; her nerve endings flickered and fizzed, her senses seemed heightened and yet she felt as if she weren't really there at all.

"When you came into Dad's office, I was trying to get some sense out of him. He disappeared after you left last night and he didn't come back. Mum put his food in his jacket pockets." He sighed. "This morning he looked like he'd slept in front of his computer. I told him if he doesn't stop working so much, Mum will walk out and go back to London without him. All the time I was talking he hardly took his eyes off the screen. Are you hungry? Do you want something to eat?"

He produced crisps and put them on the balcony between them. Their hands touched inside the packet.

"Can I ask you something?"

Yingyang blinked. There was a sound from the apartment but Andrew didn't seem to hear it.

"Do you have a boyfriend?"

Yingyang licked the salt off her fingers and shook her head.

"I'd like very much to kiss you."

213

He was staring at the crisps but he flicked his eyes up to her face for a second. As he leant in towards her, cupping the back of her head in his hand, she saw Bristol come into the bedroom.

She pushed Andrew away, a sound escaping from her throat. It took him a moment to see his father out of the corner of his eye.

He hesitated, then stood tall and rolled his shoulders back. Bristol was standing by the little fridge, making it look as if it belonged in a doll's house.

"Dad," said Andrew. "You've kind of interrupted something here." His voice hovered between amusement and fear.

Yingyang tried to catch Bristol's eye. *I pushed him away, I didn't want that.*

"Andrew," said Bristol. "I need to speak with Yingyang."

"Dad, this is my room." Andrew stood in the doorway, looking from his father to Yingyang. "Yingyang and I were talking."

"*You* were talking. Yingyang doesn't talk."

Yingyang shrank into the concrete barrier. *If I were Jessica, I'd sit on there and threaten to let go. Would you lose consciousness before you hit the ground?*

"Oh, for Christ's sake," hissed Andrew, stared down by his father. He snatched his iPod from his bed, trying to read Yingyang's face, and when she wouldn't look at him, he left the room.

Bristol came out onto the balcony, running his hands through his hair.

He said, "What are you doing to my family?"

Yingyang touched his arm gently. He shook her off. If she hadn't taught herself long ago not to cry, the tears would have come now. He had never been further from her.

Bristol looked down at her. "I did nothing to be ashamed of," he said flatly.

She shuddered. His voice was so cold. She shook her head, thinking that if he would only take her in his arms, everything would be clear and there'd be no need for all these ugly words. She folded her arms tightly to stop herself from reaching for him.

"The best thing for everyone is for you to go away for a while. You need time," he steadied himself against the barrier, shutting his eyes for a moment. "You need to get away from Jessica."

Yingyang wondered what Jessica was doing now. Had Bristol fed her valium so she would sleep?

"You haven't had it easy," he said.

His phone rang and he jumped, checked the screen and cut it off. "And you've been a good daughter to Jessica. But it's time you decided what to do with your life." He looked down at the scene far below. "There's an artists' retreat on an island off Phuket. It's called Bamboo Grove. You can write there. There'll be young people. From Europe maybe."

Yingyang stared at him. He was sending her to Phuket? On her own?

"You can make some friends, write your stories, I don't know. Just take some time to think." He checked the screen of his mobile again. "I can't support you forever. It wouldn't be right. God, especially not now." He sighed, rubbed his face with his hands. "I will give you some money. And your board at Bamboo Grove will be sorted. But I want you to stay there at least until after Christmas. Do you understand?"

Yingyang wondered how it would be to escape the weight of Jessica's moods, to see another place, other people. And at the same time she knew it was impossible, because when Jessica fell into a black gloom or spun into a place where no one could reach her, she had to be there. She had to take her home, feed her valium, watch for the times when she was most a danger to herself.

Last night she had drawn on some unfamiliar power but it must have burnt itself out because now she seemed more than ever at the mercy of this man who had got inside her mind. She was trembling, cold in the shade.

She looked at him and shook her head slowly from side to side, *no*.

"Yingyang." He breathed in and let the breath out sharply. "I'm not giving you a choice here. I'm telling you that this is what you are going to do."

She thought, *I am not your son or your snivelling wife. Don't try to control me.*

"I hate this," he said. "I don't want to hurt you. I hope you will look back and see that I am doing what is best for you. For all of us."

She put her hands over her ears. She tried to go back through Andrew's bedroom door but Bristol stepped in front of her. He pulled her hands away from her face and held her fast by the shoulders.

"Yingyang," he said sadly. "You have no choice because I hold the purse strings. Without me you have nothing and nowhere to go. But I have your best interests at heart. I always have. So trust me. Do as I tell you."

Yingyang stood still, looking into his face, until eventually she nodded. She'd trust him: let him send her to some island while he tried to make peace with his miserable wife.

She reached into his pocket and pulled out the leather diary and a fat silver pen. He watched as she tore a page from the diary and wrote, *Check on Jessica. Every day.*

PART FOUR

29

Maggie had secured her hair with a pencil and was carrying a clipboard around the studio.

"Mike," she called. "Can you turn up the yellow?"

The light glowed hotter. Pippa wiped the sweat from under her nose.

"And ... go with the fan!" shouted Maggie. "When you're ready, many as you can."

The model was very young and very hourglass. She had a face Pippa wanted to look at; the smoothest, creamiest forehead and the roundest, shiniest eyes. A tiny nose and a sweet mouth with timid little teeth that took up no more space than they should. In Gypsy Magic clothes, she looked like a delicately embroidered angel.

The fullness of her hair and her skirt was displayed beautifully in the gently rotating fan. Maggie's tame undergraduate shot photographs six to the second.

"Lovely!" cried Maggie.

Pippa slurped the remains of her mocha cinnamon latte and checked her phone for messages.

"Maggie, these bracelets go with that dress. OK?"

"Just a mo', Pips."

"No mo's. These bracelets go with that dress."

Maggie put her chin into her shawls and sighed.

"Every single colour," said Pippa. "Ten every arm."

Maggie looked up. "Right," she said. "Yes, of course."

Pippa's phone buzzed in her pocket and played a brief fanfare. She turned away and looked at the screen. The message had been written in Romanian with an English text predictor, and yet somehow it conveyed anger.

She squeezed the phone, shook it as if this could shake her brother's head. *He's beyond help*, said the part of her she had begun to dislike. An incomprehensible text and a drunken, abusive phone call from time to time. *Forget Mick. Forget you had a brother.*

"Maggie, we've got to move. Simeon needs the studio, yeah?"

"Two minutes! Give us a red, Mike!"

Pippa pressed 'reply' and began to type. 'Missing you. Missing–'
No. She deleted the text, turned her phone off and tucked her bob behind her ears. She needed her roots done; maybe Marina would mind the shop a bit longer so she could go to the salon.

The model had her arms above her head in the manner of a flamenco dancer and her foot on a little stool.

"Superb," said Maggie. "It's a wrap."

~

Yingyang carried with her only a small suitcase and a nervous expression. Sitting very still on the boat, she thought that if a hundred of Bangkok's tallest buildings were spread out in a fan, they would still be swamped by the glittering amethyst universe that was the Andaman Sea.

The boy brought the boat to a stop and stepped over a man who was lying on the prow, talking on his mobile. He uncoiled a heavy chain. The padlock on Yingyang's suitcase bumped against her anklebone as the anchor hit the seabed. She pursed her lips and swallowed.

The man put his phone back in his pocket and sat up. He was a short, fat Thai and he wore jeans and a pressed white shirt. Yingyang was close enough to see that he had a torn right earlobe. Two flaps of flesh had curled apart and grown hard. She looked past him at the platinum beach and the dark green hills. At the huts on stilts on the sand.

The boy secured the anchor.

"Come, Madam," he said.

He lifted her suitcase above his head and jumped into the sea. The water reached his waist. She screwed up her eyes against the glare and heaved her bottom onto the rail. Her thighs splayed pink and fat on the wood and the skin grazed as she slid down into the water.

The man with the torn ear was speaking in rapid Thai on the boat behind her. Following the boy with her suitcase on his head, she began to wade. Her shorts clung to her. She couldn't think where she had seen this man before, but he was somehow familiar. The hem of her T-shirt dragged in the water. She could see her feet stomping along, stirring up clouds of sand.

The boy set her suitcase down. He pressed his hands together and bowed his head. She did the same. Then he swam back to the boat and leapt over the side.

Yingyang sat on her suitcase and watched her clothes dry out. A woman collecting shells in a bucket was looking at her, and she was conscious of her puffy pink face and tangled, dirty hair.

She felt in her pocket for Bristol's card. It was wet through. He'd told her to show it and she'd be given a hut. The woman with the bucket sat down and began to count the shells, wiping each one with a cloth. Yingyang didn't want to show her the card. She stood and dragged her case up the beach towards the hills.

A tall thin man was sitting under a coconut tree with his eyes shut, looking as comfortable as if he had emerged from its roots. He had dark skin and it was impossible to tell his race or nationality. His long bony legs were pleated underneath him in a lotus posture and his endless elbows were draped across his knees. Black hair cascaded from his head and his chin but he had no eyebrows. He was draped in a rough cotton garment revealing six toes on each long brown foot, the bones as spiky as a bat's wing.

He inhaled deeply. A hair was drawn into the current of air and got stuck to the underside of his nose.

Yingyang wanted to brush it away. How could he stay so still with hair in his nostrils? Surely he'd sneeze any moment.

Behind her, in the shallows, someone was trying to start the engine on a speedboat. It revved just short of success and then choked.

"Hi," sighed the impossibly long, thin man, without opening his eyes. Yingyang stepped back. His voice reverberated in the bottom of her spine. Was this word part of the meditation or was he speaking to her? She squinted under her hand at the boat that wouldn't start. Two men were wading waist-deep, calling instructions. "Good to see you."

The man under the tree opened his eyes and stretched his arms miles above his head. His elbows clicked.

Yingyang looked at him. He thought she was someone else. She gave a half-smile and turned away.

"We've been waiting for you," breathed the man, sending vibrations across her chest. She turned back and raised her eyebrows. *Me?* "I am Moses. They told me you would come."

Moses pulled on an invisible bar and sprang upright. He rolled his head from side to side. Yingyang thought that if there were such a thing as a double-jointed neck, this man had one.

The boat engine started up. The men cheered and clapped each other's hands. Moses stood very still. His arms lay flat at his sides. He had bluey-green eyes that stared unblinking at Yingyang for long seconds. Slowly, he raised his hand to her cheek, but he didn't touch her. He let his fingers hover there as if she were too magical to touch. "You don't speak," he said.

Yingyang shook her head.

"Silence is some religion." Moses finally unstuck the wisp of hair from under his nose. Yingyang coughed to stop herself from laughing.

Above the man's head, in the tree, were three ripe coconuts. How often, Yingyang wondered, do coconuts fall onto people's heads? She had to keep looking at them to stop them from falling. If she looked away – *stop it, stop it. Mad woman. Like mother like daughter.* She squeezed her eyes shut and shook her head. When she opened her eyes, there would be no more looking at coconuts.

"Come and find me," said Moses, dipping his head and pressing his hands together. Then he moved away towards the sea, leaving six-toed footprints in the sand behind him.

Flower mosaics floated in barrels at the foot of each set of steps; a sunshine of yellow petals in a sea of orchids. Yingyang dragged her suitcase up the steps, sweating in the direct sun. She slotted the key in the lock and pushed the door. The room was dark. She opened the curtains on the far wall and saw the path leading to the other terraces.

The inside of the hut was small; just space for a mattress and a cane chair and table. But Yingyang smiled, because she didn't have to share the room. She didn't have to hide behind a screen, squashed into a corner by other people's cast-offs.

She had a notion, which she was trying hard not to give any time to, that Bristol might have sent her here so that he could follow her.

Somewhere they could be together away from the demands of Jessica's churning moods and Linda's misery. But she had learnt where fantasy could lead, and when she found herself lying back on the mattress and imagining Bristol wading in through the shallows, she sat up and opened her eyes wide.

The uncomfortable mix of excitement and dread that this plan had struck in her was still with her. She felt freer than she could ever have imagined and yet this freedom panicked her. What did you do with freedom? When you didn't have donations to distribute or a crazy mother to protect? When anyone who could tell you how to be was miles away. *I am sixteen and this is the first time I have seen the sea. I have more money in the silk wallet Bristol gave me than I've had in my whole life before.*

And, whilst Yingyang had always thought of herself as weak and worthless, it occurred to her now that she might in fact be quite strong. That she had an unusual ability to rely on herself for company. That she didn't cry like Linda or lash out like Jessica. This bizarre exile that she had brought upon herself was something to explore. To see where it led. It might be the first step out of the fog.

30

"Wake me up before you go go," sang Bristol through gritted teeth. "I don't like it when—"

Two Chinese men and a woman, all in navy suits, nodded their heads and slapped their legs in time to the beat.

"He's good!"

"Yes!" bellowed Sam, over the thud of the backing track and the shouted conversations at the other tables. "We should put his name down again." He stuck up his thumb in the direction of the stage, where Bristol stood grim-faced behind the microphone.

"Take me dancing tonight."

The audience whooped. Bristol hung his head and weaved his way to the table.

"Bastard," he whispered. "Get me a drink."

"Good man!" said the Chinese delegation. "Like George Michael."

Bristol laughed heartily.

"Oh daddy dear, you know you're still number one–"

"Jesus," he muttered and took a deep breath. "So. It's getting late. Shall we retire somewhere quieter?"

Sam deposited a round of tequila slammers on the table. They knocked them back and the woman suggested a small sushi bar she knew.

In the sushi bar, they were the only customers. Faint piped music. No flashing, colour-changing lights; only wall-mounted bulbs with a soft glow. Bristol sat cross-legged at the low table and wiped his face and hands with the cold flannel he was offered.

"So you were impressed by the refurbishments at Tranquillity Place?" said Sam, nodding.

"Excellent standard," nodded the delegation.

"Good. Good."

"When the pool extension is finished, it will be twenty-five metres at its widest point."

"Very wide."

"Excellent facility."

Bite-size tuna rice rolls appeared and a salmon dish covered in sliced ginger.

"As we said, very much the luxury end of the market," continued Sam, cradling his green tea and nodding.

"Our offer is very much open," said the chief navy suit, bowing his head a little.

"Ah."

Sam looked at Bristol, who was looking at the ceiling.

"It is important to us that Tranquillity Place and Summer Towers are left in the right hands," said Bristol. He bowed his head. "Mutual respect," he added.

"Of course," said the woman. "Mutual respect."

Sam sucked a piece of ginger. The rice rolls were dipped in soy and finished. The waitress poured more tea.

Eventually, Bristol said, "Have you had a chance to settle on a figure between yourselves?"

"Same figure," they said, smiling.

In the gents', Sam thumped the condom machine and swore.

"I sang a Wham song," said Bristol. "And it got us nowhere."

"I'll sit at that table all night if–"

"I think it might be an omen," said Bristol quietly. He leant against a basin.

"What?"

"I feel kind of – superstitious – about Summer Towers and Tranquillity Place. They're where we started. Our first major investment. They're like a touchstone. If we–"

"You're drunk," said Sam. "Sentimental drunk."

Bristol picked at a scab on his knuckle. "It balances out. You're getting arsey drunk."

"I'm arsing not."

They laughed stiffly.

"You know what I think?" Sam shoved his hands in his pockets.

"Always," said Bristol. "We've been married long enough."

"I think our builder friend committed suicide in that lift well. He'd had enough shit and he knew it would crush him. What he didn't know is, he was taking us with him."

Bristol said nothing. He washed his hands and opened the door.

"Come on, cuz," he murmured. "Let's see what we can do."

~

As night fell, Moses would come down onto the sand with a young white man and two girls, one Thai and one so dark she might have passed for Thai if it were not for her round eyes. Yingyang watched them make a fire. The young man hung a shirt from a stick to dry in the heat of the flames.

Moses lay on his back with his arms and legs stretched wide. Yingyang crouched in the shadows, watching. Their faces were gold where the firelight hit them. A chain around the man's neck glinted. The girls sucked a joint.

The man in the necklace smiled into the fire. Yingyang wanted to stare at him. The line of his jaw, the glow of his eyes, the spiral on the back of his head where his hair began. Dark chocolate half-curls that caressed his face where they fell. He twisted his chain, brought it to his mouth and sucked on it, laughing softly. He was heavy, his arms and legs chunky and his middle bulging over the waist of his denims.

Yingyang's fingers rubbed together of their own accord. They wanted to touch the chain, trace the line where his hair met his forehead. Liquid warmth spread around her stomach, oozed into her groin.

They spoke in rich undertones that passed between them like the joint; Yingyang felt sound but couldn't make out any words. She watched the young man drink from a coconut, wipe his mouth with his hand, nod at something the Thai girl said.

"Come and join us, silent one," breathed Moses. He was still splayed out on his back, gazing at the stars.

Yingyang held her breath. No one was looking at her. She could turn and run.

A flame pounced, singeing the shirt. The young man pulled the shirt away and crushed the burning corner in his fist. He gasped and licked his hand.

"The lonely girl has come to find us," said Moses, rolling onto his side to face the others. "Look."

He stretched out an arm in Yingyang's direction. Yingyang thought he waved like the King. She laughed behind her hand.

All four of them looked into the darkness at her. She stayed motionless, crouched, her hand over her mouth. The man sucked his chain, squinting, trying to focus after the glare of the fire.

Yingyang's knees hurt.

Moses folded his arms behind his head.

The Thai girl stood, wobbling a little. Her bare feet made delicate footprints in the sand. She was tiny, like a child next to Yingyang.

"We are your friends," said the girl, holding out her hand. Yingyang stood painfully, her knees clicking. She let the girl take her hand and sit her at the fire.

"Hi," said the young man, letting the chain fall from his mouth. He squeezed Yingyang's arm. The fire was hot on her face.

"I am Wendy," said the Thai girl. "This is Laetitia."

Laetitia was slender with very short hair and dark eyes. Looking into Yingyang's face, she passed her the joint. Yingyang inhaled, held the smoke in her mouth like she'd seen them do and counted to five. Then she gasped for breath and they laughed.

"How long have you been in Thailand?" asked the young man, looking sideways at her. Yingyang smiled.

Moses reached around the fire, nearly catching his toga in the flames, and pulled the stick out of the ground.

"Write your name in the sand, silent girl," he said. He held the stick out.

She took it. She smoothed a patch of sand with the side of her hand and wrote *Yingyang*.

Moses' toga trembled. Grains of sand slid off.

"Yingyang?" The word sounded beautiful on his lips. "That's your name?"

She nodded.

Moses knelt beside her and took both her hands. Her fingers were dwarfed by his, swallowed up in his huge palms. She blushed. She hated her thick pink hands; they were clumsy, sweaty, square, dirty. But Moses made them feel beautiful. She didn't want him to let go.

"Much can be taught," he intoned, "by remaining silent."

~

Jessica sat on Yingyang's mattress, staring into the sunbird screen as if it might tell her what to do. Alexis had been obligingly crass when he'd picked Yingyang up in the little minibus he ran the tours in. He strode in the door, lifted her case and said things like, "All set?" and "Allons-y!" Jessica had stood by the window as silent as her daughter, knowing that if she spoke she would cry and not stop. And even she saw that this would not have been fair. Yingyang looked at her and then at Alexis, who held the door open and saluted. And in her face, where there should have been betrayal, Jessica saw only fear. They hadn't touched. And then Yingyang was gone.

Now Jessica was more alone than ever. Sitting in the corner of the room where her daughter had slept and where, years before, Noah had slipped stoically away. The idea that Bristol might now abandon her was so painful and so inevitable. And Sam had had so little to say to her recently, she knew that night would be his last. But she felt the self-pity at a distance; the fury had left her. The seething rage she'd felt when she'd seen in her head an image of Yingyang with Bristol, the violent revulsion that had swamped her mind, had burnt itself out. She was empty, weak, hollow.

"She's better off without me," she said aloud, and curled up with her head on her daughter's pillow. It was almost as if Yingyang had never been; there was so little material evidence of her existence in the world. Most of her life was in her little suitcase. Jessica looked at the notebooks she had left behind, tied up in complicated knots. She stroked a red ribbon with her finger. So many pages, so many words. A tiny puff of laughter came from her lips. Yingyang knew her mother; she hadn't left her stories here on trust.

~

Pippa stood beneath Lazuli's prismatic chandelier, coloured lights dancing on her face and her yellow dress. She let the door shut behind Lazuli and she was alone in Aladdin's cave, breathing in and out a flow of liquid crystal.

Lazuli's voice sounded cold. Whoever had rung the doorbell wasn't welcome. Pippa hoped she wouldn't let them in. She could say she had a client with her, and then they could lie back down on the curved daybeds and sip the wine they'd poured into glasses the size of peonies in full bloom.

"Excuse me but I'm mindful that I don't actually know your name and your manner is making me uncomfortable." Lazuli had taken *Holistic Assertiveness*.

"My sister is here. I know that, and now you take me to her."

Pippa felt a thump deep within her chest. He sounded drunk, aggressive. But she wanted to cry with relief and lie with her head in his lap until she fell asleep.

"Mick?" she said, opening the door and looking into the amber-bathed front hall. "Oh my Mick, my brother."

He was very thin and the skin on his face sagged and puckered so that she was reminded of their grandfather in the days before he died.

Lazuli didn't shut the front door but stood by it as if she was showing him out not letting him in.

"Pippa. How are life, babe? You are looking so grand now in this English clothing." Mick sniffed and wiped his nose with the back of his hand. He smelt of stale cigarettes, sour breath and week-old sweat. His T-shirt was smeared with grease and his jeans were held up with string.

Pippa looked at the wall.

"Shall I ask him to leave?" asked Lazuli.

Pippa shook her head. "No," she whispered. "He is my brother. He brought me to this country. He is my family."

They stood like that for a minute or more; Pippa looking at the wall and blinking, Lazuli with her hands on her hips, biting her lip, and Mick striking a pose with his hands in his pockets and a smirk on his face.

Finally, Lazuli shut the door.

"Drink?"

"Good lady!"

"Tea only," said Pippa, clutching Lazuli's arm. "Perhaps he has been drinking enough."

"My little sister say I drunk enough! Now so much a lady you are the boss!"

"Your English has not improved." Pippa's face was scathing. "What are you doing? Do you have work?"

Mick shrugged. "Garage," he said. "Also delivering."

"Delivering what?" muttered Lazuli. "Come into the kitchen." She shut the door to her living room haven.

Pippa looked at her brother's back as he followed Lazuli to the kitchen. She wanted to wrap her arms around his emaciated middle and rest her head between his shoulders.

He sprawled in the easy chair by the fireplace. Pippa sat stiffly at the table, her hands clamped between her knees, wishing Lazuli would say something – anything – as she pushed cups and teaspoons around the marble worktop.

Mick yawned so widely that the wrinkled skin was pulled taut across the bones of his face. His teeth were yellowed, with black holes where he'd lost some. Pippa felt sick.

"So now," he said. "A beautiful residence." He took the cup from Lazuli and put it on the floor beside him, slopping tea.

"Your hands are shaking," said Pippa flatly.

Lazuli sniffed and sat at the table, sliding a cup towards Pippa. She leaned back, folded her arms and watched the grotesque lizard contaminate her Tranquil Corner.

"How did you find me?" Pippa forced a blankness over her face.

"I find anybody." He bared his teeth and widened his eyes.

Anger rushed from her centre like vomit. "I am not anybody! I am your sister. Look, Pippa!"

"My sister," he smirked, "her name is Piroshka."

Her face was burning hot. Involuntarily, she glanced at Lazuli. "My name is Pippa."

After all these years, her stupid brother, who acted as if he cared about nothing and no one, was going to ruin them both. She wanted to scream, *If I am not Pippa, I am no one! Leave me to the life I have made.*

He shrugged, sticking out his bottom lip and snorting mucus back through his nose to his throat. He swallowed.

"Newspapers, *Pippa*. You have some friends in the newspaper?"

Pippa thought instantly of Eve. Of the party, where she drank sweet orange-flavoured pop until her head became a vortex and she watched her own mind and heard her own voice from far away. She looked into her tea and hung her head.

"You're babbling nonsense, Mick. If you've only come to sneer at us and stink my house out, I'd be grateful if you'd leave now." Lazuli cleared the untouched teacups and tucked her chair squarely under the table.

"I come for see little sister," he said, in a mock-childish voice.

"And now you've seen her, and she's doing very well, so you can go back to whatever hole you emerged from and do whatever you do there."

Mick laughed. "You so funny lady. What you name?"

Pippa clenched her fists. "For God's sake," she hissed. "Are you trying to speak English so badly?"

"You don't need to know my name," said Lazuli crisply. "Now, I must get on. Pippa and I have work to do."

He nodded. "Lot of work. Good ladies. So now…"

Pippa put her head in her hands.

"If you lended me a tenner?" said Mick, standing. The cushion he'd leant back against seemed to shrink away from him.

"Don't." Lazuli glared at Pippa.

"Little sister? I see you soon OK."

Pippa looked up, her blank mask in place. "I will give you some money," she said. "But then you are on your own."

Lazuli put her palm across her forehead. "Pippa. It doesn't work like that. Your brother is taking drugs. Illegal, expensive drugs and if you give him money now he will come back until he has bled you dry."

"I am not stupid," muttered Pippa. "I can see the drugs in his eyes."

"And his skin and his hair and his clothes and his stench. Tell him you'll see him again when he's cleaned up his act."

Mick laughed.

Pippa said, "My bag is in the hall," and led the way out.

"Pippa, listen to me. I lived with an alcoholic for seven years. It only gets worse. Mick doesn't love you, he's not the young boy who was your brother."

Pippa took out her wallet, patent black with a fat silver zip.

"For goodness' sake, Pippa."

"Good girl. Now I buy some food and can look out good job. We stick close, this family." Mick took the money and sauntered away down the path.

Pippa slipped her wallet back into her bag and leant against the jackets hanging on hooks behind her.

"Please say nothing," she whispered. "I am sorry he has come to your house."

Lazuli reached out and drew Pippa to her, saying nothing and hating all men everywhere.

31

For Yingyang, who was used to the sprawling infinity of Bangkok, the island was life on a miniature scale. A shop, a bar, the three terraces of huts; hers, which overlooked the beach and the other two at the foot of the intense green hills.

In front of the shop was a fountain with an enormous ceramic fish spouting water into a pool. The surface of the water was decorated with petals in every colour arranged in the shape of a dragon. And watching over it was a tree sporting fat ripe coconuts and juicy green leaves.

Yingyang watched a young couple enter the shop, speaking a foreign language. They had their arms slung round each other's waists, the man's hand rested on the woman's buttock. They slipped off their shoes at the door and she did the same.

"Sawadee ka," said the assistant, bowing in the wai greeting. She was tightly, roundly pregnant. Yingyang smiled at her.

The foreign couple were examining a shelf of Buddhas. Fat, beaming wax Buddhas, a striped Buddha, a shining bronze one with a long face. The woman stroked the felt one, showed it to the man. He laughed and circled her from behind with his arms, rubbing her stomach.

Yingyang picked up a notebook. The cover had tiny shells sewn into it. She could start a new story. What would she write, now that she was so free? She went to the little till, where the man was paying for the Buddha.

"Where are you from?" asked the pregnant girl in a soft, delicate voice.

"Sweden," said the man. "We also have a baby coming." He gestured at her middle, smiling.

"Same-same," she said, nodding. "*Chok dee ka*," *good luck*.

Yingyang put the notebook on the counter with the money.

"Welcome," said the girl. "See you again."

Moses was asleep. Yingyang watched the rise and fall of his body, the flickering patch of sunlight across his wrist that had broken through the shade of the coconut tree. She wondered what was in his dreams.

A small child turned a cartwheel on the beach. His mother was rubbing the feet of a man talking crossly on the telephone. Her hands moved quickly, expertly, her eyes on her child. Yingyang was never going to have a child of her own. Even thinking about it made her feel she were stood on the very edge of a cliff.

The little boy caught Yingyang's eye and squealed. Yingyang looked away and in that moment she saw the man's torn ear. The man having his feet rubbed was the man she'd arrived on the boat with.

Jessica had never said, "You'll make me a grandmother one day," or even, "your prince will come." She had never once asked Yingyang, "What are you going to do with your life?" And Yingyang had thought about it less than most, because her head was always taken up with keeping Jessica from harm and writing stories. She put her hands over her face, pressing her knuckles into her eyelids until the pictures in her head fragmented. When she opened her eyes, the man with the torn ear was pressing baht into the hands of the masseuse. He was looking in Yingyang's direction. When their eyes met, he gave a fractional nod and looked away. Still she could not scratch the itch in her head that said *you've seen this man somewhere before.*

She scooped a handful of powdery white sand and watched it cascade from her grasp like a million tiny diamonds. In order to live, you needed money, and in order to make money, you needed work. What kind of work could Yingyang possibly do? She would be Bristol's captive for years to come, unless she found a way to make a new life. Which would mean abandoning Jessica. She knew the island wasn't a life; it was an escape, like a dream, but Yingyang wanted to stay asleep just now.

The masseuse lifted her child onto her hip and kissed the top of his head. The little boy didn't react to the kiss, as if he was quite used to them. Yingyang watched them disappear up the path, away from the water. The woman didn't ever look up at the coconuts above her head. Yingyang had to look at them for her. Would it be worse if the child was hit by a coconut or the mother? Would it be better for the coconut to hit them both so that neither had to face that unspeakable loss?

Moses had woken up. He had a visitor. A woman with a black plait halfway down her back and big sunglasses. She knelt in front of him, nodding at something he was saying. He took her hands in his and smiled. Yingyang felt inexplicably jealous of the woman. Moses' smile was like a gift. It was a lazy, quiet smile. He let go of the woman's hands and she hooked wisps of her hair behind her ears, glancing away. After a moment, she stood and walked away down the path, staring straight ahead.

Yingyang sat on the beach, looking at the people with whom she was sharing this secret place. The woman who had given her the key said the guesthouse had not been open long. She meant it as an explanation for the lack of a phone line and running water. There were taps at each end of the terraces, but they didn't work yet. Two men lugged great buckets of water from the sea all day, emptying them into vats. Then people plunged in the tin washbowls provided in their huts and scooped out water so they could wash.

~   .

Jessica found that if she shunted each end of the apothecary's cabinet in turn, she could gradually move it away from the wall. By the time she'd pushed it enough to get behind it, she was sneezing.

The dust had compacted under its own weight, creating a thick wad that ran the length of the cabinet. Spider webs with antique spiders and trapped insects had finally broken as she disturbed them. And a ball of green mould had grown around some unidentifiable scrap of food. She knelt to gaze at the foul display she'd uncovered. She couldn't bring herself to touch the mould-ball, but the wall of dust fascinated her. It stuck to itself; she rolled it and it formed a wheel.

She tore lengths of the tape she used for sealing the Phetbin boxes and stuck them to the wall, ripping filth off in satisfying strips. Her nails grew black underneath the chipped red varnish and she smudged her face wiping her nose.

And then someone knocked at the door. She considered staying where she was, hidden behind the cabinet.

"You're in."

Bristol. She let out a long breath.

"OK. I'll go."

She jumped up and opened the door. He looked tired; his eyes were dull. It made her feel insecure, unbalanced.

"How are you?" she said.

"Stress on all sides. I've been trying to practice mindfulness. I read a leaflet about it. But there's a part of my brain that won't stop for mindlessness – mindfulness – whatever. Anyway."

They looked at each other for a while.

Then Jessica said, "I thought–"

"Thought what?"

"I thought you'd never come. That you were so angry, or guilty, or – whatever. Anyway."

"No guilt. I did nothing. I wish you'd believe that."

She sneezed and rubbed her nose.

"You're cleaning." Bristol looked stunned.

"Yes. I'm going to categorise Noah's remedies."

"Jessica, they're fossilised. He's been dead ten years."

"Longer. They don't go off."

"Not like the rest of us then. Can I come in?"

She stepped back, drawing herself in so that they wouldn't touch as he passed. He sat on the floor opposite the cabinet, rubbing his back against the wall.

"So. How are you?" he said.

"That sounds more like a reprimand than a question."

He shook his head.

"No, sweetheart. I gave up trying to get you to behave years ago."

Jessica slumped down against the opposite wall and put her hand to her forehead.

"I'm horrible, aren't I? Don't answer that."

"Look," he said, scratching vigorously behind his ears. "Yingyang needed to get away from us. From you. She's sixteen, she needs to work out what she wants from life. I just wish we'd thought this through before–"

"Don't say it!"

"There's nothing to say. Nothing happened except a confused little girl – young lady. Maybe something inside her wanted to rock the boat, to be sent away."

"She was always free to go where she wanted. She didn't need to be *sent* away."

"Jessica Jane," sighed Bristol. "Yingyang would never have left of her own accord. The poor kid became your minder the minute she was born."

"That's not true! How dare you?"

Bristol raised his eyebrows and she fell silent.

"She's terrified," he said. "She made me promise to check on you every day."

Jessica looked up sharply.

"Well you broke that promise straight off."

"You look funny when you pout. And I didn't break my promise. I have my spies. I'd know if you were dancing on the roof."

Suddenly, Jessica was sobbing. She cried until she gagged, her shoulders shuddering and her fists clenched. Bristol waited, watching her from across the room.

"I should–" she said at last, spitting the words out.

"Ssh," murmured Bristol, looking at his watch. "Yingyang's fine on Bamboo Grove. I have it covered. She'll love it."

Jessica stopped crying and scowled.

"I should have had her adopted," she said. "It was so so selfish to keep her. I'm more of a curse than a mother."

Bristol shook his head.

"It's a close-run thing," he said, "but on balance... well, she's unique. She has a future ahead of her – she could maybe make a living out of all that writing." He looked at the notebooks by the screen, their ribbons lying loose. "What's it like? Is it good?"

Jessica bit her lip.

"I haven't really read much."

"Bullshit. I bet you had your paws on them before she was at the bottom of the steps."

She shrugged. She gestured at the notebooks.

"Her stories are incredible," she said quietly. "There are whole lives in there."

Bristol nodded. "Wow."

Jessica laughed.

"Including yours."

His eyes widened.

"And mine." She swallowed. "I can see why she's kept them secret."

Bristol laughed, but then he sat on his hands and gritted his teeth. Jessica put her head on one side.

"I can give you something for the itching."

He smiled.

"What I need," he said, "is something for damaged Feng Shui."

Slowly, she came to sit near him, legs crossed, arranging her skirt to hide her knickers.

He gave in and scratched his knees through his trouser legs. She pulled in her tummy and sat up straighter. There was the rumble of talking on the stairs outside.

"Does mindfulness not work for psoriasis?" she whispered. He smiled again. "Is the Feng Shui problem home or work?"

He stretched out his arms in front of him and then sat on his hands again.

"Feng Shui deserted me domestically long ago," he sighed. "I must have the mirrors on the wrong wall or something. No, it's Emerald City. The poor bugger who passed away in the lift well has – contaminated – Eastern Vision."

"Passed away? That sounds rather peaceful."

"It sounds more sensitive than 'crushed to death'."

Jessica reached behind her for a bottle of Coke and slugged some back. She passed it to him.

"We have to free up capital." He tipped his head back and drank half the Coke in one go. "But what we've been offered for Tranquillity Place and Summer Towers won't get us anywhere. As if paying less makes up for the bad fortune that comes with the deal."

Shuffling closer, Jessica took Bristol's right arm and began to massage it gently. He rested his head back on the wall.

"You seem well, considering," he said, closing his eyes.

She rubbed his thumb and then pulled it, cracking the knuckle. She started on his index finger.

"I've been taking something I bought in Chinatown."

Bristol opened his eyes and frowned at her. She clicked his index finger.

"Don't look at me like that. It's doing me good."

He squeezed her hand.

"Jessica. Next week you'll be screaming for valium. You know this herbal shit is no use."

Jessica snatched her hand away.

"I'm fine. I've got my head straight. I will not be 'screaming for valium'."

He finished the Coke.

"You have so many personalities it's scary to come near you. I never know who I'll find."

"*Me*. You'll find *me*. And you do come, so I can't be that scary."

He stood.

"I have to go. Just promise me you will take your lithium."

She looked up and scrambled to her feet.

"Really," he said. "I have to get back to the office. Sam will be making me do karaoke again if I don't come up with something. Now be a good girl and take your tablets."

~

Pippa wore huge earrings, white jeans, tan suede pumps and a pale gold T-shirt. And the sun did her the favour of shining through the front of the shop so that her stock was bathed in light.

"OK, good. If we could just have you looking at the scarves. Drape the blue over your arm – and – look at me – glance over your shoulder."

The door tinkled and the photographer jumped, fluffing his shot.

"Oh Good Lord, I'm interrupting!"

It was Lazuli, beads swinging and petticoats swishing. She held up a hand. "I'll leave you to it, shall I?"

The photographer scrolled through his shots.

"No stay. We can be beautiful together for the magazine." Pippa folded the scarf back onto the pile and scrunched her hair. Now it was layered, she had to use mousse and muss it up from time to time – it was in fact harder to keep messy messy than sleek sleek.

"Oh, well, if you insist!" Lazuli slipped off the uppermost of her pashminas.

"Marina is not coming, she has a wedding catastrophe," said Pippa. "So it would be good to have you here."

"Well, then. Where do you want me?"

Pippa laughed. "We are at your mercy," she told the photographer.

He coughed.

"Yes. Right. Well, ladies, maybe if – I'm sorry, I don't know your name?"

"Lazuli."

"If you could stand behind the till there. And Pippa, we'll put you here by the jewellery, and you can look as if you're calling across an instruction or something."

The part of Lazuli's neck that showed above her shawls went blotchy.

"OK," she said. "Fine," and she positioned herself as elegantly as she could at the cash desk.

~

Yingyang lay on her front and opened her notebook. She stared at the sea, letting it wink at her until her eyes dazzled.

She drew a chain with fragile little links, in the exact curve that the necklace had fallen round the man's neck. She wrote that his eyes were the colour of the sea. She wrote that he was here because his heart was broken. And her fingers twitched remembering the careless way his hair framed his face. Chocolate. Dark chocolate hair. How she'd wanted to stroke it, put a finger through a curl.

The stretch of her body felt good on the sand. She slid her hand under her middle, pressing her palm into her stomach.

Suddenly, she knew he was there. On the beach. The man with the necklace. She had one hand on her notebook and one holding her stomach. She could rest her forehead down slowly and pretend to be asleep. But what if he'd already seen her? He'd think she was ridiculous. Maybe he'd seen her edge her hand underneath herself and sigh. She swallowed.

He waved. He wore the same collarless shirt with the singed corner that had hung by the fire, and a pair of faded sawn-offs. If she blurred her eyes, Yingyang could make him disappear, blend him into the dazzle of the sea behind him.

He came towards her. His feet were bare, coated in sand. She moved only to shut her notebook. He dropped to his knees in front of her and the palm tree embraced him in its shade. Yingyang swallowed again. The hand underneath her felt squashed. She wanted to move.

He put his head on one side, looking at her, and a smile flickered on her face. Then he lay down beside her and smoothed a patch of sand with the side of his hand. *Joe*, he wrote.

Joe. Yingyang drew a circle around his name.

32

Alexis lay on the office sofa with his eyes shut, replaying the previous night in his head. That delicious boy had been waiting for him; he'd seen it in his eyes. For a week, Alexis had stayed away from Patpong, imagining the boy dreaming of him as he stood on the balcony overlooking the throngs of people. He would accept work, other men, other women maybe, but it would be only to fill his pockets with baht. Alexis knew that what he really wanted, what ate away at his insides, was to be with him every night. So he stayed away. He counted nights. Tuesday, Wednesday, Thursday, Friday. And then on Saturday, he sauntered into the bar, ordered a drink, flirted with a dancer, and all the time he felt those deep brown eyes on him. The boy sulked. He slumped against the balcony and got kicked by the bar manager.

Alexis breathed deeply, rolling onto his side on the office sofa, remembering the boy's face as he finally approached. Wordlessly, he'd wrapped his arms around his waist and steered him into an alcove.

"Mister Lexis!" There was banging on the door.

He crossed quickly to the desk and grabbed a file.

"Come in."

It was Tina from reception.

"Escu' me. Is problem. Big problem coming."

Alexis looked up slowly from the file. "Nothing the Eastern Vision empire can't handle, I'm sure."

She sucked her lips as if she was trying to stop the words coming out. "I work Easter' Vision many year. Very good company."

"And you are a loyal employee." Alexis smiled paternally, though she was several years older than him.

"Mister Lexis, my cousin work in City Government. He make to me telephone." Again, she seemed to swallow her own lips as the words formed.

Alexis frowned. Where was Sam when he was needed? And Bristol was no doubt drip-feeding valium into the mad witch from Surrey.

"What's the matter, Tina?"

She glanced behind her at the door and her hands formed a wai of their own accord. "He say me Summer Towers and Tranquillity Place buildings must be – demolish. Land for some new building." Her chin was on her chest now, her palms pressed tight.

"Tina, Eastern Vision built the apartments because they bought the land. The city fathers can't just have it back when it suits them."

Tina gave a minute shrug and began to back out, still in her cowering wai.

"Wait. What exactly did your cousin say?"

"Not my cousin fault. He see email. He want tell us quick. They say papers wrong, land not belong Easter' Vision."

Reaching behind her for the handle, pushing the door open with her bottom, she bowed out.

Alexis put his hand on the telephone and took it off again. He clicked down the inbox on the computer screen. He rammed his hands in his pockets and stood by the window-wall, grinding his teeth a little. He wished very hard that Sam or Bristol had received this news first.

~

Jessica carried the box up the steps, her swollen feet painful in her battered red heels. There was a new family, fresh from Holland, delighted to give her a plastic crate of toys and toilet rolls. She wondered if it was tactless, giving people toilet rolls and plastic tea sets when they were about to lose their homes.

Easing the box down by her door, she felt in her jeans pocket for her key. Before she could put it in the lock, the door opened and Bristol said, "Let me carry that for you."

She let him take the box, standing with the key still held out.

"Since when did you have a key to my apartment?"

"I cut it years ago, Jess. I've let myself in God knows how many times when you've been comatose. You've just never thought to ask."

She went inside and opened the drawer of the apothecary cabinet. It was back against the wall.

"Lithium," said Bristol.

She rummaged in the drawer as though he hadn't spoken.

"This is a tedious game, beautiful."

She smiled and looked up.

"Where have you hidden it this time?"

"Kiss me and I'll show you."

"Jess."

"I think I left it in my knickers."

Bristol laughed. "Trollop," he said.

"Bastard."

"You promised me you'd take lithium."

"You've made promises to me along the way and I can't see those going anywhere."

"Jess."

"Stop saying my name like I'm a particularly tiresome puppy."

She caught his eye. They both gave a little snort.

"You look shifty," he said. "And you're a touch too full of yourself."

"Shiftiness is in the eye of the beholder, mister. And it's nice to be full of myself. It makes a change from self-disgust, suicidal thoughts and so on."

"Jessica. Give me strength."

"OK. I'll give you a massage."

"No, gorgeous, I have to go. We are Having A Crisis."

241

"Sounds dramatic."

"Tragedy not comedy."

"Don't look so tense. Sit. I'll just rub your shoulders a bit."

She glared at him until he sat on the beanbag. Jess arranged herself behind him, her legs resting against his backside. She used her knuckles on his shoulder blades, pummelling and thumping. She rubbed his neck and he dropped his head a little.

"Mm."

"Take your shirt off."

"Er, no."

"Then I can use oils."

"Jess, my psoriasis is not good. Oils would make it worse."

"No oils."

"I don't want you to see my arms, OK? Leave it. I have to go."

He stood up, rolling his shoulders, reaching for his jacket.

"I still didn't take my lithium."

Bristol gritted his teeth. "So take it. I have trillions of baht to lose if I don't at least try to sort out this crisis."

Jessica sighed and went into her bedroom. "Money's more important to you than I am."

"Don't," he said. "Just swallow the stuff so I can go."

"It makes me thirsty."

"So drink more."

"I have to wee. All the time. It's hard when I go out. And I'm getting so fat. Look, middle-age spread. Am I middle-aged?"

He grabbed the packet from her hand, popped two tablets from their little pockets and squeezed her cheeks until her mouth opened.

She giggled. "Pass me that Coke," she said, the tablets still on her tongue. "I don't know why I need these. I'm not mad any more. No madder than you."

When she'd swallowed the tablets, she took his hands. "Before you go," she said, "I want to tell you something. You don't have to reply. Just let me say it."

"Best not. You don't have to say everything that comes into your head."

"I have to say this. It's bursting my mind and I'll explode if I don't let it out."

"I'm going. I might see you tomorrow. Sort the stuff out. You've got a backlog here and a slumful of needy causes waiting for you."

"I love you. More than Linda does."

Bristol raised his hand to push her away but instead he stroked her face. "I know," he said. "I've always known."

~

Pretty-as-a-picture Pippa checks the displays in her Gypsy Magic boutique.

She looked wider than she would have liked, in the main picture. But her hair was fantastic. A touch of wild chic.

"So we have now some satisfactionry coverage," she said, laying out the magazine on the counter. "Look at this one! *Pippa's assistants are in awe of her success and look to her as a mentor.* Lazuli will be so cross, it's right under her picture!"

Marina laughed briefly, stiffly.

Pippa looked at her, sighing.

"In fact," she said, "It's for the best. He wasn't right for you."

Marina began to cry again. After a while, she said, "He was better than your bloody brother."

Pippa went over to a rail of skirts and separated them so that the distance between each was exactly the same.

A young couple came into the shop without acknowledging them, and walked silently around the displays. Yawning, the girl turned over a brightly painted teapot and glanced at the price sticker.

When they'd gone, Pippa said, "He texted me. He asked me how you are."

Marina grunted.

"I hope you told him I have no drugs in my house."

"He knows that. We have told him many times."

Marina kicked the cash desk.

"I wish…"

Pippa left the skirts and leant on the counter.

"What do you wish, pretty friend?"

Marina shook her head.

"Nothing, pretty, kind, clever friend."

They held each other as close as they could, considering there was a cash desk between them.

"Perhaps," said Pippa carefully, "you could marry Moses instead?"

When the next customer pushed open the door, she found the two shop assistants snorting and trying to catch their breath.

~

Moses borrowed a boat. In the dark of late night, under the stars, they all swam out and climbed in. They stood dripping on the little deck, the five of them squashed up together.

Yingyang looked down at her chest. Her T-shirt was slicked to the bulges of her breasts and stomach. Her nipples looked like drawing pins.

Wendy laughed softly, hooking a strand of hair behind Yingyang's ear. Her finger felt like velvet. Five people could fit easily on the little speedboat, sitting down. But as they were all standing up, they were very cramped. Laetitia sighed and tipped back her head to look at the stars.

They settled themselves along the padded benches on either side and Moses flicked a knot on his shoulder so that his toga fell to the deck. His penis was hard and tall. He adjusted his swinging testicles.

Yingyang tried not to stare. She looked out to sea, into the blackness where the water met the sky. Moses steered away from the shore. The boat moved so slowly that only a triangle of water rippled out from beneath it. Wendy and Laetitia trailed their hands in the water. Joe lay on his back on the prow.

Yingyang sat in her wet clothes, shivering.

"You'll dry quicker if you take them off," said Moses, scrunching his pubic hair with his free hand.

Yingyang blinked at him. She wasn't sure if he was joking.

Laetitia wrapped her arms around Wendy and began to kiss her. They wound their hands in each other's hair. Yingyang watched, her breathing growing deeper.

Moses cut the engine. Joe sprang up and passed the long, heavy anchor chain through his hands. They were alongside another island, only about a hundred yards wide, where there were no other boats. Shingle shone like jewels in the moonlight. A steep cliff towered over the tiny wisp of beach, and up above trees grew thickly.

The girls slid each other's clothes off, kissing, murmuring. Moses sat on the deck in the lotus position and watched, his hand idly on his penis.

Joe took Yingyang's hand.

"Here," he said, "come with me."

Yingyang stared at him.

"The beach, we can wade in." He blushed. "You thought I meant – God, no. Sorry." He laughed.

Yingyang smiled. She liked the warmth that had spread underneath her wet clothes. Joe dropped into the water. He held up a hand for her to take. She stepped off and stubbed her toes.

"OK?"

They waded in, their thighs shunting water ahead of them.

"Don't put your feet down too heavily. It's worth feeling about a bit."

She stumbled. He caught her before she fell and she grasped his arm. She felt stupid, dragging her whole weight on him like that.

"This island belongs to the animals at night," he said. He sat down, wedging himself into a curve in the rock at the foot of the cliff.

Yingyang looked up into the dark tangle of trees above them. A shadow-play of creatures swung in the branches, chased each other through the undergrowth and snatched at invisible prey.

"People come here in the day, mostly for diving." Joe lit a cigarette.

The sea was treacle-black from where they stood. The boat shifted gently on ripples in the water.

"Underneath," he said, "it's magical." He blew a stream of smoke, his mouth a perfect 'O'. "The colours are delicious. Like stained glass."

She blinked at him.

"We'll go diving," he said, "on Christmas day. Is that a deal?"

Yingyang had never smoked until the joint they gave her on the beach. She watched the spark move and the way Joe's face was lit up when he brought it to his lips.

"What is it?" he said.

She squatted in front of him, reached out her hand and took the cigarette. His fingers stayed stranded in the air where he'd held it. She inhaled, coughed a little, laughed'softly. She sucked again, threw her head back and blew the smoke into the air.

Joe brushed his fingers along the back of her hand.

"Your laugh," he whispered, "what a beautiful sound."

Yingyang blinked. The thrill of his touch sent her skin flickering, wanting to be touched again. She twisted her hand round and held the cigarette to his mouth. He closed his lips around it, inhaled, took it back between his own fingers. She didn't move away, so that her hand cupped his for a moment.

Yingyang knew that she would remember this. She would watch it over and over behind her eyes, stroking her fingers over her hands to feel his touch again.

33

Jessica had washed and left the house with wet hair, but she hadn't gone a hundred yards before sweat was sliding down her face and underneath her clothes. Her thighs rubbed together; she felt elephantine, a waddling giant beside the miniature beauty of two women in skirt suits, giggling over the screen of a mobile phone.

She felt calmer than she had since Yingyang left. As so often after the storm, the self-disgust had followed. To be so jealous of her own daughter's youth, her virgin sexuality, her self-possession. It was revolting. But now her thoughts began to shunt themselves heavily, slowly, into some sort of order. She had a sense that her foul jealousy might in fact bring about something positive. Yingyang needed her freedom, deserved to grow up without her mother's stifling instability.

She walked faster in the intolerable heat, stamping out the rising self-pity with thoughts of the eviction. The slum clearance. She felt a new urgency to do – what? To stand spread-eagled in the path of the bulldozers? She slapped a mosquito on her hand. Sleep with whoever was in control of such things? She closed her eyes and steadied her breathing. Poey. Little Mai. Orphans, widows, people with so much less than she had ever had, despite herself. And they still woke up every day to work or beg for their bowl of noodles. These proud people were about to lose their homes.

With a pocketful of condoms for Poey and change for the children of the broom seller, she stood at the entrance to the alley. The invisible slot in the street, where one world gave way to another. Three young men swaggered towards her, nudging each other. They stopped; grouped around her, grinning.

"Sawadee ka," she said, smiling back.

"Where you go, Khun Jess'cah?"

"Nowhere," she sighed. "Maybe I'll go and see Poey. And look in on Toi's grandmother. Toi's so busy with college, I think she's a bit lonely up there."

Jessica knew they'd lost the thread of what she was saying, but it was a relief to be speaking at all after her guilt-ridden retreat.

"Have a nice day," they said, and wai-ed and winked before ducking into the alley.

She'd seen them grow from naked babies. Played with them by the spirit house in the little space by the khlong. They knew their homes were about to be destroyed and they were laughing. Jessica walked slowly down the alley, chewing the inside of her mouth.

~

Pippa struggled into the rainbow office with a large cardboard box newly delivered from the factory, slit the tape with the floral Stanley knife and sighed. She rummaged amongst the contents; packs of tarot cards, crystal balls, strings of beads, fabric posies. She was gazing into a turquoise crystal ball when she heard someone stamping up the stairs outside.

Marina shoved open the rainbow door. Before Pippa could look up, she shouted, "Your bloody bloody brother!" Pippa gripped the box. "He came to my home when Sasha was there, full of drugs. My son was there! That man swore and spat and fell over where my son could see and hear. He said I owed him money from before, that when we were together he got nothing from me. He said if I would not give him money, he would take it."

Pippa's head was in her hands. "I am sorry. Sorry sorry. Sasha should not see such things."

"I know you are so upset, Pips. But my first importance is my son. You tell your bastard brother if he comes again to my house I will ring the police."

Pippa jumped. "Marina, please. If you ring the police I'll end up being sent back to–"

"I thought you wanted to go home?"

"Not like a prisoner. Marina, please."

Marina huffed, scooping a handful of crystals from a wide golden platter. "I pick the wrong men."

"You are feeling sad at the moment," said Pippa to the floor. "But that is because of a different man. Not because of Mick."

"No drugs in my house," said Marina. Pippa put a pack of tarot cards on top of another as if this needed doing. Marina balanced crystals on her palms. Red, yellow, purple, black, green, blue. "Have you ever believed this crap? If I give you these crystals in a bag, will you select the one that helps you most?"

"I will try anything just now. My brother is 'bleeding me dry'. That is what Lazuli told me. And you forget – maybe I also forget – that I was born in the Romanian countryside where gypsy magic is normal. So maybe yes. Maybe I believe the crap."

"So take a crystal."

"Marina," Pippa rubbed the back of her hand across her nose.

"Go on, take one."

"Crystals are for healing," murmured Pippa.

"So we can heal your bloody brother? Too late. We'll heal ourselves."

Pippa let her eyes blur as she looked at the crystals. Her hand reached out.

Black.

"Black," she said. "*New beginnings after natural endings.* So what?"

The office smelt mustier than ever. As if the walls were growing mould in lonely protest.

"I don't know, Pippa." Marina swirled her finger amongst the crystals. "Perhaps black has another meaning."

Pippa threw her crystal back amongst the rest. She sighed. "If he comes back, I'll tell him to stay far away from you and Sasha. I'll threaten him with the police. OK?"

~

She could hear the baby crying. Maybe one of the nurses had taken her away again. They didn't think she was capable of caring for a baby; they said she couldn't even care for herself. But she was going to show them all. Jessica Jane could be a mother to all children. She already had Yim Sao holding her hand and following her in the slum where she was going to change the world. And now she had her own little baby; so tiny, born before she was ready but she was strong. Jessica rolled over in bed, feeling the familiar surge in her breasts of milk they wouldn't let her use because they said it was poisoned. She'd find the baby. She pushed herself up and staggered out of bed in the dark. She had been thinking of names. She'd asked Noah, when the child was still safe inside her, what she should call it. And Noah had told her with a smile that babies chose their own names.

And now the little girl was here and an idea was forming in Jessica's mind, as if the child really had put it there.

"Yingyang?" she called. "Yingyang! I'm here and I will feed you. My milk cannot be poisonous. It is the most natural food you can have."

She found the door with her hands and pushed it open, a soft smile on her face. But this room wasn't so dark and through the windows the moon lit only a silk screen where a lonely sunbird waited patiently below silver branches.

Jessica was awake now. There was no sweet little nurse folding blankets and shaking bottles. Only a vast apothecary cabinet full of medicines that had lost their magic the day Noah died.

"I'm sorry," whispered Jessica, cold and suddenly thirsty. She found a bottle of lemonade with no lid and drank the flat sweetness. Then she lay on the mattress behind the screen, remembering the smell of Yingyang's head when she was new and softly furry.

~

"In conclusion, Fortune Hotels is unique in this way. Unlike our competitors, and as I have demonstrated, each of our hotels is designed to merge with the space it fills, to become a part of the – I'll use the word 'growth' rather than 'development' – of the area. We are excited by Bamboo Grove. We can make that island the Eastern Vision paradise you envisage and we will work in close collaboration so that the expertise of our two organisations is combined to maximum effect."

The immaculately-suited young English man clicked off his PowerPoint and actually made a wai gesture. He clearly hadn't quite decided on this one and he came up reddening a little.

Sam leant back and folded his arms behind his head. He'd visited Fortunes in Italy and Provence, and he knew that they saw Bamboo Grove as their ticket to South East Asia and beyond. They had plans for Kenya on the backburner.

Alexis raised his eyebrows. If they signed with Fortune today and Bamboo Grove was sorted, he could tell Sam and Bristol what Tina had found out about the luxury condoms. Beside him, Bristol checked the screen on his phone.

"Perhaps you could leave us for a moment before we continue?" said Sam, pushing back his chair. "Tina will find you some tea."

Alexis showed the young man out. As the door shut behind them, he said, "Wink and a nudge, mate, I'm gunning for you."

"Thanks." He'd dropped his presentation voice. "If I secure this, I'll climb the final rung, if you see what I mean."

Alexis slapped his back, looking at his bum. "Tina, would you serve this gentleman some tea, please?"

Back in the boardroom beside the office, Sam was on the phone.

"Shit, I know she's no angel. This is not news. But we're on the verge of signing the Bamboo Grove contract and you know more than anyone how much time and money has gone into this."

Bristol looked at his watch. Alexis flicked through the Fortune brochure.

"No, not under our roof, I appreciate that. But if she's started sleeping with him she's not going to stop now." Standing at the window, Sam sighed and picked some wax from his ear. "A bastard. I know. AIDS? I'd kill him. She's more intelligent than that. Look, I'll call you. All right, I'll call her." He threw the phone on the table and leaned forwards on the back of a chair. "So. We're a long way down the line with Fortune. Reasons to continue, reasons to pull back."

Bristol doodled on the sheaf of notes in front of him. "Well, we have time to negotiate their dubious marketing strategies and they seem open to collaboration. You've been fairly convinced by the actual establishments, Sam?"

Sam's mobile made a drum roll on the table.

"Shit," he said, grabbing it. "Yes?"

Alexis flattened the spine on the brochure to look at the artist's impression.

"Tilly," said Sam. "I am in a meeting." He held up a finger, mouthing, "One minute."

Bristol nodded, staring out of the window.

"I realise she is not your mother. To all intents and purposes, however, she is your stepmother. It will get you nowhere to— No, you're right. It's your business and your business only. But not if you flaunt it in everyone's faces. Tilly?" He turned the phone off. "Sorry. Right. Phone's off."

When the contract was signed, and the Fortune rep had been shown out with his laptop and a barely suppressed grin on his face, Alexis began to chew his lip.

Bristol rubbed Sam's shoulders.

"The women in your life making waves?"

"Tilly's latest boyfriend is a twenty-nine year old shithole who seems to want to move in with us."

"Great."

"However. Fortune. Signed, sealed. Bamboo Grove can begin once Christmas is over and done with."

"Sam," said Alexis. "Bristol. Could we have a quick word on an unrelated matter?"

"Fire ahead."

"Probably nothing. Storm in teacup."

"But?"

"Tina has a cousin who works in administration in City Government. She tells me— He's apparently seen an email. Probably nothing."

"For fuck's sake, Alexis." Sam checked his watch.

Bristol looked at his cousin. "Do you wonder," he said softly, "when we, how we, got like this? We used to be so – careless – in the way we spoke. And now we snap like our gorgeous wives." He punched Sam's arm. They laughed. "Except you're not actually married to yours, you lucky bastard."

"Might as well be. Alexis, you were saying."

"Right. Yes." Alexis ran his hand over his freshly-clippered hair. "There's some nonsense," he said, "to do with ownership of land."

"Bamboo Grove?" It was hard to tell if Sam or Bristol spoke these words as their faces froze in unison, and the fists they clenched on the table formed a symmetry.

"No, no, obviously I wouldn't have – God no, Bamboo Grove is *sorted*. Signed, sealed, delivered. The question mark seems to be hovering over Tranquillity Place and Summer Towers."

Bristol frowned at Sam. "What fucking question mark? Will you stop being so fucking gay and tell us what you've heard."

Alexis pouted. "Bristol, I realise you have issues of your own to deal with. I will let that remark pass and flutter over my head without a ripple."

Sam sighed. "Now you're putting it on. Bristol, sit down. Let's hear about this."

"The email said that the land on which the luxury condominiums are built does not legally belong to Eastern Vision. So we cannot sell them. As such." He coughed. "The authorities plan to bulldoze them to the ground and sell the land."

Neither cousin spoke. They stared at Alexis, and then at the table. Finally, they looked at each other.

"We have the documents," said Sam.

"Can they do this?" said Bristol, twisting his signet ring, revealing a patch of raw white skin underneath.

Sam said, "You completed. The week after–"

"Anna died. Yes, I did. On Tranquillity Place. You were more compos mentis by the time we secured for Summer Towers."

"A friend of mine," said Alexis, his voice squeaking a little from the cough stuck in his throat, "tells me there are precedents. The authorities effectively can do what they like. If they claim the land is theirs, we'd be mad to take them on."

~

"Clarify the dynamic of your being," said Moses.

Wendy opened one eye. Everyone else seemed to be clarifying their beings so she shut it again and tried harder.

"Elongate your spine," murmured Moses, "and let the sound come from deep within your core."

Wendy waited. She wasn't sure what sound her core would make if she left it to its own devices. As the others hummed uncertainly from deep within their cores, she opened her eyes.

Yingyang and Joe were side by side, Yingyang breathing slowly out while Joe produced an endless 'Om'. Laetitia sat across the little circle, between Moses and Joe. Her hair had gradually bleached in the sun and her face was as bronzed as if she had been born Thai.

Her body was as lean as a boy's but for her little round breasts. The faded vest she wore had slipped as she elongated her spine and Wendy could see almost down to her nipples.

"Feel the shift in gravity as your perineum begins to elevate."

Wendy swallowed a laugh and immediately began to hiccup. Joe's mouth quivered. Laetitia was concentrating so intensely her face was puckered with the effort. But Yingyang's face was soft and she seemed far away. Wendy hiccupped into her fist and felt suddenly jealous of Yingyang's serenity. She thought how easy it must be not to speak, to shut yourself off from where you didn't want to be. She sometimes felt that Yingyang was deaf when she chose as well as mute.

With his legs still pleated and his eyes still closed, Moses bent backwards and lay flat on the sand. Joe stretched his arms up towards the sky and grinned. He let out a long sigh and winked at Wendy.

Laetitia put her head in her hands. Her shoulders shook.

"'Titia?" said Wendy, stifling a hiccup. She reached out to her, but Laetitia scrambled to her feet and ran towards the huts. Wendy stood, biting the back of her hand.

"Leave her," whispered Moses without opening his eyes. "Meditation connects us with a universal wisdom that can shift our sense of self. It would seem that Laetitia is undergoing a process of internal change."

"For fuck's sake, Moses," snapped Wendy, "you can't see inside her head. I know you make up most of this shit."

Yingyang opened her eyes and blinked. Joe rubbed the nape of her neck and smiled gently.

34

"I think I need a fag."

Pippa and Marina looked at each other's reflections in the endless mirror.

"I have never seen you smoke," said Marina.

"Look up at me and hold still." The makeup girl brandished a red-gold lipstick. "Relax your lips. You don't need to pucker, that's right."

"I never smoke," said Pippa. "But today I feel so scared my hands are shaking. Look."

"You. Will. Be. So. Fine," said the makeup girl. "You look stunning and your accent is beautiful."

The tannoy buzzed as an advert break began. "Gypsy Magic to the sofa. Gypsy Magic to the sofa."

"I might wet myself," mouthed Marina into the mirror.

The sofa was a smooth arc of squashy red leather. Glimpsing herself on the monitor, Pippa rolled her shoulders back and sat up straighter. Marina wiped her nose repeatedly, suddenly panicked that she had a speck of snot on view.

"Sorry, could I adjust your mic?"

He was down on one knee, reaching up to the ruffled edge of Pippa's blouse. As he unclipped the little microphone, his knuckle brushed her décolletage. She looked down on his gently spiked, softly greying hair and knew suddenly what was meant by an aura. Thought temporarily suspended by nerves, she leant forward and kissed the top of his head.

The studio audience went wild. They whistled, stamped, applauded and laughed so that as the broadcast resumed they appeared to be welcoming the red sofa guests as no guests had been welcomed before.

Pippa and the sound technician looked into each other's eyes for less than a second. Pippa began to analyse the look, to replay her bizarre action, even as the presenters spoke her name and the noise from the audience subsided.

"Gypsy Magic really is an overnight sensation! You must be dazzled by the sudden glow of the media spotlight?"

She'd been told they'd start with, *Tell us what Gypsy Magic is all about,* and she was going to say, *Blazing a trail in style, design and ethical trade.* Eve had written it on a card and she had it in her pocket. The sound technician was still there, just to one side of the set. She couldn't see him but his aura was very much still present, mesmerising.

"Thank you," said Marina. "We are so pleased to be here. However, like other overnight sensations, we have been working for many years." She smiled humbly, shyly, and the presenters nodded.

"Absolutely. I'm sure many celebrities would attest to that."

"Celebrities!" Marina nudged Pippa, partly to shock her into speaking.

The man with the plucked eyebrows laughed heartily.

"So," he said, "what's Gypsy Magic all about?" He settled himself into the sofa, angling himself slightly in Marina's direction.

"Oh yes," said Pippa. "Blazing a trail in style, design and ethics."

The woman reached for her water glass; a translucent blue globe that might have been a tea light holder.

"Indeed," she said. "And this is a winning combination. Women can wear unique outfits and accessories and be part of an exciting new partnership between East and West Europe."

"However," said Marina, her shy smile in place, "now there is no East and West but only Europe."

~

Jessica watched her thoughts break apart and rearrange themselves in a nauseous kaleidoscope effect. She was disappointed, because she had been, as Bristol remarked, 'impressively rational' for a while. But, as always when the scribble-thoughts set in, it felt now as if this was all she ever knew. Those times when she thought more clearly, saw the world in focus, breathed without thinking about it, seemed impossible. She had been taking lithium. Most days. She'd been, all things, considered, remarkably adult for someone so far off forty. And she was to be rewarded with a great wave of bleakness and confusion.

She saw her feet shuffling around the apartment, from window to door to the apothecary cabinet that was gathering fresh dust already. She watched her fingers open and shut the tiny drawers, fussing with the charms that hung from each handle. She touched every jug, every bottle on every shelf, wondering what she was looking for until she found a packet of disposable razors she had bought from Phin's garage shop. She shaved her legs, her toes, the hard skin on her feet. She shaved her armpits and then her arms. For a while, she held the razor over her head. But there was enough of her mind still intact to leave her hair untouched.

Rapid-cycling. That's what they'd called it, in her old life, the life she hardly thought about. She had a memory of her mother telling her father, "She's rapid-cycling," and Geoff peering at his newspaper as if she hadn't spoken.

~

No East or West but only Europe:

The ethos of Gypsy Magic transcends fashion, enterprise and even their innovative production and distribution processes. An air of mystery surrounds effervescent, quirky directors Pippa and Marina, who go only by their first names and will not be drawn on their work pre-Gypsy. As their unique designs take the fashion world by storm, spawning copycat lines on the high street and attracting the attention of ethical trading campaigners and politicians, they continue to run the modest boutique very much hands on and feet on the ground. In a rare interview on 'Full English Breakfast,' the pair revealed that the driving force behind their work is a shared dream of a fully integrated Europe. Ambassadors for the old Eastern Bloc, holding their own in the competitive world of Western business, it's anyone's guess what these entrancing young women will do next.

~

Moses told Laetitia to wear the stone next to her skin. To rub it between her palms, to blow on it, to put her lips to it and whisper what was inside her.

Laetitia made a face. She tossed the stone high into the air and caught it, laughing. But Yingyang saw her slip it into her knickers.

As they sat by the fire that night, Moses asked for the stone. Laetitia reached her hand into her knickers and took it out. Wendy smacked her palm against her forehead and sighed.

"Listen to him," Laetitia told her, "I want to know what he sees."

"What I *feel*," corrected Moses. "The images are rarely concrete enough to *see*, they are sensations to be *felt*."

"Yes, exactly," said Laetitia, holding out the stone.

Joe swigged from a bottle of beer and rubbed Yingyang's shoulders with his other hand.

Moses held the stone in his cupped hands. He rubbed a circle with the pad of his thumb.

Yingyang loved the feel of Joe's hand on her shoulder. He was sitting close to her, stroking her back. Once he put his face into her neck and left the whisper of a kiss behind her ear.

"Laetitia. I see good fortune. In the conventional sense of the term. There is stability here if that is what you want. The stone is solid," said Moses, "but it is also heavy. There's a sense of heaviness."

Wendy said, "Moses, it's a stone."

Joe caught her eye and shook his head just a fraction. She held her hands up. Laetitia sat very still, watching Moses' face.

"Rock solid," intoned Moses. "Do you hear what I'm telling you?"

Laetitia nodded.

"Can you handle that?" Moses stroked her face. Little tears seeped out of her eyes and she knocked them away. He wrapped his long arms around her, pulling her right into his chest, and lay down on the sand. She cried softly into his toga.

Joe squeezed Yingyang's hand. She looked at him.

"Come on," he whispered.

They padded away across the sand, leaving Wendy looking into the flames and Moses and Laetitia rocking gently together.

"I think Laetitia is going home," said Joe. He walked right at the water's edge, bare feet covered in wet sand. "Back to France. To work." His voice had an edge to it, a harshness Yingyang was unused to. She looked sideways at him in the dark.

"It's inevitable," he said quickly, scratching his head. "This is only a hiding place. It's just so easy to pretend it's real."

Yingyang knew the island was a hiding place, because Bristol had hidden her there. But Joe sounded so – destroyed – by the thought of Laetitia going home. She'd wondered at first if it was Laetitia, if Joe couldn't bear for her to go, but he seemed so absorbed in his own regret.

"Sorry," he said. "You don't need this."

She took his hand.

"Laetitia has to leave, because it's impossible for anyone to stay forever. Except Moses. She'll get a job in France. A - fucking - job!" Joe let go of Yingyang's hand and kicked the water so that a fountain of sand sprayed up around his foot.

He was crying. He lashed out at his tears, furious with himself, trying to shake them away. Yingyang wanted to comfort him. She wanted to hold his big, squashy body against hers and rock him like Moses was rocking Laetitia. But she didn't know how to touch him when he was so angry. And she couldn't just walk away, so she stood helplessly watching him.

"I'm sorry," he said again, after a while. "Yingyang, Yingyang." He looked at her and sighed hugely. She gave him an upside-down smile.

"Sometimes," he said, "I know I'm pretty pathetic. But if I give up now, if I take a job and live a proper life, it would be the beginning of the end. Of me. Of my – fuck it, my hopes, my dreams."

Yingyang put her hand on his back and gently kneaded.

"I try to stop myself writing poetry," he said, and laughed.

She put her arms round his middle and squeezed, resting her head on his back. He felt solid. Rock solid.

"If I wrote poetry I'd be a lost cause. But sometimes I do, I can't help it. Fucking poetry."

Yingyang, with her cheek against his shirt and her hands just meeting around the bulge of his middle, began to suck her tongue. She opened her mouth and blew out and then she wet her lips.

"I write stories," she said.

The sound was quiet and rough because her lips and tongue were too blunt to shape the words, but Joe heard it. He stopped breathing for a moment, waiting. But when she didn't say anything else, he put his hands over hers. They stood like that for two minutes or more, *I write stories* hanging in the night air.

"What are your stories about?" he asked, stroking her fingers.

Yingyang led him further up the beach and they sat with their arms around each other, as close as they could get.

"I write about the people around me," she said slowly. "In Bangkok there are stories wherever you look." She sounded as if English were not her own language.

"Have you always lived in Bangkok?"

"Yes, always."

He buried his face in her hair. She told him that she was different, that she wasn't farang and she wasn't Thai, that she wasn't rich and she wasn't poor. That she had no one but her mother, Jessica.

"You're lucky, Yingyang. A writer should be born into a story like that."

"Everybody has a story."

"Yingyang." He pulled away from her, trying to look at her in the dark. "I would love to read your stories."

35

Jessica shook, inside and out, a tremor in her hands and a skip in her belly. Too excited to eat, too agitated to sit or stand or lie in any position. She tried to pirouette, wishing she had trained as a ballerina, a dancer, maybe street dance or hip-hop. She wasn't sure what that was but she wanted to move fast, to spin and jerk to the rhythm in her head, to sing or rap just as fast, just as recklessly as the dance that was pouring from her. Her brain danced inside her head, her blood spiralled in her veins, her muscles pulsed to the disco in her ears. She pivoted on the ball of her left foot and she was twelve years old and playing wing defence on a school netball court, holding the firm orange ball and the power to send the game in any direction. She felt the ball in her hands as she pivoted round and round in an endless circle then stopped dead. Froze on the spot. Spun in the opposite direction and shot the ball – chest pass. The words were still there and she hadn't been near a netball court for so many years, too many years; netball was a fantastic game, she should find a team, take it up again. Or badminton. Badminton was fun. You could thwack the – what was the word – shuttlecock! How rude! The image shuttled to and fro before her eyes and she rocked her head in time, giggling at her obscene little joke until she fell to the floor in a streaming mess of laughter.

~

Laetitia slept all night on the sand with Moses, and in the morning she left on a longboat. Wendy wouldn't talk to anyone. She walked up into the hills on her own.

Joe and Yingyang sat in the shade, reading each other's notebooks. Moses was nowhere to be seen. The man with the torn ear was some way up the hill overlooking the beach, talking on his mobile phone.

"Who is he?" said Joe, squinting up at him.

Yingyang shook her head. She turned over the page without looking up.

"You write like a real book," she murmured.

"It's superficial," he grunted, "artificial."

Yingyang looked at him.

"I have actually considered committing a crime," he said, running his hand through his chocolate curls. "Just to have something to write about. That's how desperate I am."

She put the book down and smiled at him.

"I have to go home and get a job. I'm in so much debt. But what if that's it? What if I'm swallowed up and I never get to write anything real?"

"When? When are you going?" Yingyang felt the thud between her ribs.

He put his hands over his face and blew into them.

She gritted her teeth to stop the drumming panic rising inside her. Tears were forcing their way through, unfamiliar, choking.

"Not yet," he said, reaching out for her. "Not yet. How could I go anywhere knowing you're here?" He pulled her into him. "Breathe all the way out," he said. "There, that's better. I frightened myself for a minute. I'll stay a while. We'll think about it after Christmas. OK? We'll worry about it then."

"What will you do for money?" Yingyang sniffed, twisting his shirt in her fingers. She sat up, smiling, wiping her eyes. "How does Moses live?" she asked. "Couldn't you do whatever he does?"

Joe looked out to sea. "No," he said, "I think not."

Yingyang gave an after-sob. It felt odd, crying. Like being shaken by some great hand that grabbed hold of you and wouldn't let go. "I never cry," she said. She wriggled her feet so that they buried themselves in the sand. "My mother, Jessica, cries a lot."

"Oh?"

"She wouldn't know what to do if I cried."

Joe swept away the sand from her feet and caught hold of her toes.

~

The long, thin mirror had cracks across it and smudges that wouldn't come off. Spitting on her cuff, Jessica rubbed harder but she only made it worse.

She took a deep breath with her eyes shut, drawing her arms in a great arc. When she opened her eyes, she looked just above her head and allowed her focus to blur. She waited.

"Fuck it," she spat at her reflection. She couldn't see her aura. How could she cleanse something she couldn't see? Tentatively, she raised her arms again and tried bringing them down gradually to find the edge of her auric field. Perhaps she had no aura. No flowing, pulsating

261

rainbow to protect her. That explained it. Giving birth to a child split your aura and with part of it destroyed, the rest shrivelled and died.

As she stripped off her shirt and then her wide, flapping trousers, she muttered, "Yingyang has stolen my aura. It's not enough that she drained my insides. Not enough that she forced herself on Bristol, little slut. She has destroyed my aura and I have no protection."

Jessica freed her breasts and ripped the elastic on her knickers so that they fell to the floor. She flung the tight red shoes across the room.

And now she stood, naked before the mirror, trembling. Stubble had begun to grow on her arms and legs.

"Wait there," she whispered and yanked open a drawer in the apothecary cabinet. She returned with her box, which she emptied on the floor around her. Taking a long white ribbon, she twined it round her arm and glued the ends onto her skin.

"White is for the life force inside."

Then she put a string of blood-red beads around her neck. "Red," she grinned, "red is for power."

She tore at a strip of hazelnut silk and tied some of her hair together on top of her head. "Brown like the earth," she whispered. "I need to be part of the earth beneath me."

She laid out embroidery threads in purple, pink, shimmering blue and gold and tied them so they trailed from her fingers. She could feel the rebirth beginning, the strengthening and cleansing of her aura. She shook now with relief.

"I have more colours!" she cried. "In my room. Just wait." She stumbled to her little room and seized an armful of makeup. Lipsticks fell to the floor and the lid of an eye shadow snapped off.

"Shit." She dropped more with each attempt to pick up something else. "So shitting clumsy."

She scooped everything onto her sheet and swung it over her shoulder.

Now amongst the ribbons, beads, fabric and sequins were the sticky tubes and pots of street-stall makeup. She squished her thumb into a circle of muddy bronzer.

"I'm going to unblock my stagnant chakras," she said, running her thumb in a line from her forehead, over her nose, lips, chin, the dip of her neck, circling each breast and down to her navel.

She looked at her pubic hair and wondered how she'd ever borne it. She'd have to bleach it. It should be white. Why hadn't it turned white when her hair did? Why *grey*, as if Maureen and that man really were her parents?

A constantly flowing, pulsating rainbow. Right. Red lipstick. She drew a line, beginning at her right shoulder, down one side of her arm, round each finger and up the other side. Down her body, past her belly, over a rounded hip, past her knee, her shin, around her foot, all the way up her inside leg and down the left leg in the same way, up until she reached her left shoulder. Now, hands steadier, she trailed the lipstick up her neck and through her hair, down until the line met the place it had begun.

Her breathing quickened. *It is possible to replace a shrivelled aura.* She could write a book about this. Develop a technique and sell it all over the world.

She grabbed a purple eye shadow. Was that next? She screwed up her face, trying to picture the door of the rainbow office. Red. Orange! It was orange. She could mix the bronzer with the red. But it didn't make orange and now her hands were covered in the colour of menstrual excrement. She wiped them on her stomach. *Orange. Orange.* Scrabbling amongst the makeup and the beads, she found a sheet of gold star stickers she didn't remember buying. But gold was like orange so she took one after another after another, sticking them all over herself. She spread her arms and admired herself in the mirror. *Now I am the sky at night and I can see everything.*

But she wanted purple. She knew her aura was largely purple. She swept three fingers in circles on a little plastic tray of eye shadow and gave herself streaks of purple down her arms and legs and swirls around her breasts. *Now that my aura is purple I can tell the future. Everyone will want to read my books now. Everyone will want to see me.*

She grabbed a black eyeliner, but it had lost its lid and gone blunt. She bit it, trying to detach the bitter wooden casing from the charcoal inside. Her lips and teeth were smudged as she spat out the wood and found a stub of black. Pinching the stub, she drew big circles around her eyes and then copied the crack in the mirror so that her body would still have the jagged line when she moved away from it.

"Yingyang!" she cried. "Where the fuck has she gone? Now I'll have to look for her."

Jessica strode out of the door, leaving it open, calling for her daughter.

Naked, trailing carnival ribbons, decorated with gold stars and coloured streaks, she ran down the steps. When she reached the bottom, her foot caught on a nail in a slab of broken concrete.

"Sorry!" she called out. "I forgot to put my shoes on."

~

Across the desk in the shop, Pippa held Marina's hand in hers to inspect the new ring. "I always knew he was the man for you," she said. "Now he is back and you can be happy again."

Marina raised her eyebrows.

"But you said–"

"Of course I said such rubbish. When he left you I couldn't say he is fantastic." She let go of Marina's hand. "But he is back and your wedding will be one big party."

The ring was bigger than the one Pippa had made her hurl into the Thames. This time she had an oval opal rimmed with gold. It rubbed a bit on her other fingers so she was trying not to use that hand too much.

Pippa knelt and began to scrabble on the shelf under the cash desk.

"We need to find a new office," she muttered. "The web orders are a mess. And the rainbow office is still piled with stock and papers. We have to find some time to empty it. The bulldiggers will come and smash it all to the ground with the bricks."

Gazing at her opal, Marina said, "Bulldozers. Why do internet orders have to use any paper?"

"We have to have copies," said Pippa, straining to reach some that had slipped behind the shelf. "Records."

The door tinkled and she stood up, banging her head on the edge of the desk.

"Arse," she said, slamming a fistful of orders beside the till.

"Hi."

The sound technician. The man she fantasised about last thing at night and first thing in the morning. The cause of her public humiliation and private desire. In her shop. Watching her bang her head and swear.

"Hi!" said Marina. "Maybe you want us for the telly again?" She laughed at length, nudging Pippa with her foot. "Or you want a crystal ball to see your future?"

Pippa's face was hot and her mouth was dry.

"So," said Marina. "Lovely to see you, Mr Sound Man. Isn't it, Pippa?"

"Thanks," said the Sound Man. "Rob. Rob Wenton."

"Hi," she said, thinking that it might be ridiculous to shake his hand when she'd already kissed his head.

Marina shuffled the pieces of paper on the desk, holding each one to her face as if she were short-sighted and rearranging them was an essential task.

"Beautiful," said Rob, smiling straight at Pippa. "It's a beautiful place. I love the—"

He never told her what it was he loved, because behind him the door jangled fiercely, blasting the shop with alcohol fumes and cigarette smoke. The sparkle and colour of the displays seemed suddenly to fade.

"Mick, I told you not to come here."

Pippa couldn't look at the Sound Man. She gripped the cash desk. Beside her, Marina had stopped her urgent paper-shuffling and was standing with her hands on her hips.

Rob glanced in turn at the three of them and then at a photograph of the Suceava Women's Collective engaged in smocking blouses by hand.

"Yuk," said Marina. "You are more disgusting every time. You stink like a drain."

Rob turned his attention to a basket of crocheted hair accessories.

"Thank you, I am so nice see your pretty face." Mick burped and laughed. "You have got more fatter."

Marina stepped out from behind the till, jabbing a finger at him. "You will get out now or I will phone the police."

She moved towards him, arms folded, her breath coming in snorts. Rob took a step in their direction.

"Bitch woman," spat Mick. "I like sleep in police station. They has a blanket."

"God," whispered Pippa. "Do you really have nowhere to sleep?"

Marina was close to him now, scowling at the stench.

"My sister not sharing the dough!" he shouted. "I bring to her better life and she leave me sleep cold."

"Mick, please. I want to help you–"

"Bitch woman! Two bitch. My sister my girlfriend so greedy."

He sucked a ball of saliva noisily behind his teeth and spat it at Marina's feet.

Rob was there before it hit the floor. He put an arm between them.

"I suggest you leave, Mick."

"Who fuck bastard you?" bellowed Mick and swiped at the side of Rob's jaw. Marina backed away, steadying herself on the central display of shawls.

Rob was bigger and had the advantage of being sober. He grasped Mick by the arms and held fast.

"Nine nine nine," he grunted. "Pippa, ring the police."

Mick struggled free, laughing as Rob tried to tackle him to the ground, toppling a rail of tiered skirts.

"I leave. I leave."

Pippa hadn't moved. She hadn't even looked at the phone.

"Good," she said stiffly. "Look, he's leaving now."

Rob stood, holding up his hands. They watched Mick stumble to his feet, smirking, treading on the skirts, kicking the rail. He swung the door so hard the chimes broke.

Pippa turned her back on the shop, where Marina was wrestling the skirt rail and Rob was gently folding a shawl. The metal poles on the rail clattered to the floor again.

"It's broken," snapped Marina, throwing a hanger on top of the mess.

266

Silently, Rob bent to look at it.

"Is your face hurt?" croaked Pippa into her hands.

"No," said Rob. "I'm fine."

"It's red," said Marina. "You will have a bruise."

"Will he come back?"

"Not for a while," said Pippa, pinching between her eyes and sniffing.

Rob slotted the poles into place and rested the skirt rail against the wall.

"The feet need fixing," he said. "They've lost a screw somewhere."

Pippa still didn't turn to face him.

"I'll go," he said quietly.

Pippa bit her lip.

"I'll go," he said again, and let himself out.

~

"Police?" Sam swapped the phone to his other ear and scowled at Bristol. "What the hell has that nightmare woman done now?"

Bristol ran his hand through his hair, sweat sticking it up in tufts at crazy angles.

Sam put the phone down. "They found her in the fountains outside Emporium, offering to baptise people."

"Oh, for fuck's sake." Bristol grabbed a telephone directory and flicked through the pages millimetres from his face. The air conditioning was down.

"Naked. Painted. Three o'clock this morning."

He punched his fist into the mahogany bookshelf.

Sam sighed. "Nothing to bruise your knuckles over. Just Jessica being Jessica. She was obviously somewhat - out of touch with things."

"In touch enough to tell them to ring here."

"Maybe she slept it off. I expect it will cost a few baht to get her out."

"I'll pay them to keep her locked up."

Sam pulled on his jacket. Glancing at his Blackberry, he said, "If

Aquamarine Inc deign to call, tell them I want to meet this week. And Fortune need to send a rep to Bangkok. And not that wet blanket they sent last time." He made for the door.

Bristol's voice caught in his throat and came out as a squeak. "It's OK," he said. "I'll go."

Sam's hand was on the door.

"Really." Bristol put his jacket on. "You stay and see if you can speak to Aquamarine or Fortune. I'll probably have to take her home."

"Or to hospital?"

"Jessica is the most expensive mistake we've ever made." Bristol left without looking back.

Sam smiled grimly. This was far from the truth. If Aquamarine and Fortune didn't come up to scratch with the Bamboo Grove contract– Jessica was the least of their problems.

~

At the police station, Bristol slipped the officer a roll of baht and waited while he unlocked a thick metal door.

Jessica sat hunched on a ledge, wearing a man's T-shirt and some knickers so small they cut into her flesh. She had been scrubbed and her skin was red. She eyed Bristol through damp curls and sniffed gently.

He looked round the cell as though there were anything to see except a small, barred window just short of the ceiling.

After a while, scratching her palm, Jessica said, "Hey."

Bristol looked up at the window.

"Are you cross?" She sounded like a child.

He looked at her, eyebrows raised.

"Will they make you pay to get me out? I don't mind sleeping with one of them if you'd rather."

He put his head in his hands.

Simultaneously, for a brief moment, they laughed.

"You are going to take your lithium," said Bristol. "You are going to take it every day and see a psychiatrist once a month."

"Is that it? I don't get a lecture?"

"I don't have time for a lecture. I am supposed to be preparing a damn PowerPoint."

"Bristol?"

"Yes?"

"Bristol, will you hold me? Just for a minute. Just once." She was staring at her hands, where a crumpled gold star was still attached to a fingernail.

"You're poison," he whispered. "You're fire and deep water. You'll swallow me whole one day."

"Sounds fun."

"Be serious."

"That coming from you."

He nodded towards the door. "Come on," he said, "I'll take you to the hospital. You're taking lithium if I have to ram it down your whining throat."

Jessica let out a little sob, wobbling as she stood.

He rubbed his hands over his face and sighed. Then he took her arm to guide her to the door, but she didn't move.

He turned to her, taking her other arm as well, drawing in a deep breath.

Her face trembled with the tears behind it. She dropped her head onto his chest, inhaling his sweat and the starch spray on his shirts.

He circled his hands round her elbows, watching his own head drop until his lips were in her hair.

36

Tenant: Eastern Vision. Further to our previous communications on this matter, I write to give you final notice that the building must be confirmed derelict and sealed by the end of this month. Any property remaining therein will be deemed unwanted and demolition will commence—

Pippa put the letter on the desk and looked around her. It was ridiculous, really, that she still had anything in here at all. As storage it was hardly ideal; deliveries had to be lugged up and down the stairs and the place stank of mildew. The electricity was intermittent now and the banisters unreliable. She rented a warehouse but somehow she'd never quite broken ties with the old rainbow office. If she blurred her eyes, she could see Moses in his orange robes straining to pull his legs into the lotus position. In the clutter on the desk, amongst her own belongings and early Gypsy Magic paperwork, faded Eastern Vision fliers advertised an exhibition of Oriental Monastic Relics.

She picked up the floral Stanley knife and dug out the long blade, smiling a little. Marina had said it was to protect her manicures and Pippa had never told her she'd broken her nails just getting at the tools.

Her mobile sang "Walking on Sunshine," and she dropped the knife on the desk. Mick? It was the same every time, this surge of panic.

The screen said, "Withheld." She put the phone to her ear carefully, as if it might bite.

"Hello?"

"Hi. Pippa?"

Not Mick. A rich, warm, red wine voice.

"Yes it is."

"Rob here. The Sound Man."

She suppressed a grin. But she could hardly pretend the scene in the shop had never happened.

"How are things?"

"I am well. Thank you. Are you also well?" She could feel her English deserting her.

"I am also well."

"Good."

Two seconds of silence was too long and Pippa said without meaning to, "How did you get my number?"

He laughed.

"That sounds like an accusation. Do you mind me ringing?"

"No."

"Your friend gave me your number. I went back to the shop."

"Marina?! She didn't say nothing!" Pippa laughed, thinking *he came back, he came looking for me.*

"I wonder – well, we were rather interrupted when I last saw you." He paused. "Are you OK? With your brother? Sorry. It's not my place to ask."

"What you saw is nothing different. He has become – horrible." It felt like a confidence, a confession.

"I'm sorry."

Pippa blinked several times.

"You said 'I wonder.' What do you wonder, Sound Man Rob?"

"I wondered if you would agree to have lunch with me."

She stopped blinking and beamed.

"That is a nice idea."

"Very soon."

"Yes. Very soon is fine."

~

Wendy came down from the hill as night fell.

"That man," she said, "the one who speaks on his mobile phone all the time."

"Who is he?" said Joe, lighting a cigarette from the fire. "What's he doing?"

"I heard him talking," said Wendy. "He wants to build a hotel on the beach."

Yingyang looked around her.

"It's not big enough," said Joe. "You couldn't build a hotel here."

"He's planning to cut into the hills. Three hundred bedrooms."

Moses folded his legs in the lotus position and swept his hand through the fire.

"Are you sure?" said Joe.

"I'm just telling you what I heard."

Yingyang bit her hand. A hotel. It was like stealing. The man with the torn ear was stealing the island.

Joe stood up. He walked away from the fire, towards the sea. Moses reached out his hand to Yingyang and touched her arm.

"There are other islands," he said.

"How can you say that?" spat Wendy, her face pinched and tense.

271

"There'll be cranes and bulldozers. This beach will be destroyed by fucking monsters and the island will be finished."

"That word," murmured Moses, "*fucking*, where's it coming from? It's a painful word, Wendy, you're feeling pain."

"Fuck fuck fuck," she said, waving her head from side to side and trying to look scornful when in fact she just looked tearful.

Yingyang pulled her knees up to her chest and hid her face in them. She tried not to hear Wendy sobbing. She tried not to see visions of a monstrous machine with hundreds of angry, biting heads.

"Meditate with me, Wendy," said Moses softly. "Hum away the pain."

"Don't be ridiculous," she said, her breath hiccupping and her nose streaming.

"You've upset the silent girl."

"Her name is Yingyang."

Yingyang hugged her knees tighter. *If I count to three hundred before I look up it will be OK.*

"You'd just sit and meditate while they destroyed the place, Moses. They'll have to shovel you away with the sand to get rid of you. And what will I do? Where will I go? I have nowhere to go!"

Wendy was shouting. No one shouted on the island. People would come to see what was happening. Yingyang lost her place, what number had she reached?

"Keep talking, Wendy. Find your pain."

Wendy cried some more, sniffing, gulping. Yingyang thought of Jessica. Moses let out a low hum.

"I can't go back. I have nothing to go back to."

Yingyang stopped at a hundred and fifty. She looked up.

Moses pulled Wendy towards him and lay down.

"Home is something you find inside yourself," he said into her hair, "it's not sand and shade and trees. It's not here or there, but the balance between the two."

Yingyang looked around for Joe but he was nowhere to be seen. Through the fire, she watched Moses embrace Wendy. He rubbed his hands over her back, ran them through her hair, pushed them up inside her T-shirt, and she gradually stopped crying. Yingyang wanted Joe to rock her like that, to rub the pain out of her. She wondered if he would disappear if she offered herself to him.

Moses propped himself up on an elbow.

"Yingyang," he said, "come here. Don't be lonely. Never be lonely."

She shuffled around the fire, letting him pull her down beside him. He stroked her hair with one hand and Wendy's with the other.

"Bamboo Grove will always belong to us," he whispered.

~

In the yard behind the temple, an elderly man in a grey uniform swept Post-it wishes and shrivelled orchids into an incinerator.

Bristol made a gesture of apology and called Sam back.

"Why did you block my call?" said Sam, as soon as he picked up.

"I was meditating."

"Meditating."

"I had reached quite a serene place within myself."

"Bristol, we cannot afford serenity right now. We need to sit down with a stubby pencil and sort out this shit."

Bristol looked at the sky. A thousand miles away, a plane was heading west.

"Bristol? Come into the office. I need you here."

Jessica came into the yard with two large milkshakes. Bristol winked at her.

"I will come in. Half an hour, OK. The solution may present itself."

"The solution is on an island in the Andaman Sea. We have to press fast forward on that one."

Jessica sucked her milkshake through a straw.

"I have a feeling," said Bristol, "feast is on the way."

"And what if this rubbish about ill fortune follows us to Bamboo Grove? The ghost of that squashed builder might decide he's caused enough chaos here and hop on a plane to Phuket."

"Do ghosts fly on planes?"

Jessica laughed, spilling milkshake down her cleavage. Bristol raised his eyebrows.

"No doubt this one will," huffed Sam. "He's brought Emerald City down and now he's cursing everything we've ever touched. I cannot believe that superstition can actually bring down the value of real estate."

"Bamboo Grove will be fine. This hotel will be so gorgeous there'll be a waiting list. Now go and get a milkshake and I'll see you in half an hour."

"A milkshake?"

Jessica handed Bristol his huge plastic cup.

"Strawberry and melon," she said.

~

"Veils are for virgins."

Pippa stroked the white voile Marina was modelling.

"And you resemble curtains."

There was a gasp from behind the veil. Pippa opened her mouth to try and dig herself out, but Marina said, "A veil is a sort of curtain. The groom pulls it back. Like unwrapping a present."

They were sitting on Pippa's bed, on a new design Gypsy Magic bedspread. Marina took off her veil and shook it out.

"Your wedding will be beautiful," said Pippa, lying back on the bed.

Marina folded the veil loosely into its box. She let out a long sigh.

"I hope—"

"I know. He will be there. Do not panic. You are good for each other."

"Thanks, Pips. In fact I am nearly glad I met your bloody brother. Because he brought me my best friend."

"Me too."

Marina lay down next to her.

"And the Sound Man? What really happened after lunch?"

Pippa chewed her lips and put her fist to her forehead.

"I made," she said, "a fool of myself."

"I'm sure you didn't, beautiful friend."

Pippa sniffed.

"We ate sushi at a long table with many people."

"I know. You have described every part of the menu."

"We talked and laughed."

"About the boutique, making television and his cricket team. Even the kiss on the head."

"And I drank wine."

"You drank wine. He had a beer. And that's where you stop. You don't have to tell me."

Pippa shut her eyes.

"I told him I'd have sex with him."

"At the table? Did everyone stop talking to listen?"

"At the door. Quietly. I said, 'Would you like to come to my flat?' and he didn't say anything for too long."

Marina whispered, "And did he come?"

"No. He said, 'What does that entail?' I didn't know what 'entail' meant. And then he kissed my face here–" she brushed her cheek, "and I said very quietly we could have sex."

"Right."

"He said, 'Not yet,' and he smiled. And I feel stupid." Pippa put her hands over her eyes as if she could stop herself seeing the memory. "He stroked my face and whispered, 'You are worth waiting for. And I can't wait to see you again.'"

"That is brilliant!" Marina took her hand and smiled at her, nodding.

"It is brilliant," said Pippa. "And I feel so stupid. He's special but he–"

"Thinks *you* are special. He came to the shop. He came back even when he had seen Mick. A man who meets your bloody brother and still wants to see you again. He thinks you are special. Believe me."

~

In the morning, Joe said, "We have to do something. We have to speak to the man with the torn ear."

"He won't listen to us," said Wendy, eating rice with her fingers, "he's the sort who will only listen to money."

"Where's Moses?"

"Telling fortunes."

Yingyang looked at Moses' tree. He was reading the palm of a white man with a laptop case. She felt the strange stab of jealousy she had felt before, watching him tell fortunes. His touch last night had been so comforting, she craved it again. She wanted the warmth of his breath on her face. She wanted him to look at her and only her.

"I'm going to follow him," said Wendy. "I want to hear more of what this man says." She wiped her bowl with her fingers, sucked them, and stuck it in a bag swinging from her shoulder. Joe and Yingyang watched her walk away, more buoyant than they had ever seen her.

"You OK?" said Joe.

"Everything's wrong," said Yingyang, massaging her temples.

"It might not happen. It's OK."

"But it will happen. And the island feels different now. Like it's already being dug up. You'll go away, and the island will be destroyed, and I will be–" she choked on the word and had to force it out. "Alone."

"Oh Yingyang, no. No. That's not the way it's going to be." Joe shook her gently, grabbed her wrists and pulled her hands away from her face. "I won't let it happen like that."

"Joe, if we have sex, will it change everything? Will you still be with me?"

Joe let go of her hands and coughed.

"Now I've said it and that's enough."

Yingyang turned away. He took her hand.

"Yingyang, I would love to have sex with you. It's just you're so young, and I wondered, I thought maybe you were a virgin." He looked at the sand.

"I've never done it. I've – thought about it a lot."

Joe coughed again. He blushed. He scratched his head.

Yingyang said, "I've embarrassed you."

"No, not at all." He sounded very polite, as though she were a stranger apologising for stepping on his toe. "But I won't be able to think about anything else now." He grinned sideways at her. "Will you do me the honour?"

He took her to his hut and drew the curtains. He pulled his shirt over his head and unbuckled his belt. She sat on his bed, looking at him.

"I know, I'm fat," he said, pinching the roll of pink flesh.

She shook her head. She took off her T-shirt and unhooked her bra so that her breasts felt the air. She found herself trembling.

He began to kiss her with his tongue, kicking off his cut-offs. She unzipped her skirt and let his legs push it down out of the way. His erection was warm against her skin.

When they lay together afterwards, soaked in each other's sweat, Yingyang kissed his cheek.

"You won't disappear now? You wanted that too, didn't you?"

He laughed, shaking his head. "Yes," he said, "I wanted that too."

"Joe?"

"Yes, lovely?"

Yingyang had never heard the words spoken, but she heard herself say, "I love you."

Joe threw his arm across his eyes.

"Joe?" Yingyang felt her throat constrict. "It's supposed to be a beautiful thing to say, I…"

She tugged his arm gently away from his face. He blinked at her and swallowed.

"It just came out," she said, her voice shaking. "I'm sorry."

He sat up.

"No, no, don't be sorry. It's–"

"I've spent years saying nothing and now look what I've done. My thoughts come straight out of my mouth and ruin everything."

She sat up and hugged her knees. The blissful warmth they'd been wrapped in had curdled as soon as she'd said *I love you.*

"Yingyang, you haven't ruined anything. I think you're incredible–"

"But you don't love me."

"It's not that simple!" He started to pull on his clothes crossly. "I wouldn't have just done – of course I love you, in a manner of speaking. I don't go round taking young girls' virginity without–"

"I'm a young girl now! A child!" Yingyang shook, clenching her fists, feeling the humiliation of Bristol's rejection flood through her as if it were yesterday. "I thought – who was I kidding?! I'm as stupid as my bloody mother, falling in love with anyone who's kind to me and now I'm no better than her because I've thrown myself at you."

She grabbed her clothes, pulling them clumsily, shakily on, sobs burning her throat as she refused to give in to them.

Joe reached for her.

"Yingyang, please. Calm down. Will you just let me hold you? You did not throw yourself at me. And you are not a child. You are the most incredible young woman I have ever ever met and I want to get to know you so much more."

Yingyang stopped stamping and tugging and stood still, her arms folded tightly across her chest.

Joe put his hands on her shoulders and looked into her face.

"Yingyang, you are very special. Don't ever think otherwise."

She hung her head.

"But you don't love me," she whispered.

"I love you," he said, "in a manner of speaking. And as time goes past and we talk and talk and – if you like – have more sex but that's not important, that can just happen if it happens, maybe in time we'll find…"

Yingyang tossed her head and shook herself free.

"Let's pretend this never happened," she said, and forced herself to leave.

37

Jessica's heart beat a wild drum roll. Three o'clock in the morning and the city's underbelly was still up. Stoned perhaps, drunk, but awake. She kept her head down, with her hair beneath a shawl, her fists in her pockets clutched tightly around the matches and the telephone.

Perverse child, what are you playing at?

She shook her parents out of her head. A boy sat beside a motorbike, rolling a cigarette with the clumsy concentration of a drunk. Jessica turned her head away to look at the road. Then, taking a deep breath, she dived down the first alley of shacks.

It was black. She waited for her eyes to adjust, hearing a siren in the far distance.

Treading carefully in her bare feet, she entered the maze and made her way to the patch of ground where the children played. She rang anonymously to report a fire and, shoving the phone back into her pocket, she took out the matches and squatted by the bench.

A mosquito hit her ear and she slapped at it, trapping it inside. Scraping it out with her nail, she began to shake violently. Inside a shack, someone coughed. She crouched, her head on the bench, her breathing irregular.

Now she could hear only the sound of distant traffic, of insects in the swamp at the edge of the khlong. She struck a match and used the light to find a piece of wood from the ground. She held up the flame to see the corrugated iron wall of the first home. Her fingers burnt and she blew quickly, wincing.

Evil witch. You should burn yourself alive.

"I have to," she whispered. "There's no alternative."

Then, lighting a second match, she held it to the bench until the leg caught. She grabbed the stick of wood and beat the wall with it again and again, louder and louder.

Flames licked the bench, growing taller and taller. The spirit house blazed suddenly into life, illuminating itself for one last brief moment before it sent its prayers flying into the night sky. The fire was moving towards the walkway. Jessica slid behind the shack, closed her eyes and counted to twenty. Then she ducked around the spreading fire and roused family after family, yelling, "Fai mai! Fai mai!" *fire, fire!*

The fire gathered speed as people raced to escape. Now shouting filled the air so that every alley was crammed with people running, arms loaded with children, television sets, dogs, fans, purses. Jessica backed against a wall, beating it with her stick, screaming that they must run for their lives.

~

Moses found Yingyang sitting on a rock. She was tearing pages out of her notebook, shredding them into hundreds of pieces and letting them fall into the water.

He stood behind her. He took the book gently from her hands and laid it on the sand.

"Duhka," he said.

Yingyang looked at him.

"Suffering in all its forms. It makes no difference if you tear that up, because nothing is permanent. Not you, not me, not whatever it is you write in those books all day."

She sat very still. She watched a longboat move further and further away into the distance.

Moses laid his giant's hands on her head. She felt pressure and then release, as if her scalp were sighing. Tears slid slowly down her face. More crying. She had cried more in these past few days than in her whole life before.

He moved his hands down her neck onto her shoulders and pushed hard. It made her breathe more easily.

"Yingyang," he said, his voice warm and deep, "your worth belongs to no one else. Be still, forget."

She thought, is this what Jessica feels? This inertia where any movement is too much? Where the pull of the sea is so strong, I could slide into the water and hold my breath easier than not?

I love you was wrong. Joe's eyes changed when she said it. He kissed her again but without his tongue and she felt him close up. How could he reach inside her for the tears and the words and then leave her as exposed as the naked cliff that would be hacked apart by the diggers? She felt there was nowhere to go from here. Except to sit very still, holding fast to the rock when the sea called out to her.

Moses said, "Come to me, come and find me," and kissed her eyelids.

~

If anyone is dead, you should set yourself on fire. Jessica could hear a hundred voices in her head, as if the world knew what she had done. *Jessica,*

you have surpassed yourself this time. What were you thinking? Perverse child.
Pyromania now, to add to the list. I despair.

And underneath the voices, cutting through them, the screams of people running for their lives. The smell penetrated the thick, polluted air of the streets around the slum. As Jessica approached, she breathed in shallow little gasps that made her already exhausted brain dizzier still. She had stayed to watch the fire fighting, the explosion of people stumbling from their homes, the futile attempts of police officers to establish order. And as the sun rose and the smoke settled, she had slipped away with ash in her hair and terror on her face.

Now she forced herself to keep moving towards the source of the smell. Past the wok wagons and the shuttling traffic, the immaculate women and the oil-splattered cooks in the plastic roadside restaurants. Past the entrance to the sky train, past a group of laughing, spitting tuk-tuk drivers gathered ready for business. All as if Phetbin were so immaterial, so transient that its passing was barely to be remarked upon.

At the far edges of their burnt out estate, Jessica found the residents sitting quietly. She stepped over a melted, knotted bicycle and a smouldering rug and searched the faces.

"Jess'cah!"

Poey stood, wobbling on her feet, grinning. Her mother cradled a dark brown bottle, swigging at it rhythmically.

Jessica took Poey's hand and they sat together.

"Khun Jess'cah, you saved us," Poey told her.

Jessica frowned at her and she nodded vigorously.

A young man picked his way back through the ashes and the twisted metal, carrying the corpse of a dog.

"See," said Poey, "that dog is dead. But we are all alive because you saved us." She squeezed Jessica so tightly she could hardly breathe.

"I'm sorry, I have to go. I will come back. I will bring you new things."

Her feet were swollen in her battered red heels, but she ran, sidestepping traffic, street stalls, schoolchildren in her hurry. When she could no longer smell the fire, she stopped, shivering from the heat.

38

The restaurant was almost entirely red. The squishy bench just inside the door where a man with his tie at half mast waited for a takeaway, the paper globes dangling on string from the ceiling, the calendar tacked to the wall; all were a deep velvety red. Combined with the smells of gloopy sauces and spitting oil, the whole effect was of a warm, slightly sticky cocoon.

Pippa nibbled at the edge of a prawn cracker that disintegrated like damp oasis in her hand. She was being demure; she'd even ordered green tea instead of Tiger beer. A cheongsam-trussed waitress with a bright red face to match the decor balanced an iron dish on the little scaffold above the tea light on their table.

"Thank you," said Rob. He waited whilst the waitress served them a spoonful each and shook out the starched napkins that were far too thick to wipe your face on. And when she backed away, he said, "Pippa, you are very special." She stuck her finger in the sweet and sour sauce, which was still burning hot, and sucked it. "Careful." He took her hand and stroked the finger, watching her face.

The waitress made a U-turn away from their table, hovering indecisively with a bowl of soup. Rob smiled at her and she blushed and set it down for them. They prodded the edges of the boiling food, licking spoons and stirring.

"If you weren't so – direct–" he said, "I'd probably have been stuck admiring you from afar and having rude fantasies." A cackle of laughter escaped her lips, and her fork slipped on a pineapple chunk. She squidged the pineapple between finger and thumb and fed it to him.

"I could blame my foreignness," she said, "for making me so embarrassing. But I won't. I think I am simply a bit brazen." She sighed and drank from his beer.

"Pippa," he said, grinning like a schoolboy, "that day in the television studio. There was nothing wrong with your microphone. I just wanted an excuse to get near you."

She dipped her head, gazing into her soup, and her king prawns looked back at her knowingly.

~

In a cave on a mountainside, where snow lay heavy for most of the year, lived a girl with no mouth. She had eyes to see the town below her and ears to hear the conversations that floated up. But with no mouth, she couldn't call out...

Yingyang's hand went into spasm. She relaxed her grip on the pen and massaged her palm. Then she dropped her notebook and lay flat on the sand. At the International School, they'd studied magnets. Now the lessons came back into her mind and she saw that she was a magnet that changed its pull. She attracted, closer and closer, drawing first Bristol and then Joe towards her. But as soon as they touched, they bounced away, repelled by the force she couldn't control.

~

Sam was with the solicitor representing the Summer Towers Tenants' Committee. Bristol was in his office; two tenants on the sofa, a third refusing to sit and a fourth on the telephone.

"I won't insult you by explaining that the Bangkok authorities invent their own rules," he said, to the telephone and the assembled company. "You are not the first to be given notice like this and you will not be the last. In a desperate bid to raise capital, the government are reclaiming and reselling any land they can get their hands on."

"Any land with loopholes," said the British man who refused to sit. "When I rented this apartment for my family, I was new to the area and I trusted that the agent knew he was marketing a bona fide property."

"The agent believed he was doing so," said Bristol, from the script. "And we had no reason to doubt the binding legality of our ownership of the land."

The woman at the other end of the telephone hung up.

"It is imperative," said the Frenchman on the sofa, "that we all use the same solicitor." He spoke to the Brit and the German beside him as if Bristol were not in the room. "I suggest Bedlow and Mackay. I know one of the partners."

Bristol opened his mouth to speak but the German had stood.

"To employ a solicitor," he said as he made for the door, "would be wastage of our time and moneys. We are in Thailand. We cannot live by European rules. I will pack my possessions and rent a new place. Still I have a nice place with a maid and a guard at the gate." He left the room, nodding a generalised farewell.

The Frenchman sighed. "Maybe we should just burn the buildings down ourselves," he said.

"I think that might be going a little far," murmured Bristol.

"This is not such a joke. The slum at Phetbin was also under threat of eviction." He nodded slowly.

"Good Lord," said the Brit. "The one that burnt down?"

"Precisely," said the Frenchman.

"What are you suggesting?"

"My sources tell me that although the authorities reclaim land if they decide it is not legal, they nonetheless pay compensation to people who have lost their homes through fire."

"But those people surely didn't own their land." The Brit was all ears.

"No, of course no. But they will receive some compensation. If there was no fire, they would be evicted now with nothing."

~

"Good morning! It is a pleasure to welcome you to Gypsy Magic."

The customers hadn't even opened the door wide enough to make the new chimes tinkle.

"Good morning," said the woman, and the younger woman who was clearly her daughter glanced vaguely at Pippa.

"We have many delights to show you."

"Well," said the mother. "We have a very specific request."

"Specific is also fine."

Marina came forward, smiling.

"Excuse my colleague," she said. "She is very excited today."

The daughter was looking half-heartedly at some necklaces.

"My daughter is getting married," said the mother, for some reason sticking out her chest.

"Fantastic!" said Pippa. "Marina is also getting married."

The mother pursed her lips a little, pulling in her chin. It wasn't flattering.

"Congratulations," she said, rather dismissively.

"Sorry," mouthed the daughter, rolling her eyes.

"Congratulations everybody!" said Pippa. "So now."

"We are planning a gypsy theme."

It was a trump card. Pippa actually squealed.

"Marina is wearing white stuff," she said. And added in a stage whisper, "*So boring*. So. We can design a special dress and send it to the Suceava Women's Cooperative to make up."

"Excellent." The woman nodded. "And if we could continue the theme through table dressing, my hat and the cake decorations."

Pippa nodded back.

"Cake decorations?" said Marina.

The woman looked at her.

"Flowers," she said, as if Marina were being purposefully slow to follow. "We need the icing to pick up on the colours and style of the fabrics."

"Of course." Pippa tutted at Marina, who held up her hands. "We do cake icing here."

Marina widened her eyes.

"And hats," she said.

"Of course," said Pippa.

When phone numbers and appointments had been noted, the customers left with a catalogue to begin working on preliminary sketches. The bride yawned as they left. She looked pale.

"Weddings," sang Pippa. "We are now weddings experts."

She took the invitation out of her pocket and smiled broadly at it.

"*Marina and Ahmed request the pleasure of the company of Pippa and Rob*. Pippa and Rob. Rob and Pippa. Do you think the men will be friends like us?"

"Well–" said Marina. "Not like us. But I'm sure they'll get along. I'm sure."

"I am also sure." Pippa took Marina's hands and danced a polka around the central display. "Marina and Ahmed," she cried, "Pippa and Rob!"

~

285

Jessica strode down the newly-carpeted corridor as if she was used to meeting with city officials. The lady at reception had said "through the double doors," and as she approached them she cleared her throat. She swung open both doors and stopped short. Her way was blocked by a trolley piled high with hardback notebooks. If she moved too suddenly, she felt they might topple, crashing to the floor.

"Excuse me?" she called. "Sawadee ka?"

Somewhere behind the trolley, a telephone rang.

"Hello!" said Jessica, nudging a little wheel with her foot in the hope that the trolley might roll gently to one side.

"Ah. Khun Jessica."

She couldn't see past the notebooks to the man addressing her.

"Yes, it's Khun Jessica."

She waited, shivering in the fierce air-conditioning.

"One moment please."

The man shunted the trolley aside and Jessica wai-ed, willing him to understand, to help.

The notebooks began to fall; a sharp corner grazed her shins. Torn between jumping away and jumping forward to halt the landslide, she stood helplessly and did nothing.

"No problems," the official said. "A lady is coming now. Please come this way."

Jessica picked her way over the books and followed him down the corridor.

"What are they?" she asked, as one more lost its balance and fell behind them.

"Records," he said.

"Ah."

"All the exit and entrance of employees and visitors to the building are logged by the guards."

They entered a small boardroom where two further officials waited.

"Of course," said Jessica, and they all nodded.

"Please, sit."

The three men stood until Jessica was seated, straight-backed, hands clasped primly in her lap, a hint of a smile on her face.

"Some tea."

A buzzer was pressed and a tiny woman appeared with a wooden tray of ceramic shot glasses.

"Kop Khun Ka." Jessica wai-ed the maid, who bowed low.

"How long have you lived in Thailand?" asked one of the men, in a broad Manhattan accent.

Jessica thought. "Maybe twenty years." Better to round up.

"How old are you?"

"Thirty." Better to round down.

"More tea?"

"Kop Khun Ka."

They all smiled at each other across the table. Jessica coughed quietly.

"My friends in Phetbin," she said, her head on one side. "We are not sure where they can live now."

"Yes. This is a problem since the fire."

"Yes."

"And the land is required for development," drawled the American-speaker, shrugging.

Jessica sipped her tea.

"And so a new site is required," she said, "for their simple homes. The compensation money must come with somewhere to build."

"Of course. Indeed."

They all nodded again.

"We must give this matter some thought."

"Absolutely."

"Yes."

They all stood, bowed their heads briefly and smiled.

"Kop Khun Ka," said Jessica, realising that this was as far as she would get today.

As she stood at the threshold, the sound of a hundred hardback notebooks hitting the ground made them all jump.

"When do you think you will find somewhere?" she asked, eyes wide.

"Not too long. You can be assured we have this matter in hand. A site is presenting itself just now."

39

Moses dreamt that he was suffocating. A creature so vast it filled his vision was throttling him with a thousand tentacles. The tentacles threaded their way up his nose, into his ears, lassoed each finger and toe, thrust their way up his back passage and strangled his insides. He couldn't draw air into his lungs and his body deflated like a balloon with a pin in it.

When he woke, clawing at the sand and shivering, he knew that he was dying. This dream was too vivid and too physical to be a by-product of his mind's meanderings. It was a premonition. He did not have long to live.

He lay in the gradually dawning light, watching the sky turn from black to grey to gold then gleaming blue, and the sea reflecting each colour in turn. Thirty-eight. Was that a good age to head for the Spirit World? He told himself he'd be busy up there, visiting people still on the earth and giving them the benefit of his wisdom.

It was a while since he'd called himself a Buddhist and he wasn't sure he'd be reincarnated. He wondered what he would come back as, if reincarnation were an option. Stretching his limbs and yawning, he decided it would really depend on who made the decisions.

The question was why he'd been given this knowledge. What was he supposed to do with it? Certainly there was little point in heading back to the mainland to see a doctor. This premonition was the impending end of his life, whatever he chose to do with it.

If he'd spent his life living up to the expectations set out for him, he might now head for a Bamboo Grove and live out his remaining time in an orgy of self-indulgence. He laughed aloud. It was a rare sound and there was no one there to hear it.

~

Tranquillity Place was almost empty. Bristol sat with his suit trousers rolled up and his bare feet dangling in the pool. Leaves dotted the surface and a dead frog blocked the filter beside him. He kicked his legs, creating a small whirlpool, and forced himself to think.

They didn't have even half of the advance they had agreed with Fortune for the work on Bamboo Grove, and Fortune wouldn't ship the machinery until the finance had cleared. The oil project had been a bum investment; that money was down the drain. Summer Towers was wasteland now. But already people had started building shacks there. Whole streets of little huts had been constructed from the broken pieces of Eastern Vision; planks, window panels, doors, mounds of rubble where the children sat and experimented with cigarettes.

The wife and children of the young man crushed in the bowels of Emerald City would maybe end up there when the luxury home he'd given them was razed to the ground. Dragging himself to his feet, carrying his shoes, Bristol made his way up to their apartment to tell them there were only two days left.

~

The building was derelict now but for the remnants of Gypsy Magic, formally Eastern Vision London. Marina scooped a pile of laminated cards from the shelf and dropped them into a crate. She swore as they slid against each other and scattered messily.

"Do we have space in the warehouse?"

"We have space," said Pippa, tossing fabric posies into a plastic sack. "And it is good that this horrible building will be destroyed."

"I think I will miss that rainbow," said Marina. "Shall we paint a rainbow on the shop door?"

Pippa laughed. "I think maybe I have had enough of rainbows."

A crash on the stairs made them both start, turning to the door.

"The key. Pippa. Where is the key?"

Pippa searched frantically among the papers on the desk; the hole-punchers, staplers, the floral tool kit and the slippery document wallets.

Marina tripped on her laminated cards, sending them flying as she flung herself at the door.

"You listen me you bitch girl! I am your brother, I bring you to this country."

Unable to find the key, Pippa gave up and leapt to push on the door with Marina. She strained her arms and legs. Marina jammed the door with her shoulder, shuddering with the effort.

"Say nothing," she whispered. "Keep silent."

"You must to be a sister for me! Let me come inside!"

Mick thumped his fists on the door and whooped like someone egging on a fighter.

"He is very bad today," mouthed Pippa, twisting round to press against the door with her backside and give her arms a rest.

He kicked hard. Again and again.

"The key!" said Marina. "There. On the shelf."

They looked at each other.

"You can't hold this alone," said Pippa.

"Go," hissed Marina. She rammed her shoulder and her foot against the door.

The kicking stopped and before Pippa could move, a different sound began, level with their heads. The flimsy wood of the door was being smashed and splintered.

"The banister that was broken," said Pippa, fighting tears of panic.

"Stop!" shouted Marina. "If you stop we will open the door. OK?"

The crashing and thumping grew wilder.

"Mick, stop please! You are not yourself!"

The banister broke through, pushing a chunk of battered rainbow before it.

"Stop!" The two women shrank away from the door, Pippa running too late for the key.

Mick rammed the banister at the door until the rainbow lay in pieces on both sides. Then he shunted what was left and stepped in, wielding the weapon in front of him.

"Good afternoon, ladies," he said. "Nice to meet you."

They backed away, close together.

His hair was greasy and full of tiny flakes of scalp. His cracked lips merged into sores and pus-filled spots. The grimy T-shirt he wore sagged.

"So," he said. "You have for me some money? This business has a lot of cash. Dough." He swaggered across the room and Pippa saw the border guard from years ago in his swagger. She screamed, "Get out! I never want to see you again. Get out! You are disgusting!" She seized the platter of crystals and flung it at his head. It hit him side on on the cheek and a cut glass kaleidoscope sprayed around him.

"Bitch woman!" he shouted, grabbing her sweater.

Marina jumped behind him, trying to wrestle the banister from his hand. He turned on her, both hands holding it high.

He brought it down hard onto Marina's head. Pippa backed up against the desk, feeling behind her amongst the mess, afraid to look away.

Mick struck Marina's ear and she roared in pain, clamping her hands around his feet and trying to bite through the foul cloth of his trousers. With a smirk on his face, he raised the banister to hit her again, but before he could bring it down, Pippa had the Stanley knife to his throat.

Clutching the back of his T-shirt, she pressed down hard and sliced fast. The banister clattered to the floor. Mick's hands flew to the hole in his neck spouting blood. He fell forwards onto his knees and Marina had to roll away to stop him pinning her down. Her face was white and her eyes blank.

Pippa stood shaking, teeth chattering, the floral knife in her fist dripping with her brother's blood, until she too fell to her knees.

"Miklos," she sobbed, "my brother."

Miklos had become so thin that they were able to lift his body into a crate. Without speaking, they rolled up the blood-soaked rug and stuffed it on top of him.

"Now we take turns to watch while we wash our hands," said Marina.

Pippa stared at the knife she'd dropped and didn't know if she'd faint or vomit.

"Pippa. Pull yourself together. Somebody may have heard the noise."

Pippa shook her head weakly.

"It's fine," she said, in a child's voice, "the offices are shut so close to – Christmas." This last word came out in a whisper.

"I'm going to wash my hands," said Marina. As she opened what was left of the door, the lights finally gave up. Pippa was left in the dark with the smell of her brother's blood.

"Miklos," she whined softly.

A sound on the landing made her jump, her heart racing. She backed away from the door.

"It's me. Marina. Now go and wash your hands."

Pippa watched her feet take tiny, fragile steps out of the room towards the toilet. The tap produced only a trickle of left-over water. She rubbed the blood off her hands, her wrists, her arms, and her stomach thrust its way into her throat. She threw up violently, clutching the chipped green sink and choking on the endless stream of vomit. Then, shivering, she washed again and tried to swill her mouth with the foul-tasting water.

In the office, she said, "Marina. What have I done?"

"You have saved my life and yours. He would have killed us."

Pippa's legs felt as if they would give way but she couldn't sit down, not in here. She said, "And now we must go to the police. I must tell honest truths."

"We're not going to the police. Like you, Mick has not existed for many years and so it is easy for us to forget this."

Pippa couldn't take her eyes off the crate. In her mind, she saw again and again the moment she had done it. The feel of the knife in her hand as it slit through the skin. The way he fell forwards and Marina rolled from under him.

"If I had time to think, perhaps I–"

"*I* would be dead. And probably you as well. I am glad you had no time to think." Marina pushed broken pieces of door aside with her foot. "Now find the other tools and we will fasten the top of this crate. Then we get out. Leave the rest. The building will be destroyed and Mick will go with it."

Moving like a sleepwalker, Pippa dug around in a box for the floral screwdriver and the little hammer. She heard her brother's whisper in her ears, *It's different in the West. They're wringing us out. It cannot last.*

40

Jessica handed coins to the noodle-seller and took the plastic bowl.

"Kop Khun Ka," she murmured.

The noodle-seller reached behind her and handed Jessica a flannel. Jessica smiled weakly and wiped her streaming face and neck. Handing it back, she dipped her head and went to squat against the window of a Seven-Eleven store.

A young western couple carrying rucksacks stopped beside her and caught her eye.

"Hi," said the girl. "Do you speak English?"

"Not that often," said Jessica, squinting up at them.

They laughed. The boy gestured at the noodle wagon.

"Will this stuff give us the runs?"

Jessica shrugged.

"What do you think the meat is?" asked the girl, looking into Jessica's bowl.

Jessica scooped up a fistful and sucked it, letting the noodles slide up her chin.

"Well," she said, chewing, "they bash the animals in the head down by the slums and sell the recognisable bits. Then they mince the rest for this sort of thing. It's fine." She hooked a crumb from inside her cheek. "The head's good."

The couple smiled uncertainly.

"Pigs, cows," said Jessica. "Whatever."

"Thanks," said the girl. She looked at her boyfriend. "Go on then."

He looked at Jessica.

"You're like someone off that film," he said.

Jessica slurped straight from the bowl.

"It's about seventeen years," she said, "since I saw a film."

As they moved away, peering at their coins and waiting behind a man in a bulky leather jacket, Jessica heard the boy say, "Doesn't she know she's a walking cliché?"

Jessica finished her meal. Ignoring them, she tipped her bowl into the soap bucket and wai-ed the noodle-seller.

Have the clichés followed me across the world, across the years? Am I still my own worst enemy?

She stubbed her toes on a concrete slab. In a burst of self-pity, tears welled up in her eyes.

I am no better than Poey's mother who swigs cheap whisky and condemns her daughter to a life of paid sex, disease and drugs. What have I done for my daughter?

A tall, thickly-made-up lady with a tight dress and sleek black hair smiled coyly at her, absent-mindedly adjusting his genitals. Jessica smiled back. She blinked away her tears and wiped her nose on the back of her hand.

Stooping to admire a display of bracelets spread on a blanket, Jessica set her jaw. She had never stopped to wonder what it was she felt for Yingyang. Now she found herself asking whether she was any better a mother than Maureen. And she knew then that Maureen had tried. Maureen never stopped trying; meeting chaos with calm, fury with reason, and hatred with her best attempts at love. Jessica's birth mother, whoever and wherever she was, had escaped the nightmare that was Jessica's upbringing. And Jessica in turn had fled from her own daughter.

She looked up at the sky, blinding her eyes in her effort to see. Moses had told her once, as they walked the streets of London long ago, that she had a lot of unseen help. That in the Spirit World, a young girl who had taken her own life was watching out for her. That an elderly woman who had lived an entire lifespan was steering Jessica when she lost her way. Gazing blindly at the sun, unaware of the people dodging past her, she hoped Moses was right. And that somewhere up there someone was looking out for Yingyang.

~

"Rob."

Pippa's voice was a cracked whisper. She was surprised to hear that she could make a sound at all.

"Pippa, are you ill?"

"No. I am really fine. You sound very busy. You must be in the studio…"

"Darling, you're crying. Look, I'm going outside where I can hear you properly. Shall I call you back?"

"No! Please keep speaking. Say anything. Please speak to me."

"OK. Here I am speaking. Speaking, speaking. I'm going through a door that says 'no exit', I'm in a glamorous little courtyard where the bins are overflowing and there's cat shit on the ground and—"

"My brother is dead."

Rob swallowed.

"Please don't say you are sorry," said Pippa. "Say that he was a ruined man with no hope for the future and it is good that he is gone."

"Darling? Where are you? What's happened?"

Pippa crumpled to the floor beside her bed, shivering, gripping the phone as if it were Rob's hand.

"I – I – Miklos, he—"

"Where are you?"

"Home."

"I'm coming now. Hold tight. It's going to be all right."

Pippa's hand shook too much to turn her phone off and Marina grabbed it and pressed the little button, scowling.

"Be careful. Maybe you should not talk to him yet. You are still very screwed up."

Pippa twisted her fingers together.

"Screwed up?" she repeated.

"It's something Sasha says. It means—"

"I know what it means. Of course I am screwed up. I am a guilty killer."

She curled up on the floor like a baby in the womb and rocked.

Marina went to the window, waved at the lollipop lady and shut the curtains. Sliding down to sit with her back against the wall, she steadied her breathing.

"Mick died of an overdose," she said again.

"And where is his body?" sobbed Pippa; again. She wiped her nose on the broderie anglaise valance.

"In the river," said Marina weakly. And then, after a while, "but he'd be washed up."

295

Pippa coughed and couldn't stop. Choking on phlegm, she staggered to the bathroom and vomited. When she came back, Marina said, "He doesn't have to be dead. He can just stop turning up. No one asks 'oh, how is your brother?' He can just be gone. Forgotten."

Pippa threw herself on the bed.

"You have no heart. I do not understand you can be not a caring person, I have cut the neck of my brother I am a guilty killer hating myself, it—"

"Stop it!" Marina was on her feet, shaking Pippa roughly by the shoulders. "Speak proper English! Stop rolling about in his blood and forget you had a brother."

"Mama, Papa…" murmured Pippa.

"They too will be relieved. They are old and won't have to put up with an evil son."

Pippa sat up, her face on fire.

"*I* am the evil person!"

Marina hit her hard across the cheek and they sat staring at each other.

"Don't tell Rob," whispered Marina. "You can't tell anyone. You know that."

They reached simultaneously for each other's hands. Pippa's breath became slower, more regular. She drew her fingers through her hair.

"Moses used to say," she said, "that Bristol and Sam could do anything. I remember—"

Marina looked at their hands and nodded.

"I remember many years ago when I was nothing," continued Pippa, "when I first worked in the rainbow office—"

"Yes?" said Marina.

"That crazy witch Jessica came into the office and Moses said, 'We'll get you a passport. Bristol and Sam can do anything.'"

She stood, wiping her face with her sleeve. Marina said quietly, "Jessica was a spoilt little girl with a neat little birth certificate. Of course she could get a passport."

"I think we will find a way," said Pippa. "Bristol and Sam are powerful, clever people who know other powerful, clever people. I think perhaps they can arrange a passport for me."

She laughed and Marina stared at her.

"I feel," said Pippa extravagantly, her voice shaking only a fraction, "that my time has come to travel to the East."

~

Round the fire, as the sea and the sky turned back again from blue, through gold and grey to black, Moses watched Wendy and Yingyang plait each other's hair.

"Tell me," he said. "Who will watch over you when I am gone?"

Wendy frowned, holding a strand of Yingyang's hair in one hand.

"Moses?" said Yingyang. "Is something wrong?"

Moses put his hands together slowly like a priest at an altar. He turned to her, reached out a hand and touched her lips.

"Someone has put words into your mouth." She nodded, looking at the stretch of his vast palms held out towards her. The lines were so deeply ingrained and so complicated. She spread out her own palms and examined them. The lines on her hands seemed random; scattered messily, vaguely so that she thought it might be impossible to see any story at all.

"Will you tell my fortune?" She blushed, growing flustered under his gaze.

He stroked her half-plaited hair away from her face and rubbed his thumb on her forehead.

~

The broom seller's son scooped leaves from the surface of the pool with a long-handled brush. Poey watched, smiling, and then blushed when she caught sight of Jessica. Jessica gave her a thumbs-up.

There was something Parisian about the way the alleys fanned out from the centre, where the pool was fast becoming the focal point of the community. The pump was borrowing electricity from a neighbouring condominium, where the tenants' committee had got nowhere with their campaign to stop the slum spreading on their doorstep.

Jessica stepped carefully over a mountain of smashed concrete; the huge building reduced to rubble by the six hands that had pawed her at once. She watched a group of children run laughing towards the pool. They leapt in, oblivious to the slab of wall beneath the water that might have broken their legs. The broom seller's son abandoned his task and went shyly to sit beside Poey.

A melancholy fatigue had settled over Jessica. She rubbed her face, sighing. She would have liked to lie down on the neat stack of roof felt that had appeared the previous day and shut her eyes. But she left the new residents of Summer Towers to their work and play and followed her feet through the streets.

As darkness fell, she squatted beneath the sky train steps. The white Christmas tree outside Emporium was three floors high. She blinked and diamonds danced on the branches. Bright pink bulbs alternated with red around the rim of each window and a laughing Father Christmas flashed on and off over the door. She thought of Poey, dreaming of the broom seller's son, and Toi, whose future was so far from her past.

She picked pale marshmallow-coloured varnish off her fingernails, sniffing. Thirty-five. Half of seventy. Five years off forty. A naked baby slept on a stall of watches and bracelets. Its father sat gazing across the road at the lights of Emporium, slurping noodles from a plastic bowl. Jessica wanted to hold the baby. To feel its skin. The soft fuzz of its hair. She imagined the tiny fingers curling round her own, like Yingyang's used to do all those years ago. Maybe she could have another baby. This time she'd love her properly, close her eyes and drink the feel of her, let days go by just stroking and kissing.

The man at the stall saw her staring and placed his hand on the child's back. She looked away, miserable. Did she look like someone who would hurt a child? Mothers are supposed to put their children first. Do you get a second chance ever? I could be a good mother. Look how Little Mai comes to me and Poey tells me when her own mother sends her to her ruin. As if I could rescue her. You see, Jessica told herself, I don't just get rescued, sometimes I do the rescuing. I can be a proper person with a functioning mind of my own. Dragging herself to her feet, choking a little as a moped went past with a black exhaust, she set her jaw. *If I have to spend Christmas on my own I will drown myself in the khlong. Bristol must know that I can't be alone, he must have thought of something.*

Her feet led her to his apartment off the Sukhumvit Road. She was in the lobby before she had time to think. A young girl dressed as an armed guard nodded at her with a half-smile. She nodded back. The Christmas tree was beside the lift; eight foot tall, sprayed with pretend snow and draped with gold tinsel. A reception desk was hung with plastic flower garlands. Jessica could see the swimming pool grinning at her and she imagined diving under the water, washing the grime from inside and out.

What exactly are you doing here? Visiting Linda? You'll have to ask the guard, you don't even know what floor they're on.

"Excu' me, Madam, I help you?" The guard's voice was gentle and sweet.

"I don't know," mumbled Jessica. "Maybe I'll come back later."

"Goo' evening Madam," said the guard over Jessica's shoulder. Jessica turned and froze.

Bristol had pushed open the door and was holding it for a woman with immaculate highlights and a scowl on her face.

He looked at Jessica and mouthed, "No! Not here," shaking his head. She didn't move.

"Lind, you go on up. I'm just gonna take this call." He produced his phone from his top pocket and held it to his ear. "I'll lose the connection in the elevator."

He stepped back outside the door then, and Linda pressed the lift-call without acknowledging him. She touched her heel where her shoe had rubbed and tutted.

Jessica watched her disappear through the grey metal doors, and then she followed Bristol outside.

"There'd better be a good reason for this." Bristol rammed his phone back into his pocket.

Jessica focussed on a parade of ants heading underneath the building.

"Jess? This is not a good time, beautiful."

"I want us to be together for Christmas." She began to count the ants.

Bristol sighed. "Is that it? I've just lied to my wife for some garbage that–"

"You've told her bigger lies."

"I know." He rubbed his temples. "Jess, are you OK? I'd like very much to wrap you in my arms but you'll forgive me if I don't. The neighbours, you understand."

"I thought you wanted a divorce?" She looked at him now, up into his face.

"It's not going to happen."

"You've never loved her."

"That's not entirely true. She is my *wife*, Jess."

"Because her daddy pulled a shotgun. Get over it, Andrew's out the way and you can move on. Grow up."

Bristol gave a dry laugh. "That's rich," he said, "coming from you."

She smiled. "So? Give me a promise kiss and I'll let you go up to your ratty little dinner à deux."

"Thanks. That's generous of you. However," Bristol's face grew serious, "Linda's father was our first major investor and if things continue as they are, he may well become our last. This is not the time for talk of divorce."

Jessica folded her arms. "So you're leaving me on my own?"

He sighed. "I'm in a corner here."

"Will you get me pregnant?"

"What?"

"I want a baby. You stole my first child and I need another one."

"You crazy witch." He stroked her tightly folded arms.

"Please. Just sleep with me until I'm pregnant. I won't ask you for anything more."

~

Ceiling after ceiling collapsed one onto the next, crashing down into one great mountain of rubble. Floorboards, concertinaed staircases, shattered door frames and shards of glass lay quivering as if the building were taking its last breaths. Contorted slabs of concrete shifted in a cloud of plaster dust and asbestos and an arm flopped out from underneath.

Pippa woke, adrenaline churning in her veins and bile in her throat. Rob made her sit up and open her eyes wide to rid herself of the dream.

"Well done, baby," he murmured, stroking her matted hair. "Good girl. Has it gone now?"

In truth, the rubble was fast becoming landfill and Miklos' corpse with it because the site had been acquired by the council for its twenty-first century academy, which was essentially a vast comprehensive school with a lobby like a five-star hotel. The plans were pasted on the boards surrounding the area, with seven-foot posters of model-gorgeous teenagers at computer terminals.

"Pippa, baby." Rob stroked her back. "You know what I think? I like your idea of travel. You've worked so hard for so long and you can afford to escape, explore a bit..."

Pippa wiped her eyes and sipped from the water glass beside her bed.

"Would you come with me? We could go and see Moses." She laughed a little and it made her cry. "Moses is really something. I'm sure you have never met a man like him."

"This is the walking sperm bank we're talking about here?"

Pippa laughed and this time she didn't cry.

"He is more than a bank of sperm. He is a bank of wishes. He actually tries to bring people what they wish for. That silly girl Jessica was stuck in her boring life and he magicked her away. Alexis had no job and Moses gave him Eastern Vision." She glugged the rest of her water and lay down again, pulling the covers around her. "And there are many ladies with a baby for which they wished very hard."

Rob lay down beside her and punched his pillow into place.

"Moses the magician," he said. "Yes, it might be fun to meet this stud."

Pippa nestled her head into his armpit.

"Let's go to Thailand. I'm getting a passport. And anyway I got to England with no passport—"

"Pippa. You are going on a passport. You are a successful business woman with bank accounts and a mortgage. No one will think you're trying to sneak anywhere by the back door."

"Rob. Will you do something for me? Only when we are alone?"

"Mm?" He kissed her head.

"Will you call me Piroshka? Just sometimes."

She let tears fall slowly down her cheeks but the adrenaline was gone; the sick fear underlying every part of her body.

"I love you, Piroshka," said Rob. "How's that for a start?"

41

Tiny spherical sweets had arrived in the shop that day. They had pastel wrappers that caught the light when you twisted them. In the heat of the fire, the wrappers stuck to the sweets so that Wendy had to scrape bits off with her nails.

She popped a sweet into her mouth and licked her fingers. She hadn't yet worked out what flavour they were and whether they were all the same.

Yingyang rolled a sweet between her palms, thinking of Joe sitting alone somewhere in the hills.

"Moses," said Wendy, for the third time that evening. "You are avoiding the subject. If we don't do something, Bamboo Grove will be bulldozed to the ground and concreted over."

Moses nodded slowly.

"I will turn my attention to that perhaps. I am mindful of Yingyang's desire for psychic counselling and I would like to address that first."

"You're talking bullshit, Moses. The future of Bamboo Grove is not something to put on a to-do list. I've been following Torn-ear man and I'm not sure we've got time to talk bullshit." She shoved another sweet in her mouth and bit down hard.

"We will come to it. I feel something in the air, in the glint of the sinking sun on the water, and the message is clear. Yingyang, give me your hands."

Yingyang's heart began to beat faster. She gave him her upturned palms, but he clasped her hands between his and breathed deeper and deeper until he was almost snoring. Wendy lay back on the sand and untwisted a sweet wrapper.

"You'll meditate while Bamboo Grove is bulldozed around you," she muttered, but his eyelids didn't flicker.

Yingyang trembled inside. Would Moses see that Joe was coming back to her? What if he said she'd lost him and that was it? Perhaps he'd say that an American man in Bangkok was thinking of her every night. She wasn't even sure what she felt about that anymore.

Moses sighed. "Close your eyes," he said. "What do you see?"

"The sunbird. He wants to fly."

"And now?"

Yingyang whispered, eyes tight shut, "My mother. Homeless and wild on the streets of Bangkok."

"Are you with her?"

"Inside her. Just beginning. She doesn't know I'm there."

Moses was jolted from his trance. Yingyang opened her eyes and they faced each other in the firelight. He coughed.

"What do you see, Moses? Will he come back to me?"

"I see happiness. Many people will read your books. I see love. But I also see loss."

Yingyang's throat constricted. "What type of loss?"

"I can't be sure. You will of course lose me, because my time on this earth is to come soon to a conclusion. However, I feel there is something else."

Yingyang pulled her hands away. "Stop saying you're going to die. There aren't any doctors on Bamboo Grove so who's put this into your head?" She clapped her hand over her mouth.

"Yingyang?"

"Do you have AIDS?" she whispered. "Like Noah?"

Although he shook his head, Moses' face took on an expression she'd not seen on him before. He looked — vulnerable. Uncertain. Maybe he did have AIDS. He was thin, but his eyes had none of the sunken blackness that Noah's had as he sickened beyond the help of his own magic.

Eventually, carefully, Moses said, "I will live on. In the roots of the trees—"

"Which will soon be dragged out of the ground," said Wendy, scooping a handful of sand and sieving it through her fingers.

"I am deep in the earth, I am in the tranquil waters of the Andaman Sea. And I tell you this now because I have no shame but only pride – I will live on in the many, many children I have fathered."

Wendy sat up. Through the flames, Yingyang and she stared at each other.

"The women who come to me," he said, pulling his legs into a lotus posture, "are aching for a miracle and I have a gift for the particular miracle they seek."

"You screw them and get them pregnant?" Wendy glared at him.

"I perform a ritual with the clients whose path leads them to me. And the ritual can take many forms. But you are right, though you have a rather naïve way of describing what I provide. My body produces a powerful semen and there are many lives I have begun."

Moses turned to Yingyang. "Tell me," he said, in a very different voice, "what is your mother's name?"

"Jessica," she said. "People say she looks like Marilyn Monroe and acts like Robin Hood. On spiked drugs."

Wendy hooted with laughter, thumping the sand and spraying grains into the air. But Moses sat perfectly still, gazing at Yingyang's face.

Yingyang frowned, looking into his eyes until Wendy stopped laughing and sat up again.

"Do you know her or something?" said Wendy, feeling as separate as if she were watching them on film.

"Yingyang," said Moses, in a voice that came from deep within himself. "You are my first child. I am your father."

~

Bristol stared across the road at Tranquillity Place. The great neck of a JCB hung limp and stupid. Peeping over the boards, the top of the spirit house was just visible. An intricate little roof with a gold piping gutter, standing defiantly beside the tower it was built to protect.

On Christmas Day, he'd have to sit through dinner with Linda and

Andrew, Andrew's new girlfriend, Sam, his other half and the twins, but just now he couldn't imagine how. He'd drink a lot, he supposed, and Linda would huff and bitch at him. He'd be silent until he broke under her temper, and maybe then he'd tell her steadily that it was over. Their stifling marriage, the farcical little empire that was Eastern Vision, the paradise that would have been Bamboo Grove hotel and spa, which they had dreamed up on a long ago Christmas in Phuket. All of it burnt out like a firework display.

And what would he say then? That it was Jessica he loved, Jessica he had always loved despite everything? That Linda could finally have her way and go back to her beloved London. With her share of what was left when their lives had been dispersed and poured into the cavernous pit of debt.

Bristol scratched his scalp with dirty fingernails and laughed at his own spectacular arrogance. He turned to walk back up the Sukhumvit Road towards his apartment, where his restless evening waited. And as he did so, he glimpsed a woman in a pale green cardigan sliding out of a taxi across the street, a cell phone pinned to her ear. She looked appraisingly at the remains of Tranquillity Place, spoke quickly into the phone and popped it into a silver handbag. She stood on tiptoe to peer through a gap in the boards.

"Hey, Tina!" bellowed Bristol. She swung round, gripping her bag to her chest. "Happy Christmas! Goodwill, peace and so on."

She bowed her head a little and when he kept grinning at her, she tossed her hair and walked away in the direction she had come.

~

Yingyang stared at the blank page but her right hand had become as stubborn as her mouth had once been. She looked out to sea, watching boats ferry people home for Christmas and bringing others to escape it. She saw newcomers wade through the shallows, sweating in the sun, their luggage held high by the boat boys.

A woman with scrambled auburn hair stepped onto the beach. Did she have a head full of wishes that only Moses could grant? Another brother or sister to add to the endless family Yingyang had never known she had. Again, the sensation that she had been kicked in the stomach.

Wendy knew. Wendy had known who Yingyang's father was at exactly the moment she had known herself. He'd robbed her of the chance to take it in, to decide for herself when to tell people.

The auburn-haired woman stood with her hands on her hips, gazing up into the dark green hills in the centre of the island. Her lips were moving as if in silent prayer.

Yingyang felt Joe's presence before she turned to see him. He looked into her face and she kept her expression blank.

Tentatively, he crouched and then sat. They watched the girl from the shop pad down the sand, her pregnant belly ready to burst, holding an umbrella over her head. She paddled her toes in the water.

"Wendy told me."

"She had no right."

"I don't know what to make of it. Do you think it's true?"

Yingyang nodded. She said flatly, "He says he was blonde until he was six. That his mother looked–" she swallowed, "just like me." Her voice had fallen to a whisper so tight it might snap. "His father is a children's author." The tears fell at last from her eyes. She watched from a distance as they streamed down her face.

Joe dug his hands into the sand. The pregnant shop girl squatted slowly to splash water onto her forehead.

"Can I hold you?" asked Joe.

Yingyang shut her eyes.

He twisted round to face her, pulled her close and, with one arm round her back and the other cradling her head, he rocked her gently.

She soaked his T-shirt in her tears. Her body sagged against his. The rocking slowed until they sat still and the tears had exhausted themselves.

"All my life," said Yingyang into Joe's shoulder, "I have been lonely. I didn't know I had a father. And now I find I have brothers and sisters in another continent."

Joe's fingers were wound now in her hair. He nodded, though she couldn't see him do it.

"All my life," she said again, "I have been lonely."

42

Moses didn't come with them to see Torn-ear man. He said he had to meditate over a black crystal, symbolising new beginnings after natural endings. But as she climbed up the hill behind Joe and Wendy, Yingyang glanced back to see the auburn-haired woman waiting under his tree.

She shook her head rapidly from side to side. She'd met her father, known him without realising, seen him masturbate for heaven's sake. And, before he told her who he was, he had told her he expected soon to die. Above her head, a monkey swung from one branch to another, seeming to grin at her. The haze of gnats grew thicker as they climbed. Her shins began to ache.

"There!" Wendy held out her arm and they came to a halt behind her. Joe put a hand on Yingyang's shoulder.

"Excuse me, we'd like to speak with you," said Wendy.

Torn-ear man turned quickly to face them, stuffing a piece of paper into his pocket. His expression changed. He seemed to make a decision.

"Yingyang," he said. "Yingyang. Wendy. And Joe?"

They looked at each other. Wendy frowned.

"You are right," she said. "The island is small so you've heard our names. Unfortunately for all of us, we have also heard your telephone calls. In fact," she added, "I've never seen you speak to anyone on the island. You only talk into your mobile."

Torn-ear man grimaced. "I'm afraid you are correct. Such is business."

A seagull squawked above them, dropping a splat of white excrement onto the ground.

"It is this 'business' we want to talk about," said Wendy, folding her arms.

Joe touched her elbow.

"Shall we sit somewhere? On the beach?" He batted a mosquito.

"No," said Wendy. "I want the truth before he has a chance to make stuff up."

Torn-ear man held up his hands. "OK, OK," he said. "What is it you are interested to know?"

Before Wendy could speak, Yingyang answered quietly, calmly.

"Bamboo Grove," she said, "is our retreat. We each have reasons to seek one. It has become our shelter and our home. And," her voice broke a little, "a place of friendship."

Joe cleared his throat.

"We are concerned," he said, "that you seem to be planning a development of some sort. Perhaps you don't realise that what you envisage would destroy the very thing you are trying to market."

Torn-ear man nodded. "There is reason in what you say."

"So what the fuck are you doing?" cried Wendy, her hands on her hips. "Bamboo Grove was uninhabited before the artists' retreat was built and they've preserved its—"

"What stage of negotiation are you at?" asked Joe steadily. "I imagine Eastern Vision is not entirely in the dark about these plans?"

As Torn-ear man clasped his hands together and breathed out at length, Yingyang remembered where she'd seen him before. Shaking hands with Bristol and getting into the lift.

"I work," he said, "for Eastern Vision. The – development – you refer to is the next phase of their plans."

Wendy's mouth fell open. Yingyang and Joe turned away to look down the hill where the beach was just visible through the trees.

~

Bristol stood with his hand on the dresser, fiddling absent-mindedly with a tinsel wreath.

"You're grinding your teeth," said Linda, from the sofa.

He grunted. *Summer Towers and Tranquillity Place.* He remembered teasing Jessica, years ago, when the idea of investing in real estate was so glamorous, such a grown-up game. *At least admit they're cool names.* And now, it seemed, the luxury condoms had been built on sand. Insubstantial, impermanent, corrupt sand. And Emerald City was a white elephant. A tower of untouchable luxury. They had pumped money into it, only to see it stand empty, guarded by the ghost of the tragic builder. Bristol scrunched the tinsel in his palm. The oil project too; he had a clear vision of bank notes swamped in stinking greasy oil, swirling in a vortex to land in a hole deep in the seabed.

"Bamboo Grove," he said, through gritted teeth. "It's all we have left but how do we fund it when we've become financial lepers?"

"That's a revolting image," said Linda.

Bristol brushed bits of tinsel from his fingers and went to sit beside her.

"I'm sorry," murmured Linda. "I can't imagine the stress you're under. I worry about you."

He smiled weakly.

"You worry? About me?"

"You're my husband, Bristol. I've known you forever."

"Yes," he said. "God knows how you've put up with me." He rubbed the stubble that had crept onto his chin and swallowed. "You deserved better. I should never have let you tie yourself to me. We could have—"

Linda sniffed.

"Financial ruin has made you quite prosaic," she said. "I'm not sure it suits you."

He reached for her and pulled her into his chest, trying to bury his head in her hair. She was still for a moment and then, gently, she pulled away.

"Bristol," she said, and she sounded not like a forty-three year old reluctant ex-pat wife but like the young PR star she'd been years ago. "When Andrew goes to college, I'm moving back to London. I've been talking to a contact of Dad's."

He nodded. He scratched his elbows through his shirt sleeves.

"Right. Yes. I see."

She squeezed his hand.

"Maybe you can make a go of it with Jessica. Hm?"

He stared at her and she looked unblinkingly back at him.

"I—"

"Don't try, Bristol. Just accept. I won't drain you dry in the divorce; I'd have picked my moment better if it was money I was after."

"Oh God, Linda."

She stood, brushed down her dress and shook out her hair.

Bristol took a deep breath and stared at his feet.

"Is there – I can't believe I'm saying this – is there someone else?"

Linda smiled.

"Two or three actually. I haven't quite decided which to settle for. I'm going out. I'll see you later. Try and meditate or something. You'll give yourself a heart attack if you're not careful."

~

White gold turned to soft peach as the rising sun warmed the sand. The sea came to life as it reflected the lights coming on in the sky.

Yingyang watched the shifting colours from the shade of her father's tree. She sat cross-legged, a sarong from the shop draped over her legs. She waited while the sun grew hot and the boat boys began to pull up anchors and rev reluctant engines.

The auburn-haired woman appeared, looking about her, eyes pinched against the sun. She fidgeted with the knot on her headscarf, slowing as she neared the tree.

Yingyang sat up very straight.

"Welcome to Bamboo Grove," she said. "Are you lost?"

"Sorry. Thanks," said the woman, smiling. "I was – erm – looking for Moses?"

"You will need to look another day," said Yingyang, pressing her palms together and dipping her head.

The woman's face fell and Yingyang thought she saw tears behind her eyes. She said, because it was the first idea that entered her head, "With Moses the time must be exact. He will descend from the hills and you will know he is ready to perform. Rituals," she added quickly as the woman's face flushed puce.

"Right. Maybe he could – well, I'll be about. I'm here over Christmas. I have to leave on the twenty-seventh?"

Yingyang nodded. "In Bamboo Grove, time is measured by the wax and wane of the moon and the pull of the tranquil waters. Days and dates have little relevance here."

"No, of course. It's just – well, I have to get back for work, but – well, thank you." The woman wai-ed hurriedly and scuttled off.

Yingyang grinned and a great bubble rose up through her middle until she was laughing more in one single outburst than she ever had in all her life before. She wiped her eyes and bit her fist, shook her head and giggled until she sank back against the trunk of the tree with aftershocks hiccupping their way up through her throat.

When finally she looked up, feeling exhilarated calm, Moses was there.

"You have never looked more beautiful than you do at this moment."

"And you," said Yingyang, squinting up at him, "have never looked less sure of yourself."

"May I sit with you?"

She nodded, aware of her own heartbeat, and he folded himself so that he sat holding one knee, the other flopped out to the side. He gazed into her face.

"Did you really not know until you tried to tell my fortune?" Her eyes flicked down to her hands.

"You and I saw it in the same moment, Yingyang."

They sat in silence. Yingyang's fit of laughter had burst a layer of the armour she'd worn all her life. She felt as different as if she'd swapped bodies with someone else.

"Silence," she said, "is some religion."

Moses put his head in his hands. "Yingyang, I ask you to forgive me many things. Including the bullshit that I am in the habit of speaking."

She laughed and he looked up, scraping his hair away from his face.

"I am angry," she said. "All my life my mother told me different stories about my father but she never told me you were here." She knocked her head back against the tree and squinted at the vast leaves above her. "And," she said through gritted teeth, "neither did you."

"Yingyang, I didn't know. I never thought. I never asked. I've been so full of my own crap I've seen only what I chose to see. You were conceived in London." He put a fist to his forehead and looked away. "In the stock cupboard. And then Jessica came to Thailand. I came soon after, but I only ever passed through Bangkok. I was seduced by the island game."

"The stock cupboard?"

Moses nodded. He had the look of a schoolboy caught truanting. "In the rainbow office. It's where Eastern Vision began, before the Bangkok stuff or Bamboo Grove were even thought of. Unfortunately," he said, scratching his armpit, "there was a whole stack of fertility symbols in the cupboard. I didn't think, at the time."

Yingyang stared at this man who had brought her so mindlessly into the world.

"Didn't you love Jessica? Why did you let her come to Thailand on her own?"

"We all loved Jessica. She's indefinable. Bristol loved her the minute he met her off the plane. And Sam did as soon as he could see through his grief. It was the summer his wife killed herself."

"Oh God, I never knew."

"When Jessica arrived in the office, she was like a coconut dropping into the fountain. The water was never going to settle the same way."

"She has that effect."

Yingyang's hands were clenched. She scrunched up her face, eyes and mouth tight shut.

"Yingyang? Are you so angry? Do you hate us?"

"Didn't you know what she was like? Didn't you know she refuses her medicine? That she wants to save the world in the middle of the night and then she doesn't move or eat for days? Did you think it was safe to let her go to Bangkok alone, to look after a child?" Yingyang was sobbing now. "A child. I was a child. And you left me to look after her. Yes I'm angry. Yes I hate you. You – have – no – idea." She couldn't speak any more, the sobs shook her body as much as the laughter had.

Moses waited. Yingyang smashed her fist on the ground and shook her head to fling the tears away. And slowly, as he reached out his hand to take hers, he began to cry some dry, rusty tears of his own.

~

Bristol and Sam sat side by side on the sofa in the chocolate office, silent and morose.

After a while, Sam sighed.

"I'd sell Emerald City for almost nothing, just to have something to put behind Bamboo Grove. There has to some bastard somewhere stupid enough to invest in us. Bamboo Grove could be great, it just needs time."

Bristol scratched his scalp. His cousin's incessant churning over of their financial ruin was giving him the most revolting psoriasis he'd ever known.

Sam stood and pressed his head on the huge window.

"There's something to be said for reducing overheads," he said. "This office can go. The secretaries have voted with their dainty little feet. Oddly enough, we'll keep Alexis. The tours are looking less like an add-on and more like a way of paying bills."

Bristol coughed.

"By the way," he said. "Linda's left me."

Sam turned to look at him, his eyes wide. At last, he said, "I didn't know she married you for your money," and gave a hoarse bark of laughter.

Bristol put his head in his hands.

"I'm a heartless bastard, Sam."

"Sure you are," said Sam, "I've always admired you for it."

There was a bossy knock on the door and they turned to look at it.

Bristol pulled himself together and stood.

"Hello?" he called.

The door opened and in walked a woman with bobbed hair and a fitted T-shirt over jeans.

"Good morning, gentlemen," she said.

"Pippa?" said Sam.

"Yes. Associate Director, Eastern Vision, London."

She extended her hand to Sam and then to Bristol.

"You got your passport."

"Yes, indeed. This was not a problem. It is quite clear to immigration that I have ties in the United Kingdom and will be a visitor only in this country."

Bristol gestured for her to sit on the sofa.

"It's good to see you."

"And your good selves," said Pippa, sitting down and crossing her legs. "How is the great empire?"

Sam leaned against the window and Bristol sat on the edge of the desk.

"It seems it may have had its day," shrugged Sam. "We find ourselves in something of a financial crisis."

Pippa raised her eyebrows.

"I heard Bamboo Grove is lovely. We can surely market it in many countries as a very special product."

Bristol smiled.

"Yes," he said. "It's more of a cash flow thing. We're rather in need of an injection of funds and what we're faced with is more of a haemorrhage."

Pippa looked from Bristol to Sam and frowned.

"Eastern Vision London is still growing," she said. "We have gone from strength to strength. Perhaps it is time to re-establish the links and remember that there was a day when Eastern Vision Bangkok was just an off-shoot. An experiment. Such a very lucrative experiment that Eastern Vision London was left behind like a forgotten little sister. But now maybe it can grow up."

Sam grinned.

"You're quite something, Pippa. I had no idea you still traded under Eastern Vision."

Bristol rubbed his eyes.

"Good on you, girl. I feel like the biggest shit for abandoning you like we did. Bangkok just took over and then when Moses and Alexis came over, we really just let you go."

"On the contrary," said Pippa, sitting up very straight. "You left me with an office, a network and a name. And I built my own little empire."

Bristol nodded. "So I don't need to feel like a big shit?"

"That is entirely up to you," said Pippa. "Now, what is the size of the injection required?"

43

A pavilion at the edge of the park offered a star-shaped patch of shade. Pippa sat on the slatted bench and watched sunlight bounce off the little lake. She liked Bangkok. She liked the way the air was full of talking in so many different languages, and the streets were so busy it squeezed thoughts to the very edges of her mind. She had to focus on dodging past people, stepping into the road to pass a food stall without being hit by a taxi, smiling at people trying to sell her things. It didn't smell like London and it didn't smell like home; it smelt of far away where no one knew her and she could be Pippa or Piroshka or whoever else she chose.

She was excited about Emerald City and Bamboo Grove. In her mind they were already buzzing with life. She only wished Marina could be with her as she chose furnishings for the show apartments; it would have been fun to do this together, sorting through silks, picking mini-chandeliers from the glittering lighting shops. But Marina had a wedding to plan. And this time she had got as far as invitations – she wasn't about to let the guilty demise of her ex-boyfriend stand in her way.

Pippa strolled to the lake and watched a little boy launch a paper boat. Under a tree nearby, a couple of older boys smoked and played draughts with bottle tops on a cardboard box.

Sam had asked her to come for Christmas but she was intrigued by Bamboo Grove. Perhaps it was a need to keep moving, a restlessness she wondered if she would ever lose now. But Bamboo Grove sounded unlike anywhere she had ever seen. And it would be interesting to see Moses after all these years. She'd never been sure if she loved him or hated him and she suspected both were true. The little paper boat absorbed water, its colours blurring and its sides collapsing. Elegantly, it fell in on itself and vanished under the sparkling blue water. Rob had said he would come. If she could get him to bring a cameraman with him, they could make an advertisement of sorts, a little film that would help them to sell their Paradise. It would mean being polite to Alexis, but she would persuade him to let them use the minibus. Bamboo Grove; Artists' Retreat. In the far corner of her mind, her brother's voice murmured, "A murderer's retreat," and the rice she'd eaten earlier hurled itself back up through her throat. She swallowed it, choking a little on the foulness. Crouching down, she scooped a handful of water and splashed her face with it.

Bamboo Grove, Emerald City; she repeated the words like a mantra in her head. She was a new breed of businesswoman: Romanian-British-Thai. Quirky, eclectic, bijou, innovative, ever-flexible. She began to walk fast around the perimeter of the park, smiling at anyone who would catch her eye, raising her face from time to time to the steaming sun.

"My plan is to market Emerald City as accommodation for the long or short term business traveller," she announced later. "I envisage companies may purchase apartments for their foreign guests and foreign companies can rent family-sized accommodation for people posted here."

"Pippa, when did you start using words like 'envisage'?"

Sam plonked his glass down and droplets of whisky splashed into the air.

Pippa looked at him, expressionless. Bristol shook his head.

"I'm sorry, Pippa. Ignore the drunk in the corner. I like the concept. You've bypassed the whole curse thing by appealing to the foreign market."

Pippa squared a sheaf of papers on the desk and nodded.

"I have calculated my capital input, loans required and an initial five-year forecast," she said. "Based on the working of Emerald City and the great success of Bamboo Grove which you will achieve with the resulting income secured."

Bristol and Sam stared at her and she stared back for a long moment before pushing a spreadsheet across the desk.

"I trust, gentlemen, that my proposition is acceptable."

Bristol threw back his head and laughed.

"Pippa," he said. "You are as of this moment a full and equal partner of Eastern Vision International."

He stood and they shook hands while Sam stared into his empty glass.

"I'm sorry," muttered Sam. He cleared his throat. "But which banks are going to lend us investment capital on this scale?"

Pippa leant back in her chair and clasped her hands behind her head.

"There are plenty of banks writing me letters about loaning money to me. That is no problem. I have a successful quirky bijou boutique, an expanding internet shopping site and I employ three hundred people in my factory in Romania."

Bristol grinned.

"If I remember rightly, it was Moses who brought you to the party."

Pippa looked puzzled.

"Which party?"

"I mean that he introduced you to Eastern Vision. He turned up with you one day and said he needed you as an office junior. Those were his words. 'Office junior', smarmy bugger."

Pippa smiled carefully.

"I was sadly grateful," she said, "to be the office junior. It was a curse, in those years, to be born Romanian. But we now have entrepreneurs and business travellers in Eastern Europe too. We will spread wide our marketing net for Emerald City and Bamboo Grove and they will thrive."

"I'm hungry," said Sam. "Shall we adjourn to the Chinese?"

Pippa's smile relaxed.

"Yes," she said, "I'm starving. Show me where business tycoons grab their snacks."

~

Bristol looked at his watch, mounting the steps two at a time. Tranquility Place was being pulled down and Summer Towers had become a slum. But if Pippa really could help, then the future of both Emerald City and Bamboo Grove might just be secure.

He thumped on the door.

"Jess? Quick, beautiful. I *have* to get back." He thumped again, looking at his watch. "Are you there?" He could hear movement. Shuffling, dragging, getting closer to the door. "For God's sake, are you *trying* to drive me mad?"

The door opened and Jessica stood dressed and made up, her hair washed and smooth. Beside her was a small rucksack, straining its zip.

"What's the plan?" he said, his pulse throbbing at his temples and in his eyelids.

"I'm going to Bamboo Grove," said Jessica.

"Sure you are."

"I'm serious. I want to be with my daughter for Christmas. You can't deny me that."

"Have you taken your sweets this morning?"

"I've packed them."

"But you've taken some?"

"Can't remember."

He smashed his fist on the door frame. "This is getting tedious. I have to go." He turned away to stop himself hitting her.

"I need the money. I'm going to the airport."

With his back to her, he said tightly, "Try listening for once. Money is not exactly flowing freely right now."

"Please." Her voice shook.

Bristol found himself leaning on the flaking wall, digging his nails into the creases of his elbow where his skin itched worst.

"A flight to Phuket is nothing to you. It's on a different scale. But to me it would mean the world."

"You asked me – you blackmailed me – into sending Yingyang away. And now you can't bear to be without her?"

"I was angry," she said quietly. "Please."

"The flights might be full."

"There'll be a seat. I'll wait by the desk until they let me on."

Bristol rubbed his face.

"You'll have Andrew home for Christmas. And your sweet, loving wife. And you're telling me I'll be fine in this little apartment on my own? That I won't drown myself in the khlong while you're scoffing Tutu's roast potatoes?"

"Jesus, Jessica." She picked up her rucksack. "You can go on the minibus. On Christmas Eve. Alexis is picking some people up. Maybe Moses will magic you a baby. I've heard he's doing well on that score."

"Meaning?"

"Ask him."

"He's there? On Bamboo Grove?"

"Yes, sweetheart. My spies tell me he and Yingyang are thick as thieves."

44

The air felt heavily, intensely hot. The sky was thick with a cocktail of pollution and rain-stuffed clouds.

Jessica rubbed her eyes with the backs of her hands and remembered too late that she was wearing mascara.

"Shit," she mumbled, trying to wipe it off her cheeks with the pads of her thumbs.

"All set?" said Alexis, making an odd little gesture halfway between a thumbs-up and a high-five.

"All set," said Jessica and climbed into the bus.

"Hi there, good morning," said the driver, "how do you do?"

Jessica smiled. "Sawadeeka," she said. "Pretty good, thank you."

Alexis yanked the door shut and settled himself by the window.

Please don't try to make conversation. Jessica stared hard out of the window, trying to look lost in thought when the truth was her thoughts had jammed themselves to a standstill. She'd reflected, regretted, analysed and wished until a sort of mental gridlock had set in.

"We're going via the airport, Jess, to pick up our film crew."

"Film crew?" She looked at him.

Alexis had adopted a nonchalant expression and now he stifled an irritating yawn.

"We're making a little docu-ad about Bamboo Grove. I'm fronting it; seems sensible, with my background."

Jessica said, "Oh," and shut her eyes.

The traffic was agonisingly slow. Intrepid policemen stood in the midst of the smog-filled chaos, their toes under constant threat of being crushed by trucks and taxis, cars and tuk-tuks.

Jessica leant her head on the window but the glass vibrated too much and she couldn't get comfortable. Now that she was so near to Yingyang, so determined to – what? Speak to her? Hold her? Beg for forgiveness? Make friends with her and find out who she was? – it was torture to make such a slow start. She made herself breathe out and then deeply in, thinking of Bristol's attempts at mindfulness. As they found the expressway, the minibus picked up speed and Jessica's agitation settled a little. She gazed out at billboards with vast images of shiny white people and glittering apartment blocks, inviting her to buy into 'Idolised Living' or spray herself with imported perfume. Layers of roads criss-crossed, leaving concrete caves beneath them where litter turned slowly to urban compost and people at the very bottom of the Bangkok heap curled up at night.

At the airport, the driver became instantly stressed and stressful.

"No can stop here!" He repeated, jumping in and out of the bus.

"All cool, mate. Hover if you can, drive round if you have to. Give me five at most OK?"

Jessica sat tight, tearing a cuticle from her thumb and sucking it when it bled.

"No can stop here!"

The driver revved urgently, drove forwards a few yards and turned off the engine. Behind them, a taxi horn blasted.

Jessica tried a bit of mindfulness for a while. The hooting became intermittent and then stopped. She looked out of the window and saw Alexis striding ahead of two men who were carting a tripod, a selection of cameras and a sound boom. Behind them, beaming, was a woman pushing a trolley of luggage and duty-free bags.

The driver leapt out to load the equipment and the baggage while the woman took hold of one of the men round the waist and planted kisses all over his face. "No can stop here!"

The driver scuttled back round the bus and jumped in. As he revved and hooted, the men nodded at her, settling themselves into seats, and the woman grinned and scrunched her hair.

"All set!" called Alexis, tapping the back of the driver's seat.

Jessica looked at the smiling woman and something shifted in the gridlock of her mind. A memory from the edge of childhood, the smell of spray paint, the scowl of a girl in a rugby jersey and a sarong. The woman sensed that she was being stared at and looked at Jessica.

The boyfriend shuffled in his seat and cleared his throat.

"Rob," he said, leaning across to offer Jessica his hand.

"Hi," she said, enjoying the firmness of his grasp.

"Pete," said the other man, giving a little wave.

"Hi."

Now the women looked again at each other and Jessica found a rather sheepish little smile flickering across her face.

"Pippa?" she said.

"I certainly am," said Pippa. "And you are Jessica Jane."

Alexis coughed.

"Ah, yes, of course," he said. "You ladies will have worked together at Eastern Vision London."

"Many years ago," said Pippa. And Jessica felt, inexplicably, like crying.

"How are you?" said Pippa.

Jessica couldn't think of an answer; her lips moved a little as if she was trying to speak but in the end she smiled tightly and looked away.

"Argh, my knees," said Rob. "Not only do you economise by having us arrive on Christmas Eve, you don't even get us into business class."

He tickled Pippa and she squeaked.

Pete didn't seem to feel any such need to help fill the silence, or else he was too tired. He let his head loll back and quietly poked his finger about in his left ear.

Pippa snuggled into Rob and rubbed his knees.

"God, I have missed you with all my heart," she purred. "It is the most wonderful thing in the world to see you."

Rob laughed.

"You too, Pippa," he said, and he kissed the top of her head.

Jessica swallowed. She chewed the inside of her cheeks, shreds of skin catching in her teeth. Bristol had kissed the top of her head, standing in a police cell not so long ago. She'd lived for sixteen years nursing the memory of each consecutive promise kiss, sometimes weeks or months apart, and punctuated by dream-come-true nights when his love for her was in his eyes, his touch, his kisses and the way the contours of his naked body fitted so exactly with her own.

They all fell asleep on the bus, even the driver, though fortunately only for a few seconds and they were alone on a country road at the time. Pete slept longest and deepest, unaware of the gasses releasing themselves from his bowel as he relaxed. Rob and Pippa slept with their arms folded together and bliss on their faces. Alexis snored and grunted, muttering from time to time, and Jessica drifted in and out of a state where she wasn't quite asleep and she wasn't quite awake.

~

Jessica trailed her fingers over the side, creating a ripple that merged with the wake of the boat. The Andaman Sea was the biggest crystal of all. Tomorrow, she would swim. She'd strip off her clothes and dive right under, letting the waters erase all trace of what she had been. When she emerged, she could start afresh. She could be a mother to her daughter, a friend to herself, and find a man who loved only her. She didn't know where she would go, but she knew that when she stepped out of the water and let the sun dry her hair, it would be clear.

"It's good that you came, Peter," Pippa was saying. "I am grateful to you and it is such short notice."

"I jumped at it! This place is awesome." Pete kicked off his shoes, rolled up his khaki chinos and lay on the prow of the little boat with his hands behind his head. "*The Beach* is my favourite book."

Rob was checking the camera equipment, which he was attempting to keep dry.

"We'll be wading in," said Alexis, preparing his jeans for the event. "We'll need to hold everything up out of the water. Obviously," he added, and stuffed his trainers into an oversized satchel.

First, Jessica must ask Yingyang's forgiveness. Her silent daughter who had never known a childhood or the warmth of friendship. Who had looked for love only to be sent away by a mother paralysed with jealousy. What would she say when she stood with Yingyang? *Happy Christmas? Forgive me? I never knew how to love you but I want to learn. I want to build a life for us, I want to start again.*

I have nursed a man while he died of AIDS, I have given food and clothing to hundreds of people. I have set fire to their homes so that they could start again. But to the one person who I should have given most, I have given nothing.

It was odd, thought Jessica, that her eyes were dry. Had she finally, after all these years, turned off the waterworks? She thought of Maureen and Geoff whose lives she had destroyed and tried to imagine them living in some sort of peace. Lifting her face to the sun, she shut her eyes.

"The concept here is 'docu-ad'" said Alexis. "I'm thinking twenty to thirty minutes—"

Pete coughed. "I thought we said more ten to fifteen."

"Let us play this with our ears," said Pippa. "We will explore, we will film, and we will have a Christmas to remember forever."

The boat slowed and Jessica opened her eyes to watch Bamboo Grove come into view. A golden beach flanked by coconut trees. Huts on stilts and behind them dense green hills. Here, she would find her own peace.

She could see people now, moving slowly in the afternoon heat. A small boy sieving handfuls of sand through his fingers. A tall figure sitting statue-like beneath a coconut tree. A couple holding hands. Jessica scanned the beach for Yingyang, straining her eyes. My daughter is here in this paradise. She imagined she could see her, right in the centre of the beach, watching her mother and waiting. Jessica's stomach cartwheeled. All around her, the others were wielding tripods and camera bags, passing things tentatively over the side of the boat.

Rob waded ahead, a tarpaulin-wrapped bundle held high above his head. Pippa was laughing, her skirt tucked into her knickers, her kit bag slung across her shoulders.

Jessica stood and breathed in.

"Oh, God," she whispered.

Jessica put her rucksack on the sand and looked up into the dark green hills. Bamboo Grove. Where people came to hide.

"It's beautiful," she whispered. "It's heaven on earth." She laughed silently.

Along the beach, a lady lay on her front whilst a masseuse pulled an arm behind her back to touch the opposite leg. A little boy sat watching them, drawing in the sand. A young and very pregnant woman squatted in the shallows, splashing herself with water.

Jessica thought of Bristol and his attempts at serenity. His inability to achieve mindfulness. If he would only stop fretting about money, money, money. Deals, emails, contracts. He should come here. She sighed. If tranquillity were possible anywhere, it was here. She would be as still as the water, as golden as the sand. Though even here in paradise, her stomach fluttered at the thought of seeing Yingyang, and knotted itself when she dared to think she might be forgiven.

She hooked her rucksack over an elbow and, leaving the others to fuss over the equipment, made her way up the beach to where a hippy sat under a coconut tree. His head was hung and his long hair fell forward, drying in the sun. He was sitting in the lotus position.

"Excuse me," she said quietly. "I'm looking for—"

"Yingyang." He lifted his head and his hair dropped away from his face.

She knelt and they took in the detail of each other's faces. She saw the creases that hadn't been there seventeen years ago. The incredible beard that was a continuation of his hair. And the depth of the peace in his eyes. She knew that he saw a plumper, older, tireder woman than the girl he'd known so briefly.

"Moses," she said. "They told me you were here."

He nodded.

"Mark. Just Mark. I am glad to see you, Jessica."

She smiled, looked up at the coconuts. "Do you ever worry that they'll fall on your head?"

"Don't you remember?" said Moses. "I don't worry."

She laughed suddenly. "I liked you better as a Buddhist monk."

He laughed.

"Why," he started. They looked straight into each other's eyes. "Why did you never tell me?"

Jessica looked away.

"I'm not sure," she said. "Perhaps you didn't look like someone who'd do milk and nappies."

"And after that?"

"I was in love."

"And you still are."

She nodded.

"Bristol," she said. "I wanted him to be Yingyang's father."

He raised an eyebrow.

"It wasn't Yingyang's choice," he said, "to come here."

She picked up her rucksack.

"Where is she? I need to find her."

She stood, shading her eyes against the last of the sun.

"Take a hut," said Moses. "I'll tell you when the time is right."

Jessica looked around her, frustrated, stubborn.

"Jessica," said Moses. "Please trust me. Tomorrow is Christmas Day and Yingyang is going diving. With her boyfriend–"

"Her boyfriend?"

He smiled.

"Yes. Her boyfriend. It's very sweet that our daughter has a–"

"*Our* daughter! You can call her that after all these years? How dare you? You can't just *own* her like that, she never knew you!"

Moses sat still, letting a tiny breeze blow a strand of hair into his eyes. He ignored it and it drifted back again. Jessica glared at him.

"Let her have Christmas Day," he said. "She'll be on the other side of the island and you can find some peace before you see her. You need some time to clear your head space."

"Head space? You still talk rubbish. I'll see my daughter when I choose."

Moses shrugged.

"I suggest you time your reunion carefully. Do you know what you are going to say?"

"No, I–"

"Good. When the time is right, you will see her and you will know what to say."

45

"And...Action!"

Alexis punched the air in lieu of a clapboard and executed a little twirl in the sand.

Ironically, the instruction cued quite the opposite. Moses became absolutely motionless in his customary position. He exhaled slowly and inhaled deeply, though he was careful to keep his shoulders steady so this wasn't really noticeable. The advanced state of mindfulness involved was impressive but invisible so when Alexis said "And...cut!", it was hard to tell what had been cut.

"Awesome," said Alexis.

Moses opened his eyes slowly.

"Thank you," he said. "Your awe is appreciated."

Pippa wriggled her toes in the sand and grinned.

"I'd like to get some shots of artists doing the art," she said. "There is a lady called Wendy who is set ready to paint on the beach, and a man who has agreed to write, possibly on a rock."

Rob extended his hand to Moses.

"Thanks, mate. That should be a good little piece of footage."

Moses pressed Rob's hand between both of his.

"My pleasure. If you're selling Bamboo Grove as a place of tranquillity, I imagine the more violent of the development proposals have been reconsidered."

Pippa nodded.

"Do not distress yourself, Moses. I will be allowing only pacifist architecture and there will be no aggressive tourism."

Moses bent his head back to gaze at the coconuts above him.

"You are as magic as ever, my little gypsy princess."

Rob cleared his throat, brushing specks of sand off the boom. Moses looked at him and found it within himself to blush.

"Sorry. Strictly speaking, she is *your* little gypsy princess. She was never mine."

Alexis became very busy with a mobile phone, which he shook and peered at intently.

"No signal," he muttered. And then he added, somewhat

uncertainly, "Show some respect. Pippa's the big boss now, guys."

Pippa laughed.

"I certainly am," she said.

~

Moses washed his hair in coconut milk for the last time. He combed it through with his hands, wondering when it would happen. It was close now. And there was something precise about passing away on Christmas Day, the idea appealed to him.

The shock of meeting his first child had changed him. He would have liked to see them all now, to look into their faces before he passed. Perhaps he'd look down from Spirit and find some way to protect them. Like a father.

Placing his hands together, dipping his head, he fell into a deep meditation. He floated above the island and saw its future. He saw his own life; in orange robes with a shaven head, taking the virginity of a mercurial young girl, pacing the office through the night after the journalist began to chase him. Telling fortunes and looking into the eyes of his child. And now sitting in the lotus posture he had at last perfected, wearing a recycled, ethically traded, unbleached organic cotton toga.

~

"Noodles for Christmas dinner!" said Pete. He scooped up a great tangle of them and chopsticked them messily into his mouth.

Wendy smiled at him. Alexis said, "Here's to that!" and opened another beer.

Further down the beach, Jessica watched them; Pete, Wendy, Alexis, Rob and Pippa. They were inseparable, those two. Jessica would have been envious but her heart had no room for envy; it was too full of Yingyang. She knew Moses had made sure that Yingyang and Joe left early for their snorkelling, and his plan had worked because here she was still waiting. She sighed. Tonight. They'd come back and she would – she would know what to say when the time came. Moses seemed determined to make her wait. As if he wanted to speak

327

to Yingyang first, to warn her. Jessica scowled at the thought. *I am her mother!* The voice in her head raised its eyebrows: *but you gave up that right when you sent her away. Remember 'Get – rid – of – her'.* Pippa called out to her.

"Come and have noodles and beer!" she said.

Jessica looked at the cosy circle; Wendy was laughing and talking as if she had known the others for ages. Pete raised his can of beer and smiled broadly.

"Merry Christmas!" he said.

"Merry Christmas," she repeated softly and moved uncertainly towards them. They made space for her, between Pete and Alexis, and she knelt down and accepted a bowl of noodles and mushrooms.

"You must be looking forward to seeing your daughter again," said Rob politely.

Jessica blushed.

"Yes," she said. "Yes, I am." She glanced up at Moses' tree, under which he was absorbed in serene meditation. "But Moses tells me she has gone snorkelling for the day. With a boyfriend."

Wendy slurped some noodles and, as she chewed, she said, "Yingyang knows that Moses is her father. He told her. He said you were his first customer."

Jessica's face burned a deep red. Wendy looked from her to the others, to Moses and back to Jessica in search of an explanation. Alexis choked on a knot of noodles and Rob got up to thump him on the back. After this there was silence until Wendy mumbled, "Sorry. I shouldn't have opened my mouth."

"It's fine," said Jessica, twirling a ringlet of hair around her finger. She wasn't sure *what* exactly was fine but she felt she'd ruined their party with her presence.

Rob cleared his throat.

"We should all go snorkelling," he said. "Not that we have an underwater camera, which is a–"

Jessica stood, leaving her bowl of uneaten Christmas dinner on the sand.

"I'm sorry," she muttered, "I'm just going to see Moses."

She walked up the beach, shaking a little as she thought about Wendy and what she'd said.

"Moses," she called as she drew near. "Mark."

He opened his eyes but the rest of him stayed motionless.

"Wendy said you…"

"You don't want to take too much notice of Wendy. She has problems of her own."

"Look," she said. "Have you told Yingyang I'm here? I have to see her."

Moses cracked his knuckles and she winced.

"You will see her first thing tomorrow morning."

"Tomorrow? No way, I–"

"Trust me. Christmas night is for lovers. Let Yingyang have her peace on earth before you, well, she will be readier to – forgive."

He spoke this last word tentatively, with a question mark in his tone. Jessica blinked a long blink and walked quietly away, her jaw tight set.

~

A crystal mirage. A cut-glass rainbow that melted under their touch, sending slivers of light in all directions. Fish swam in and out of reeds in a silent ballet. Joe put his hand to his snorkel and then out to Yingyang as if he were blowing a watery kiss. She smiled, clamping the rubber grip between her teeth.

He reached out for her hand, pointing between two rocks at a neon orange fish with a white stripe. As they began to push upwards for air, a whole cloud of fish blew towards them. Ribbons of blue fins and black stripes danced in synchronised chaos. Yingyang laughed and choked on the water she sucked in. She kicked herself to the surface, spluttering, eyes shining. Joe emerged suddenly behind her and blew a whale-fountain from his snorkel, pulling her into his arms. Treading water, they spat out the rubber grips and kissed.

Diving under again, holding hands, Joe winked at her from behind his mask and Yingyang nodded a slow-motion nod. Only the sound of her own rhythmic breathing broke the silence in her ears. Here, she could suspend the inexorable approach of the bulldozers. She could see only Joe, and the underwater fairground, and know that it was Christmas Day everywhere but Bamboo Grove.

46

Yingyang woke shortly after eight the next morning, her head on Joe's chest. He let out a soft snore and she laughed quietly.

Then the bulldozers started up. The hut shook with the violence of the machines and she squeezed her eyes shut, trying to erase the awful images of destruction. She could believe anything of Eastern Vision now. To begin the demolition the day after Christmas. She felt ashamed to have lived off the business, to have wasted so many hours dreaming of a man who didn't exist. She felt nothing for Bristol now. Let him stay with his wife, he deserved no better when he thought only of profit and gain.

The thunder of the machines lasted only minutes. Yingyang tried to hope there was some last-minute reprieve. That Moses had seen sense and stood in the way. She imagined him spread-eagled naked in their path and grinned despite herself. Maybe Torn-ear man had been touched by their protests and called a stop to the plans.

Joe stirred.

"Yingyang," he murmured, pulling her towards him. "What's that noise?"

"Ssh," she said, "I'm coming back. I won't be long."

She pulled on his T-shirt and tied her sarong round her waist. Joe rolled over, smiling, his eyes half-closed.

She came out into the morning sunlight, but she saw no sign of any bulldozers. She walked all the way round the huts and peered into the hills, but the island was still asleep. The lights had come on in the sea, the diamond flecks that would shine more brightly as the sun climbed higher. A boat-boy lay on the prow of his boat, arms folded behind his head. A young woman arranged fresh petals in the barrels at the foot of each set of steps.

Moses sat beneath his tree as though he hadn't moved all night, as though he had fulfilled his prophesy and departed, leaving behind his shell on the earth.

Yingyang shook her head. Perhaps the trembling had been the approach of thunder. Perhaps she had imagined it on the edge of sleep. She turned to go back into Joe's hut and there, on the steps at the far end of the row, was her mother.

"Yingyang," she said. "Please don't walk away."

Yingyang didn't move. Jessica's face was clear of make-up and she had flattened her hair with yellow silk. She had bare feet and she wore a man's shirt that fell to her hips and past her hands. She walked slowly toward her.

"I came to find you."

The petal mosaics finished, the young woman bowed a little wai greeting and left them. They smiled, the same fleeting, nervous smile.

"Khun Jessica," said Yingyang. "Welcome to Bamboo Grove."

"Your voice," said Jessica, "it's beautiful. I've waited a long time to hear your voice."

47

It was then that the great wave hit Bamboo Grove. Deep in the seabed, the gods of the underworld had unleashed a storm that would kill and kill. The first thing we were aware of was shouting; a sound alien to Bamboo Grove. Then a roar that gathered strength as we turned towards it. The shore had drained far from the beach. Boats slumped sideways with no water to hold them. Fish thrashed and crabs scuttled under the sudden exposure. The great roar took shape as a tower of water stretching right across the skyline, moving inexorably for the island.

Some people started to run. One of the boat boys stood by his boat staring at the wave as if it were an illusion. The little boy whose mother did the massages picked up a fish. He stuffed it in his pocket and scooped up another. But Wendy was sprinting away from the wave.

"Run!" she screamed. "Fucking run! That's a tidal wave!"

The masseuse ran in the opposite direction, crying out for her son, her arms flailing in the air.

These things all happened within the space of a minute, but I can play them like a film frame by frame in my head.

Joe appeared in the doorway of the hut, pulling up his shorts and frowning. Pippa and Rob emerged, looking around, dazed. Jessica reached for me, still staring at the wave, and then Joe shot down the steps away from us, calling "Run! Go up into the hills as fast as you can!"

"Joe! Where?" I shouted, but Jessica was tugging at me, dragging me down the steps. She kept my hand firmly grasped in hers and Rob pushed me onwards, bellowing, "Pete! Where's Pete?"

I don't remember when I realised that Wendy wasn't with us, and I'll never understand how we came to lose her when she'd been one of the first to run. I remember Rob panting, "I hope to God Pete's in the hills and not on the beach," and I remember when the girl who did the flower mosaics caught us up. But my mind was so full of Joe and visions of his stupid heroism that I didn't shout for Moses. My father was there. *My father*, meditating under a coconut tree while the coast of south-east Asia was destroyed. And I left him there.

Halfway up the hill, we came gradually to a breathless halt and stared white-faced through the gaps in the trees. Jessica tightened her grip on my hand. The wave swallowed the beach, smashed the huts and the shop, tore apart the fountain, hurled the boats into the air and then sucked in its breath for a second onslaught.

Moses must have been slammed against the trunk of his tree, bombed by coconuts shaken from its branches. He'd have preferred that to drowning, as a cause of death.

And as we stared and shook, Joe stumbled up through the trees just below us, the masseuse's son clinging koala-like to his body. Joe sank to his knees and rolled the boy off him. A bright orange fish slid lifeless to the ground. I sobbed. I crouched beside Joe and buried my head in his wheezing, heaving chest. Pippa picked up the little boy and murmured to him in Hungarian.

Each successive pendulum-swing of the wave was less violent. There were bodies; men, women, children, dead or dying as the water receded. Shattered glass, splintered wood, tiny pieces of ceramic, branches jammed at angles in the sand. And everywhere the smell of rotting fish.

At first, we thought it was only Bamboo Grove. We came shakily down onto the beach when the sea finally settled. We stared at swelling corpses and held the hands of the dying. Rob said, "Where are the helicopters? There must be someone somewhere on the mainland, anywhere, who has seen the sea behaving strangely. God, they can predict earthquakes on computer screens, surely tidal waves show up?" Pippa kept her distance, the little boy's head on her lap, turned away from hell. A woman whose head had been badly damaged made a tiny sound. Joe crouched beside her and put his fingers inexpertly on her wrist. Jessica bowed in a deep wai.

I bit my lip and squeezed my eyes shut until I had turned away. I walked up the beach to Pippa and lay down, curled like the child she cradled. Pippa didn't move. She kept murmuring in Hungarian, words from her childhood, rubbing the boy's earlobe between her fingers. Joe and Rob padded up the beach and sat with us. I felt suddenly that I might blink us all back in time and we'd be in a circle round a fire, with Moses offering profundities and Wendy rolling her eyes. We sat in silence for a while until Rob cleared his throat.

"I think there was an earthquake," he said. "The hut shook, but I went back to sleep."

"A very small earthquake," said Pippa, "for such a big wave."

Joe ran his hand through his hair.

"The epicentre could have been far away," he said.

I heard a little squeak escape my throat.

"Then Bamboo Grove might not be the only place that was hit," I said slowly. Then, speeding up, panic racing through me, "the whole of the coast, all the islands…"

We sat digesting this idea and avoiding each other's eyes. Jessica stood at the edge of our little circle for a moment as if she needed permission to join us. I looked up.

"Mum," I said. "Are you OK?"

She blinked at me. The *Mum* took her by surprise. She sat down, cross-legged, wrapping her arms around herself.

"I keep thinking," she said, "that Moses will just appear from somewhere." She gestured towards the hills. "Moses wasn't – terrestrial – enough to die. He's just gone to meditate somewhere else." She laughed, full of tears.

"You are so right," said Pippa. "Even a tidal wave could not interrupt Moses in his lotus position."

Moses would have been proud of us. I picture him sitting on a cloud up there, straight-backed, full lotus, allowing himself a little smile as he watched us living on coconuts for twenty-four hours. They dropped all night, thudding to the ground where they had been loosened by the wave. We slept a little, in the hills because we didn't trust the sea. Pippa and Rob kept the boy between them. Joe and I lay side by side, squeezing each other's hands from time to time when one of us felt the tears come. The woman who did the flower mosaics told us her name was Hing. She was Burmese and didn't speak much English or Thai. She curled up tightly on the ground and Jessica curled up next to her, stroking her thick dark hair.

It was a clear blue-black night and the stars seemed rude in their refusal to be dimmed. I imagined a helicopter – in my half-waking dream, it was Bristol's helicopter. I saw him hovering over the island, landing on the sand. Even in the midst of such a grotesque situation, I found myself wondering how I'd feel when I saw him again. Would I blush with shame for the mute child who had no one else to turn her affections to but a man who could have been, for all she knew, her father? I hoped fervently he'd be ready to forget that child and her ridiculous crush. He'd see that I was an adult, with a voice and a future. And – I glanced at Joe – a lover. I began to cry and cry then, because he was alive and so was I.

At first light, drinking coconut milk and eating the woody white flesh, we reassured each other. And this reassurance was not empty, because of course Bristol and Sam knew that Bamboo Grove had been hit along with everywhere else and they were on their way.

They arrived on a little speedboat, shielding their eyes and straining to see their island paradise. We ran, all seven survivors, down onto the beach to meet the boat. We must have made a horrible sight, a line of blank-faced filthy people flanked by corpses and ruins. They waded in, followed by their driver, and stared at us.

Then Jessica cried out and flung herself into Bristol's arms. He held her tightly and began to shake.

"Moses?" said Sam, looking down at his feet. "Alexis?"

334

"Sorry," said Rob quietly. "And Pete, my cameraman."

"Right," said Sam, and he too started to shake. "Are you all OK?"

I nodded.

"We are alive," I said, and Bristol let go of Jessica and looked at me.

"Yingyang," he said.

Bizarrely, I began to make social introductions.

"This is Joe," I said. I pointed along the line. "Hing. You know Pippa, I guess. Rob. And the little boy's mother died. He hasn't spoken yet."

"No," said Bristol. "Of course. My God. Is there anyone else?"

"We've searched," said Rob flatly, "everywhere. The sea has – swept a lot of people away."

The boat man crossed himself and mouthed a prayer. Sam and Bristol looked up into the hills. Pippa stood tall and drew in a deep breath.

"We will rebuild the island," she said, "we will clean it up and make it beautiful again. Beautiful in a pacifist, mindful manner with no aggressive architecture," and she broke down in tears. Rob stroked her hair and failed to think of anything to say. "Moses," she said eventually. "He was so outrageous we should have a statue constructed."

Acknowledgements

I would like to thank Lindsay, Richard, Shelagh, Viv, John and Tim, who taught me to write; Gwen Davies, who encouraged and supported me through the painful process of rewriting; Aim, who showed me Bangkok and the Best Quality Slum; Woody, who is secretly more Moses than Bristol; Dee, who keeps me going; and Charlie, who loves me even when I'm Jessica.